◆ Shadows of Glass ◆

Also by Kassy Tayler

Ashes of Twilight

Shadows of Glass

·

Kassy Tayler

St. Martin's Griffin ⚑ New York

This is a work of fiction. All of the characters, organizations, and events portrayed in this novel are either products of the author's imagination or are used fictitiously.

SHADOWS OF GLASS. Copyright © 2013 by Kassy Tayler.
All rights reserved. Printed in the United States of America.
For information, address St. Martin's Press, 175 Fifth Avenue, New York, N.Y. 10010.

www.stmartins.com

LIBRARY OF CONGRESS CATALOGING-IN-PUBLICATION DATA

Tayler, Kassy.
    Shadows of glass / Kassy Tayler.—1st ed.
        p. cm.
    ISBN 978-0-312-64176-4 (paperback)
    ISBN 978-1-250-03268-3 (e-book)
    [1. Survival—Fiction. 2. Government, Resistance to—Fiction. 3. Social classes—Fiction.
4. Coal mines and mining—Fiction. 5. Science fiction.] I. Title.
    PZ7.T211487Sh 2013
    [Fic]—dc23

                                                                    2013011254

St. Martin's Griffin books may be purchased for educational, business, or
promotional use. For information on bulk purchases, please contact Mac-
millan Corporate and Premium Sales Department at 1-800-221-7945
extension 5442 or write specialmarkets@macmillan.com.

First Edition: July 2013

10 9 8 7 6 5 4 3 2 1

For Hayes Hudnall Holby
Let's make every day an adventure.

In memory of Levi and Addison Masencup

Acknowledgments

Thank you to my husband, Rob, for his neverending patience with my special kind of crazy. My mom for all her support. My wonderful agent, Roberta Brown, who is always there no matter what. A special thank-you to my awesome editor, Holly Blanck, for making me kick this story up a notch, and to Aleks Mencel and the rest of the gang at SMP for making sure my books are getting noticed. Thank you to the Saturday morning breakfast gang at King Kitchen. And as always, thank you to my wonderful and supportive friends, the werearmadillos. This business has its ups and downs, and I'm happy to share the ride with all of you.

Shadows of Glass

· 1 ·

*T*here *are moments* in history when drastic change comes about. Whether it is for the better or for the worse can only be told after time has passed and stories are written by those who witnessed it. The question that often puzzles me is how do you pinpoint the exact moment, the precise word, or the final action that changes everything for everyone? My own history has to have such a moment, yet I have no idea of how it occurred. When did our forefathers decide that it was necessary to save our race by going inside a dome? Was it the moment they saw the comet in the sky, or was it later, when they realized the deadly implications of its existence? Was one voice responsible for the decision, or were many involved? These things are not taught to us, only that the decision was made.

Was it only a few days ago that our history was taught in two stages? The time before the dome was spoken of in reverent tones, while the time since was nothing more than a cautionary tale to keep the unprivileged in their proper place. There was no alternative to our lives but death. For some of us, that was not enough.

We had questions, and we would not stop until we had the answers. As I step out of the slash in the earth that was our home, I realize that our future has changed. There is no going back from this point. I, like my friend Alex, have seen the sky, and only death will keep me from seeing it again.

I can only hope, when future generations look back on this day when we spilled forth from the earth and found that the world was not engulfed in flames as we had been taught, that I will be remembered kindly. That, like the scientists who built our dome, I only did what I thought I had to do to stay alive. Still I cannot help but wonder, as I think about all those who lost their lives, how many deaths will I be held accountable for? Or will the historians even remember my name?

The sky is blue . . . Alex's last words run through my mind as I stand next to Pace and we stare in wonder at everything that lies before us.

The words that could be written about this moment are meaningless in comparison to what we see. Pace takes my hand beneath the vast expanse of sky, and I realize that Alex's last words did not do the sky justice, because there is so much more to it than the color blue. There are colors I have never seen that are brighter than I can comprehend. The distant horizon is full of them, one fading into the next and the next and the next until I don't know where to look. I don't even know what to call them as they are beyond my understanding. They are more than the reds, purples, and oranges that I have seen before. Those colors were faded and old, covered with ash and soot. The colors that I now behold hurt my eyes as I stare in awe. My mind insists that they could not possibly be real and I have to convince myself that *this* moment *is* real. I tell myself over and over again that I am awake and not trapped in a dream.

Cat calls out to us and I turn to the sound. He stands on a large flat rock that starts in the sand, close to the cave entrance, and goes on to jut into the sea. Cat is not happy, and his complaints let me know that I am, indeed, awake. A wave crashes against the rock and showers over him. He lays his ears back in distaste and cries out again, urging us to come back to the safety of the cave.

Pace and I had run ahead of the others who escaped from the flood that destroyed our village beneath the dome. How long will it be before the rest of us find their way out? I take a moment to search the sky for the canary, Pip, who we were chasing when we realized that the underground river would lead us to the outside. I slowly turn and look at the large wall of rock that rises behind me. Somewhere above is what is left of the dome. I shield my eyes with my hands as I search for a spot of yellow. Will we ever see Pip again? Even though I know Pace would miss him, I honestly cannot blame the tiny bird if he chooses to fly away from this place that was our prison. I certainly would fly if I had wings.

I turn back to look once more at the sky and find Pace watching me. His love, so recently declared, shines in his beautiful blue eyes and he lowers his head to gently kiss me. I know from the touch of his lips that he wants me to know how important this moment is to him, no, to the two of us together. My breath catches in my throat at his kiss and I hold it and onto him, until he finally pulls away. When he does, I have to force the breath out and my chest hurts with the effort. I ignore the pain because I see the most glorious thing as I turn to the west. A golden orb hangs right over the water, like a hand dipped into a bowl, part of it beneath the surface and part of it above. It is so very bright and my eyes water with pain, but I can not tear them away from the sight. I blink and blink again because I don't want to miss anything even though my throat feels as if there is a tight band around it.

The orb looks as if it will slide right into the sea. The realization that it is the sun and I am looking at the edge of the world fills me with so much wonder that I tremble. The sea is vaster than anything I have ever imagined, but the sky, the sky is limitless and beyond my comprehension. There *is* a world outside the dome. It is not flame or fire as we were always told. Instead there is this inconceivable openness that never ends, which makes it close to impossible for my mind to comprehend it. I keep a tight hold of Pace's hand because I am frightened that without him I will fly off into the oblivion that stretches before us. It is hard to understand that everything we've been told our entire lives is a lie. My mind is at war with itself so I try to take a deep breath just to collect myself, but instead all I can do is gasp.

My chest burns and my lungs convulse. I cannot breathe. I am suffocating and I drop to my knees on the sand. My hands clutch at my throat as if someone has wrapped a band around it. Nothing is there, yet the constriction is real. There is nothing I can do to stop it. I don't want to die. Not now, not when I am so close. Not when my dreams have finally come true. Not when I finally have everything I ever wanted.

"Wren!" I hear Pace shouting my name as if he is far, far away. I want to answer him but I cannot speak. I open my mouth and nothing comes out. I claw at my throat as if I can free it from the vise that holds it shut. I pitch forward with the effort to draw a breath. Salty water splashes into my face and my eyes burn and tear. All I can do is blink. Pace catches me and turns me over so I am halfway in his lap. I see him above me, as if he's at the opposite end of a tunnel and his face is full of fear. I grab his arm as my lungs labor for air. A horrible spasm wracks my throat and I feel my eyes bulging. I know I am dying and there is nothing I can say, yet there is so much I want to tell him.

Is this how Alex felt? This desperation to make sure that nothing was left unsaid? He had to welcome death over the unbelievable pain he felt. I was not burned by flame, but my lungs feel as if they've dissolved into ashes inside my chest.

Suddenly Pace flips me over. He bends me over his arm and strikes my back. My insides feel as if they are coming up my throat, and I gag. Thankfully I am able to draw a breath, but as soon as I do I begin to cough. I cough and cough and something black comes out. I feel as if someone has stuffed thick fabric down my throat. I keep gagging and coughing and it keeps coming up, black and horrible and thick. It has been inside me, all this time, killing my lungs, and killing the rest of my body slowly. I want it out. I want all of it out. I want my insides to be free of the coal the same way my body is free of the dome.

I don't know how Pace can stand it. I look at the mess in the sand that has come out of my lungs and it makes me sicker, if that is possible. My stomach joins in the upheaval. I feel as if my insides are coming out, one small piece at a time. I am exhausted. I have nothing left to give, yet it keeps coming. Pace rubs my back and scoops handfuls of seawater and dribbles them on my neck until I slump over his legs, exhausted. I hear voices behind me; the others have found their way out. I should tell them to go back, to ease their way into the air that is so fresh and clean that I feel as if it will kill me. But I can't say a word because my world has once more turned to shadows and I feel myself slowly sliding away into the darkness.

◆

There are times in our lives when we dream so vividly that it is impossible to tell what reality is and what our minds trick us into believing is real. We stay in the dream, mostly because it is so much better than the monotony of our everyday life until something jolts us to awareness and we wake up, not certain of where we are or where we belong. When it happens to me I close my eyes tight and try to recapture that part of the dream that led me away into a different world, as if I could will myself into that place once more.

I find myself trapped in that half-dream state. My mind cannot settle on what is real. The sounds around me are different than what I am used to. My bed feels strange and my body aches all the way into my bones. My throat feels raw and I am so very thirsty. I lick my lips and taste nothing but salt. Someone nudges me and I have to force my eyes open.

It is Ghost, my favorite pony from the mines. He is curled up against me, and my head is on his side. He nudges me once more with his nose as he does when he wants a treat, and I place my hand on the side of his face to let him know I am awake. Cat lies beside me and sits up as I move.

I blink and gasp at the beauty and wonder of what is above me. The sky is full of points of light: some bright, and some so distant I can barely see them. They are everywhere; no matter where I look I see them.

"You're awake." Pace's sweet and handsome face blocks my view.

"What are they?" I manage to croak out as I point upward.

Pace kneels down beside me. He puts a hand on Ghost's head to keep him still as he looks over his shoulder at the sky. "Stars," he says. "Sailors of old used them to navigate the seas."

"They are beautiful," I whisper and he turns to look at me once more. I see in his face that something is horribly wrong, and the beauty of the stars is forgotten as I quickly sit up. My head swims and my stomach rolls in protest.

"Stay still," Pace urges me with his concern plainly showing on his face. "You should rest."

"The others?" I ask.

"They're here, except . . ." Pace's voice trails off and my head fills with horrible thoughts of what more could befall us. Panic fills me. I climb to my feet, trembling with weakness and terror. Pace sees that there is no stopping me, so he helps me up, always steady, always there. Ghost scrambles to his feet behind me, and Cat frantically jumps away. He is still nervous and not happy about the circumstances, and he lets us know by meowing fretfully. How easy it would be just to sit down and cry out my fears, but I cannot. Not now. Not ever as long as I remain strong.

The lamps we carried from the tunnels sit on rocks that are scattered about the shoreline. Because I am a shiner, I can see fine without them, but Pace cannot see as I can in the dark. Still the light is comforting. The sandy beach we came out on is much smaller now, so small that I fear that we may run out of room and have to retreat back into the cave if the water comes any closer. The ponies that came with us stand huddled against the cliff wall. The openness has to be frightening to them, because they can't see. They knew the tunnels. How can they survive in this unknown world since they are blind? I know Ghost is frightened because he stays close to my back, as if he's still in the harness and I'm leading him through the mines.

The children that joined up with us during our escape are gathered close to the cave entrance with a lamp. They are recovering the things from our village that have washed through from the flood, and I hear their excited chatter as they pull something from the water. Alcide, who is a year younger than me, is with them as they pile the things they find close against the stone wall that towers behind us.

James and Adam are nearby. James sits with his head down and scrubs his hands through his hair. Adam watches the children. How long has he been awake and waiting to see if the body of his wife—and my best friend—Peggy, who was also James's sister, washes out of the cave? She was lost in the flood, and the pain of it, of watching the water rise around her and knowing there was nothing we could do, is still fresh in my mind, along with the cries of Adam. They had only been wed a day when the flood came, caused by an explosion in the caves after we were attacked by the bluecoats from above.

"They just woke up. They had the same problem as you," Pace explains. "It wasn't as bad with the young ones, just a few spasms and they were done." I look at him, at his handsome face and his beautiful blue eyes. He, like the rest of us, has been through so much, and I feel like I let him down because he had to take care of all of us once we came outside, while I was sick and unconscious. He has to be worried about his mother also. My father was holding her prisoner when the explosion happened. We have no idea what happened to those above, and now, since we are outside, we have no way to find out.

"They haven't been deep in the mines yet," I explain, grateful at least that the children did not have to suffer. "They are still too young." We don't go into the mines until we're thirteen and have finished our schooling. Most of the children we found were between five and twelve, and had been in school when the attack came. Alcide is fifteen, so it makes sense that he would recover before the rest of us.

"I set them to working, so they wouldn't think about their families," Pace said. "I thought it best if they kept busy. I wasn't thinking about what else they might find."

"Bodies?" I ask.

Pace shivers as he nods. "At first they cried, especially the little ones," he explains. "Now they look at it as helping them, even though the people are dead."

"That's because of you," I say, wanting to offer him some comfort and gratitude for what he's done. But I also have to ask because she is . . . was . . . so dear to me. "Peggy?"

"Not yet," Pace says as if there is some slim hope she might still be alive. I know better than to grab onto it. I know there is no hope left for her.

I look once more at Adam and James. They both seem done in, as if all the life has been sucked from their bodies, and I know I must look the same if not worse. I wouldn't wish what I'd been through on anyone, not even James, who I'd been at odds with since this strange journey began, and especially not Adam, who had suffered so much for our cause. I know how they feel. Bringing up the coal from my lungs had nearly killed me, especially since I was weak from the battles I'd fought. Adam and James had to have fared better than me because they were stronger, but those who were weak and had years of coal dust inside of them, how would they survive? Even now my lungs feel strange and sore and my throat is raw.

"I'm sorry I wasn't any help," I say, even though it won't change anything. Then suddenly a chill washes over me that has nothing to do with the night air that surrounds us. "Where are Hans and Mary?" They are the oldest of all of us, all that was left of our tribe of elders as all the rest had been swept away in the floods.

Pace hesitates, as if he's searching for the right words. "They didn't make it," he says. "It was too much for them."

No . . . I don't want it to be true. I wouldn't believe it was true, not until I saw for myself. "Where are they?"

"With the others," Pace says and his voice breaks. He looks away for a moment yet keeps a strong hold onto my hand. I don't know how long I was unconscious, and because I was, because I wasn't strong enough, Pace had to endure these things by himself. It was weak of me to leave him that way, but I don't know what else I could have done. Maybe I shouldn't have rushed outside, maybe I should have warned the others before they came out. If only I had known what being outside would do to us. Like everything else that has happened in the past days, every decision I've made has been diffi-cult. Every decision I've made has led to as much bad as good. I don't know why this has fallen on me. I don't want it any more. I don't want to be responsible for all this death.

"This way," Pace says. He pulls on my hand and I follow, regret-fully, yet resolved, since I have to know. Pretending something hasn't happened won't make it so. We walk toward the children. As we approach James and Adam, they struggle to their feet and join us. They are both quiet. Considering all that has happened, I am not surprised; still it worries me, because I don't trust James, not after everything that has happened. Not after everything he's done. We are a strange group, the four of us, with Ghost and Cat following along after us as we walk to where the river joins the sea. What if we are the only ones who survived? Surely, with all the people that live in the dome, some had to have escaped. I think of our friends from above. Lucy and David, Jilly and Harry, who joined us in the fight, and my father, Sir William Meredith, who is the Master General Enforcer and the one we battled against in our effort to escape the dome. Was he the one who sent the bluecoats down with the flamethrowers? I cannot help but think it would be fitting if his decision to come after the shiners resulted in destroy-ing the very thing he was trying to protect. How will history remember him when these chapters are written? I guess it will de-pend on who does the writing.

We come to where the river spills forth from the cave. I look at the mammoth slash in the earth. How long has it been here? Did our forefathers know of its existence? Was it written down someplace that this could be a way out, or did they deliberately hide it from the inhabitants when they finalized the dome? How simple it would have been for all of us, if we had just simply known about it from the beginning. From the looks of it, I'd say it has been around a very long time, since way before the dome. Possibly since the beginning of time. Was this something else my father kept hidden from the people to preserve the bloodline of the royalty that he values so much?

The children have been busy, sorting and stacking the things that have spilled forth from the earth, with Alcide directing them in their endeavors. Pots and pans, blankets, clothing, bits and pieces of furniture, and some toys lay on the sand, the only remnants of our village. Cat stops to sniff through the things. I stop and ask one of the children, whose name I do not know, to lead Ghost over to the rest of the ponies.

I give Ghost a reassuring pat as the little boy takes the halter. I should learn his name; I should learn all of their names, as we might be the only ones left. Before they were just part of the innumerable group that went to school and played in our cavern, all belonging to someone. I had no time to worry over them as I was wrapped up in my own life with my own group. Are we four, me, James, Adam, and Alcide, along with these children, all that's left of the shiners? Is this loss because of me and the decisions I made? Was making sure Alex did not die in vain worth all these lives that were lost along with his?

Adam and James splash across the water and Alcide follows them. Pace waits for me. He stretches out his hand, and I realize I am frightened to take it. I don't want to see the faces of those who have died. I don't want to know that Hans and Mary made it out, only to die because of the fresh, clear air. I don't want to know that so many people drowned, but I must go on. I cannot change the things that have happened; I can only hope to learn from them. If only the lessons did not come with such a steep price.

Hans's son, Freddy, who is twelve, sits beside his father's body. Hans lies on his back with his head against the cliff wall and his feet pointing to the sea. Beside him in the same position lies Mary, who was the oldest of us after my grandfather died. Both had been kind to me, when I didn't deserve it. Hans especially, because he knew that I had Pace hidden in the tunnels and he did not turn us in. What we will do now without their wisdom and guidance? They were the last of our elders. Who will we look to when a hard decision has to be made?

Their faces show the strain of their deaths, and as I look at them I also see the horrible death that Alex suffered by being burned alive, and my grandfather's, when he was crushed. All of them dead now because I wished to see the sky. All of them dead because I made decisions that affected them and changed their lives. What made me think I should be the one to decide for all of us? I should have left it to wiser heads than mine to make the difficult decisions. I should have thought things through before I acted. I had this ideal in my mind about how things should be. Now that I am faced with the harsh reality of how things are, I'm not so sure anymore. I am not sure of anything, especially not the decisions I made.

Freddy leaves his father's side and comes to me. He doesn't say anything; he just buries his head into my chest and breaks into tears. I am at a loss as to what I can do for him, what I should do for any of us. All I can do is put my arms around him and hold him while his body shakes with sobs. He's lost both his parents and his home. He's tried to be brave, but there comes a point when you have to give in to the sorrow. I wish I could cry like Freddy. Have Pace wrap his arms around me and just cry into his chest until the tears come no more, but I can't. I'm afraid that if I start I won't be able to stop. I console Freddy as best I can until his sobs subside, gone as suddenly as they came. He smiles briefly, nods, and then steps away as if he is embarrassed by his display of emotion.

There are more bodies beyond Hans and Mary. So many that I

cannot count them. Alcide has tried to lay them out, but some of them are so broken that it was an impossible task and they lie at strange angles with their arms and legs in awkward poses, beaten by the floodwaters and the stone walls that they tumbled past on their way to the sea. It is heartbreaking to see babies among them. The last minutes I spent in the village were with Jasper's wife and small son. I can still hear the boy's laughter as Pace entertained him with the tricks he'd taught Pip. So many lives lost. The cost is immeasurable.

"Who have you found?" Adam asks Alcide, as if it would make a difference.

"Abner," he says and looks at James. "Your parents are here. Jasper and his wife . . ." his voice trails off. There is no need for Alcide to list them. We know everyone who was in the village is dead, including Peggy. Still Adam asks and Alcide shakes his head.

"Do you think everyone is dead?" Freddy looks up at me with a tear-streaked face. "My mother?"

"I don't know," I say. " We won't know . . ."

James interrupts me. "Until they show up."

"James," I say in frustration. Freddy shouldn't have to deal with these horrors. None of these children should, yet there's nothing else we can do at the moment. We have no place else to go. Before I can chastise James any further, we are interrupted by a shout from the children.

We turn to look and they point at the water coming from the cave. Another body has washed down. Adam takes off at a run and we follow him. His cry rings off the cliff walls as he picks the body up from the water. Peggy is limp in his arms, like a cloth doll. I catch a sob in my throat as James runs to help Adam. She was my best friend and all I can do is watch as they lay her gently and tenderly in the sand. A horrible sound comes from Adam as he takes her hand into his and pushes the hair back from her face with the other.

"Oh Peggy," I say and my heart breaks for all of us. I'd tried to be strong, but the sight of Adam with her body does me in. I crumble beneath the weight of my grief. Tears consume me, and I turn away as I try to choke back the sobs. I don't want anyone to see me, to see the pain that I suddenly cannot control, yet there is no place to hide and no hiding from the grief. I cry for Adam, who lost his wife; for James, who lost his sister; and for me, who lost my friend. For all these children who are now orphans and have no one but us to depend on. I cry because I don't want the responsibility of all these lives, and guilt threatens to overcome my grief because I am the one responsible for both the living and the dead. Pace reaches out a hand to console me but I push him away. He cannot help me and he can't make it go away any more than I can. I step away from him, from everyone, but there is no place for me to go. I try to make it stop but there is no stopping it.

"What right do you have to say anything?" James moves quickly, leaving Adam's side in one instant and standing before me in the next. I wipe at the tears and choke back a sob as he moves threateningly close, his face only inches from mine. Even though my eyes are full of tears, I clearly see his hatred behind the shine of his green eyes. Eyes that are the exact same color as Peggy's were, yet very much different in what they reveal of the soul beneath. "All of this is your fault, Wren." His words spew out with the same disgust as the coal that choked up from our lungs, and my grief suddenly gives way to fear. "All of it."

James's words are like a dagger into my heart. Especially since I know them to be true.

· 2 ·

There comes a time in your life when you realize there is no turning back, that the decisions made by you and by others around you have led to this exact time and place and there is no way to change it. But you cannot but help ask yourself: Would you change things if you could? If you had a choice, would you go back?

If it meant that the lives recently lost could be restored, then yes, I would turn back the hands of the time without a moment of regret. I would go back to the moment when Alex flew over the pit and tell him that he had nothing to prove to Lucy. That he should be good enough for her, just the way he was. Then I would make sure that he did not follow her to work the next morning, that he did not see her with another man, and that most of all he did not get burned alive after finding a way to escape the dome. If I could change those few simple things, then the rest would not have happened. Peggy would still be alive, and my grandfather, and all the rest who died needlessly.

Changing these things would mean I would not have met Pace.

As much as I care for him, as close as we've become, it's a sacrifice I would gladly make. I have to believe that if we were meant to be together then we would have met, regardless. At the moment it's the only belief I have. I put my hand on Pace's arm to stop him as he steps between James and me. I don't want a fight between them. Not again, and especially not now, when so many of our friends are dead.

"You are as much at fault as anyone," Pace says to James in a voice that is scary because he sounds so calm and logical. "You are the one who blew up the fans. You're the one who brought them down on our heads."

"On our heads!" James spouts back in evident anger. "You are not one of us! They came down because they were looking for you. Wren never should have brought you down below. You were the one they were after." James is shorter than Pace, but that doesn't stop him from getting in his face. "I only did what I had to to protect my people. If not for you and her none of this would have happened. My sister would still be alive and my parents. Everyone would still be alive!" His angry shouts ring off the cliff walls behind us.

Pace's arm beneath my hand stiffens, and I know he wants to punch James, just as much as I do, even though I know it won't help the situation at all. It's not fair that he blames us, not after everything that has happened to all of us, yet I have to agree with him to a point. Most of what's happened is because of the decisions I made. If not for me being captured by my father's team of enforcers, James would not have felt the need to blow up the fans, although knowing James, I'm sure he would have eventually found an excuse to blow something up. I also know his grief is what is behind his words, but that doesn't excuse his hate.

"That's enough, James," I say.

"What makes you think any of us will listen to you anymore?" James turns to me, giving me an equal share of his hatred. "We never should have listened to you at all. You betrayed us. You betrayed everyone by throwing in your lot with him."

I can't hold Pace back any longer. This fight has been brewing between them for too long and it's been interrupted too many times. Pace swings at James and hits him square in the jaw. James staggers back several paces before lowering his head and charging into Pace's stomach, wrapping his arms around him and taking him to the ground. They roll up against my feet and I fall backwards, landing on my tail in the sand. I manage to turn over and try to scramble away and get a face full of sand when they roll on top of my feet and calves. Hands pull me up and away and I spit out a mouthful of sand as Alcide helps me to my feet.

Adam watches the fight with dead eyes. He moves away with Peggy in his arms as if he can protect her from any more harm. I realize it is up to Alcide and me to stop them. I have no idea how.

Somehow Pace and James stand up and go at each other again. The looks on their faces are intense and, with a sickening thought, I realize that they truly want to kill each other. I never would have thought Pace capable of such violent emotion, but it is plainly written on his face. They pound at each other mercilessly, aiming at the face and then the gut. I don't know how they stay on their feet with the blows they give and receive. Pace is bigger and stronger, yet James has a wiry strength and speed that are deceptive.

Alcide and I circle around them. I don't know what to do. "We've got to stop them before they kill each other!"

Alcide shrugs his shoulders helplessly as Pace and James suddenly come together, grappling for the upperhand. Their bodies are locked with one arm while they pound at each other's guts with the other. They turn in a circle with sand flying around them. I am suddenly aware of the children. They stand back, watching the fight with tear-filled eyes, and the littlest ones are crying.

Pace and James topple over, James finally giving in to the greater weight of Pace. As soon as they fall, Alcide wraps his arms around Pace's waist and pulls him off James. He pushes him at me and I jump in front of him as Alcide grabs James and drags him in the direction of Adam.

Pace is livid, his face full of anger and hatred. He shoves at me, but I stubbornly hang on, my feet planted in the sand. "STOP!" I scream. "You're going to kill each other!" I hear Alcide yelling something similar at James behind me. I grab Pace's face with both hands so he has to look at me. "You're scaring the children."

His eyes come into focus and he looks at me. His eyes flare in recognition and he shakes his head up and down as if he is afraid to speak. I release him and take a step back. I'm not sure what to do next. I'm so very scared of his anger. I know to expect it from James, but from Pace it is shocking. I thought I knew him. He was so calm and supportive through everything that happened to us, but I guess even his patience had to come to an end at some time.

Pace's face is battered and bloody, and he touches a finger to the corner of his mouth where it is cut. He stares at James for a moment over my shoulder, and then he turns and walks away, splashing back across the river to the ponies.

I turn to see Alcide breathe a sigh of relief. The past few days have hardened him, and I'm suddenly aware of the resemblance he has to Alex, who was his cousin. It's as if he's grown up, overnight, or maybe it's just that I've been so wrapped up in my own problems that I didn't notice.

"Stop it, James," I say. "We shouldn't do this. We shouldn't fight, especially not tonight and not in front of these children." There is too much regret to add any more. It's a burden none of us should have to carry, yet I feel the weight of everything pressing down on my shoulders. We are all at fault, yet none of us should have to bear the blame. And like the lives that are lost, the words and the blows James and Pace exchanged are something that can never be taken back. They accomplish nothing but damage and pain.

"Why should I stop?" James says. "He threw the first punch. I didn't say anything that isn't true. He's not one of us. You never should have brought him below. Like I said. It's all your fault."

"Don't," Adam says quietly, back with us once again. "Just don't."

"Now see what you've done," James spouts once again, once more turning his hatred to me.

I want to protest at James's ridiculous assumption, but the grief on Adam's face stops me. "We need to do something for these children," I finally say.

"How about we get them settled for the night?" Alcide suggests. "I'll take Freddy and get some fresh water." Alcide, the younger of us, acts with the most maturity. I nod in agreement, relieved at having something constructive to do. I lead the children to the ponies while Alcide, Freddy, and an older boy and girl gather up some pails and go back into the cave. I have always sought the company of the ponies when I was troubled, and as much as I want to feel sorry for myself after James's accusations, I can't. The children have suffered enough for one day. The ponies always calm me when I'm upset, and I'm hoping they will do the same for the children, who are all quiet now after their scare from the fight. I have a feeling Peggy's body showing up filled them all with a sense of finality for their own families. They were all in school when the explosion occurred. Their mothers and smaller brothers and sisters were in the village while their fathers and older siblings were guarding the tunnels. The chances of any of them surviving the cave-in and floods are very small. At least in that respect I am lucky. After Peggy, the only one I had to lose was Pace, as I have no family left at all.

Pace has moved on, farther down the beach. He stands at the edge of the water, staring out at the impending darkness. I decide to leave him be, for now. I am not certain that I can talk to him calmly at this point. I feel betrayed, for some strange reason. I depended upon him so much in the past few days to be steady and calm. This sudden upsurge of anger and violence from him is disturbing.

As soon as the ponies sense my presence, their unease subsides. They are patient to wait for me to take them wherever they must go; the problem is I have no idea where that is. For so long, escaping the dome consumed every moment. I guess I thought we would find some sort of paradise outside the dome. Instead we are trapped upon this sandy beach until we see what daylight will bring us. At least the water is receding now. Pace calls it the tide.

I am so weary all I want to do is sleep, yet my mind will not let me rest. The children have curled into the sand with their backs against the wall at my urging, and I concentrate on settling them among the ponies. I put Cat, who has become my shadow, next to a little girl named Stella, who stares up at me with tear-filled eyes.

"Why can't I sleep in my bed?" she asks me. The answer is so simple yet so complicated. How do I explain to her that her world is no more?

"Because our houses are gone," a little boy answers for me. "Everything is gone."

"Will we find it in the water?" Stella asks another impossible question. "Will we find my mommy and daddy in the water too?"

I smooth her tangled hair back from her face. I don't even know who her parents are . . . were . . . and I search my heart for some sort of answer, something that will give her hope, which I desperately need for myself. Instead of answering, I turn away from her in relief when Freddy and the other two children arrive with fresh water. Several cats trail after them and Cat jumps up to greet them. As I watch them sniff in greeting I cannot help but think, if the cats survived the flood then maybe some of our people did too.

Freddy offers the children dippers of water, and I gratefully take a drink when the girl who went with him offers me one. "What is your name?" I ask, guessing her to be around ten years old.

"Nancy Neal," she replies.

"Peter's sister?" I can see the resemblance in her eyes. Peter has to be dead. The last time I saw him he was running straight into the battle where the explosion was.

"Yes, ma'am."

Her calling me *ma'am* shocks me. What if we are the elders now? Me, James, and Adam. What if we have to be responsible for all these lives? I don't want it. When it was just my life I could make decisions because it was only my life at risk. This responsibility I cannot live with. I've already seen the results. The price is too high. "I'm so sorry," I say.

"Thank you," Nancy replies. Her lower lip trembles, and I know she's trying to be brave. She does not realize that my apology has everything to do with what led to Peter's death, that it is not just my condolences I am offering.

I drink deeply, emptying the cup in one gulp. My throat feels raw and my stomach empty, even though I had a decent meal right before everything happened. I drink again, to soothe my throat. "Make sure the ponies get some too, after the children are done," I tell Nancy and she nods in agreement to my bidding. If only everything else could be so easy. We need food and we need shelter. Perhaps both could be found in the caves eventually, but I do not see going back inside as an alternative. Not after we fought so hard to get out. I am so weary. How much time has passed since the world, as we knew it, ended?

I see Pace in the distance, still staring out to sea. In the opposite direction are Alcide, James, and Adam. I am stuck in the middle between them, a bridge that needs to be joined in order for all of us to survive. But first some sort of decision has to be made about the bodies. It is our custom to burn them, and I see no reason why that should change now.

The children settle in among the ponies. It is a peaceful scene, if one forgets the tragedies that led up to it. Some of the cats explore the beach while others, including the one we call Cat, who has adopted me, curl up beside the children.

I look up at the sky that is as black as the tunnels I lived in. Stars spread across it like dust. This is what remained hidden from us for all of our lives and the lives of the generations before us. The beauty I've seen tonight is beyond anything I imagined. Yet my father led me to believe that outside was dangerous. It is hard to believe that this peaceful setting could hold danger, yet I cannot help but think of the weapons that his agents used and the fact that he traded young women and men to get them. Could the enemies he feared be watching us? And what about Jon, the boy who was captured with me and went outside when my father sentenced us both to go? Where is he now? Is he looking at the sky now and wondering what has happened to all of us in the dome, or did he take off and get as far away from it as he could?

Alcide leaves Adam and James and walks down the beach. Pace meets him halfway, they talk for a moment and then come my way, gathering up the lamps and turning them down as they walk. I conjure up a small smile. At least in all this, I am not alone. I have someone to lean on. Someone to cling to. Someone to share the wonder of this new world, along with the grief from the old. If not for him, I would be totally alone. The least I can do is be patient with him. Understand that he has issues also. That he is as scared and confused as I am.

"Adam and James will keep watch for the rest of the night," Alcide says. "We'll have services for them in the morning," he adds. "Perhaps the others will see our smoke and will find us." There's hope behind the weariness of his voice. It's something for him to cling to. His family could still be alive. Still, a shiver runs down my spine at the thought of who else might be out there.

"We should get some rest," I say. There is no need to invite fear. For now I believe we are safe on our narrow strip of sandy beach, but I cannot help but dread the coming of a new day, because I have no idea what it will bring.

Alcide drops on the sand next to a pony and without another word curls up on his side. Pace and I move off a bit and sit down with our backs against the cliff wall. Even though it is full night, Pace moves easily, and I realize that he can see fairly well in this darkness. It is not oppressive like the tunnels. The stars, along with the lamps, lend the landscape a soft glow of definition.

"We have water to drink . . . and wash the blood off," I suggest. He has new bruises, mingling with the older ones from his first fight with James, and from the beating he took when he first escaped from the bluecoats who accused him of killing his best friend.

Pace touches his thumb to the corner of his mouth and winces. "Alcide says we look about the same."

"You have to know you can never win against James," I say. "He never forgets and he never gives in."

"As long as he keeps his mouth shut the rest won't bother me," Pace says. "He shouldn't have said those things about you. Or about me."

"He didn't say anything that isn't true."

Pace looks out into the darkness for a moment and then nods. "I guess it is just the way he says it."

I have no answer for that so I go to get Pace some water. He takes it gratefully when I return. I wet my kerchief and carefully dab off the blood at the corner of his mouth. He watches my face as I work and cups my hand in his when I finish. I notice that his knuckles are bruised also, but he squeezes his fingers over mine before I can minister to them.

"I'm scared, Wren. I'm not really sure what's going to happen to us out here. It's not what I expected."

"It's not what I expected either," I confess. "Hopefully things will seem better in the morning." We lean back against the wall of stone that rises behind us. "I'm sorry about Pip," I say as Cat moves next to us. He takes a moment to lick the sand off his paws before he steps onto Pace's lap and starts kneading his leg as he purrs.

Pace slides his arm around me. "He'll be back come daybreak," he assures me.

"It's bigger than I expected," I say as I lean my head against his shoulder.

"What? Outside?"

"Yes," I say. "I didn't expect it to be so . . ."

"Forever?" Pace suggests. "You sound disappointed."

"I don't know," I admit. "Maybe I am."

"Wren, you can't blame yourself for all this," he says.

"I know, but . . ."

"But no," Pace says firmly. He shifts so he's facing me, which disrupts Cat, who meows indignantly as he stalks a few steps away. Pace places his hands on either side of my face and stares into my eyes. I cannot help but notice once more how blue his eyes are even in the darkness that surrounds us. How they change in hue with the light, or the lack thereof. How I feel like I am staring into his soul when he looks at me. My shiner eyes have an advantage. I wonder what he sees when he looks into mine. Does he see my soul when he looks inside, or does he merely see a reflection of what he thinks I am?

"No matter what James or anyone else says, you are not responsible for the decisions other people make. And there were several of them made that led to this. Some of them were right and some of them were wrong. Yes, there were lives lost. You are no more at fault for those than I am."

I appreciate what he's saying, more so for the reason why he's saying it. He cares for me, deeply, so he doesn't want me to hurt. And because I do not want him to hurt, I nod as if I agree with him.

I don't like lying, I never have, yet it is something I've done a lot of lately, almost like I'm making a habit of it. Is protecting people from the truth worth it? Should we lie to the people we love because we don't want them to get hurt? Pace lies to me and I lie to him. But it makes him feel better to think he's made me feel better, so I do it. I lied to my grandfather because I didn't want to hurt him, and he ended up dead and he knew I'd lied. It's a never-ending circle and I don't know how to find my way out of it. So I smile at Pace and nod.

Pace smiles his sweet smile, nods his agreement with me, and leans against the cliff wall once more. I lower my head to his shoulder and look out over the water. The sound of the tide lapping against the sand is a lot like the creaking of the water wheel back home. I slowly close my eyes and let it lull me into a temporary peace that I know will be gone come morning. For the first time since I can remember I am not looking forward to the light coming to my world.

· 3 ·

The light wakes me. For a long moment, while I lie in that state between dreams and awareness, I think I am on top of the buildings beneath the dome waiting for the light to come, as I did every morning before. The sounds are different however. There is no constant roar of the fans, or the *clank-clank* of chains from the workers riding their baskets up to clean the dome. Instead there is a strange quietness that is unsettling. I sit up with a start as the happenings of the past day catch up with me. The light is faint, like the dome on one of the worst days, more a hint of what is to come than the actual gift of morning.

I stand and slowly turn a circle, fascinated with the new sights before me. I look up the cliff wall and see that it isn't flat, like I originally thought. Instead there is a trail that gently slopes upward, much like the tunnels we used to inhabit beneath the earth. The height is higher than the dome, but not by much. At the top I see a platform that juts out over the cliff wall, with iron girders beneath it and a strange and twisted contraption atop it. The look of it makes me think that it was built around the time of our dome.

The beach where I stand is blocked on both sides by the cliff that curves outward and into the sea. I suppose with the tides we might be able to get around it. I think that the trail up the cliff might be our best chance. There have to be other survivors, somewhere.

The children are all asleep, as are Pace and Alcide. The ponies are awake but peaceful, waiting for me to tell them what to do next. Cat stretches and yawns beside me and stalks off, sniffing at the sand as he goes. I notice the rest of the cats are scattered about the beach curiously sniffing at the sand and pawing at the surf. One splashes in and quickly retreats with a small fish in its mouth. Another one chases a crab into a hole, and tiny birds on long legs skip ahead of the rest of them as if they are running a race. The cats have quickly adapted. I can only hope that we can do the same. The issue of food is foremost in my mind at the moment. The children will be hungry when they wake, as will the ponies.

I look down the beach and see James and Adam on the same side of the cavern as me. I wonder if any more bodies came down during the night. Adam sits with his head against the cliff wall with his eyes closed. He looks tired and defeated. I am afraid for him. Afraid that without Peggy he will just give up.

The sea looks much as it did the night before: a flat surface with a gentle swell of the tide as it slowly laps against the sand. In the distance I hear the sound of cries, but I can't identify the source. It could be birds, or it could be someone. It is too far away for me to know for certain. Things litter the beach, bits of wood, formerly tables and chairs or perhaps even doors and the water wheel, all of it washed down from our village that no longer exists.

The world is awash in shades of grays and blues and the sky is brightening, much like the dome, yet more wondrous, the colors muted, yet vibrant. This beauty has been hidden from me my entire life, and I hope I never take it for granted. My body yearns for the light to come, as it has become a habit with me. I ache to see the new wonders that this world has to offer. I still feel the responsibility of all those lives that were lost. I desperately need to see something, or feel something, that will make me realize that their sacrifice has some value. I still fear it is too steep a price to pay.

A familiar chirp rings out, then a flutter of wings. Pip flits around my face and settles on my shoulder. It isn't exactly the sign I was looking for, but it cheers me to see him. Pip holds something in his beak, and he tilts his head back and forth until I hold my palm beneath him and he drops it into my hand. It is nothing more than a sliver of something soft. I pick it up carefully, afraid that I will lose it. It is deep green in color and I hold it under my nose. The smell reminds me of the leaves on the rooftop trees within the dome.

"What is it?" I ask the bright yellow canary. He blinks his bead of an eye at me and glides to where Pace still lies in sleep. One of the cats looks at him like he's planning his next meal, and I stomp my feet in the sand to dissuade him. Cat stalks over to Pace and takes a position next to him while Pip nips delicately at his shirt button.

Pace shifts and his eyes open. A wide grin spreads across his face when he sees Pip. "I told you he'd be back," he says as he sits up.

"He brought a gift too," I reply. I hand him the wisp that Pip dropped in my palm. The morning has brightened enough that Pace can see too. He runs a fingertip over it and smiles.

"It's a blade of grass," he says. He looks at Ghost and the rest of the ponies beyond. "Sweet grass for you to eat."

"Send him back out," Alcide, who has yet to open his eyes, says grumpily. "See if he can find something for us to eat too."

I can't help but laugh and the sound stirs the children. They wake with sleepy eyes and confused faces. The littlest one, Stella, cries. "I want my mommy," she says and I go to her. I pick her up and soothe her as best I can.

"We'll see if we can find her," I say and look helplessly at Pace.

"Boys this way," he says and tilts his head down the beach.

"I'm hungry," one of the little boys grumbles.

"We'll see what we can find," Alcide says, and the two of them lead the boys down the beach away from us.

Nancy climbs to her feet and takes a young girl's hand in each of hers. The other two follow me and we go behind the ponies to give us some semblance of privacy as we squat in the sand and then cover it up in the same way that the cats do. I try to keep a cheerful face in front of the little girls. They are still sleepy, probably hungry, and very much confused. I know exactly how they feel.

The light around us is brighter now and the sky is streaked once more with color. The cliff above us blocks the sun and the air is chilly without the heavy dampness of the earth that we are used to. A breeze tugs at my hair and I comb it back with my fingers and tie it up with my bandana. I am not one to worry about my appearance much, not that it matters now. At the moment there are much more pressing things to think about.

Pace, Alcide, and the boys join us once more. Adam and James stand up and stretch away the weariness of their night. Decisions need to be made.

"There's a trail up," James says as a greeting when we all gather together.

"I saw it," I reply.

Pip sits on Pace's shoulder as he looks up and studies the cliff wall. James shakes his head, more than likely disgusted at Pace's love for the little bird. Since the sky has brightened, a plume of gray smoke is visible now against the blue shades of the sky. "That must be from the dome," Pace says.

"There have to be survivors," Alcide observes.

"I certainly hope so," Pace says. I know he's worried about his mother.

"We need to take care of our own before we worry about anyone else," Adam says. His words sound harsh, but I know it's only because Peggy is among the bodies laid out on the beach. More had to have come down during the night.

"He's right, we should," I agree with Adam. "If we gather up all the wood, we should be able to make a suitable fire."

"It's wet," James says.

"Not all of it," Alcide offers. "And there is a can of oil that I found last night." His stomach rumbles as he speaks and he places his hand against it. Food is at the forefront of my mind also.

"The children can dig for mussels," Pace says.

"And what good would that do?" James asks.

"It's food," Pace explains. "I read about them in a book. We can cook them and eat them."

"You've got an answer for everything don't you?" James asks. "Just because you've read a few books." Reading is something we learn for necessity's sake. The only book any shiner has ever had access to is a Bible. Mine, the one I gave to Peggy and Adam as a wedding present, is lost in the flood, like the other few things I owned. The type of reading Pace has done is frivolous to us. Books are too valuable to be wasted on the likes of us. Thinking about books makes me wonder if the library that held so many of the past world's treasures has survived the explosion that destroyed *our* world.

"If it's going to put food in my stomach then I'm glad of it," Alcide declares.

I watch the lines being drawn, the sides being taken. I know Pace and James well enough to recognize the signs of their anger. James is crafty and sly, and Pace showed his limits last night when he took him on. James is smart enough to goad someone else into throwing the first punch, while Pace retains a calm façade that does nothing to reveal the anger he's feeling inside until it erupts. I know by the blaze burning in his very blue eyes that he's out of patience with James and his prickly know-it-all demeanor. Pip senses it also and darts off, a bright spot of yellow against the drab rock cliff.

We all know it will do us no good to fight amongst ourselves. Yet neither James's nor Pace's pride will let them back down, even when one or the other is wrong. I know that anything I say will only make matters worse. Both are fighting for leadership and for the right to make the decisions for all of us. As far as I'm concerned they can have it.

Thank God for Freddy. "Can you show us?" he asks Pace. "So we'll know what to watch out for?"

Pace keeps his gaze on James as he speaks. "I can," he says to Freddy. "We'll need the pails."

"Can you make sure the ponies are watered too?" I ask Freddy.

"I will," he says and dashes off to do as I asked with Nancy following on his heels.

"Come on, Wren," Pace says and holds out his hand.

I don't take it. I have an obligation that I need to fulfill. "You go search for food," I say. "I'll help Adam and James get the bodies ready."

"I think you should come with me," Pace says again, his eyes on James.

It would be so simple now. To take Pace's hand and just walk off without a care. But these are my people who died, and it is because of me that they are dead. It is my responsibility to tend to their needs now, with the respect I owe to them. There is more at stake here than Pace and James fighting for control of our little band of survivors. I will not allow myself to be the source of contention between the two of them.

James's self-satisfied smirk isn't helping things either. For the first time since we met I feel really awkward around Pace. I take his hand and he thinks I'm going with him, but instead I just pull him far enough away that James cannot hear our conversation.

"I have to do this," I explain.

"I don't trust him," Pace replies, and I realize he's not really listening to what I have to say because he's still watching James. My temper flares and I lose patience with him. I know it's because I am tired, scared, and worried. I need Pace to be supportive of me, just like he has since all this began.

"I've known him a lot longer than you and don't trust him either," I snap. Pace's eyes finally turn to me and they widen in surprise. "But this has nothing to do with who trusts who," I continue. "This has to do with my people who have died. I owe it to them to make sure they are respected until the end."

"We can help them after we find food," Pace argues.

"Or I can do it now while you find food."

"They're dead Wren, they can certainly wait." His tone is dismissive and callous, and I know his thoughts are more about James than me.

"I won't let them wait any longer than they already have," I return in a voice I barely recognize.

"I've got people that are missing too," Pace says. "And unlike you, I don't have any way of knowing if they are alive or dead. I don't know what's happened to my mother. What if she's hurt someplace? There's no one to look for her. There's no one to care for her."

"I know," I say. "And I'm sorry." I really am sorry, but I'm also angry that he's putting this pressure on me. I have enough on me as it is. "There is nothing I can do about it now. Right now I have to take care of what is in front of me, then I will worry about the rest." I turn and walk away.

"Wren!" He whispers my name loudly so James and Adam, who have moved down the beach to the bodies, won't hear. I ignore him and keep on walking until I get to the pile of debris from our village. I gather up as many pieces of wood as I can carry in my arms in one trip and splash across the stream of water to where James and Adam have laid out the bodies. I am strangely angry and do not want to talk to anyone, especially James who I know is watching me.

I make several trips back and forth across the water for wood, gathering up the pieces that litter the beach. I am soaked up to my knees but I keep going. What's a bit of water to me when others have lost their lives? The day becomes brighter around me, but I don't notice as we are still in the shade from the cliff walls. I see Pace in the distance, standing over the children as they dig. He kneels and picks up something from the sand. It must be what he was looking for because he drops it in the bucket and the children go back to work with a clear purpose now.

I suddenly realize that Alcide is missing. Did he go for water with Freddy and Nancy? I look to the ponies, who are still huddled in the same place, and see Freddy and Nancy watering them, but there is no sign of Alcide until I hear a shout. I look up and see him on the trail that goes up the cliff. Alcide waves at me and I wave back as he makes his way down.

He's a bit out of breath as he trots up to join me, Adam, and James, who stopped what they were doing when he arrives. "It goes all the way up," he informs us.

"Is there any sign of life?" I ask.

"I didn't see anything or hear anything, except for some birds," he says. "But there has to be something up there, some sign of the dome, and survivors," he adds hopefully.

"We need to finish this," Adam says. While I've been gathering the wood, Adam and James have moved the bodies into a circle, placing husbands and wives together with their children. I didn't pay much attention to what they were doing, not because I dismissed it, but because I didn't want to look at the faces of the dead. I carry Alex's death with me, so close to my soul that I see him right as I fall into my sleep and am suddenly jerked awake with the horror of it. I don't need more faces to haunt my dreams, yet I fear they always will.

"Bring the oil," James adds. "We're nearly ready." They'd placed the bodies close to the water. The tide is out now, but when it comes in, it will wash the ashes out to sea. I'd always wondered if that's where the ashes went, when we placed our dead on the funeral pyres on the river that ran through our village. I'd always hoped it was the sea, and not deeper into the earth. Generations of shiners spent their lives underground and, to me, their remains deserved to be free of the constraints of the earth. Pace told me stories of the before time, when people buried their dead in the ground. When my time comes, I want my ashes thrown from the cliff tops and carried away in the wind that swirls around us so that I can fly like the birds and not be buried once more in the earth.

Alcide finds the can of oil he'd stashed earlier and hands it to James. Then he runs down the beach to where Pace and the children are still hard at work to bring them back. It is time to pay tribute to those of us who have passed on.

My grandfather's funeral is the last one we had. It was just a few short days ago, yet it seems like a lifetime . . . many lifetimes. It is our custom to talk about the one who has passed, to list their attributes and how they contributed to the village. I realize there aren't enough words to speak about those who lie before me. How do you pay tribute to so many people who died in vain?

The children come, slowly, dreading what is to come as much as I am. They all have family members among the bodies, and if they aren't here then they are surely dead. Some of them, like Stella, are too little to understand the finality of it all. She just knows that she misses her mother and wants her back.

Pace doesn't cross the water with the rest. Instead he collects the pails from the children and gathers bits of wood for his own fire. I watch him for a moment and wonder if James will take offense at Pace not joining our circle. I realize it's a no-win situation for Pace. If he came across, James would be just as likely to tell him he's not welcome.

I nod, to let him know I'm in agreement with his decision to stay away, and he ignores me, even though I know he was looking right at me. It is ridiculous that we allow James to come between us, because that's exactly what he wants. I need to put my anger away for now, out of respect for those who have died.

The smaller children hang back. Just like me, they don't want to look on the faces of the dead. Little Stella has tears streaming down her face. I pick her up and urge the rest of the children closer to the circle.

"Why don't they wake up?" Stella asks.

"Because they are dead," the little boy who had the answers the night before says. "They will never wake up again." His dry way of speaking reminds me of my grandfather.

"Everyone here has lost someone they loved," I explain. "And we need to tell them good-bye."

Peggy's body is the last one to go on the pyre. Adam places her on top, against her parents. He smooths her hair back from her face and places a kiss upon her cold lips. It tears at my heart to see it and the tragic look on Adam's face. They truly loved one another, which is a gift in our world. When there are so few to choose from, a lot of couples settle for compatibility. Adam and Peggy were truly blessed.

I steal a quick look at the faces on the bodies, committing all who have died to memory. I see Adam's father and realize I never even thought about him losing his only remaining parent. So many lives gone and families shattered. I was the one orphan among them; now we are all orphans. All that is left of generations of shiners.

James dumps the oil over the pyre and, without a word, lights it. His jaw is tight and I know he is full of anger. I fear that Pace and I will bear the brunt of it, when it comes out, as it is bound to do. Even though it is damp, the wood catches quickly because it is old and splintered. The flames shoot up and the wind spins them round and we step back as one from the heat. Stella buries her head in my shoulder and cries. "My mommy isn't there."

"Hush-a-bye, baby," I say, quoting the lines to an old lullaby. I don't know if her mother is on the pyre or not. It could be nothing more than a wish on her part. There were so many faces, and I don't want to confess to her that I don't know who her mother is.

The heat is unbearable. So many bodies at once have created a huge fire, with flames leaping so high it seems as if they will touch the top of the cliff. Surely if there are survivors above they will see the smoke and flames.

And what of the others, the unknown army that my father feared? What if they see it and come with their superior weapons to attack us? My father traded with them, giving them young men and women from the dome for weapons that could drop you in an instant from far away. We would be at their mercy if they showed up. Especially now.

My skin feels like it is blistering from the heat. Every part that is exposed to the flames burns. The children are crying and my eyes water painfully. But it isn't because of tears. My eyes feel like they are on fire too. The smell of burning flesh brings back the memories of Alex once more, and my gut wrenches in protest. The only thing saving me from puking is the fact that it is empty.

I look around even though it is painful to my eyes. We are all feeling it. The children continue to cry and James, Adam, and Alcide all look as if they are in pain. I lift my hand to shield my eyes and see that my skin has taken on a red hue.

I look up at the sky and feel as if someone has stabbed my eyes with a red-hot poker. My vision is gone, replaced by a white light. I still have Stella in my arms, and I need to move. I need to cover my eyes, wash them out, something to make this horrible pain go away. I am terrified to take a step, terrified to release my hold on Stella because I've lost all sense of where I am.

I am blind.

· 4 ·

The cold hard truth of our world is if a baby is born with defects then it is not allowed to live. It is not something that is talked about because it does not happen that often, but upon occasion a baby has been born with a mouth that did not form right, or with twisted or missing limbs, or even blind or deaf. The child is killed mercifully, if there is such a thing, and the family mourns and then moves on because it is for the best. It is not something that I like to think upon because I cannot say what I would do were I to find myself in the same situation. I've been told it is for the greater good because everyone must be able to contribute to our survival. A child that is a burden has nothing to give back to the community, yet we take care of our ponies, which are born blind, because they can work, even though they cannot see.

These thoughts go through my mind as I try to calm myself. I cannot see anything beyond a searing white light and I'm holding a crying child. Meanwhile my skin feels as if it is on fire.

"Get out of the sun!" I hear Pace yell behind me. "It's what's burning you."

I hear everyone moving around me. Some of the children are crying. I keep my hand on Stella's head to keep her face buried in my neck to protect her as much as I can.

"Don't look at it!" Pace yells again, too late for me but hopefully the others will be safe. I feel tears streaming down my face and my eyes burn as if they are in the flames. Alex's eyes were red; the whites of them burned just like his skin. Is that what I look like now? I blink against the tears and I cannot tell if my eyes are open or closed.

"Alcide," I call out because I remember he was the closest to me. "I need help."

"Wren?" he replies. I can tell he's close and I reach out my hand. I feel it flailing in the wind as if it is no longer connected to my arm. My entire body feels disconnected from this world that I can no longer see, as if I'm locked in a box and beating on the sides to be let out. If I cannot see them, can they see me?

"I can't see," I whisper because I don't want to frighten Stella any more than she already is.

"Wren?" Alcide whispers back.

"Take her," I say. I feel his touch as he takes Stella from me. She cries louder and clings to me, pulling my hair, which is caught up in her hand as Alcide takes her away.

"Pace!" Alcide yells and the loudness of its startles me because he is so unexpectedly close to my side. "Wren can't see!"

I am suddenly alone as Alcide steps away with Stella. This is how it is for the ponies. Forever blind and just waiting for someone to guide them. I don't want to be a burden to anyone. I stand in place, unsure of where to go or what to do. The fire is burning somewhere close by and the water is beyond it. I could easily be lost in just a few uncertain steps.

Panic builds up inside me. What if no one helps me? What if they just leave me here to die because I am no longer of any use? I take a deep breath and another and another while I begin to shake uncontrollably.

"Wren!" It is Pace. He grabs my arms and throws something over my head. His jacket?

"I looked at it," I say. "I looked at the sun."

"Oh God," he whispers like a prayer. I feel my body move as Pace picks me up and runs with me in his arms through the water. Suddenly I feel the cool shade and smell the familiar dampness of the earth. Pace carries me back into the cave and sets me down on a rock. My ears are filled with the sound of the falls, and in the distance I hear the cries of the children. He pulls his jacket away, and I turn my head in different directions, trying to make sense of where he is.

"My eyes," I have to ask. "What do they look like?" I imagine them gone. I can still feel the tears on my cheeks, and I wonder if it's not tears but my eyes that have melted in their sockets.

I feel Pace's hand on my face. My skin stings, especially when he touches it. He pulls my kerchief from my hair. "Don't move," he says. How could I? I'm terrified and suddenly I realize this is what it was like for Pace, when I first brought him below. He was as blind as I am now, totally lost in the darkness and dependent upon me, as I am now dependent upon him.

There is no luxury of a lamp for me. Pace did not answer my question about my eyes and desperation fills me. I need to know, but I am so very afraid, more so than I've ever been, even with everything that's happened. I raise my hands to touch them but Pace stops me before I can. He puts the bandana over my eyes and the cold water instantly cools them.

"My eyes," I say again in a shaky voice.

"They are still there," he assures me. "They look the same."

"What happened?"

"The sun is so bright, especially to your shiner eyes." He dribbles some water on the back of my hands. "It's like getting too close to a fire. It burns your skin because we're not used to it."

"The others?"

"You're the only one who looked up, Wren," Pace confesses. "All of us have red skin right now, from the sun, but you're the only one who . . . ," his voice trails off.

I am so frightened now I am shaking. I reach out into the darkness and grab onto Pace's forearms. "Is it forever? Will I be blind for the rest of my life?"

"I don't know," he admits, and his voice sounds just as shaky as mine.

"What am I going to do?" I ask as the fear burns its way into my bones.

"We'll figure it out Wren," Pace says. He touches the side of my face and smoothes my hair back. I lean into his touch as if it will save my life. "But for now, you're just going to have to be patient." My words to him are coming back to haunt me now. He takes my bandana from my face and moves away. Once more I feel so very alone. "Here, keep this over your eyes." He hands my kerchief back, once more dripping with water. "Maybe it will help." He puts his hands on my shoulders. "I'm going to check on the others. Don't move. You should be safe as long as you stay still." And then he is gone.

I am too frightened to move; still I manage to make my body smaller by pulling my legs up and wrapping my arms around them.

I put the wet bandana against my eyes. The coolness does help, but my fear will not let me take any comfort from it.

I can't stop shaking. I have no concept of where I am. We ran through the cave so fast when we realized that it led to outside that I didn't pay attention to it beyond recognizing the opening and the light beyond it. The roar of the falls fills my ears. It makes me feel even more isolated, if that is possible. I turn my head back and forth, trying to make sense of the noises that surround me. I have no idea how far from the entrance I am, or how close to the river, although I imagine it is very close.

I drop my head to my knees in an effort to calm myself. Something brushes against my side and I jump, panicked. I brace myself against the rock because I'm afraid I'll fall off and then be totally lost. I hear a meow and realize it's Cat who is beside me. He bumps his head against my arm and I manage to find him and pull him into my lap. His rumbly purr is a reassuring sound in my darkness.

I have no way of knowing how much time has passed. I feel as if I am totally cut off from the world. Was this what it was like for Pace when I left him to fend for himself in the tunnel the first day? He was in total darkness, with nothing to let him know he was alive except for Pip in his cage. He was alone for hours. For me it has been only minutes and I feel like I am about to lose my mind.

I don't want to be underground again. Just the thought of going back into the earth, especially since I fought so hard to leave it, makes me feel even more desperate. I am afraid that once I am back beneath the earth, I will never be free of it, that I will be stuck within forever with the bodies from the days before the dome when they buried their people in the ground. Even with my blindness I can see the bony limbs reaching for me. It is a sight that closing my eyes will not make go away, just like Alex when he was burned.

I cannot share this fear with Pace. My blindness is an encumbrance that I would not wish on anyone. How can I ask him to make sure I'm not left in a place that will frighten me when all he is doing is taking care of me the best he can?

What will we do now? Have we traded one type of prison for another one? Did we leave the dome, only to be trapped forever on this beach without food or shelter? To become cooked during the day by the sun? Perhaps my father was right after all. He warned me about the world out here. Even though there are no flames, there is still fire.

The irony of my situation is not lost on me, and I am certain my father would enjoy it. Thoughts of my father lead me to think about how the people of the dome survived the cataclysm. We saw a part of it caved in from the explosion during our escape. How many from above died in the explosion that destroyed our world? What of Pace's mother, whom my father was holding as a hostage against us? What of the other seekers like us who lived above? Lucy, David, Jilly, and Harry. What of the royals and the scarabs and all those in between who worked in service to the dome? I can't help but think of Max, the dome-washer, whom I saw every morning when I went up to watch the light come to the dome. What has become of him? What will become of all of us?

Mostly I am afraid of what will now become of me. I will be nothing but a burden to everyone. It is nothing more than what I deserve. I deserved to be punished. I should be dead instead of Peggy, instead of all of those whose bodies lay smoldering on the beach.

I hear a splash that has nothing to do with the falls. I have no idea where I am in the cave, and I have no way of knowing if I am turning my head in the right direction or not.

"It's me Wren," Pace says, and I sigh in relief. I am so lucky that he cares about me. Where would I be without him?

"How is everyone?" I ask. My voice is still shaky and I hate that I sound weak.

"Everyone is fine," Pace says. He sits down next to me on the rock. I can feel him by my side but I keep my hands on Cat.

A long moment passes, during which I feel terribly self-conscious. Is Pace looking at me? Is he trying to decide what to do with me? Is he about to tell me that the group has decided to abandon me because I am now a burden to them all? "You should think of a name for him," Pace says when he finally speaks. "There's so many of them around now that you can't just call him Cat anymore."

"I'll think on it," I say, and I'm relieved that my voice almost sounds normal. It should be easy for me to come up with a name for Cat. I don't have anything else to occupy my time at the moment.

"I think as long as we stay in the shade, everyone should be fine," Pace says. "We managed to cook some mussels," he adds. "The children are eating."

"Was there not enough for everyone?" I ask.

"It's hard work," Pace confesses. "Especially when you don't really know what you're doing."

"At least you knew what do to," I say. "And how to protect us."

"I should have thought of it sooner," he says. "If I had . . ."

"It's not your fault Pace," I say, repeating back the words he said to me earlier. "I guess my father was right. There really is fire out here."

"There's so much more than just fire," Pace says. "There's an entire world out there for us to see . . ."

I sob. I can't help myself. I feel Pace move away, and I put my hand over my mouth to keep in the rest that threatens to follow.

"I'm so sorry Wren," Pace says. "I wasn't thinking."

I shake my head. I'm afraid to speak, afraid that the tide of tears will drown me if I let them loose. I really need to stop feeling sorry for myself, but I cannot help it. I was all ready to fight because I really didn't think I'd get hurt. Now that I am, all I can think about is giving up. But I can't give up. I think about Ghost and the other ponies, about how they don't even know what they are missing because they've never known what it is to see. About how they depend on me.

"The ponies need food. And water," I finally say.

"I know," Pace replies. "We've talked about it. We're going to go up the trail as soon as the sun goes down. There has to be grass up there, and trees, and hopefully more survivors and shelter."

I nod and wonder if they will take me with them or just leave me here to sit for hours on end. *Stop it . . . Stop being so morbid.* "You have to watch out for the ones who live outside," I say. "They have weapons, like the one used on David. My father told me about them."

"We know," Pace says. "We've talked about that also."

We know . . . Suddenly it is "we," when before it was Pace against James, with me trying to maintain peace. Now they are making plans together and I'm the one left out.

"I want to go back outside," I say. "I don't want to be in here alone."

"I think you should stay in here. You don't want to risk any more damage to your eyes."

My hand goes to my neck where my goggles still hang, so much a part of me and the life left behind. "I can wear these," I say. "And cover my eyes with my bandana."

"I still think you should wait." Pace says. "At least until the sun isn't so bright in the sky."

I have no choice but to comply. If he doesn't want to take me out, I'll never find my way on my own, and while I would have no problem asking Alcide for help, I don't want James to see me this weak.

Still the prospect of the long lonely hours ahead isn't helping. I lower my head to Cat, and the smell of the sea and sand wafts up to my nose from his fur.

"I've thought of a name for him," I say.

Cat meows as Pace scratches under his chin. "What is it?"

"Have you ever heard the story of Jonah? From the Bible?" Pace continues scratching Cat's chin and as his rumbly purr is all I hear, I go on. "Jonah tried to run away from God's commands, so God sent a whale to swallow him. My grandfather showed me a painting of a whale in the library, because we had just read the story. I did not believe it possible until I saw the painting."

"I know the painting," Pace says. "I've seen it."

I try to remember the story as best as I can. I was so small when Grandfather read it to me from his well-worn Bible, now lost in the flood. I couldn't imagine a fish large enough to swallow a man whole until I saw the painting and when I did, just a few weeks after we read it, it came back to me again. How could a man survive in the belly of a whale? Only through God's intervention, because he had plans for Jonah.

I continue with the story. "Jonah realizes that he is trapped and without God he will be held forever in the whale's belly. So he agrees to do as God tells him and the whale spits him out on a beach."

"Do you think what we've done was part of God's will?" Pace asks. "Do you think he's punishing you now for something?"

"I don't know what to think," I admit. "I just know that what happened to us is a lot like what happened to Jonah. He was more scared of being trapped than he was of what he was asked to do."

"And you feel the same way," Pace concludes.

"We were swallowed by the earth and it spit us out on a beach," I say. "Just like Jonah. And just like Jonah, I don't want to go back into the belly of the beast. I'm afraid I'll never find my way out again."

Pace takes my hand into his. "Wren, I would never abandon you. You could have left me, when I was trapped in the tunnel, but you didn't. You've got to know that I would do the same."

"If I had truly known what it was like for you I never would have left you alone," I confess.

"You had to leave me. It was the only way we could both stay alive." I feel his hand cup my cheek. "I promise I will not leave you behind."

It tears my heart out to say it, but I realize I must. "If it means someone's life then you have to."

"Wren . . ." Before he can say more we are interrupted by a shout.

"That came from inside the cave," I say, instinctively turning my head toward the sound.

"Don't move," Pace says, and leaves me. As if I could move without his help. I hear the splash of water and then Pace's voice again. "There are people coming," he says, and I can hear the joy. "They're shiners. I can see their eyes from here."

"Thank God," I say, genuinely grateful despite my circumstances.

"This way!" Pace yells, and I hear him moving away from me, back up the river inside the cave. The echo of excited voices gets louder.

"Wren!" someone calls out. I try to identify the voice in my mind as they get closer and become louder. I hear the *baa* of a goat and the whicker of a pony. There are survivors other than the few of us.

I am so excited that I climb to my feet, cautiously, with my hands out to keep my balance. Jonah meows indignantly at the removal of his comfortable bed and twines between my ankles. I have no idea how big the rock is I'm standing on and the last thing I want to do is fall into the water.

"Who is it?" I call out.

"Rosalyn!" she calls back. "And Sally and Sarah."

"George!" Another voice, "Eddie!" And then, "Peter!"

"Peter . . ." I gasp, astounded that he is still alive. The last time I saw him he was running into the battle. "How did you survive?" I call out.

"You know the rules, Wren. Always have an escape plan," Peter calls back and the rest call out hearty agreements.

He is right. We always have an escape plan for every cavern. But we never dreamed we would have to outrun a wall of water. And there is something that we can't escape: what going out into the fresh air does to our lungs. And Peter already has the horrible cough that signifies the start of the disease that kills our lungs from the inside. He might not survive going outside. None of them might.

"Did anyone else survive?" Rosalyn calls out. Rosalyn is a council member also and just a few years older than Adam. The fact that another council member is alive fills me with such relief. I don't want the responsibility for all these lives. Sally is the teacher and she knows the children. It is as if a great weight has been lifted from my shoulders.

"Adam, James, Alcide, and several of the children are with us," I say.

"Stella?" Rosalyn shrieks. "Is my Stella with you?"

Tears run down my face and I can barely speak because I am so happy that Stella's mother is alive. "She is," I manage to say loud enough for her to hear.

"Where?" Rosalyn starts but is interrupted when George calls out.

"Look at the light!"

"Is it outside? Is it safe?"

I hear them coming closer, faster. I am suddenly very self-conscious of my eyes. Will they be able to tell that I'm blind? What will they think? What will they do? I hastily chastise myself. I should be grateful they are alive—and I am, very much so—instead of worrying over how they will treat me.

I hear the sound of running feet and the next thing I know, I'm lifted in the air and swung around. I grab onto Peter and hug him tight.

"Wren! Wren! You were right! Alex found the way. You saved us. You saved all of us!"

I didn't save all of us. Some of us are dead. I think most of us are dead. I can't stand the thought of any more of us dying. I keep a tight grip on Peter's sleeve so he cannot move away from me. "You can't go outside yet," I say.

"What do you mean?" Peter laughs and then he stops suddenly. "Wren? What's wrong?"

"The sun burned my eyes," I say. "And the air does something to your lungs. We are so full of coal that it's painful." I keep my grip on his sleeve, afraid if I let go he'll slip away from me. "Mary and Hans did not survive it."

"Mary?" Sally says. "Where is my mother?"

"Where is Stella?" Rosalyn calls out as they come closer.

"You should stay here," Pace calls out over their voices. I hear their voices, all raised in questions about their loved ones, and then suddenly they stop. Even though I can't see them, I can feel their shocked stares.

"I'm blind," I say. "I looked at the sun and it burned my eyes."

"Wren . . ." Sally begins in sympathy.

I shake my head. "It's not an easy transition," I say. "The outside is beautiful but it has its dangers. Your lungs will be purged and the sun will burn your skin. Make sure you wear your goggles. Do not look at the sun."

"So there is fire out there."

"But no flames," I say. "It truly is beautiful," I add. "The things we saw last night . . ." How do I explain a sky full of stars and the colors of a sunset to someone who's never seen them before? It is something they will have to witness for themselves. But first they have to survive going out there.

"Where is Stella?" Rosalyn demands again.

"Stay here," Pace says. "I'll get her. I'll get everyone."

"So you're saying we traded one kind of hell for another," George begins. "You had all those people die for no reason?"

"I didn't . . ." I begin. Even though I can't see them, I feel the accusatory stares. "We have to learn to survive out there, just like we learned how to survive underground, all those years ago."

"Is there food?" Eddie asks. "Water?"

"You're standing right beside water you fool," Peter snaps. "It's not Wren's fault. If you want to blame someone, blame those arses who brought the flamethrowers down into the tunnels."

Before the words can escalate into an argument between George and Peter we hear a shriek. "Momma!" It is Stella, along with the excited voices of the others. I listen with a smile on my face as I realize that George and Eddie both have children among the survivors, and I hear the rush of Nancy coming to Peter and Peter's exclamation of joy as they stand beside me.

"What of my mother?" Sally asks.

"She died, along with Hans, when we went outside," James explains. "We all nearly did, except for him." I know he is referring to Pace, who has moved next to me. Beyond James's callous words I can hear Adam talking to Sally, offering her words of comfort.

"It's how much coal dust you have in your lungs," I say. "It didn't bother the children much at all."

"We can't just stay here forever," Peter exclaims. Of all of them, I am worried the most about Peter. He actually dug out the coal, along with Eddie and George. James and Adam worked on demolition with my grandfather. Sally taught the young ones and Rosalyn kept inventory and distributed our goods. Peggy worked with her. Everyone had their purpose in our community. Now we have to join together in the shared purpose of staying alive. Joining together might be the most difficult thing we've ever attempted.

"You can't go charging outside," Alcide says. "It might kill you."

"What of the others who died?" Eddie asks.

"Their bodies washed down from the village," Alcide explains. "We burned them this morning. We never thought there'd be more survivors."

"The water was on our heels," Rosalyn said. "I caught up with Sally and Sarah and we managed to get above it in one of the tunnels. We found George and Eddie, and then we ran into Peter. We heard the goats and followed them out."

"Do you think anyone else survived?"

"Those that were around the lifts could have survived," Peter says. "If they climbed up. I was just coming in when the fool with the flamethrower shot it into the chute below the lift."

"Oh please let it be so," Rosalyn says hopefully. "My Colm was with the fighters."

"The last time I saw him he was alive," Peter offers.

"I thought the lot of you survived it," Rosalyn said. "I saw you from the other side when the waters came through. I knew the council chamber would lead you above the waters."

"It did," James says. "But it was nipping on our heels the entire way."

"I'm sorry about your Peggy," Rosalyn says to Adam.

"Thank you," Adam replies softly. "She's with the rest now. Her ashes have washed out to sea."

"So the explosion was in the chamber on the other side of the village, which is why the wall crumbled," James asks.

"I took off running as soon as I saw what he was about to do," Peter explains. "I managed to find a tunnel that went up and caught up with this group where the ground had given way beneath the dome."

"I wonder how bad the damage was above," Pace wonders aloud. He is worried about his mother. There is no way for us to find news about her.

"What if they're all trapped in it," Alcide adds. "At least we had a way out. They have no fans, no way to keep the air circulating."

"They have a way out," I say. "The way Alex went. The way they took me."

"There's only one way to find out what's happened above," Adam says. "We're going to have to go up the cliff because we can't survive here."

"At least we've got food for today," Pace says.

I hear a *whoop* from Alcide and another one from Freddy and then splashes from something in the water.

"What is it?" I ask Pace.

"A dead goat," he says. "We can roast it."

The prospect of roasted meat in my stomach suddenly makes my mouth water, and I feel somewhat optimistic about things. Maybe my blindness won't be permanent. Other shiners have survived. We are outside and the world is a beautiful place, at least that small portion of it that I've seen. Maybe, just maybe, things will be all right for the lot of us. At least for the moment, we are all safe and for that I will be grateful.

· 5 ·

Words, especially those spoken without thought, can wound you as deeply as any knife thrust or burn. They can also heal when they are spoken from the heart, and I am most grateful for the words Pace speaks to me.

"I'm sorry for what I said before." We sit in the entrance to the cave with our backs against the wall. Everyone moved inside after the meal, including the animals, because there was no shelter to be found outside from the sun. It is merciless in its attack upon our skin, making it dry, raw, and itchy beneath its rays. I expect in time we will become accustomed to it. Just as our shiner eyes adapted to see in the dark, we will once more be able to stand beneath the sun. We have to, or else how could our forefathers have survived all those years? They sailed the seas and worked the land in all kinds of weather and so must we in time. I can only imagine what we all look like. Pace told me everyone's skin is pink. In my mind I can't quite grasp the color, as it would appear on our skin.

Jonah is beside me and his constant movements and loud purrs lead me to believe he's licking his fur clean from his recent meal. The world around us is quiet except for the sound of the river, so much so that my blindness leaves me to think we are alone, but Pace's hushed tones lets me know that there are people around us. "About the people from your village who died."

"You spoke in haste," I say. "I know you didn't mean it."

"It was disrespectful," Pace continues. "You were right to do what you did. I shouldn't have put you in that position."

"You can't let James get to you," I say. "Once he knows he can do it, he won't stop. If we're going to survive this, we're going to have to work together."

"Whether we want to or not?"

I open my mouth to explain why we have to work together, and then I realize Pace is teasing me. Because I can't see his face I don't know the intent behind his words, but I do remember what he looks like and I can easily visualize the look on his face at the moment. How long will it be before that memory fades?

We are so lucky. All of those who showed up today survived the purge. I don't know if it is because they knew what to expect or because they eased their way out into the pure air, sitting for a while at the cave opening before venturing forward into the new world, but they somehow managed it. It is another thing to be grateful for, along with the meal of roasted goat we just finished.

More things have washed down now. Things we can actually use. Clothing and blankets, which have been spread on the sand to dry. A bag of feed that, while damp, was not moldy and was there-fore rationed among the ponies and goats. Personal things, such as brushes and combs, plates, cups and bowls, even Pip's cage, were found strewn along the banks of the river within the cave, and Pip is in it now, sleeping away after his flights of adventure, according to

Pace. The things scavenged from the banks of the river are not much to testify to the community we had beneath the ground, but to those of us who survived with nothing more that the clothes on our backs these things are great treasures.

"You should try to get some sleep," Pace says. "We all should. We don't know how long it will take us to get up there."

"Or what we will find when we do," I finished. I am worried about the others, the band of roving outlaws that had my father so intimidated with their strange weapons that could drop a person from far away. We all saw the results with David, and I will never forget the sight when the filcher who held me was hit by one of the same weapons in the head and his blood splattered all over me. I never want to experience that again.

Pace's suggestion of sleep takes root in my mind and I yawn loudly. It isn't as if I have anything else to do. The ponies have been cared for and are in the cave with the rest of us. I no longer have to worry about the children because Sally is with them. Pace gently kisses my forehead and then steps away. I yawn again and I stretch out on my side and fall asleep, lulled into peace by the sound of the river that reminds me of home.

I dream of a meadow. It is from a painting I once saw. It is a wide open expanse of grass and flowers, things I've never actually seen before, except in the beautiful pieces of artwork on display in the library the few times I was permitted to go. It is the most beautiful place I have ever seen, more so because in my dream I know that it actually exists. Colorful insects fly past me with beautiful wings. Butterflies. The word comes to me, even though I am not certain if I've ever heard it. I stand in the middle, among all the bright colors, and feel the soft kiss of a breeze on my cheek that smells so very sweet. The sun is shining overhead but it does not pain me.

Ghost and the other ponies are in the meadow and at my feet Jonah chases an insect. All around me I hear the chirping of birds, and there are so many more than what I've ever heard before and they are as colorful as the flowers. I reach out to touch a flower that wavers on its stalk next to me. It is as high as my waist, and as I cup the deep pink petals I realize that my hands are remarkably clean. There are no coal stains around my nails and no cuts or scrapes mar the surface of my skin. My arms are bare and I see that I am wearing a dress of the purest white and the softest fabric that flutters around me in the quickening wind.

I look up. Something has blocked the sun from my view. It is the same as if I am on my back on the rooftops, looking up at the milky glass of the dome. It grows larger, and darker, and I realize that it is a whale. It comes at me from the sky with its huge maw open, dark and bottomless like the pit where Alex flew. I try to run but I am not fast enough. It scoops me up into its mouth and swallows me whole, and I feel my body falling into the eternal blackness.

It is the falling that startles me from the dream and I slowly open my eyes. Everything is dark, yet I see movement and shadows. At first I am frightened because I cannot see, then I realize that I can see more than I did before I slept. That has to be a good sign, doesn't it?

I try to stare through the darkness, as if my will alone will make it go away. It is as if a heavy piece of fabric is over my eyes. I do not know at what I am looking. I just know that there is something there.

I am alone, except for Jonah, who I can feel stretching beside me. Should I call out for help? Should I tell them I can see? I decide I won't, in case this is as good as it gets. It is better than it was before and for that I am grateful. Instead I place my hands against the cave wall and slowly stand up. Surely someone will see and come for me. I cannot help but wonder, where is Pace? Why did he leave me alone for so long? Does he not want me anymore because I am now blind? Does he consider me nothing more than a burden now? The thought makes me feel like a petulant child, and I ask myself why he should stay by my side every minute. It is no different than what I did with him when I brought him into the tunnels.

I listen carefully to the sounds around me and realize that either I am alone or else everyone is sleeping. I don't even hear the shifting of the ponies or the restless movement of the goats that were close by before. I am completely alone.

A cold chill fills me and I wrap my arms around my body. Did they leave me here? Are they climbing the cliff right now and left me behind because I would be a hindrance to them? What will I do? I can't find my way up the cliff on my own and I can't survive staying here. I am panicked, so much so that I cannot breathe.

Take a breath Wren . . . I breathe deep, making my body and my mind relax, and then I turn my head, trying to remember the brief time I was in the mouth of the cave, and try to discern if there is light because that will be the way out. All I see is shadows. None is brighter than the others. None helps me determine where I am. What if it is night now? What will I do?

I can't help myself. I have to know if I'm alone. "Hello!" I call out. "Can anyone hear me?" My words echo around me, taunting me with my solitude. What am I going to do?

"Wren?" It is Alcide who comes to my rescue. I am grateful it is Alcide, actually grateful that it is anyone but James. I don't want him to see me as weak, even with my blindness. "Is something wrong?"

"I just woke up alone," I explain and feel foolish and ashamed when I hear the words.

"Pace said to let you sleep as long as possible. He's hoping it will help . . . with your eyes."

I don't mention that I can see shadows. I see enough to know where Alcide is standing. "Where is everyone?" I ask.

"We're ready to go up the cliff. I was just coming to wake you."

Alcide was coming for me. Not Pace. He takes my arm in a firm grip. "We've got the supplies wrapped up in blankets and tied to the ponies' back. We're going to put the children on the ponies and the rest of us will lead them up," he explains. I wonder if I'm included in the useful lead them up part. I want to be seen as useful.

I can sense the world brightening around me as we walk. The noise of the ocean is much louder now, and I can hear birds cawing above me. We have to be outside, but I have to be sure that I am actually seeing something. "Has the sun gone down?" I ask.

"No," Alcide answers. "It's just low in the sky. It doesn't hurt our skin to be in it now. I think the middle of the day is the worst of it."

So I am seeing something, or maybe sensing it is a better word. Still it makes me feel optimistic about my eyes eventually returning to normal.

"I'll take her," Pace says as he meets us. He kisses my cheek and it feels strange, as if he's placating me. The kisses we shared before were so much more, so deep, so lingering, as if he was pouring all his emotions into that single instant. Even the one we shared after we came out of the cave had such meaning. The past few have felt more obligatory than anything else. "How did you sleep?" he asks.

"Deeply," I reply as the dream about the meadow comes back to me.

"Good," he replies. "Did Alcide tell you the plan?"

"Yes. Put me with Ghost. He's used to me. The rest of the ponies will follow on his tail if he's in the lead."

"You know them best," Pace says.

"I know Alcide checked the trail," I say. "What did he say about it? Is it steep? Are there rocks or holes we should look out for?"

"He said it looks like it was man-made because it's a lot like the tunnels below. It's smooth and wide and it appears to go all the way to the top by angling back and forth."

"It was probably made at the same time as the dome."

"Maybe they used it when they were building it to carry things in from the sea," Pace says. "The catwalk above certainly looks like it could be in the dome."

"Is the smoke still there?"

"I haven't seen it, but it could be because the wind has changed. Can you feel it? It's blowing in from the sea."

Yes, I can feel it. It is rougher, yet inconsistent. When it comes it tears at my hair, which is loose and wild around my face. I instinctively reach for my kerchief, but it's gone. It must have fallen when I stood and I didn't know it.

"Your kerchief?" Pace asks. "It must be in the cave. I'll go get it."

"No wait," I begin but he is gone and doesn't answer me. Now I feel even more useless as I have no idea where I am standing or where anyone else is, and Pace is wasting his time on a trivial errand for me. Just a few minutes ago I felt as if I was an obligation for Pace and now I feel even worse as he's running after something as insignificant as my bandana. Are the others waiting and watching? Do they see me as a nuisance now?

I turn my head to the left. Pace said the wind was blowing in from the sea and since I can feel it on my cheek, I hope that I will see more shadows when I look toward the cliff. I do. Is my sight getting better still? I look up and I see a definite contrast between the cliff wall and the sky.

I hear the noise of the others close by. The shifting of the ponies, the ramblings of the goats, and the quiet chatter of the children. I can't see them. They are lost in the shadows of the cliff wall.

"Wren!" I recognize Adam's voice. Neither he nor James has talked to me since this morning. Since I went blind. I instinctively turn in the direction of Adam and will my eyes to see him. There is nothing but shadows, but shadows are better than nothing at all.

"Adam," I say when I feel him close by. In the past Adam and I have never really talked to each other. We always had Peggy around as a buffer between us. I always felt he only tolerated me because Peggy and I were friends. But I also know him to be fair. Even though he and James are best friends, he doesn't automatically go James's way. I've always respected Adam for who he is. There is nothing sly about him, like James. I know my grandfather thought well of him, or so he told me many times. Maybe he wished that Adam would have chosen me instead of Peggy. But there was no denying their love. It was obvious to everyone who saw them together.

Adam doesn't say anything. Instead he puts his arms around me. He pulls me tightly into his embrace. My arms are trapped within his and all I can do is put my hands on his chest as he squeezes me against him. I feel him shaking and realize that he is fighting back tears.

"Adam?" I ask tentatively.

"She loved you so much," he says after a brief moment when I imagine he was trying to keep his emotions under control. "She was so worried about you."

"Peggy?"

"Yes."

"I loved her too."

"I know." Adam sniffs back his tears and releases me. "I just wanted you to know that. Before . . . before things get any crazier than they already are."

"Adam," I say. "Do you think what we did was wrong?"

"I think we all made mistakes, Wren. I think I made the biggest one of all by not stopping James when he wanted to blow up the fans. If not for that . . ."

"You are not responsible for her death . . ." I begin.

"In a way I am," Adam says. "In a way we all are. For all of them. But none of us any more than the others. It's a responsibility we all share. And because of that, we have to make sure some good comes of it."

"You and Rosalyn have to lead us now," I say without letting my relief show. I don't want to be the one making decisions any more. I can't make any, not the way I am.

"Don't sell yourself short, Wren," Adam says. "You are wiser than you believe you are. You just have to believe in yourself more."

"I thought I did," I confess. "Now, after everything that has happened, I'm not so sure."

A shadow crosses my vision and I feel Adam's hand on my cheek. "Follow your heart, Wren. It won't lead you wrong."

I smile and nod at Adam. "Will you take me to Ghost?" I ask.

"Ghost?"

I had forgotten that no one would know my pony's name, except for me. And Pace, since I did introduce him to Ghost before the flood. "The white one. He's the lead."

"Your guy is coming," Adam says. "Don't you want him to help you?"

"Only if you mind doing it yourself," I say.

"I don't," Adam says and he takes my arm. "Do you know our plan?" he asks.

"I do. Adam," I have said this before to Pace, but I want to make sure, "you know there are others that live outside. And they have the weapons like the one that injured David. We have to watch out for them."

"We're aware," Adam says. "There's not much we can do about the weapons, but we will watch out. We don't know what's up there, Wren, we can only hope that it is something better than what's down here."

"Adam. I am so sorry about Peggy."

"Me too, Wren. But at least we had a few moments. It's more than some." He takes my hand and puts it on Ghost. I immediately recognize the feel of his shaggy mane. "Here's your beast then," Adam says.

"Thank you, Adam," I say. "For everything."

"You too," he says and walks away.

Ghost is glad to see me. He butts his head into my chest. I find his head with my hands and lower my forehead to touch his. "I'm like you now boy," I say. "Trapped in the darkness. Hopefully between the two of us we'll find our way out." Ghost snuffs at my clothes and nips at my sleeve. I know I smell different to him. I no longer smell like coal and earth. Now I am covered with the salty smell of the sea.

"Are you ready?" Pace asks me. He puts my kerchief in my hand and I use it to tie my hair back.

"I am ready," I say. I wrap my hand around Ghost's halter. "Show me the way," I say and we move forward once more into the darkness.

· 6 ·

We are all creatures of habit. It is easy for me to pretend that I am once more in the tunnels, just putting one foot in front of the other without thought because there is only one way to go. Either down into the mines or back to the stables. That was my circuitous route, night after night as I worked my shift, guiding the ponies with their loads of coal. Walking up this trail isn't much different from what the ponies and I are used to.

My vision is returning. It is not my imagination as I kept telling myself over and over again before. I can clearly see the outlines of people in front of me and know that Adam, James, and Pace are leading the way and they carry some sort of weapons. I cannot tell what they are for sure, but I imagine they are stout pieces of wood. All three of them have small knives, as do Peter, Alcide, George, and Eddie. The shiner men always had a knife in their belts and handy things in their pockets, such as twine and scraps of metal. You never knew in the tunnels when such things would come in handy.

"Has anyone thought about what we're going to do if there isn't any shelter above?" Freddy asks. Freddy is leading Ghost while I keep my hand wrapped in his halter. Pip's cage is tied to the bundle on his back and he contributes an occasional chirp to the trip, as if he's offering directions to Ghost. Jonah and a dozen or more cats scamper with us, running up the trail, and then waiting for us to catch up with questioning meows before they take off again on the next leg of the journey.

"There has to be," I say. I cannot fathom there not being any shelter. The dome is up there, somewhere close by. My sense of direction, so much a part of me, tells me that the dome is above us.

"What if they don't let us in?" Freddy asks.

"Do you want to go back in the dome?"

"It depends," he replies. "On what else is out here."

I have no response for that, nothing to allay his fears, since he is only voicing what I have thought and said over and over again since our escape.

The wind is rougher now, swirling around us like a demon and bringing back memories of the way it roared up from the pit. It tugs at my hair and my clothes and brings a damp chill with it that is familiar and strange at the same time. My eyes feel dry, so I pull my goggles up from my neck to protect them. I don't want to take any chances with my eyes now. Every time I blink my vision seems better to me, as if the fabric over my eyes is becoming more sheer as the moments pass.

"The sky looks strange," Freddy says.

I automatically look up but cannot see well enough to see what he is talking about. "In what way?" I ask.

"There are things in it. Like piles of feathers."

"Clouds," I say, as I remember another painting in the library.

"Except these aren't white," Freddy continues. "They are gray, like the fur on your cat."

"Jonah," I say. "His name is Jonah."

"Like the story with the whale?" he asks.

"Yes, Jonah and the whale." I have no idea what it means to have clouds in the sky, especially gray ones, but I have heard of a thing called rain, when water comes out of the sky, and I wonder if perhaps we will see it. I also hope I am right and there is shelter above. A low rumble sounds in the distance, much like the explosion that caused the flood, and everyone stops in their tracks. Ghost tosses his head in distress, jerking my hand, and I quickly comfort him.

"Did you see that?" James says.

"What was it?" Alcide calls out from behind me.

"A light flashed across the sky over there," James replies and I can actually see his arm extended against the sky. I turn in the direction that he is pointing and to my surprise I see another flash of light, followed a few seconds later by another rumble.

"We need to move faster," Pace says. "We don't want to be on this cliff when that gets here."

"What is it?" Adam asks as we start forward once again at a quicker pace.

"I think it's a storm," Pace says. "Rain, lightning, thunder, and wind."

"Something else from your books?" James asks.

"Yes and no," Pace says. "I've heard thunder before," he explains. "When I was on the catwalk at the top of the dome. I saw the flashes of light too. I didn't know what it was until I looked in a book. Someone told me at the time that it was caused by the flames. But when I looked in a book it talked about a storm."

"Does he mean rain like the flood in the Bible?" Freddy asks.

"Yes," I say. "But not for forty days and nights. The Bible says he promised never to send a flood like that again."

"God destroyed the world by flood and then he destroyed it by fire," Rosalyn says behind me. "I wonder what he will use the next time we displease him."

"The world is not destroyed," I say. "It was just hidden from us."

"For two hundred years," George calls out. He huffs with exertion as he speaks. "So far I'm not impressed with what I've seen."

"And you think others don't think the same about you?" Rosalyn calls back to him. I've always admired Rosalyn because she isn't afraid to say what she's thinking, which is why she was chosen for the council. Since there are only two members left, that we know of, another will have to be elected. James was removed from the council for his rash actions in blowing up the fans, but only a few of us know that. Hopefully we will find more shiners who have survived. Hopefully *we* will all survive.

The wind picks up, violently, and pushes against us as if it wants to throw us off the cliff. I hear Stella crying behind me and Rosalyn trying to comfort her. The goats, which trail after us, baa their distress. The cats yowl their displeasure and Jonah slinks under Ghost for what little bit of shelter he provides. Ghost tosses his head once more. How can I explain to him something that he's never known and cannot see?

Lightning streaks the sky again and more thunder rumbles. With every burst of light I can see better, and I realize that my sight really has returned. I could almost sigh in relief but I do not because now my biggest fear is of being blown off the cliff. We are more than halfway to the top and I pray that the storm stays out to sea until we find some sort of shelter.

My prayer goes unanswered as lightning streaks again right above our heads. A strange tingling goes down my back and my ears pop. Ghost rears and jerks both Freddy and me in his effort to get away from the strange sensations around him.

"I've got him," I say to Freddy. "Help Rosalyn."

"But you can't see," Freddy says.

"I'll be fine," I assure him as I calm Ghost. I rub his neck and talk to him, assuring him that I will protect him, although I don't know how. The rest of the ponies are just as spooked as Ghost and dance around in an effort to escape the unknown. "Hold on to them!" I yell. "They'll go right over the side if you don't!" Right over the side with the children on their backs, if they hang on. Getting off isn't much better, not where we stand. Freddy goes back and grabs the halter of the pony behind us and Rosalyn takes Stella from its back.

"Come on!" James yells at us. The trail has doubled back on itself, the last turn before we reach the top.

"Wren?" Pace calls out.

"I'm fine! Just keep going." There's no time. The storm is upon us. There is another clap of thunder, so loud that I can't help but jump, and then the sky opens up and we are soaked before I can take a breath. Pip squawks angrily in his cage but there is nothing I can do for him. I put my head down and yank hard at Ghost's halter. "Keep them close!" I yell back. "As long as they know another is in front of them they should keep on walking!"

"Just go!" Peter yells from the back.

"That's easy for you to say," George adds.

"Come on boy," I encourage Ghost. I can see well enough to watch his milky eye roll back as he tosses his head but he moves, thankfully, in the right direction.

I have never imagined anything like this. It is almost like being under water. I wipe the water from my goggles as I move on and up. The rain pelts against me like rocks and the wind swirls so that

I feel like it will pick me up and blow me away. Stella's cries have stopped, but I do not turn around to see why. I can only trust that they are still behind me as we make the turn to the top. My head is down so that I can only see the next few steps in front of me so I jump when Pace grabs my arm.

"You can see?" He has to yell because the rain pounds so loud.

"Yes." Lightning flashes again and thunder rolls right over our heads. Pace grabs my shoulders and pulls me close enough to kiss, hard and fast, on my mouth. Then he grabs Pip from his cage and carefully places him inside his coat.

"Keep going," he says and I move past him, his kiss still burning on my lips. It wasn't a placating kiss, it was wonderful and full of emotion and I can't help but grin a little as I trudge on through the rain.

"Come on! We're almost there!" Adam turns around and calls out. I look up and see the metal catwalk right behind Adam. A contraption hangs from it, perilously twisted and broken. The wind rattles it and it bangs and clanks as if it might let go of its hold and go crashing down the cliff side. The cats slink by me, crying their distress and searching for a dry place.

James is at the top. He stops and puts a hand up to stop the rest of us. I don't know what he expects us to do. We can't turn away and go back. The storm has pushed the sea onto our little beach and there is no place for us to go. I quickly catch up to Adam and I stop Ghost while everyone else piles up behind me. Pace runs back up to where we stand and moves forward to join Adam and James with Alcide and Peter right behind them.

"What's going on?" George asks.

"Shhh!" James hisses. I don't know what he expects us to do. We can be quiet, but the cats are yowling to the heavens.

"We need to make sure if it's safe," Adam says.

"It cannot be any worse than this," Rosalyn says.

"Is there shelter?" Sally asks.

"Quiet!" Adam says again.

I turn around. "Please, let them make sure there is no one about."

"What do you mean no one about?" Rosalyn asks me in a loud whisper. Stella stares at me with her big eyes. Raindrops cling to her lashes and she looks pale as a ghost. She has her thumb in her mouth and she is shaking.

"I was told there are people who lived outside," I say. "We do not know what they are like."

"God help us," Sally says. She holds Sarah in her arms with her head pressed into her neck. They both shiver from the wet. I hear Peter's hoarse cough and once more the order to be quiet. We cannot stay here; we must move on and face whatever it is before us. "Can you see now?" Sally asks suddenly.

"I can," I say. I look once more at James, Adam, and Pace, all peering cautiously over the top. James wipes the water from his face and stares once more into the sheets of rain. "Come on." I tug on Ghost's halter and we start walking, past Peter and Alcide, past Pace, and past Adam.

"Where do you think you are going?" James hisses as we walk past him.

"I'm going to get these people out of the rain," I retort.

There's a steep slope the last few steps up. It is slick from the rain and I slip, falling to my knees before sliding back a few steps. Determined, I use my hand to leverage myself up while pulling Ghost after me until I reach the top. I need a moment to catch my breath and there is a cramp in my side from the strange angle I had to use to crawl up the slope. I am also covered with mud on my knees and my hands and all I can do is wipe my hands on my pants. While I take a moment to recover, the cats, including Jonah, bound past and disappear into the rain.

"She can see again?" Alcide's voice shows his surprise.

"Yes she can," Pace says. I hear him and Alcide both scrambling up behind me as I look at the scene before me.

Grass as high as my waist swings back and forth in the swirling wind. The cats have all taken cover within. In the distance, I see the dome, dark and gray like the clouds that are so close above us that I feel like I can touch them. The rain would have to sound like drumbeats on the dome, but with the constant roar of the fans, there is no way anyone would ever hear it, unless they were right against it and that was strictly forbidden. The fans are not running now. What do the people inside hear? Are they frightened at the unknown noises and flashes of light? Is rain falling inside from the hole that the smoke was coming out of?

Between the grass and the dome there are trees and the ruins of buildings that create a dense maze of cover that could either shelter us or shelter someone who wants to hurt us. "What do you think?" Alcide asks as James and Adam join us.

"I think I want to get in out of the rain," Pace says.

"Me too," I agree. "The rest will need help getting up."

"Pace and I will help," Alcide says. "You three go on and find us a place."

My respect for Alcide is growing with leaps and bounds as we try to survive this disaster. He may be younger than me by a year, but he already knows how to placate James, who wants to prove that he is a capable leader for all of us.

James steps into the grass, Adam follows, then me with Ghost. It feels like walking into the water where Pace and I swam with the glowfish. It surrounds us and then the surface ripples out around us before tossing back into us, like waves. Ghost sniffs at the grass, which tickles his nose, with his ears perked up and then stops in his tracks to bury his head in it. He tears off a clump by its roots and chomps it down. Jonah appears before me and with a quick meow, disappears back into it, with nothing but his tail showing like a rudder on the wooden boats we used to sail on the stream in our village.

"This isn't dirt," James says. "It's more like rock."

I look beneath my feet and see that the grass grows in thick tufts between cracks in the stones. "Cobblestones," I say. "Like the promenade."

"Then this was part of the city before?" Adam asks.

"I think so." I look around. "It's just fallen into ruin."

"It has been two hundred years," Adam says.

"And a fiery comet," I add. The rain is still pouring down on us while the lightning and thunder continue, but we are so wet that it doesn't matter what we do now. Ghost keeps his head down now, oblivious to the rain as he continues to eat.

"Leave him for now," Adam advises and I let go of his halter. There is no need to drag him if he wants to eat, especially since it has been several days with nothing but a handful of grain for all the ponies. The rest will bring him along when they catch up. I look behind and see Pace and Alcide pulling the rest of our group up. Those who are up look around with the same sense of wonder that I feel.

A jagged bolt of lightning suddenly streaks down from the sky. It hits the contraption that juts up from the decking and an explosion sounds around us, so loud and so violent that we are thrown to the ground. Ghost rears in terror, up and down, up and down, screaming until I slip and scramble through the grass and grab his halter.

I immediately turn to where the rest of our group had gathered at the cliff's edge. I hear a loud tearing sound, as if the fans inside the dome were torn from their braces, and see the contraption that once reached up into the sky now twisting and turning as it tears away from the deck and falls first on the earth and then, in a desperate dance, topples into the darkness beyond.

"Pace!" I scream his name because I cannot see him. All I can see are the ponies bucking and jumping in terror and the goats running into the tall grass. We take off as one—me, James, and Adam—running to our friends through the sheets of rain.

As we get there one of the ponies falls over the cliff, lost in his blindness and terror. Eddie was holding onto his halter, and his son was on the pony's back. They are all gone in a blink of an eye. I hear their screams as they fall and then, just as suddenly, all is quiet and I know they are dead. My stomach heaves with the realization while my mind refuses to accept the finality of what just happened. I shake my head, stunned, and then realize the rest of our friends are lying on the ground, overcome, from the explosion and Eddie's fall. Everyone is in danger of being trampled by the ponies that have no way of knowing what is happening or where they are.

I go to the ponies and grab one halter, then another while I talk to them soothingly, and they immediately stop and stand, frightened and shaking, when they hear my voice. I manage to get them under control as they all turn to me, seeking something that is familiar.

James and Adam help our group to their feet. Everyone is so shocked that no one speaks. I realize that Pace, Rosalyn, and Stella are missing. Fear grips me, clenching my spine and my heart in its fist. What if they fell over the side with Eddie and his son? What if they are lying on the beach below, trapped in the water and the pounding waves, broken from the fall?

"Where are Pace and Rosalyn?" I call out.

"Here!" Pace calls out. He waves his hand over the cliff where we'd just come up.

"He saved us," Rosalyn says. Pace hands Stella up to James, then boosts Rosalyn. Adam hauls her up, and George and Alcide grab Pace's hands and pull him up also.

"Freddy, Nancy, take the ponies," I say. "Lead them to the grass." The children rush to do my bidding, their faces white from the terror they just experienced

"He saved us," Rosalyn says again as she takes Stella from James. "That thing was falling right for us and he moved us out of the way."

"We lost Eddie and his son," Alcide says and he looks over the cliff.

"He couldn't have survived that," Adam adds. "No one could."

"It could have been us," Rosalyn says, looking at Pace.

Pace shakes his head. "I nearly killed us anyway," he says. "The ground gave way beneath us." They are all covered with mud but the rain quickly washes it away.

Rosalyn puts her free arm around him. "You are very brave and I will not forget what you've done." She embraces him quickly with Stella between them.

"We should keep moving," James says. He has a strange look on his face and I cannot help but think he is jealous of the glory that Rosalyn heaps on Pace. "Before it hits again."

"What about Eddie?" Sally asks.

"There's nothing we can do for him," Adam says. "You can see the water. It's up to the wall. Even if they survived the fall they will have been washed away. They are gone."

It happened so fast that it is hard to process it. They were there one moment and gone the next. This world is much more dangerous than I ever imagined. What will become of us? How can we survive when we don't know what to expect from one minute to the next?

"Was it one of the weapons?" Peter asks. "You said there were people here with weapons."

"It was lightning is all," Pace says. "It is attracted to metal."

"More of his facts," James snorts. "From books."

"Can you imagine if it was a weapon?" Alcide ignores James. "Whoever could harness that could rule the world."

"Whatever you do, don't mention that to my father," I say. "Or else he will try it."

There is such a sense of relief among all of us that we survived that those of us who know who my father is laugh, while the rest look on in confusion.

"We should go," Adam says. "If there are people about, with weapons, this might attract them." Everyone goes quiet at this, as we are reminded once more of how precarious our situation is.

As the others move onward, I take a moment to put my arms around Pace. "I was scared I'd lost you," I say as we embrace.

"A storm cannot keep us apart," he says. I feel him tremble a bit and realize that for all his bravado, this time he really was frightened. A squeak from inside his jacket startles us.

"Pip?" he says as if he'd forgotten him. Considering the circumstances I am not surprised. Pace unbuttons the top button and pulls the little bird from within. He must have been as stunned as the rest of us who were close to the lightning. He gives his body a shake within Pace's hands and looks up at both of us with his beady eyes.

"Is he hurt?" Pace asks. "It's hard for me to tell," he continues and once more I realize we are back on familiar ground. I can see in the dark, he can't. And while this darkness is not as complete as what we experienced, it is still darkness and harder for Pace to see. I lower my head to Pace's hands and touch my finger to Pip's head. The bright yellow canary stretches his wings out and gives them another thorough shaking before folding them back in and dipping his beak into one as if he had an itch.

"I think he is fine," I say. "And eternally grateful he wasn't squashed."

Pip adds his agreement with a curious peep, and Pace places him carefully back inside his jacket. He leaves the button unbuttoned, and Pip sticks his head up from within, sheltered by Pace's chin. Pace nods and smiles and then takes my hand. We follow after the rest while my heart breaks, just a little, for Eddie, his son, and the poor pony who fell from the cliff.

✦

The grass thins as we keep on walking. We realize that is because there are foundations for buildings scattered throughout. There is no way of knowing what they used to be, homes or shops, because there are no remnants of anything else, as if time and the wind had scoured the memories away. The grass gives way and we walk into a forest of trees. The trees are thick, not leafy like the ones from the orchard on my rooftop; instead their branches are covered with leaves that look like spikes, which are as long as my fingers. The smell is amazing. It reminds me of the earth but in a much sweeter way. The foliage is so dense that the rain tapers off to nothing more than a fine mist that becomes more violent when the wind gusts.

Jonah appears once more and rushes to me. I pick him up and his rumbly purr lets me know he's not scared any more. We catch up with our group and I see that James and Adam both have their hands on a tree trunk.

"This is where wood comes from?" Adam asks.

"You've never visited the orchards?" I ask. "Never touched a tree?"

"Never," he confesses.

James pushes against one, testing its strength. "I never imagined anything like this," he confesses.

"Amazing," Pace says and everyone looks around with wonder.

"We still need to find shelter for these children," Rosalyn reminds us.

We venture on, leaving the ponies and the goats behind because they are busy eating every bit of grass they can find. I don't worry about them. Ghost will follow my scent, and they can shelter beneath the trees when they are full. At least the problem of food for them is taken care of. I can only hope that we will be as lucky.

We move closer to the dome. I have no reference as to what part of it, but I can't help but think that when we reach its outer edges we will be outside of Park Front, which is where all the royals live. We, as shiners, were never allowed to enter that part of the dome; however, Pace has been there, as his mother works as a governess for the royals' children. That is why he knows so many things about the outside world. Pace was able to study with them as he grew up, while our education only consisted of the basics, such as reading, writing, and arithmetic and the stories we were read from the Bible.

"I think this was a park," Pace says. "The ground is so level, and without someone to maintain the lawns the trees just take over."

"Even after a fire like the one the comet caused?" Alcide asks.

"The fire had to eventually burn itself out when there was nothing left to fuel it," Pace says. "And then nature just took its course."

"I don't know if I'm angry that we were deceived for so long, or sad that we've missed out on so much," Adam says.

"You should be angry," James says. "I know I am."

"At least we had the courage to do something about it." Alcide looks my way.

"Shelter please," Rosalyn says. "You can congratulate each other after we find some."

The rain, while not as fierce because of the trees, still falls. The thunder and lightning are not as close as before, but I don't know if it is because of the cover above us or because it is moving on. I can see the cats that travel with us scampering through the trees, yet keeping us in sight. I put Jonah down and push my goggles up on my soaking wet hair as we move onward. As we walk, the trees thin out and we once more see the foundations of buildings. A tree has fallen, sometime ago, because the wood is as dry as what we have down below and several of the cats are sheltered beneath it.

"Surely something had to survive," Rosalyn says. I hope so. We are a bedraggled bunch, all of us soaking wet. The children look ready to fall. Even Freddy, who has been incredibly brave and helpful, despite losing his father, is done in, if the huge purple shadows beneath his eyes are any indication.

What will we do if we can't find shelter or food? We came up here with the belief that it had to be better than what we left behind, but what if we keep making things worse instead of better. What if we've forever lost the best we would ever have because of the decisions I've made?

"I think I see a light," Adam says. We all stop and look in the direction he points to. I see it, a flicker, then another, the type a fire would give out. It is there one moment, then gone, and then it reappears for another quick moment before it disappears. We all stand, holding our breath, as we wait for it to come back, but it doesn't.

"This way," James says and moves in the direction of the fire.

"Wait," Pace says. "We shouldn't all go. Only a few of us should go, to make sure it is safe."

"While the rest of us stay here and drown?" George asks.

"You can go if you want George," Alcide says. "He's just thinking of the children."

"Make up your mind," James says. "Who goes, who stays?"

"James, Pace, and Wren," Adam says. "Do you agree Rosalyn?" he asks.

"Aye," she says, and with those comments they reassert themselves as our leaders through council. A third will have to be elected, but that is something that can wait until we are safe.

"Someone go back and gather the animals," I say.

"We'll take care of them," Alcide assures me and the three of us move on in the direction of the light.

Pace and James both have their knives in their hands. James also carries a stout piece of wood. After what I've seen, I know that neither is effective against the weapons carried by those on the outside. Pace saw it, and James saw the aftereffects, but telling James to use caution now is like telling the rain and wind to stop and expecting it to really happen.

There are more ruins now than trees. We dart from tree to stones, trying to stay low and unseen, which is hard since several cats, including Jonah, travel with us. The rain is still with us, blocking our vision, but then I realize that it is not the rain before us, but the dome. It is still several paces away, but it is before us, rising up from the ground like the cliff we climbed to get to this place. From here we can see nothing behind it because the glass is cloudy and gray. I wonder if we go close and put our hands against our eyes, will we be able to peer through as if we were looking through a window at one of the shops on the promenade?

"Whoever has the light has got to be close," Pace says. The ruins are larger now that we are closer to the dome. The trees are no more, as if they are afraid to stand in its shadow, but the ruins are more identifiable as buildings. If only there was a roof, or even a floor under which we could shelter. Every place I look isn't big enough to shelter the lot of us.

One of the cats lets out a low, warbling yowl and then suddenly another noise erupts, one that is reminiscent of some of the dogs I've seen in my life, but much louder, and sounding much more dangerous. A huge beast suddenly appears from one of the ruins.

He is a golden color and waist high, with enormous fangs bared and his mouth viciously snapping at a cat. The fur on the back of his neck stands straight up as he lunges at the cat. Jonah and the others run straight by us and then beyond, with their ears flattened in terror. The dog captures the cat in its mouth and shakes it violently before tossing it aside. The cat is stunned, and before it can get up again, the dog grabs it once more and we hear the crunch of broken bones.

"Watch it," James says. "It might come for us next."

"Should we run?" I ask, ready to turn and make a dash after the cats if they say so. I well recall the terror of running with someone breathing down my neck and last time I was caught. I am fairly certain I would not survive being caught by this huge beast.

"I think running will only make it madder," Pace says quietly.

"Beau! Stop!" A voice commands.

We immediately crouch low, hoping to be invisible to whoever it is who comes up from the ruins after the dog, who drops the body of the dead cat on the ground and nuzzles it with his nose.

It's a boy around my age or so. His clothes are ragged and worn, but they are what we are used to; pants, a shirt, and a jacket that's seen better days. His shoes look newer than his clothes. He's fairly dry and the smell of wood smoke drifts to us as he leans over to investigate the body on the ground.

"Good boy," he says. "Looks like you found us some dinner." The boy stands up with the cat's body in his hands and recognition hits me with a joyful blast as I see his bruised and battered face. His hair is brown and his eyes blue and his body is thin as if he doesn't ever get to eat his fill. He fits Pace's description, or so the filchers thought when they captured the two of us. He looks right past where we are hidden. I stand up.

"Wren," Pace hisses. "What are you doing?"

"It's Jon," I say. And then I wave. "Jon!"

· 7 ·

A week ago I never would have thought that I'd be sitting around a scarab's fire and be grateful to have it, but circumstances have led me to have different beliefs than the ones I had a week ago. In our society the scarabs are the lowest of the low. They are the descendants of those who managed to hide inside the dome when the comet came. No provision was made for their existence, so they have survived all these years on the cast-offs of the rest of us. They live on the streets in makeshift hovels and pick the trash for whatever is usable. It is from their ranks the filchers come, despicable men who wear masks and do anything for a reward. I will not hate Jon just because he is a scarab any more than he will hate me because I am a shiner. We were both captured by filchers for the reward. Me, because my father saw me as the troublemaker, and Jon because he has dark hair and blue eyes like Pace. The filchers saw us together and assumed Jon was Pace. I saved his life from the filchers and we were both arrested by the bluecoats, of which my father is the head. Then we were both taken to the exit of the dome to be traded to the rovers. That was when James and Adam blew up the fans. Jon and I shared so much in such a short time. It is a connection between us that will never be severed, I hope.

The children are settled, finally, and the ponies and goats are corralled into an area in the woods with tree branches. We still do not have food, but we do have shelter, which is a welcome relief from the rain.

Jon's shelter is the basement of a house. If we had not seen Jon come up I don't think we ever would have found it because the entrance is hidden so well. Through the basement is another room, a few steps down and lined with stone. Remarkably it still has a rotten wooden door. On the opposite side of the room is part of another door and a tunnel leads off of it. Jon's fire is in this lower room, and it heats the stone, which in turn gives heat to the room above it. I am in awe of how quickly he figured out the most efficient way of staying safe, dry, and warm. There are enough nooks and crannies in the stones that the smoke trails upward and outside without inconveniencing anyone sitting around it.

"I haven't had a chance to explore it much, but I think it leads back beneath the dome," Jon say as James peers down the tunnel off the room. The huge beast of a dog sits beside Jon and eyes James warily. The few cats that stayed close after the loss of their comrade keep a safe distance, except for Jonah, who sits in complete security in my lap. Pace sits next to me with Pip on his shoulder, who is busy at work preening his feathers. James joins Adam, Alcide, and Rosalyn, who make up the rest of our circle around the fire. Everyone else is asleep above us, except for Peter, who cannot seem to stop coughing. We can hear him through the warped boards of the door. I am worried that the rain and the damp have affected him more so than the rest of us, but there is nothing I can do for him except to pray.

We've taken off as many clothes as we can without being scandalous and have things strung and hanging to dry on every thing we can find. Having a dry place to sleep and dry clothes to put on gives me a lot of hope for tomorrow. Finding Jon alive gives me more.

"What happened after you went outside?" I ask.

"It was nearly dark," Jon replies. "After what you told me about the bluecoats trading girls and boys to the rovers I expected to find some waiting outside, but there was no one. I decided the best thing was to get as far away from the door as possible just in case they were watching, so I just took off running until I ran out of breath. That's when I found Beau." Jon rubs his hand down the big dog's head. "Or maybe it's more like that was when he found me. I was just standing there, bent over, with my hands on my knees, trying to breathe and he ran up to me. I was terrified at first, and tried to run, but he knocked me down. I thought I was dead for certain until he started licking me."

We all laugh and I stick my hand out for Beau to sniff. He obliges, lets me rub his head, and continues to look adoringly at Jon. Jon moves his hand to Beau's neck and shows up a collar buried in the golden fur. "His name is written on this," he says and shows us the letters carved into the leather.

"I wonder where he came from?" Pace asks. "He has to have people somewhere. Someone who loved him enough to put his name on his collar."

Jon shrugs. "He's the only friendly thing I'd met until you showed up."

We all know Jon means the rovers, so we wait for him to continue. "After that it was just trying to figure out what this world is all about. It was full dark by then and the only thing that I knew for certain was the dome. I could not see anything through it except for some light, occasionally, so I stuck close to it and walked until I got tired. I found a basement a lot like this to sleep in and Beau stayed right by my side, which was nice because he kept me warm. The next morning I started walking again. I could see smoke coming from the dome, so I knew the explosion that happened when we were in the passageway had to do some damage. I also managed to snare a fat bird and roasted it. I slept some more and I woke up when Beau started barking. Then I felt the earth shaking beneath me. I thought for certain the dome was going to cave in but it didn't."

"That was the methane gas going off in the tunnels," Adam explains.

"They came after us when we blew up the fans," James adds. "The tunnels caved in and our village was flooded."

"We lost a lot of people," I say and then I ask, "Have you seen anyone else since you've been out?"

"I saw the rovers," Jon says. "I hid from them."

"What happened?" Pace asks.

"I saw more smoke after that," Jon continues. "I couldn't tell where it came from and all I could do was keep walking. I walked through a lot of ruins, large buildings that were probably warehouses before. Then the ruins started getting smaller and trees started popping up. Beau started growling so I hid and saw a group of about a dozen men. They carried weapons, like the bluecoats had when they captured us. Their clothes were a lot like mine, cast-offs and such, and some had hide vests and pants. They were dirty for the most part, long hair and beards."

Jon's observations about the state of the rovers are surprising because we always considered the scarabs to be dirty. Of course it is hard to stay clean when you live in a shack on the streets. Jon's hair is shaggy and badly in need of a trim, but he does have the look of someone who tries to take care of himself. I am glad to see he's recovering from the beating he took when the filchers captured us. His face is bruised and cut, but healing.

Jon continues. "The worst part was they had a girl with them who I knew. Bess. Her hands were tied and she had another rope around her neck. One of the men was leading her by the rope. She went missing about a month ago. From the looks of her, she's had a rough time of it."

"She was traded to them for weapons," I say. "My father has been doing it for a while. He has the filchers capture them. Boys, girls, and anything else they ask for."

"Sick bastards," James says, and for once I am in agreement with him.

"They looked at the dome for a while then they went in the direction that you came from. Which is probably where I came out because I haven't come upon it so far. That was yesterday. I decided to look for a place that was safe to hide and found this. I spent today trying to find food and hoping they didn't come back."

"Did you find any food?" James asks.

"I found an apple tree, but the fruit isn't ripe yet. I set out some snares also."

"Snares?" Alcide asks.

"We made them with string on the inside," Jon explains. "To catch pigeons and rats. For food."

My stomach turns at the thought of sinking to such desperate measures as to eat a rat, but then again, who knows what I'll resort to if I go several days without a meal. We have the goats if we get desperate, but the thought that we'd kill the ponies for food sickens me so much that I can't think of it. What will we have to do to stay alive? Once more I ask myself, Is this freedom from the oppression of the dome worth the price we've paid and might continue to pay?

"Can you show me?" Alcide asks.

"I will in the morning," Jon agrees.

"The apples will ripen soon," Pace says. "And we might find other things. Our calendar says it is the end of April, which is the middle of spring according to the seasons."

James rolls his eyes. "More book stuff?" he asks.

"More book stuff," Pace says. "We should be glad it isn't winter, or we'd be freezing and the rain would have been snow."

"To every thing there is a season, and a time to every purpose under the heaven: A time to be born, and a time to die; a time to plant, and a time to pluck up that which is planted," Adam says. "It is from the Bible. Ecclesiastes, chapter 3." Time around us seems to stop as he continues, accompanied by the pop and crackle of the fire. "A time to kill, and a time to heal; a time to break down, and a time to build up; A time to weep, and a time to laugh; a time to mo . . . mourn . . ." Adam stumbles over the word, and I want to cry at his grief and his strength, but I also want to know what comes next and I do not want to risk breaking the spell his words have created for us. He gathers himself and continues.

> . . . and a time to dance;
> A time to cast away stones, and a time to gather stones together; a time to
>   embrace, and a time to refrain from embracing;
> A time to get, and a time to lose; a time to keep, and a time to cast away;
> A time to rend, and a time to sew; a time to keep silence, and a time to speak;
> A time to love, and a time to hate; a time of war, and a time of peace.

His last words seem to echo around us. A time of war and a time of peace. Which will tomorrow hold for us? "That's it," Adam says. "There's more but I cannot remember it." He gets up from his place at the fire and walks over to the doorway that leads to the tunnel.

"James, the Bible is a book too," Alcide says. "In case you were wondering." James gives Alcide a look that promises he will pay for his sarcasm, and Alcide simply shrugs in return and goes back to poking at the fire with a piece of wood.

"So you think this leads under the dome?" Adam asks from the tunnel.

"It does," Jon answers. "Part of it is caved in. I didn't want to take the chance of going any deeper because I knew there was no one to find me if something happened."

Adam and James look at each other and without a word both leave to explore the tunnel.

With Adam's leaving, the spell that held us captive while he quoted the Bible dissolves around us and I am able to think once more about practical things. "Now that there are more of us we can search more, while others look out," I contribute. The thought of running into the rovers on the outside is as nerve-wracking as running into the filchers on the inside. Neither is a safe prospect for any of us.

"I never really thought about how big the dome is," Alcide says. "Two days of walking isn't enough to circle it?"

"I wasn't walking that fast," Jon admits. "Mostly I was trying to figure out what I should do next to stay alive."

"As you should have," Rosalyn says. "And with that last bit of wisdom I will bid you good rest." She stands and stretches before going into the other room where everyone is sleeping.

We bid her good sleep and Jon asks me. "What happened after we parted?"

"I went back to the house and everyone was waiting for us." I tell Jon everything that happened to us since we'd seen him last.

"I wonder how everyone else has fared," he asks.

"We have no way of knowing what's going on inside."

"It has got to be harder now for the bluecoats to maintain control," Pace says.

"They have got to be worried about how they will survive without the fans," Alcide observes.

"We all saw smoke," I add. "Wouldn't that mean that there are cracks or holes in the glass?"

"It seems likely," Pace says. "Especially since the ground caved in."

"That means they can get fresh air, which is a good thing since the fans no longer work."

"But if the dome is cracked or broken, that means the people can see the sky," Alcide says. "They would know that there is no flame outside. If it were me, I'd want out."

"But my father is determined to keep everyone in. Or maybe it's more that he wants to keep everyone else out. All he is concerned with is protecting the royals."

Pace takes Pip from his shoulder. He holds the canary in one hand and strokes the bright yellow head with the tip of his finger as he stares into the fire. He's worried about his mother, who, last we heard, was being held by my father in hopes that Pace would turn himself in. But that was before everything happened. When my father was trying to keep the fact that the outside world was habitable a secret.

"He doesn't need her anymore," I offer. "Surely he'll let her go with all the other madness that has to be going on in there."

"I hope so," Pace says. He looks at me and I see the worry plainly written in his lovely blue eyes. "If only there was some way to find out."

I have no answers for him. No way to make him feel better, no way to take the worry away. All I can do is take his hand in mine to let him know I am here for him, just as he's been here for me throughout all the madness of the past few days.

"Maybe James and Adam will find a way back in," Alcide offers.

"I'm never going back in," Jon says.

I want to agree with Jon but the past few days have taught me that you don't know what you will and will not do until the time comes and the consequences of your actions are placed before you. I can honestly say that I do not want to go back inside the dome. But after all the lives that were lost, and if it meant saving more lives that losing them, then I would gladly go back in.

The last few days have taught me that there is a cost for everything and at times that cost is too high. The one thing I can say with confidence is I never want to pay that price again.

· 8 ·

It was easy for me to fall in love with Pace. Just being with him made it easy. He is kind, generous, and brave, and he has a wry sense of humor that sneaks up on you. The fact that he is beautiful to look at made it easy too, although I am certain he would never want to hear me say that. Every moment that we spent together until we escaped the dome was precious because we did not know if it would be our last.

"I am so proud of you, Wren," he says.

I am exhausted. Even though I slept most of the day in the cave, I feel like I cannot keep my eyes open for another second. James and Adam are still in the tunnel and Alcide and Jon, with Beau at his side, went down to check on them. It could have caved in on them, or they could have found a way back into the dome, at the moment I do not care. I just want to sleep.

Pace and I find a blanket from our supplies that is warm and dry and go to an empty corner of the basement, with Jonah, as always, trailing behind. One of the lamps glows softly in the middle of the room, a beacon of comfort for anyone who wakes up in the middle of the night. Pace puts Pip into his cage as I spread our blanket out on the stone floor. My body aches for the comfort of my bed, long gone in the flood, or at least someplace soft to sleep. I cannot help but think of the nest Pace and I made in our own little cave. There was no mattress, but several blankets and a sandy floor perfect for comfortable sleeping.

"You are?" I ask. "For what?"

"Your courage," he says. "Even when you were blinded you never gave up."

But I did . . . I thought my life was over. I was afraid Pace might not want me anymore because I was blind, and I was scared when I woke up alone. Now I find I'm angry with myself for doubting him. If only I wasn't so tired. I don't know what to say so I give him a weary smile and lie down on our blanket. Pace stretches out beside me on his side and puts his arm around my waist. I roll over so I am snuggled up against him. Jonah promptly settles into the curve made by my body, and his purr joins the other noises of our shelter.

George lies on his back and his snores are loud enough to drown out any sound that anyone might make. The children are all snuggled together between Rosalyn and Sally, except for Freddy, who sticks close to Peter and Nancy. At least Peter is finally asleep. His coughing has me worried.

As do some other things, and even though my body is exhausted, my mind will not rest. There are too many things to think about and process. My grandfather told me one time there was no need to worry about tomorrow, it will be here soon enough with its problems and I know that it will arrive whether I am ready for it not. We will still have to face the problems of food, of better shelter, and of just staying alive.

"I pray that we hear some news of your mother," I say to Pace once more. Surely my father has let her go with all the other problems that he now has. But then again, I am not certain that forgiveness is one of his strong suits. If he bears a grudge against Pace and me, then there is no telling what he may do.

"If only there was some way to find her," he says. "To know for certain."

"If only we had some way of talking to those on the inside." I am so worried about those who helped us: Lucy, David, Harry, and Jilly. "I need to know if Lucy is all right. I need to tell her what happened to her parents." They were among the dead, as were Alex's. So many people lost and I want to hold on to the hope that those that I know are still alive.

We talk quietly, so as not to disturb the others in the room, although I am certain George's snores, which seem loud enough to shake the dome, would disturb them first. We are trying to reestablish the bond we had in the tunnels.

"We will find a way," he whispers against my ear. I don't know if he's saying it for my benefit, or for himself. I feel him yawn and then he is quiet. His breathing becomes deeper and I know he's fallen asleep.

I lie there, listening to Pace's gentle breathing, the uneven noises coming from George, and the restless movements of the rest, accompanied by an occasional cough from Peter. I close my eyes because they burn with exhaustion and then open them again because I am afraid I will go blind once more. Even though I am so very tired, my body is used to being awake during the night, and I find sleep, especially under these circumstances, to be impossible.

As quietly as possible, I leave our makeshift bed. As soon as I move away Pace rolls onto his back and Jonah slides up against him. I can't help but smile at how quickly they compensate for my leaving. I stand for a moment, looking around at the scattered sleepers, torn between checking on my friends in the tunnel or going out-side. And then I realize for the first time in my life that I *do* have the choice to go outside, so that is where I go.

The rain has stopped. Water drips down rivulets and scatters from the trees with the breeze. Strange and unfamiliar noises greet my ears, a series of peeps and chirps rise around me in a strange chorus that must be as natural as the air, yet is a wonder to me. I know it has to be creatures of some kind and I wonder if they are big or small, safe or dangerous.

The clouds have parted. Some still trail across the sky and scat-tered stars drift through, dazzling me with their presence. I know to call them stars, yet I cannot perceive their purpose, other than that they are beautiful and fill my soul with a longing much like the one I had when I stared at the dome in the mornings. The only way I can identify it is a yearning for *more*. More of what, I do not know.

I make my way into the park where we'd left the animals. The ponies and goats all stand huddled together beneath the trees. I climb through the barrier we'd rigged for them and go to Ghost.

"You've got to be confused," I say to him as I comb my fingers through his tangled mane. "Your world has drastically changed in just moments." He leans into my side. "There are new sounds around you, new challenges and you can't even see them." One of the goats nuzzles at my sleeve. "This is a scary place," I add. "I just hope it's the right place for all of us."

A sound echoes in the distance. A long and mournful sound of *Ooo* over and over again. The ponies stomp nervously and the goats shift around and stare in the direction of the noise. All of the other creatures that sang to the night suddenly stop and I hold my breath—in anticipation of what, I do not know. It sounds again and another joins it, and then another. My mind identifies it as a dog, but I cannot imagine any dog I've ever seen making such a sound, unless it is a large one like Beau.

Beau is another mystery of this strange world. He has obviously known the love of a person, or else why would he take to Jon so willingly? The only people that I know to be outside are the rovers. Yet from what I've heard of them, from my father and Jon, makes me think that they are not the type to love a dog. Anyone who would chain a person would more than likely treat a dog the same or worse. Whoever owned Beau loved him enough to make a collar with his name on it, which leads me to think that there might be others, besides the rovers, who survived the comet. If the trees and grass could survive, and the creatures that make strange noises around me, and Beau, who came from somewhere, then why not more people too? People who are like us, who want to live and let live. People who love and laugh and live their lives morally. People who do not trade for young men and women and do not tie ropes around necks and lead them like animals. People who are good.

But what did they have to do to survive? How did they carry on when everything around them was burned in the flames? What did they eat or drink? Where did they live?

Just thinking of the things that they had to go through generations ago makes me feel horribly inadequate. How did they feel, seeing the dome rise up from the earth and knowing that they were not chosen to survive? How desperate they must have been, desperate enough to find a way inside, as some of them did. Yet the rest did find a way to survive, not all of them, but enough of them that there are other people about. How different all of our lives could have been if those who lived inside had chosen to open the doors when the world became safe again.

I do my best to calm the ponies as the unfamiliar howls have them and the goats spooked. The ponies move restlessly but the goats are much move vocal about it. They baa their distress and mill from one side of the pen to the other before they all stop and stare off into the darkness with their ears pitched forward.

I dare to think, no hope, for a moment that someone from our group has come in search of me. Then I realize that the goats stand with their backs to the dome, as do the ponies. They sense something that I do not, and the direction it comes from makes me realize that it is someone or something I do not know.

Ghost whinnies and stomps his foot, and I shiver in fear. Whatever or whoever is out there surely knows where we are now. I put my hand on Ghost's nose and look out into the darkness. I see the trees, standing straight and tall even though they are random in their growth. Shadows fill the spaces in between. Then I see movement, nothing more than another shadow that darts from tree to tree.

I crouch among the ponies. I am confident that whoever it is will not be able to see me until they are right on top of me. And if they can see me now then it has to be a shiner and I have nothing to fear. From my position I see a pair of legs moving between the trees. The ponies sense something and move restlessly about while the goats still peer into the darkness.

I need to do something, but I don't know what. I cannot tell if it's friend or foe. I scan the darkness to see if there is anyone else about. All I see is the one pair of legs that is getting closer and closer. It has to be a man by the size of the feet. I look around again to make sure there is only one person.

He stops when he gets to the branches we'd set up to keep the goats and ponies contained. I watch as he moves one branch, then he steps into the pen. All the animals move back as far away from him as they can get, and I join in the shuffle to make sure I am far away from him as well while still staying with the ponies, who roll their eyes wildly at his unfamiliar scent.

I smell him too. Odor from his body washes over me and my stomach turns at the sourness of it. I try to see his face but it is next to impossible with the animals milling about. A goat baas in protest as he grabs its horn and tries to pull it away from the rest of the herd. The goat braces its legs as he yanks on it, and finally the man gives up and picks the goat up in his arms. The goat bucks and tries to wrestle away, but the man is strong and keeps the goat in a tight hold. As he stands up with his burden I get a good look at him. His hair is long and unkempt and his face is covered with a beard.

He's a rover, he has to be. He fits the description of the group Jon told us about.

He's stealing our goat. I am suddenly filled with such anger that someone would just walk up and have the audacity to take something that clearly isn't his.

"I'll be back for the rest of you lot later," he says to the herd as he kicks the branches that he moved back into place. "And you are all the proof I need to get them to believe me," he says to the goat in his arms.

His words sink in. He will come back. There are more of them. If more come back what chance to we have against them? They will steal our goats and our ponies. We need the goats for milk and for cheese and as a last resort for food. And the ponies? The ponies are in my care. Just because we no longer work the coal does not mean I will abandon them, especially to someone cruel enough to put a rope around a person's neck.

I climb through the fence opposite where the man came through. I do not have a plan beyond I have to keep him from stealing the goat whose piteous cries I can hear from the trees. The other goats call out in answer, crying for him to come back. I run round the pen, without worry for the noise I make because I know the noise of the goats will hide it. I see him ahead of me, struggling to keep the goat from jumping out of his arms.

My foot hits something and I nearly trip and fall, but I am able to keep my feet as I catch my hand against a tree. I look down and see a stout branch, nearly as long as my arm and as thick as my leg, on the ground. I pick it up. It is heavy but I am able to brace it beneath my arm as I continue on, now dashing from tree to tree as the rover did.

I have to get to him before he gets into the tall grass. If I don't, his friends might see me. He might see me or hear me, but as long as I have the shelter of the trees I have a chance of stopping him.

The goat either senses me coming or decides he must help himself because he makes a desperate lunge from the rover's arm and slips to the ground. The rover dives for him and catches his leg while the goat cries out in frustration. The rover holds on as I come up behind him. I take the branch into both hands and without thinking of anything beyond saving the goat, and saving us from further attack, I bring it crashing down on his head with all my strength.

He turns to face me, and his eyes widen in shock as he puts a hand up to his head. He falls to the ground like a stone, reaches for me, and then his arm collapses onto the ground beside him. The goat jumps to its feet and takes off for the safety of its friends in the pen.

What have I done? I throw the branch aside as if it burns me and I drop to my knees next to the rover. His smell sickens me; it is so oppressive it is as if I could touch it. His hair is dark and matted; still the blood that pours from the back of his head shows up clearly to my shiner eyes. I tentatively put my hand out, reaching for his skull, afraid that at any moment he will grab me and that he isn't really . . .

Dead. He has to be dead. There is so much blood and he is so very still. I put my fingertips on the back of his head and feel a piece of his skull move beneath his hair. I pull my hand away and see that my fingers are covered with blood. I killed him; no, I murdered him in my anger and fear.

What have I done? I stagger back a few steps and suddenly my stomach heaves. I put my hands on my knees as I bend over and empty up the contents of my stomach. It's the goat meat I ate this afternoon. I killed someone for wanting to do the very same thing I had done myself. Once again I killed someone. I killed the filcher who tried to rape me and now I've killed a rover for trying to steal from me. Where will I draw the line?

I look at him again. At his dark hair, at the scruffy beard, at the hook of his nose, and realize that beneath the dirt and hair he's not that old, maybe ten years older than me at the most. As I look at him I realize I will never forget his face. Never. It will haunt me until the day I die.

What have I done? It's one thing to kill or be killed, or so I told myself after the filcher's death, but it's quite another to murder someone because you don't like what he's is doing. When did killing get to be so easy for me?

What have I done?

• 9 •

I run. I am filled with such panic, such desperation, such fear and shame that I want to get as far away from the scene of my crime as I can. I have no idea where I am going, except it is away. Away from everything.

The problem is you cannot run back into the past. You cannot turn back the clock and run to the time before everything went wrong. You cannot undo what has been done no matter how bad you want to. I stop running when the stitch in my side becomes so painful that I cannot breathe and I have to stop. I bend over, put my hands on my knees, and suck in a lungful of fresh, damp air.

The price is too high. First Alex, then my grandfather, then Peggy, and then countless others. I hold myself responsible for all these deaths but now . . .

What have I done?

I finally catch my breath and take a look around me. The dome is not as close as it was. I ran away from it and the madness that gripped me in its shadow. As long as it is in sight I should be able to find my way back to the others after my mad dash. I'm not sure if I want to. To go back means I will have to admit my guilt. If only I could just pretend like it didn't happen. Unfortunately, life is not that easy. Pretending won't change the facts, and I am certain every time I close my eyes I will see the results of my foolishness.

The dome glows from within, a warm beacon against the cold night. There is no definition of what is within, there is just light. How many generations of survivors have looked at the dome from the outside and wondered what was within, just as I wondered what was beyond the glass walls of my prison. Perhaps my father was right, perhaps he was protecting all of us instead of just the royals. And then it hits me. When the comet came, those who were left outside surely came and beat against the glass, begging to be let in. Their bones are probably still there, somewhere, lost in the grass and the trees that finally came back when the fires were gone. The tunnel that James, Adam, Jon, and Alcide explore was probably built by someone trying to get in.

I look up at the sky. Smoke still trails from within and I cannot help but wonder what kind of devastation there was that left a hole in the dome and still smolders and burns. What of the people? What happened to our friends?

The clouds are mostly gone now; just a few remain. Behind the dome I see another glowing orb, like a smaller replica, hanging in the sky as if a giant had hung a lamp on a peg.

It is the moon. Something I have always known about, like the sun, but never thought to see. My crime takes all the wonder from it. I am too undeserving to look at such a beautiful sight, but I cannot seem to tear my eyes away. If I were to stand on its surface would I see the dome glowing back at me?

I stand on a muddy wide track that reminds me of the promenade inside the dome. It is as straight and the width is consistent. It must have been a road in the past. It still is used as one. I see tracks: the imprints of bare feet, shoes, and hoof prints that are much larger than the ponies leave. They head to the dome and back again. I look to the left and see how it winds into a forest. Does it go all the way through? Is there a town somewhere, and people who lead a somewhat normal life, whatever that is? My thoughts on normal have changed drastically in the past few days.

On the other side of the road from where I came is a wide stretch of deep grass and beyond that is darkness. I can smell the tang of salt in the air and hear the crash of the waves. The stars are out again, just like they were the night before. Hundreds, no, thousands, hundreds of thousands. More than I could ever count, a number that does not even exist in my base of knowledge.

And one of them is moving. Or is it my imagination? I blink and look again. It isn't hard to find it since it is the lowest star in the sky, and it moves very slowly as it seems to grow larger. As it gets closer another light appears, and then another one that is a bright red. It is heading straight for the dome, and without thought I take a course that will lead me to it.

As the lights get closer I realize that they are part of something much larger. I see a long cylinder with another oblong shape beneath it that blocks out the stars. There are many more lights, a white one at the front tip and a red one at the back and then several beneath in the box, shining like candles in window.

I run down the road that leads to the dome. The shapes become more distinguished. The top one is one large mass and silvery white, like a cloud. The one beneath looks more like a house with a walkway and banister all the way around it. If it's a house, then there must be people and I suddenly am afraid.

I stop to survey my surroundings. I recognize the place where we came up because of the large metal catwalk attached to the cliff. I realize the thing, whatever it is, is making its way to the catwalk.

As I look up I see two shapes launch from the front of the house. They look like huge birds and they spread their wings and soar upward on the wind that blows in from the sea. The air currents catch the wings and they float right for the dome while the big thing with the house beneath comes straight for the catwalk. What is it? Surely there are people on it. Who are they? Where do they come from? Are they part of the rovers or someone else entirely?

I dash into the long grass and drop down to my stomach to peer between the stalks as I hear shouts coming from the air above me. A laugh rings out and I realize that it belongs to a girl, and then a man's voice says, "Quiet!"

I understood him. That means he speaks the same language as me. But who are they? What do they want? Why are they here? From where I hide in the grass I cannot see the two who fly above me. I slowly turn around and look up. To my surprise they are standing right on top of the dome. One of them has a lamp and they use it to send a signal back to the thing in the sky, in the same way that we would signal each other in a long tunnel.

My mind is spinning. Of all the things that have happened to me in the past few days, this has to be the most remarkable and the most confounding. It is almost beyond my comprehension. If I did not see it with my own eyes, I would not believe it myself.

Will my friends believe me when I tell them about people with wings who can fly and houses that float in the sky? As much as I wanted to get away from everyone before, now I wish with all my might that Pace and the rest were with me.

I hear a creak and a sound like steam releasing from an engine. I turn again and see the house and the contraption that holds it floating slowly to the catwalk. It is right before me now, as big as a building, bigger than any one thing I've ever seen. It is so immense that it would fill up the dome and it definitely would fill up the cavern where I lived. I can plainly see people moving about on the deck around the building. A metal ladder unfurls from the side and hits the catwalk with a clang. Someone scrambles down it with a rope attached to his waist and ties the rope to the catwalk. He gives the rope a good yank, jumps up and down on the catwalk, and then gives a thumbs up sign to those above. I hear an engine start and then a slow *creak-creak* as the rope is winched and the thing is pulled to the catwalk. Another line is thrown from the back of the deck to the man and he ties it to the catwalk also. The house settles into place, parallel to the catwalk, and a panel opens on the side. A wide set of steps folds out and into place so that all the people on board have to do is walk down the steps and onto the catwalk. I see words painted in bright blue letters on the thing above the house. u.s.s.s. QUEST and above it a rectangle with red and white stripes and white dots on a small blue square in one corner.

I am so overwhelmed with what I see that I cannot gather a thought into my head. Three people come down the steps and stand on the catwalk. One has a long tube in his hand and he puts it to his eye and looks up at the dome. His hair is bright gold and he is tall and straight like my father. He wears a pair of light brown pants made of hide and a white shirt that is open at the neck. His skin is dark, like brass, which seems strange with his golden hair.

The other two men, who are dressed similarly in dark pants and shirts, much like the bluecoats wear, move off the catwalk and stand at each end of it with something in their hands. I recognize what they hold. They are the weapons my father is afraid of. Just like the ones he traded the boys and girls, including Jon's friend, for.

A man and a woman join the first man on the catwalk.

"The storm must have knocked down that crane," the man who just arrived says. He has dark hair and a short beard and a pair of glasses perched on the end of his nose. His clothes are neat and well kept, just like the blond man. He speaks English, like me, but the accent is strange. There is a different cadence to the words that makes me want to hear more.

"Do you think the storm is responsible to the damage inside also?" the woman asks. Her hair is pale blond. She has it twisted up on her head and she wears a white blouse with a pin at the neck and a long dark skirt. The man with the gold hair hands her the tube and she puts it to her eye, just as he did. It must help them see distant things.

"Hardly," the dark-haired man replies. "Remember, we saw the smoke long before the storm."

"If there's smoke, that means there's got to be an opening now," the tall man with the golden hair says. "Because there surely wasn't one a week ago."

They were here a week ago? A sudden image flashes into my mind. Of me, lying on my back on the rooftops looking at the dome and the sight of a long dark shadow passing overhead. It must have been this airship, and now they are back. But why?

What should I do? Should I talk to these people? The thought of rising up from the ground terrifies me. They have weapons, weapons that can pierce me from a great distance. There is no doubt in my mind that they could injure and possibly kill me before I could even open my mouth.

"Hopefully we can find Beau," the woman's voice says as she hands the tube to the second man.

"If he's still alive," golden-haired man says. "I wouldn't put it past those demons to eat him."

"Lyon, don't say such a thing," the woman's voice rises in protest. "That's a horrible thought."

"I am certain he is fine my dear sweet Jane," he replies. "Bring Bella out, perhaps she can roust him out of his hiding place."

Beau is their dog. That explains why he took to Jon so quickly. And these people seem much more civilized, much more the type to put a nice leather collar on their dog with his name inscribed on it. But that still doesn't help me. If I could get back to my friends and have Jon bring them Beau then maybe they would help us.

But help us what? With food? With shelter? Could they take us away from this place, to a better place? Perhaps the place they came from, wherever that is. Could their ship hold all of us? Pace wouldn't go, not without word of his mother, but the rest of us, me, Adam, James, Alcide, even Peter and his sister, we have nothing to hold us here, nothing at all.

My mind has gotten way ahead of the situation. One moment I'm terrified and awestruck and the next I imagine myself sailing away into the clouds. That would solve all my problems if I could just sail away.

But they wouldn't take me if they knew I was a murderess. I crouch down lower into the grass, if that is possible. I'm already lying on my stomach, but I feel as if there is a sign over my head, pointing to my position, that has my crime written on it in blood.

No one will know if you don't tell them . . . But I know. I will always know.

The woman, Jane, goes back into the house and the two men stay on the catwalk with their eyes on the dome. The two with the wings must still be up there. An image comes to my mind, of two faces peering down through the hole in the dome and marveling at the activity within. Do they have any idea that there is an entire society housed within? What would my father think if they were just to stroll up and knock on the door?

The man with the golden hair, called Lyon, has an air about him that reminds me of my father. The way he stands, as if he's in command of everything, is exactly like my father. The other two, the man and the woman with him, remind me of the royals. Will they think me beneath them or will they treat me with kindness?

Once more my imagination has taken off. I need to get away from this place before I am seen. From the looks of the men with the weapons, they would think nothing of aiming them at me.

The woman returns with a large dog that looks just like Beau by her side, and my heart skips in my chest. They might not see me, but the dog surely will. Even now I can see her staring straight at me. She lets out a quiet woof and wags her tail.

"What is it Bella?" the woman asks. "Can you smell Beau?"

Bella looks up at her mistress and whines.

"Go find Beau," she says and Bella jumps off the catwalk. She comes straight for me. I turn around and take off, staying low to the ground. Can I outrun a dog? Probably not. The bigger question is will anyone come after her?

"Something is out there," Jane says. "In the grass. See how it moves?"

I don't turn around. I keep on going. Since they've seen me, there is no need to pretend any more. I take off at a run once more and pray that the dog stays between me and the men with the weapons. I don't know what else to do. I'm too terrified to think.

"Stop!" I recognize Lyon's voice calling after me.

"We just want to talk!" the other one calls out.

If only I could believe them. My fear doesn't allow me time to think. I can feel the dog on my heels.

"Going somewhere?" Suddenly there is a girl in front of me. With wings. I stop because if I don't I will crash into her. And there is the fact that she has wings. Large brass wings. She is also wearing goggles and a leather cap with a lamp on the side that fastens under her chin. She removes the cap to reveal a long tumble of blond hair.

I shake my head at this new mystery and turn to run in another direction. And run right into a boy who also has wings and is wearing the same type of cap and goggles. Both wear tight brown leather pants and jackets that accentuate every muscle and curve of their bodies.

"Zan, you're such a show-off," he says.

"I told you I'd beat you," Zan says.

I stare between the two of them, completely mystified and nearly scared out of my wits.

"Let's have a talk," the boy says. "Shall we?"

· 10 ·

*T*he dog, *Bella,* is overjoyed to see the two that wear the wings. She bounces between them with her thick tail wagging furiously and what looks like a smile on her face. Her fur is a darker hue than Beau's and has a reddish cast to it. The two take the wings off and I am astounded to see that they are like a fan. They fold into a long thick piece, and the boy and girl wrap their harnesses around them and then sling them over their shoulders.

I think about running again, but I realize I'm no match for them. I'm exhausted from running and more so from being frightened. There are three of them, including Bella, and only one of me. And for some reason, I don't think they will hurt me. They had plenty of opportunity to and they haven't.

"Do you have a name?" the boy asks.

"Wren MacAvoy."

"I'm Levi and this is my cousin, Alexandra."

She gives me a dazzling smile. "Zan for short," she says. "Levi, look at her eyes. They are extraordinary."

Levi still wears his cap and the lamp on the side shines on my face as he peers at me. I close my eyes against the brightness and tears well up. I panic for a moment, afraid that I will be blind again, and quickly blink and am relieved to still be able to see, although there is a blurry part right before me that slowly fades away.

"Oh, sorry," Levi says. He snatches off his hat and a thick wave of blond hair springs up from his head. He detaches the lamp from the hat and shines it off to the side as he looks at me again with his warm brown eyes. "Brilliant!" he exclaims. "I believe she can see in the dark."

"Seriously?" Zan replies. "Can you?"

"I can," I say and then immediately regret it. I have no reason to trust these people, yet they are so very charming that I cannot resist them.

"Really Levi, you shouldn't talk like Wren's not here. She's right in front of us and she did tell us her name."

"Oh, I'm so very sorry," Levi says. "Please forgive me." He gives me a slight bow, and I am so overwhelmed that I can only nod.

"Please come and meet my parents," Zan says. "They will be ever so happy to talk to you. And Dr. Stewart will be beside himself." I can only surmise that Dr. Stewart is the other man on the catwalk. And Lyon and Jane have to be Zan's parents because they all have the beautiful blond hair. As does Levi.

"I would ask you what happened to the dome, but then you'd have to tell it again so we will just have to wait so you only tell it once," Zan says.

"Please excuse my cousin," Levi says. "She's a bit of a chatterbox." They walk on either side of me while the dog, Bella, bounds in front of us. They are so friendly, so attractive, and so very different than anyone I've ever met before, except for Jilly, who they remind me of. They have to be near my age, yet they seem to be so confident, whereas I am a trembling mass of fear and confusion.

"Am I your prisoner?" I ask.

"Heavens no," Zan says. "Whatever gave you that idea?"

There are plenty of things that made me think that but I don't share them, instead I ask, "Can I go?"

"You can if you really want to," Levi says. "But from the looks of you I'd say you're hungry. We have plenty of food and an insatiable curiosity about the dome. Are you from the inside?"

"Yes."

"Then consider this a trade. We will provide you with a glorious meal and you tell us about the dome," Levi offers.

I hesitate for a moment. I am not the only one who is hungry. And they could be lying to me about the food, and about being a prisoner. I do not want to put anyone else at risk and perhaps they would be willing to help us if I cooperate. My curiosity about them is just as insatiable, so I nod in agreement.

"Excellent!" Zan says. She sticks her arm through mine in a heart-wrenching way that reminds me of Peggy. "How old are you? I'm sixteen and Levi is seventeen. His mother and my father are brother and sister." Levi is right, she is a chatterbox. She talks so easily while I feel completely tongue-tied.

"I am sixteen," I say.

"I simply adore your accent," Zan says.

I cannot help but smile. To me she has an accent. "Where are you from?" I ask.

"America," Levi replies. "Across the sea."

Pace told me of a place called America. But to actually meet someone that is from there is more than I can comprehend. We have come to the edge of the grass where it meets the road in front of the catwalk. The three adults stand patiently awaiting our arrival.

I see that the men with the weapons have moved off the catwalk, one in each direction away from it, yet close enough to act defensively if the need arises.

"Is she alone?" Lyon asks.

"Lyon, don't be rude, she's our guest," Jane says. Bella bounces up the catwalk, and Jane kneels to rub the giant head of the dog. "No Beau," she says to the dog, "but you did good."

Should I tell them I know where Beau is? I open my mouth to speak and then close it. I still don't know their motives, and I don't want to send them to my friends unannounced. There will be time later, and I know Beau is safe for now.

"She's from the dome," Levi announces.

"Outstanding!" Dr. Stewart says. I have to shake my head and smile. They are the most enthusiastic people I have ever met, with their words like "brilliant," "outstanding," and "excellent."

"May I present Miss Wren MacAvoy," Levi says as we step onto the catwalk, which is now brightly lit with lamps all around. There are also two chairs and a small table on it. The long metal tube that Lyon used to look at the dome lies on the table, along with a thick roll of paper. I've never seen such a large piece of paper before and my hands itch to unroll it and see what wonders are placed upon it.

"My uncle, Lyon Hatfield, my aunt, Jane Hatfield, and this is Dr. Jethro Stewart." His announcement makes me feel as if I am a royal instead of a shiner. Of course they do not know anything about me, and Levi's opinion may change at any moment.

"Do you mind if I have a look at your eyes?" Dr. Stewart says. "I've never seen anything like them."

"Just don't shine a light into them," Levi warns. "They are light sensitive."

"Am I right in presuming you can see in the dark?" Dr. Stewart asks.

"I can," I say.

"It must be a process of evolution—" he begins but is interrupted by Jane.

"Please, Dr. Stewart," she says. "Poor Wren looks starved. How about we feed her before you two start with the questions?"

Poor Wren . . . if they only knew how poor I was. I am definitely not one they would invite into their homes if we were in the dome, but we are not. Jane takes my arm in the same way that Zan did and leads me up the steps to their house.

Thick cables connect the house below to the thing above. I do not know what it is made of but it looks to be a thick fabric of some sort that is filled with air. I look up at it in wonder and feel, once more, as if I am looking at the dome.

"We call it a dirigible," Levi says. "The more common term is airship."

"That makes sense," I say. "It is a ship that sails in the sky. What is it made of?" I ask.

"Goldbeater's skin," he says, and I look at him in confusion. "Cow intestines."

Zan makes a face. "It takes several," she adds. "Believe me when I say nothing in our country goes to waste."

"They are quite elastic," Levi continues, "and able to hold the gas." Zan covers her mouth and giggles while Levi rolls his eyes at her. "Hydrogen. It is steered by a small combustion engine and we mostly float on the air currents. The main cabin," he says, indicating the house, as I called it, "is made of bamboo, which is a very light yet sturdy wood. We live in here, and the crew has quarters above, in the balloon."

"Inside?" I ask looking upward, marveling at how something so amazing could be made of cow intestines.

"We can show you later, if you'd like," Zan volunteers.

"Yes," I say and feel quite guilty. I shouldn't be here. I should be back with my friends. They will be worried about me. Pace will be worried. I should warn them about the rover. What if his friends come looking for him and find him dead? What if they steal the goats and the ponies and then find our hiding place?

"I should go," I say suddenly and turn to go down the steps.

"Please don't," they all say at once.

"At least eat something," Jane says and opens the door to the cabin. I look inside. I have never seen such luxury, never, ever imagined it, even when thinking about how the royals lived. I stand in the doorway, transfixed, and I am afraid to move, afraid I will disturb something, or damage it, that I am so unclean with my coal-stained nails that I will tarnish the room just by stepping inside.

The furniture is beautiful, tables with a highly polished sheen like my father's desk and chairs covered with fabric and thickly padded so that it looks like you would just sink into them with comfort. There is a large table with several chairs around it, and another smaller one covered with papers. Lamps hang around the room, giving it a soft glow. In the very center of the room sits a stove with glass doors and a flame that has to come from gas because there is no wood. But how do they control it? Bella walks past me and flops down on a rug in front of the stove with a contented sigh.

There are cabinets with glass doors that hold more treasures than I've ever imagined, and I cannot begin to understand what they are. And the books. They are everywhere. On shelves and stacked on tables and in baskets on the floor. As many as are in the library inside of the dome, if not more. Alongside the books I see small stand-up frames with images on them. And then I realize the images are likenesses of the people that are with me. More are on the walls, in frames. Every square inch of wall is covered with some sort of framed images.

Against the opposite wall is a huge drawing that takes up an entire space between the two windows. I cannot seem to stop my feet from moving until I am standing directly in front of it.

"What is it?" I ask.

"It's a map of the world," Levi says from behind me. I can feel him, standing there, tall and straight, and he smells wonderful, like the sea and air. I feel strange, ashamed of how I must look and smell, yet I feel warm and comforted, as if I'm back in my bed before all this madness started.

"The entire world?" I ask. He moves up beside me to stand as I look at the map. There are tiny pins stuck in various places. I have so many questions, yet I do not know where to begin.

"The way it is now," Levi says. "Yes."

"It was different before the comet?" I ask. I turn to look at him and am struck once again by his beauty. He is like Lucy, who nearly takes your breath away when you look at her. He is the way Alex was. It is as if he's from a different time or place. And I realize that he is. He isn't from my world, which has been lost in time for two hundred years. His hair has more colors in it than I can count, and his skin has a golden hue to it that is unlike anything I've ever seen. Still his brown eyes are warm and welcoming as he talks to me as if I'm the only person in the room.

"Yes it was," he says. "Has the dome been here since before the comet?"

"Yes," I say. "They built it to protect the royals."

"They preserved the royal bloodline of England? Queen Victoria and the Hanoverians?" Dr. Stewart interjects. "Outstanding! Whoever conceived of it were geniuses. I cannot wait to examine it closer. To think that everything from that period of history has been preserved. I imagine they have the crown jewels in there. Excellent!"

"Has it been closed up all this time?" Lyon asks as Dr. Stewart rambles on about things I've never heard of. It is a sad state of affairs that he knows more about my history than I do.

"Until two days ago," I say.

"Heavens," Jane interjects. "All those people for all those years? Whatever for?"

It is too much for me to just say at the moment. The questions are too fast and I am still confused and wondering if I should be here. Instead of answering them I stare in wonder at the map. "Where are we?" I ask. Pace told me about the British Isles, but I need to see them on the map.

Levi places his finger on a point in the center of the map above my head. "Here," he says, "on the coast of Wales." His finger trails to the left, across the pale blue that has Atlantic Ocean written in script. "And this is where we are from."

I look at the country, across the sea, and I cannot begin to imagine the journey that brought them here. Their country is so much bigger than mine, so much broader, so vast. I look at Wales and England again. There are dotted lines around part of the map. "What does this mean?" I ask, pointing to the lines.

"The comet caused the melting of the polar ice caps," Dr. Stewart says. "Which led to the sea levels rising. The dotted lines are what used to be land masses, which are now under water." He puts a finger above and moves it across to the right to a place called Russia. "The comet entered the atmosphere here," he says and traces his finger across Russia and onward over France and Spain, words I can read but which have no meaning. I know they are countries, like mine, England, but they are nothing more than words to me. "These countries were devastated by the fires and, like yours, are in a state of recovery now. It continued onward," he moves his finger across the Atlantic, below where Levi showed their course just a moment before, "and crashed into the land mass formerly known as South America. The devastation there was complete and brutal. The land there is just now recovering."

"After two hundred years?" I say.

"We are lucky, as a human race, to have survived," Lyon says quietly. "Lucky that we lived in America, which like Africa, was spared the brunt of it."

"And survive we did," Jane says cheerily. "I asked Cook to fix us breakfast since it's so early. Wren, would you like to wash up first? Zan can show you where."

"Thank you," I say and follow Zan. She leads me into a hallway at the front of the cabin.

"There are our rooms," she says. "Mother and Father's there," she points to a door straight ahead. "Levi's there and mine here." She opens the door on the left and leads me into a small room, just as nicely appointed as the main cabin. The bed is nearly four times the size of mine, with fabric draped around it and linens piled upon it. I have never seen a single piece of fabric so big, and she has several. A wardrobe stands open and clothes spill out of it, and I see at least five sets of shoes and boots.

"I'm sorry it's such a mess," Zan apologizes. "I dressed rather quickly when we saw the smoke from your dome."

"No, it's . . ." I do not know what to say. I certainly did not want her to think I was criticizing her.

"The water closet is here," she continues, and I realize that she wasn't really concerned about my opinion; she just likes to talk. She opens a door to reveal a small room with a strange looking hard white chair. There's a washstand of sorts with a bowl built in with different handles and knobs above it. Most surprising of all is a brass tub with a curtain around it and another set of knobs.

I am totally confounded. I stand in the doorway looking into the room and have no idea what to do.

"It's quite brilliant you know," Zan says. "Our waste is cycled for use as fuel and we are able to remove the salt from the ocean water to use for washing. It still doesn't taste as good as fresh water but it will do in a pinch."

"You use your waste as fuel?" I ask.

"Dr. Stewart is a genius," she says. "As I imagine the scientists who built your dome were." She tilts her head to look at me, and I once more feel inadequate around her golden beauty. "You don't have a system like this, do you?"

I shake my head. "No."

"Let me show you how it works," she says and goes to the wash-stand. She turns a knob. "This is hot and this is cold."

"You have hot water just by turning a knob?" I ask.

"It's heated with steam and kept in a tank until we call it up just by turning it on." I shake my head, amazed, as she lifts the seat of the chair. "This is where you go," she says. "And then you pull this chain and it goes down to be cycled into fuel." She demonstrates and I am once more amazed. "And this is for bathing."

"That I knew," I say and she laughs in delight. "Although I've never imagined bathing in something this big."

"What did you do, in the dome?" Zan asks.

"I worked in the mines, beneath it."

"Digging coal?"

"My job was to move it," I say. "But yes, I am, was, a shiner."

"Because of your eyes? They called you shiners instead of miners? You lived your entire life underground?"

I answer all her questions with one word. "Yes."

"Amazing," she exclaims. "I'll leave you now, just come out when you're done. I'm going to change out of my flight clothes," she continues as she closes the door and leaves me inside the small room.

What luxury! Is this how the royals live? If so, no wonder they wanted to protect it. If this had been my life, I would not want to give it up. I take care of my needs and go to the washstand to wash my hands. I tentatively put my hand under the water tap to feel the heat of the water. I am amazed. A bar of soap lies on the stand and I pick it up and inhale its scent. I've never smelled anything like it, but it is so very pleasant. What would it be like to bathe with it?

I put the soap back and realize there is a mirror above the washstand with small lamps on either side. Not a piece of one with the paint coming off the back like we had in our home, but a large one, large enough that I see myself from my chest to the top of my head.

My hair is a mess. Zan has a brush that alleviates that. There is a streak on my cheek and when I look at it closer I realize it is blood. My wounds from a few days past are healing but still are tender, especially the cut on my temple. My eyes seem larger than I remember and my skin looks raw. That's what the sun did to me. It burned my eyes and it burned my skin. Yet it is what makes Levi and Zan seem so golden and warm.

There are dark smudges under my eyes, and I rub at them with the water, but they do not go away. I am able to remove the blood, and when I am done I look down at my hands to make sure there is none there. There isn't, but just because I do not see it does not mean it does not exist.

I take a deep breath and open the door. I am worried about my friends. But my hunger will not let me leave.

· 11 ·

I *have never seen* so much food in one place. Not even when our
community had a feast was there such an abundance of things
to eat. I have never had bacon, or seen an orange, much less drink
the juice squeezed from one. I have never seen strawberries or
heard of a thing called whipped cream. Neither have I eaten at a
table so exquisitely set with china that is so fine and delicate that I
am certain if I hold it up to the light I will be able to see a shadow
through it. There are so many utensils that are heavy with silver that
I do not know what to do with them so I steal a look at Zan. She
unfolds the large piece of linen that lies on her plate and places it in
her lap, so I do the same and nearly shake my head at the foolishness of it. The linen is much nicer than my clothes. The utensils are
not much of a problem, except I do not know why there are so
many. Still I keep an eye on Zan, who sits next to me, and follow
her lead.

She spreads soft butter on a slice of bread that has a brown swirl
in it and I do the same with the small slices of butter that sit on their

own little plate next to mine. The taste of it explodes in my mouth with such pleasure that I touch my fingers to my lips.

"It's cinnamon," Zan explains. "A spice."

"It is wonderful," I say honestly, and both her and Levi grin at me as I take another bite. I want to taste everything, but I feel guilty at every morsel that passes my lips because my friends are hungry. Yet I do not have the power to leave. Leaving means I have to face what I've done.

My hosts wait until I have sated the worst of my appetite before they question me. "How did you get out?" Lyon asks right off. "I've been all over that dome twice and as far as I can tell there is only one way in and one way out."

"We came from below ground," I say. "From the mines. A tunnel was opened up when the gas exploded, and we followed the water until it led us out."

"Gas? Explosion?" Levi asks. Both he and Zan have changed out of their leathers and into the same type of clothing that the adults wear. Zan's shirt is decorated with lace and Levi's is much simpler. Neither has a patch or a mended place anywhere that I can see. Levi sits across from me, with Dr. Stewart next to him, Lyon at the head of the table, and Jane next to me at the opposite end.

"Wait, you said 'we,'" Jane asks. "Are there more like you?"

"Yes there are." I feel my face flush with shame. "I did not want to mention them until I was sure you wouldn't harm me, us."

"Very smart on your part," Lyon admits. "You had no way of knowing if we were friend or foe."

"You are all so very nice that I cannot imagine you being anyone's foe," I confess.

"We are quite capable of defending ourselves if attacked," Lyon reminds me.

"We are mostly children," I say. "And your dog, Beau, is with them," I add.

"You were spying on us," Lyon says with a smile.

"I had to find out if you were a threat," I say. "And I've never seen anything like this before."

"Of course you haven't," Dr. Stewart says. "The entire world is new to you. What a marvel you are. An entire city trapped in time."

"I am not so certain we would think that a marvel," I said. "For most of us, it was a prison."

"What led to this explosion you speak of?" Lyon asks.

"Wait, before you get into your story," Jane says, "tell me of the others. You said there are children? We must prepare some food for them. Surely they are as hungry as you."

"They are," I say. "There are twenty of us. Half are children and the rest my age or older. We also have five ponies from the mines and a small herd of goats. And an abundance of cats, except for the one Beau killed."

"So sorry," Levi says. "We must work on that. His manners are atrocious."

"I think he was hungry," I say.

Levi smiles a dazzling smile at me. "There is no excuse for bad manners," he replies and Zan rolls her eyes at him.

"I will tell Cook to prepare some baskets of food," Jane says and leaves the table to go through doors at the back of the room.

"If you don't mind," Lyon says and I realize it is time to pay for my meal, "please tell us your story."

I tell them everything about my world. About working in the mines. About how the coal ran the fans to keep us alive. About how we were lied to about the flames and kept under control all these years so the royals would remain safe. Then I tell them about Alex and how his death rallied us to find a way out. And then I tell them the price we all paid. The only thing I do not tell them is that Sir William Meredith is my father. I see no reason for them to know that. I also do not mention my part in it. I just let them believe that it was all of us acting as one. I want no credit for what happened. I am not a hero and I do not want anyone to think I am. Especially after what I've done.

"So you just left the dome two days ago?" Lyon asks.

Was it only two days? "Yes. The first day we sheltered in the cave because the sun burned us."

"Of course it did," Dr. Stewart says. "You must build up a resistance to it." He picks up Lyon's arm and pushes up his sleeve to show bronze skin. "This is a result of several days of sun exposure. After a bit your skin gets used to it. But you must take it in small doses." He studies me for a moment. "It must have been brutal on your eyes."

"It was," I confess. "I didn't know not to look at it. I was blinded for an entire day."

"Of course you were," Dr. Stewart responds. "You are lucky you recovered so quickly, but it may be a result of your eyes' ability to adapt. Do all your friends have eyes like yours?"

"All but one," I say. "He was from above."

"Ah, the young man you mentioned who was instrumental in finding out the truth about your friend's death. Since he lived above, his eyes would not be as sensitive or adaptable. I have a way to solve your problem with the sun. I have developed amber paint that we put on our spectacles to protect the eyes. I could put some on your goggles and you'd be all set."

"That would be wonderful," I say. "I have to admit I am terrified of it happening again."

"As we all would be," Zan says.

"I know I would," Levi adds. "It must have been frightening."

"It was," I say, recalling those moments in the cave when I thought I was abandoned. Levi smiles at me from across the table. "You are terribly brave you know." I look down at my plate in shame and confusion. He is the second person to tell me so in the past few hours, and I know in my heart I am undeserving of such praise. And I don't have the courage to tell him why so I change the subject.

"You say you've been all over the dome twice?" I ask Lyon. "When? How did you even know of it?"

"I came here many years ago with my father. He was an explorer, like me. We arrived here last week. When I informed Dr. Stewart of our discovery all those years ago he insisted on seeing it himself. We set sail from St. Louis more than a month ago."

"I think I saw you," I said. "Every morning I would go to the rooftops and watch the light come to the dome. A week ago I saw a shadow cross over and wondered what it was."

"It was probably me wearing the glider," Levi says. "I landed on top looking for a way in and took off again. It's rather amazing how thick the glass is. And how milky."

"I have a theory on that," Dr. Stewart says. "I believe the heat from the comet accelerated the hardening of the glass. Or it might be that the original builders figured the heat into the formula to help protect the people within. Whoever they were, they were years ahead in their technology. I certainly hope they saved their records."

"Getting in to see them will be the hardest part," I say. "Sir Meredith is determined to protect the royals at all cost."

"We are certainly not a threat," Dr. Stewart protests.

"Oh but we are," Lyon says with his eyes on me.

"Proof that the outside is safe is contrary to what those inside have been told to believe," I say. "Everyone's purpose is to serve the royals. Without service, their way of life will change." I stop to consider my words. "It already has changed. They no longer have coal, they no longer have the fans . . ."

"They don't need either with the large holes in the roof," Zan contributes.

"My . . . Sir Meredith will still use fear to control the population," I say. "There are other people here. People with weapons like yours. Our world does not have such weapons. There is nothing to keep the rovers, the people on the outside, from taking what they want from the rest of us."

"Except the dome," Lyon concludes.

"Wait, you mean guns?" Levi asks. "Guns were certainly around before the time of the dome. For a couple of hundred years before."

"Why would they need such things inside?" Lyon says. "They left them out to keep the peace. To keep the people from rebelling."

I see the wisdom of his words. "And it worked," I said.

"Until you came along." Levi's warm brown eyes are on me. Measuring me.

"No," I protest. "It was all of us."

"Did anyone else watch the dome from the rooftops?" Levi proclaims. "You were the one who was there when your friend was burned. You are the one who heard his last words."

I cannot deny it, yet I do not claim it. There are too many things to regret. Too many things that I've done wrong.

"I should get back to my friends," I say. "They will be worried about me."

"I'll arrange for an escort," Lyon says. "I am certain Jane will not rest until she makes sure your children are cared for. Where are you staying?"

"We found shelter from the rain in the foundation of an old house," I say. "Beyond that I do not know what there is."

"Ruins?" Dr. Stewart exclaims. "I shall have to examine them also."

"I am certain everything so close to the dome has been picked over," Lyon says.

"Everything was destroyed by the fire," I say. "There is nothing there."

"Oh you'd be surprised at the treasures Dr. Stewart has found," Zan says.

"Treasures?" I ask.

"We are treasure hunters," Levi explains. "We search for artifacts from the before time. Some are underwater now, some were simply abandoned, and others were preserved. Some we simply photograph."

"Photograph?" I ask again.

Levi gets up from the table and retrieves a frame from a bookcase. He hands it to me. It is like a small painting, only much more detailed even though the colors are faded. It is of a younger version of Levi standing with an elderly woman with gray-streaked black hair that hangs to her waist. She has feathers wrapped in her hair and is wearing a long hide dress covered with fringe and beads. They stand in front of a small dome made out of wood and a pieced-together canvas. "This is a photograph," Levi explains. "The image is created with light and various chemicals. It creates a permanent record of the subject."

"Outstanding," I say, totally amazed at what I've seen and recalling the way he said it earlier.

"I imagine there are quite a few artifacts inside the dome," Dr. Stewart says. "If they went to all the trouble to preserve the bloodline, then surely they preserved the historical artifacts also."

I recall the things I saw in my father's office. The exquisite paintings and the beautifully carved furniture along with the things I had seen in the library when I was a child. "We have a library and a museum, but the shiners were only allowed in the library one time a year and never in the museum."

"A library!" Dr. Stewart exclaims. "Excellent!"

"Don't get too excited Jethro," Lyon warns. "First we have to get into the dome."

Back into the dome is not a place I want to go. And I've been gone long enough. "I really should be going now," I say. I fold my napkin, as I'd seen the others do, and rise from my seat.

"I'll go with you," Levi says. "To make sure you don't run into those rovers."

"Me too," Zan says. "To keep you safe too, cousin," she says with a mischievous grin.

"We might as well all go," Lyon announces.

"Then make your selves useful and carry something," Jane says as she comes back into the room from the back. "I've got food, blankets, and medicines if needed." She looks at me. "Is anyone injured?"

I think for a moment. "No . . . but Peter has a horrible cough."

"Then hopefully we can help him," Jane says. She grabs a coat from a hook on the wall and puts it on, which signals the rest to get ready too.

I slip outside while they gather their things. The guards are still there, back on the catwalk where they originally were, and I realize Lyon must have moved them away when I came aboard for my comfort. The moon has traveled also. Where before it was behind the dome, now it hangs closer to where I committed my crime, as if it is a beacon telling all that a body lies here and something must be done about it.

I fooled myself thinking that whiling away the hours with the

American treasure hunters would make things easier, or make the situation go away. It is still there for me to deal with, the body and the repercussions.

Several baskets sit on the catwalk. The resources that the airship has amaze me. To have so many things at your disposal, so many luxuries that you can share so generously, is beyond my comprehension.

"It has turned into a beautiful night," Levi says as he joins me on the catwalk. "We had to stay out at sea when the storm came in. I thought it would never end." He puts on a brown leather vest over his shirt and he wears a belt strapped low around his hip, with a smaller gun than the ones the men carry in a leather holder that is strapped down to his thigh. A knife is in a similar array on his opposite hip. A pair of glasses with dark lenses sits on top of his head. Bella is with him, and she sits at the edge of the catwalk and stares off into the darkness.

"It is beautiful," I admit. "I had always known about the moon and the stars, but to actually see them . . ."

"There's a saying we use," Levi says. "Seeing is believing. Of course I never would have believed there was an entire society inside that thing until I met you."

"I could be lying," I say, because the way he stands so close to me is frightening in a way that has nothing to do with fear.

"It's too outrageous to be made up," he says with a wide smile.

"As are you," I return. "If I did not take you with me, my friends would never believe me." I do not add that James certainly would not. He did not believe me about Alex, and he was able to turn everyone against me. Would he do the same when I showed up with the Hatfields and their gifts of food and supplies?

"What were you doing wandering around at night by yourself?" Levi asks.

"I am used to being up at night," I say. "My shift was in the nighttime. It is hard to get my body used to anything else."

"So you decided to wander about and explore in the dark all by yourself? What about your friends, what are they up to?"

"Some are asleep," I say. "The others are exploring a tunnel that was found in the foundation. They think it leads back into the dome."

"And you have no desire to go inside," Levi says with a laugh.

I nod and grin, relieved that I no longer have to explain about what I was doing before I met them. The rest of the group come out. Lyon has two belts strapped across his chest with small guns, like the one Levi carries, stuck in leather holders. Several small loops cover the belts, and they are filled with small cylinders that have to be the ammunition for the guns. He also carries a long gun, like the guards, and has two long blades in leather belts. Zan wears a gun also, similar to Levi's, and has her glorious hair stuffed up inside a cap. Dr. Stewart has added a large leather bag that is placed crossways over his body so that the bag rests on his hip. Jane wears a hat and short jacket and has a bag similar to Dr. Stewart's.

"Lead on," Lyon says. "We are at your disposal." Everyone picks up a basket and we go as Lyon and Dr. Stewart shine beacons before us.

We walk into the tall grass with Bella bounding ahead. Occasionally she puts her head down and sniffs the ground and at other times she raises it up and tests the wind. Is she searching for Beau? Or does she sense the blood on my hands and on the ground up ahead? I make sure we go away from the scene of my crime and toward the dome where my friends hopefully have not noticed I am gone.

Lyon walks on one side of me and Levi on the other. I stumble over a cobblestone and Levi quickly catches me before I fall and then releases my arm with a smile when I assure him I am fine. I have never been treated with such eloquence and politeness in my life. For someone of my station to have such kindness and willingness to help bestowed upon me is flattering, yet humbling. "You are too generous," I say. "Won't this deplete your supplies for your trip back to America?"

"We resupply as we go," Jane says. "And we have quite a few things in ice storage."

"Ice storage?" I ask.

"It is a way of keeping things cold and therefore fresh for extended periods of time," Zan says. "It was all Dr. Stewart's idea."

"It was quite simple really," Dr. Stewart says. "I just use the ice to keep the ice frozen. It's like an eternal circle of success."

"I'm afraid I don't know what ice is," I say.

"Of course you wouldn't!" Dr. Stewart exclaims. "Your temperatures more than likely remained constant because of the fans and the heat from the steam engines. Quite ingenious really."

While his answer makes sense it still doesn't explain to me what ice is and Levi quickly realizes it. "Ice is water that becomes hard and extremely cold from frigid temperatures," he explains. "Remember when we said the polar ice caps melted and the sea levels rose? That is because all the water that was once frozen melted and ran into the sea. The earth finally righted itself and we have the seasons again, winter, spring, summer, and fall. Ice comes about in the winter. We harvested it and saved it and use it to keep our food fresh."

"Amazing," I say, thinking of Adam's speech. "To every thing there is a season, and a time to every purpose under the heaven."

We have crossed the grass by this time and moved into the park. It did not take long for Dr. Stewart to realize that we were walking on former streets around destroyed houses and into a park. "I really must take samples and collect seeds," he says. "Some of these species I've never seen before."

"Wouldn't that be better done in the daytime?" Jane suggests.

The wind rustles through the trees and I hear a familiar chirp. At the same time, Bella takes off with a bark at a run.

"Bella!" Zan calls out. "Come back!"

"She must smell Beau," Jane says. Lyon and Dr. Stewart shine their beacons in the direction Bella goes. There is nothing there but long shadows cast by the trees.

"It's the right direction," I say. I hear the chirp again. It isn't Pip, but it is the whistle that James, Adam, and Alcide use in the tunnels. I look up and see Alcide up on a tree branch right above Lyon. Before I can open my mouth he drops, along with James, Adam, and Pace, onto Lyon, Levi, Dr. Stewart, and Zan.

"Run, Wren, run!" Pace yells as he jumps on Levi.

"Stop!" I call out. "These are my friends." And that's when I realize I am talking to all of them, about everyone. But first I have to stop them from killing each other.

· 12 ·

My shiner friends are no match for my new American friends. In a matter of seconds, Adam is flat on his back with the point of a gun pressed against his cheek. Pace goes flying though the air, and Levi draws out his knife and goes after him. Zan's hair flies from her hat as she jumps straight up and kicks James in the chin, and Alcide is on Dr. Stewart's back until Dr. Stewart propels himself backward into a tree to break Alcide's hold.

"You're a girl!" James exclaims as Zan straddles his chest before thumping down on him. She pulls a small knife from her sleeve and holds it to his throat.

"Stop!" I yell out. "Don't hurt them! These are my friends."

Bella rushes at us and Jane grabs her collar before she can do any damage to the attackers. She growls ominously as Lyon stands over Adam.

"Why did you attack us?" Lyon demands.

"We thought you'd taken Wren," Adam replies. "We found blood on a club and thought she'd been taken by the rovers."

"I'm fine, Adam," I say. I turn a circle to see they are all at risk of death if anyone makes a wrong move. "Please, let them go," I say to Levi.

"They are young, Lyon," Jane urges, "the same age as Zan and Levi."

Levi nods, sheaths his knife, and extends a hand to Pace to help him up. Dr. Stewart does the same with Alcide, who stumbles. Lyon gives Adam a stern look and lets him up, while Zan gives James a smile that tells him she is not to be messed with again, then jumps up. James grunts as Zan "accidentally" kicks him in the side.

Pace runs to me and pulls me into a hasty embrace. "You're not hurt?" He pulls away and looks at me closely. "I was afraid you were dead or worse."

They found the bloody branch. But no mention of a body. What happened to it? "No . . . I'm fine," I say. "They offered to help us."

"What are they," James asks as he keeps a cautious eye on Zan. "Royals?"

"They're from America," I say. "They saw the smoke from the dome and came to investigate."

"From where?" Adam asks, and I realize that only I know about America, and only because Pace had told me.

"From a country across the sea," Pace says.

"How did you get here?" James asks as he climbs to his feet, giving Zan a wide berth. I notice she is smiling rather smugly, but she is also watching him closely.

"They have an airship," I say.

"A what?" Alcide squeaks. He is bent over, with his hands on his knees, trying to catch his breath.

"Lose something?" James says at the peculiar tone of his voice.

"At least I didn't get beat up by a girl," Alcide replies as he straightens up.

Zan laughs and makes a great show of shaking out her hair before replacing it beneath the cap. I can't help but notice James and Alcide watch her closely, fascinated by her movements.

"We have food for you," Jane says. "And blankets. We would like to help, if you'll let us. We can talk about the rest later."

"Food?" Alcide says.

"More than I've ever seen," I say. "The children need it."

"I vote yes," Alcide says. "We all need it."

"No one asked you," Adam reminds him but he looks at me. "Wren?"

"They are good people," I say. "They really want to help."

"And learn," Dr. Stewart adds.

"And learn," I agree. "This is Lyon Hatfield, his wife Jane, his daughter Alexandra, and his nephew Levi."

"Levi Addison," Levi says and holds his hand out to Pace.

"And this is Dr. Stewart," I conclude.

"I'm Pace," Pace says and takes Levi's hand.

"Adam." Adam raises his hand.

"James."

"Alcide."

I let out a sigh of relief. The light around us brightens and I sense that morning is not far off. Surely this day will offer more hope than the last. We gather up the baskets and the lamps that were dropped in the attack and move in the direction of the shelter. Pace walks on one side of me, Levi on the other.

"You're not a shiner," Levi says. "Wren explained to us about her eyes. I noticed you don't have them."

"No, I'm from above," Pace admits.

"So you're the one," Levi says. "She told us about the revolution."

"You mean she is the one," Pace says. "Without her inspiration, it never would have happened."

"I knew you were brave," Levi says.

"No, I'm not," I say. At the moment I am terrified. What happened when they found the branch? Where is the body?

Pace slings his arm around my shoulder. "And modest," he adds. "But please don't disappear like that again. I was terrified when we couldn't find you."

"What happened? Why did you all go looking for me?"

"I woke up and realized you were gone. I thought you'd gone into the tunnel with the rest, but when I went to look for you there, they had come up. We went outside, saw your tracks in the mud, and followed them. We found a bloody tree branch, and it looked like there'd been a scuffle of some sort. We found more tracks going away, and we knew they weren't yours because they were bigger. We were following them when we saw the lights among the trees and went to investigate. Adam, James, and Alcide could see from far off and said that you were being held prisoner."

"It must have been when you stumbled and fell," Levi says. "And I caught you."

"So we climbed the trees to set a trap."

"You're lucky we didn't shoot you," Levi says.

"It's a risk I was willing to take," Pace replies, "to keep her safe."

Pace's words speak volumes about his feelings for me, but I'm too worried about what else he said to appreciate them. "All you found was a bloody branch?" I ask.

"Should they have found something else?" Levi says.

I shake my head, pretending confusion.

"I'm just so grateful you are not hurt," Pace says. "So how did you find each other?"

"I was looking at the stars and saw one moving," I say, relieved that I do not have to lie about this part. "So I went closer and realized that it was something coming this way. I watched them from the grass until they discovered me."

"We literally landed on top of her," Levi says.

"How?" Pace asks.

"They fly," I say. I know Pace will be fascinated with the things the Hatfields have and do.

"How do you fly?" Pace asks. "I would like to see that."

Levi explains to Pace about the glider wings while we walk. I see that Adam, James, and Alcide are in deep a conversation with the Hatfields, as the three of us are. I also notice James and Zan stealing looks at each other when they think the other one isn't watching. Perhaps I should warn Zan about James. But what would I tell her? Just because James and I rub each other the wrong way doesn't mean it will happen with other people. It might just be our personalities. Our world has gotten a lot bigger now, as have our choices.

"What did you see when you were up there tonight?" I ask. "You never said."

"Because I was distracted," Levi grins. "We really didn't see much. Smoke mostly and the tops of some buildings with what looked like trees on them and a long catwalk that looks as if it stretches from one side to the other."

"It does," Pace says grimly. His father fell from the catwalk and died before he was born, chasing a criminal. "They can't clear the smoke because the engines for the fans were destroyed," Pace says. "And if it only has the one hole to come out of it will take days for it to clear."

"I believe there was more than one hole, although one looked to be more on the side."

"From where James blew the fans," Pace explains.

"The poor people," I say. "We still have friends inside and we're worried about how they have fared. We are especially worried about Pace's mother," I continue. "She was held hostage when all this happened."

"Maybe we could go inside and snoop around," Levi suggests.

"What do you mean?" Pace says. "Go in through the hole?"

"Why not?" Levi says. "It should be fairly simple to lower down to the catwalk and from there I would assume there's a way to reach the ground. The smoke would serve to conceal our actions."

"We could certainly get to David and Lucy's place from there," Pace concludes. "At least they would have news, and we could tell them how to get out through the tunnels."

"If the way is still there," I say. "We have no way of knowing if it is."

"It certainly wouldn't hurt to find out," Levi says. His excitement over the plan is obvious, and I know Pace will go because he is desperate to find news about his mother.

"How would the rest of us get there?" I ask. "You and Zan have the gliders."

"We have four gliders and the capability of carrying passengers or a load as long as they don't weigh too much," Levi says. "And there's no reason why we can't just fly the airship above and lower the winch down to the dome top. Of course we must consult with my uncle, but I am certain he would be all for it. The dome is a mystery that he's wanted to solve for years."

A shiver goes down my spine at the possibility. I do not want to go back in, yet I cannot abandon our friends who are still inside. They fought alongside us. They need to know that what they fought for is real.

"Wren and I must be the ones to go with you," Pace says. "After all, we know the streets better than anyone else." I cannot argue with his logic, yet I am still terrified at the thought of going back in. I am afraid that if I go back in I will never get out again.

We come to the place where we have corralled the ponies and goats. "They lived underground with you?" Dr. Stewart asks. "Oh my, the ponies are completely blind. Well of course they would not need sight since they live in the dark."

"We weren't completely in the dark," Alcide says. "We did have light."

"Ah yes, the waterwheel you told me about. It powered your entire underground system?"

Alcide falls back into discussion with Dr. Stewart while we pause to look over the animals. I quickly count the goats in my head and know that one is still missing. I expected to see her with the others even if she was on the other side of the barrier we constructed. Did she just wander off?

Zan steps through the barrier and goes to the ponies. "They are precious!" she coos as she pets one.

"One of the goats is missing," Adam says.

"How can you tell?" James asks.

"It's the brown one. It belonged to Hans. I just remember it because one of its horns was broken," Adam explains.

"It could have gotten out," Pace suggests.

"Or someone could have stolen it," James replies. I should tell them that it's true, but I am ashamed to confess my crime. I'm afraid of what they will think of me.

"We better set a guard from now on," Adam concludes. "If it's the rovers . . ."

"We have nothing to fight them with," James says.

"Perhaps we can help with that," Lyon says. "Help you even the odds a bit."

While they talk I join Zan inside the pen. Ghost comes directly to me and bumps his head against my stomach. "He loves you," Zan says delightedly. As she talks, Jonah runs into the pen, meowing for all he is worth with his tail straight up in the air like a flag.

"And I love him," I say as I rub Ghost's forehead and Jonah trails between my legs. I listen to the conclusions drawn by the men. They were right; we need to set a guard because the rovers will be back. Except I think they will be after more than our livestock. I believe they will be after revenge for the one I killed. And I really do not think we can survive it.

· 13 ·

Sleep is a long time coming for me, and, when it finally comes, it is full of disturbing dreams with bodies that float down from the sky and chase me through the trees. I would have much rather dreamed about taking a bath in Zan's wonderful tub. When I finally wake up, achy from sleeping on the hard and unforgiving ground, soaking out my aches is all I can think about. Because I am determined not to think about the rover I killed the night before.

No matter how badly I don't want to think about him, I can't erase him from my mind. I have to know what happened to him. James, Adam, and Alcide are still sleeping when I creep from the basement we sheltered in. Jonah, who slept by my side, as is his habit now, follows me as I go in search of food, and hopefully some answers.

A lot has happened since I stumbled down into our shelter after arriving with the Hatfields and the food. A canvas awning now covers our ruins. A table sits beneath it, with some chairs, and a small brazier supplies heat. The table has food on it, no doubt left behind by the kindness of Jane. I pick up an apple and take pleasure in the crisp fresh tartness of it, as I had only eaten dried apples in the past. Pip is in his cage, which hangs from one of the posts that holds up the canvas, and I feed him a small piece as I pass by. Two men, dressed similarly to the guards I'd seen the night before at the Hatfields' airship, stand guard with long guns in their arms and smaller ones strapped to their hips.

"Where is everyone?" I ask one of the guards. The sun is high overhead and I figure the time to be early afternoon.

"Mrs. Hatfield took the women and the children to the ship for bathing," one says. "And the men are foraging for supplies. They asked us to send you to the ship when you awakened. They plan to move your camp closer to the ship but did not want to unduly alarm you."

"I am on my way," I assure them. I go by the place where the ponies and goats are kept, with Jonah trailing after me, and I am amazed to see another guard there. I give Ghost the core of my apple and move on, pretending to go in the direction of the airship until I am far enough away that I can go to where I attacked the rover the night before without the guard seeing me.

I've got to know what happened to him. The problem is I'm not really sure where it was when I attacked him. I have just a general idea of the direction. Jonah runs ahead of me, with his tail straight up, taking delight in the sights and sounds of this exciting new world. I keep on, fairly certain I'm going in the right direction, until I see the familiar shape of the branch lying on the ground.

I pick it up and look at the blood on it. It is dried now and a tiny black ant is stuck to it, long dead after his struggles to escape. I pitch the branch away, disgusted with the thing it has wrought at my hand. Jonah runs over to investigate it as soon as it hits the ground. He flattens his ears at the smell of the blood and hisses at the branch.

The grass is flattened where the rover lay. I look around for the tracks that Pace talked about. I recognize mine, made fresh in the earth last night from the rain that had just fallen, and notice how they closely follow those of the rover. While my tracks are plain, his have a marking in them, as if he'd carved the letter *T* on the heel of his shoe. I look closer and see the goat's cloven hoof prints cross over our path where it ran back to the others. As much as I do not want to be there, I go to where the grass is flattened and look closer. A few tufts of grass have blood on them. His friends must have come looking for him. But what did they do when they found him? How many of them are there? I walk away from the grass, away from the dome, in the direction of thicker, darker woods. I keep my eyes on the ground, looking for more tracks, but the grass is so thick here that . . .

I see tracks. One set. And they have the mark on them. But how? I look back at the place where we fought and then at the tracks again. They are definitely leading away. I follow them for a few paces, my eyes looking for the patches of dirt between the clumps of grass, and I see another one.

My breath comes rapidly from my lungs, and I put my hand on a tree to keep myself upright. I look at my hand and see blood on the bark, a little above where my hand sits.

He's alive. He was able to get up and walk away. He stopped here, just as I did, before he continued on. I am filled with such a sense of relief that I slide to the ground with my back against the tree and cry. I cannot stop myself. The tears come and they are accompanied by great heaving sobs that I cannot quiet no matter now hard I want to. Jonah meows at me questioningly and then jumps up the trunk of the tree and scrambles into the leaves.

"Wren?" It is Levi. "Are you hurt?" He drops down to one knee in front of me, concern plainly written on his handsome face, compassion showing in his warm brown eyes, and I am struck, once more, by how beautiful he is. He carries a weapon that I have never seen before. It hangs by a strap from his shoulder and he puts it aside as he rocks back on his heels at my answer.

"Have you ever killed anyone?" I ask. He certainly looks capable of it, with all his weapons. They seem like a natural part of him, the way Pip seems a part of Pace.

He tilts his head sideways, as if to see me better, and his brown eyes widen in surprise at my question. I have to admit that it probably was not what he was expecting me to say.

He answers my question with one of his own. "Would it make a difference in how you see me if I had?"

I study him closely. I really know nothing about him, but he and his family have shown me and my friends nothing but kindness when they could have just turned me away after finding out everything they wanted to know. It is not something I have ever known from strangers, yet it was the very thing that kept me going when things were at their worst. The kindness of Pace, of Lucy and David, even Jilly, who is of royal blood. I cannot judge Levi for the things that have happened to him before I met him. I do not know what he has had to do to survive, anymore than he can judge me for the things I have done.

"No, it wouldn't," I answer truthfully.

Levi pulls a large linen square from his pocket and hands it to me before he sits down next to me with his back against the tree. "Wipe your tears," he instructs as I look at the pure white linen. It is like the napkin, much nicer than my clothes, still I use it to wipe my face and check it to make sure I have not soiled it too much. "Now tell me why you asked me such a deep question and why you are out here by yourself, crying your eyes out."

I cannot look at him as I speak the words. "I was afraid I killed someone."

"What do you mean afraid?"

"Last night, before you found me. I was with the ponies and a rover came up and stole one of the goats. I hid when I saw him. When he took the goat I followed him. I found a branch and I hit him in the back of the head. There was blood and he fell and I ran . . ."

"And that's what you were doing out by yourself when you saw us dock."

"Yes," I said. "And that was the bloody branch Pace and the others found last night when they were looking for me."

"But there wasn't a body."

"No. I think he was able to walk away. At least that's what I think from looking at the tracks. And the goat is still missing. I thought he ran back to the pens but he's not there now."

"So either he wasn't dead and left or he was dead and his friends found him and stole the goat."

"I think he wasn't dead." I turn my head to look at Levi. "I just wish I knew for sure."

"I never answered your question, Wren," he says. He is quiet for a moment, considering his words, and then he answers. "Yes, I have killed someone. It wasn't a pleasant experience. But I had to in order to survive."

"He was trying to kill you?"

"Yes, actually trying to kill all of us. As we said last night, the world is still recovering and not all of it is civilized. I fear your rovers might be part of the latter group."

"Is there a difference then? Is there a list of rules that justifies killing?"

"Such a complicated question, Wren. One that I'm not qualified to answer. Can you be more specific?"

"Is it right to kill someone because they want to kill you and not right to kill someone who steals from you?"

"This wasn't your first time," Levi asks. "I can see it in your eyes."

"It wasn't," I admit. "I killed someone before. Inside. Because he tried to ra . . . rape me."

"Then you were most definitely justified. There isn't a court in our land that would convict you."

"But last night I attacked a man over a goat."

"And that one goat might make the difference over your survival. Maybe not today, but in a few weeks if things like last night keep happening." Levi leans forward and turns so he faces me. "The human race has been through a terrible time, and people do what they have to, to survive. You were only doing what you thought was right, to protect the people you love."

I nod. What he says makes sense, but it doesn't make the guilt or the pain I carry inside any easier to bear.

Levi reaches out a finger and touches a tear that I'd missed, wiping it on the linen square that I have clutched tightly in my hand. "Your guilt is a good thing, Wren. It's doing something like you did and not feeling anything that is wrong. I have a feeling that the rover you bashed felt no compunction whatsoever about stealing your goat, which is why he went back and finished the job when he woke up."

"If it was him that woke up."

"I have a feeling it was. If more had come looking for him do you think they would have stopped with one goat?"

"No," I agree. "We know that they have traded their weapons for young men and women with the bluecoats in the dome." *With my father* . . . I do not say. "Jon saw them the first night he was out with one of his friends who has disappeared. He said they were leading her with a rope around her neck."

"As I said, uncivilized," Levi says. "My uncle will want to look into this. He abhors slavery of any kind. Which is why he was immediately drawn to your side of the struggle. You and your people were nothing more than slaves to those inside."

I nod. I never thought of it as being slavery, or maybe I just didn't want to consider myself to be a slave. I just thought of it as being my place, as that is what I was always told. My life was due to the unlucky circumstances of my birth. I remember reading stories of slaves in the Bible. Not specific stories of slaves, just references. I just thought it was the way things were everywhere for everyone. I never considered that the world beyond the dome would do things differently.

"Why did you confess this to me?" Levi asks. "Instead of Pace. There is something between you two, isn't there?"

"Yes, there is," I say. I think on it for a moment. Why didn't I confide in Pace? "I didn't want to tell him because he has this ideal of me as being some great leader, like a savior or something. And I'm not. I'm just me, trying to figure it all out and doing the best that I can. Yet he keeps on saying things, just like you did last night. Telling me I am brave and special. I'm not. I'm just me. Wren. A shiner."

"A shiner with a purpose," Levi says. "Do not underestimate yourself, or the things you can do."

"Now you sound like Pace," I say and he grins at me.

"What of your family, Wren?" he asks. "Did you lose them in the catastrophe?"

"My mother died when I was born, and my grandmother soon

after. My grandfather raised me. He died a few days before everything happened. He blew up a tunnel to keep the filchers from capturing Pace and I."

"I'm sorry," Levi says. "What are filchers?"

"They are like rovers, only they live inside the dome." I go on to explain. "They come from the street people, which we call scarabs because they have to scrounge for everything they have. They are descended from the people who managed to hide inside before the dome was closed up. They wear horrible masks and haunt the streets. They rape and they steal and they plunder. They also do things that the bluecoats, what we call the enforcers, don't want to do. Basically they will do anything for a reward and are to be avoided at all costs."

"Ah," Levi says. "Bounty hunters." I nod, as it sounds logical. "And your enforcers are what we call policemen. Every city in America has a police force and the outlying areas have sheriffs."

There is so much to learn about this new outside world. "Not all scarabs are bad or become filchers," I add. "I don't approve of what they do, but I believe it's born of desperate measures. Jon comes from the scarabs. Like me, he just wanted to find a way out of the dome."

"You explained about your mother," Levi says. "Where is your father?"

My father . . . "I never really knew him," I say because it is true. "He came from above." I still don't really know him. I probably never will because our worlds are so totally different, and I really don't want to explain about him to Levi or anyone else for that matter. "What about your family? Lyon is your mother's brother?"

"Yes. My father and Lyon were best friends. He was an adventurer also."

"Was?"

"My mother, my father, and my older brother were killed when their airship caught fire. I was ten at the time. I would have died also except I threw a tantrum that day because I wanted to go to a friend's birthday party. My mother gave in and let me go, and I was allowed to spend the night with my friend also, as they were taking the new ship out to test it." He grew quiet for a moment, still grieving for his parents I expect as I still grieve for the mother I never knew. "I've been living with Lyon and Jane ever since, except for a short time when I lived with my father's mother."

"I'm so sorry."

Levi shrugs. "It happens. You grieve and you go on. Isn't that what you did when your grandfather died, and your friend Alex?"

"So many people have died besides them."

"But so many survived," he says. "You say Pace sees you as a great hero and you are not. You are also not the reason so many died."

"But," I begin, and he puts a finger to my lips to stop me.

"You can't have it both ways. Denying your part in this will not bring those people back. Denying your part only serves to make their deaths inconsequential."

"What do you mean?" I ask.

"Did they ask you to stop? Did they say, no we will not leave the dome even if you do find a way out?"

I shake my head. "They didn't believe it."

"They didn't have to. You believed it enough for everyone."

I shake my head again. I am so confused and there is so much to think about. Jonah looks down from the branch above and meows questioningly.

"A friend of yours?" Levi asks.

"His name is Jonah."

"Like the story with the whale?"

"Yes!" I say and smile.

"Brilliant!" Levi stands and extends his hand to me. "Are you hungry?"

"Yes I am."

"Then you can help me hunt." He picks up his weapon. "This is a crossbow. And it doesn't make any noise. We wouldn't want to alert those rovers to our presence now would we?"

"No, we wouldn't."

"Tell Jonah to keep quiet," Levi says with a dazzling grin, and we both follow him into the woods.

· 14 ·

The sunlight dapples through the trees as we move deeper and deeper into the forest. I never would have dared to go this far, away from the dome, away from my friends, if not for Levi. He is intent on his mission and I am content to follow, along with Jonah, who seems thrilled with the new sights and sounds. Birds flit from tree to tree and call out warnings while small creatures that Levi quietly identifies as squirrels, rabbits, and chipmunks scatter through the low brush as we silently creep on a thick covering of fallen leaves and pine needles, which send up a fragrant bouquet with every step. Everywhere I look there is a new sight, a new sound, and a new word to add to my ever-expanding vocabulary.

Perhaps I should worry about the rovers, but the sight of Levi's weapons, the crossbow and the quiver of arrows, the gun and knife strapped on his hip, gives me a sense of security that I've never felt before. He sees me squinting when we walk through a sunny spot and he gives me his glasses with the tinted lenses. They fit differently than my goggles, and the thin curved wire feels strange on my ears. Levi grins at me as he straightens them on my face.

"Got to protect those beautiful eyes," he says, and I feel a red come over my cheeks that has nothing to do with the sun.

We step back into dense growth and Levi uses his crossbow to part the foliage, keeping it before him in case we come upon something. I hear the sound of water running in the distance, and its bittersweet sound reminds me of the river by the cave where Pace and I lived for a few short days. I have no idea what we are hunting until he holds up a hand to stop me and then points ahead into another clearing.

A wondrous creature stands before me. Tall, sleek, majestic, with a large array of horns upon its head, so heavy that I wonder how he can hold it upright as he dips his head to graze upon the tender shoots of grass in the small clearing we came upon. I grab Jonah and pull him close before he can dash out from where we hide and give us away. A movement catches my eye and I see three more, but these do not have horns. At the edge of the clearing is another creature with a smaller set of horns. Beyond the group is a wide stream that tumbles over huge rocks. Water sprays up from it and the sunlight streaming through the trees create a wide band of color. I slip off Levi's glasses to see it better and clearly see blue, purple, and red, and then the paler hues of orange and yellow. It is another miraculous sight of things I never thought to behold in my lifetime.

"What are they?" I mouth to Levi.

"A stag and his does," he mouths back. "Deer." I want to ask him about the other thing I see over the water, but I don't as I see he is intent on the deer. Slowly he lowers to one knee and props the crossbow on his arm. The stag stops his grazing and stares with his deep brown eyes directly where we hide. Suddenly, he takes off with a great leap and the does go with him. Before I can draw a breath, Levi lets the arrow fly. I hear the soft twang of the bowstring and see the arrow strike the smaller stag midflight before he falls to the ground.

I choke back a sob. Jonah wiggles free and dashes to where the stag lies while I stare up at Levi in shock and the survivors crash off into the forest.

"It's a matter of survival, Wren," he says. "A difference between eating today and tomorrow or not eating at all. It's a hide to cover your feet and keep you warm. It's tools and weapons. It's something you are going to have to learn if you want to stay alive."

"But he was so beautiful," I cry. "They all are."

"Then respect his beauty and appreciate his purpose." I nod and once more wipe the tears from my cheek. I've seen so much death lately and not enough beauty. I hate to think of anything that amazing being removed from this world, but I also appreciate the significance of it. Without Levi and his family we would be starving. I cannot condemn him for helping us stay alive.

He kneels by the stag, places his hand on its neck, and bows his head in prayer for a brief moment while Jonah sniffs at the place where the arrow went in. I do not know anything about hunting, but I know enough about life to realize that this was a clean kill and the animal died instantly, and for that I am grateful. I do not think I could stand it if it were thrashing around in agony.

"The older one would not have let this one stay around much longer," he says. "He would have fought him for the herd." Levi pulls the arrow from the stag and checks the tip. He wipes the blood off on the thick grass.

It is all a matter of survival I realize. The strong taking from the weak to survive. If we want to survive, we have to be the strong ones. We have to learn how or we might as well have died in the floods.

"Will you carry this?" Levi says and hands me the crossbow and quiver of arrows. And then, to my amazement, he leverages himself under the deer and picks it up with it slung over his shoulders.

"Isn't that heavy?" I ask.

"A bit," he says and his voice sounds strained. "Lead on then," he says after adjusting the weight.

"Come on, Jonah," I say and go back through the dense underbrush that we'd passed through, leading with the cross bow as I'd seen Levi do.

"Where did you learn to hunt like that?" I ask. I keep my eyes on the trail as Jonah scampers ahead.

"From the Sioux," he replies with a puff.

"Sioux?"

"An Indian tribe indigenous to the northern part of the Midwest." He takes a breath. "America."

"Would you rather wait until you can answer for me to ask you anymore questions?" I ask.

"I can answer now," he says. "I'm fine." I turn around to look at him, and his face is flushed beneath his tan. I do not believe him, but I know about young men and their pride so I continue on.

"What are the Sioux Indians like?" I ask.

"They live as one with the land. It's how they managed to survive what they call 'The Great Winter.' They have legends that even predicted the coming of the comet. Because they knew how to live off the land, they were able to survive while those who lived in the big cities died off because there just wasn't enough food." Levi's speech comes in small bursts as he carries the deer. "They have a legend about a spider who spun a web with a hole in the middle. It talks about the cycles of life: you are born and need care, then childhood, then you become an adult, and then once more you become old and need care."

"Shiners don't live that long," I say.

"What?"

"We do not live that long. Most die before they are forty from black lung. It comes from breathing in the coal dust our entire lives. My grandfather was forty-six when he died. That is old for a shiner."

"That is so sad," Levi says.

"It is the way things are," I reply. The way things always were. We were taught not to expect more. "Tell me more about the spider."

"The web he spun was called a dream catcher. Its purpose is to catch the good dreams and let the bad fall through the holes. The spider said . . ."

"The spider talked?"

"It's a legend," Levi says. "The spider was talking to a wise man."

"Go on," I say.

"The spider said there are bad forces and good forces at work throughout our lives. If you listen to the good forces you will go in the right direction, if you listen to the bad you won't."

"Did he mention how to tell the good forces from the bad?" I ask teasingly. I know he's telling me about the legend in an attempt to make me feel better about everything that has happened to me in the past few days. The fact that he does this makes me happy and strangely carefree.

"No. I guess you're just supposed to follow your heart." Levi adds, "And make sure you have a dream catcher close by. Don't you have any legends?"

I think for a moment. Do we? We don't and for some reason that suddenly makes me sad. My emotions are all over the place and I don't know why. "All we had was stories from the Bible. It was the only book any of us possessed."

"I don't think that's a bad thing," Levi says. "It is good to have something to believe in." The underbrush has cleared out and the going is easier now so we can walk side by side. Jonah still stalks ahead of us. The sun is lower in the sky now and shines in our faces when it can find a path through the trees.

"I always believed in the things the Bible says. I also believed there was a world out here," I say.

"And you acted on it."

"That still doesn't mean it was a good thing." I stop in my tracks. Jonah, ahead of us, is crouched close to the ground with his ears laid back. He lets out a low rumbling growl.

"Someone is coming," Levi says.

"What should we do?" I ask. Jonah hisses and growls again. His tail twitches angrily.

"Hide," Levi whispers. He moves in a crouching run to a dead tree and drops the stag on the ground. I follow him and together we shove the dead weight of the stag beneath the tree. Branches crack loudly and I fear we have given ourselves away. Jonah takes off and dashes up a tree while Levi and I crawl beneath the dead tree away from the dead stag. It is a close fit between the thick branches and we have to wedge our way in until we lie hip-to-hip and shoulder-to-shoulder. There is an abundance of brush before us, enough to hide us, I hope.

We hear the crack of a branch to our right and Levi eases the crossbow in front of him, pulls the arrow back into the slot, and aims it in the direction of the sound. There is a space between the ground and the brush, and another above that gives us a view of the path. We are so close that I can feel the clench of his thigh against mine, and his elbow, where it supports the crossbow, is pressed against my breast. I smell the earth, the blood on the stag, and the scent of my fear. I also smell the freshness of Levi's skin and the scent of his soap.

We hear them before we see them. "I'm ah-tellin-ya, I smell blood."

"It's because ya haven't washed off what's on ya," another voice says. "Ya smell to the heavens anyway. Don't know how ya can smell blood over your filth."

I concentrate on making myself unseen. Pressing my body into the dirt and hoping I blend with the grass and the brush that surrounds me. Levi keeps the crossbow aimed at the trees. We know there are two of them. How many more are with the two?

"If there's goats and such there's got to be people too," another voice says.

"Well yeah, since one of them ah-clubbed me."

My eyes widen in surprise. It has to be the rover that I hit. It has to be. I keep my eyes on the spot where I think they will appear and sure enough, he comes striding from between the trees, his face still grubby and covered with hair and a rag wrapped around his skull.

"I didn't kill him," I whisper with relief.

"Let's hope I don't have to either," Levi quietly replies, and there is no doubt in my mind that he would not hesitate to do so.

There are five of them. All dressed in old patched clothing and hides. All carrying the long guns, although now that I've seen Levi's and the ones Lyon's men carry I see a difference. Lyon's guns are sleeker, shorter, and much shinier. I also don't see the rounds of ammunition like Lyon carried unless they are in the small hide bags the rovers carry crossed over their chests and resting on their hips. Everything around me seems dark and desperate and I realize it is because of the tinted glasses that I wear. I do not dare move enough to slide them up.

"They don't have weapons," the one I thought I'd killed says. "Not if they're from inside the dome."

"Do ya think they were cast out?" They stop right in front of us. I am overcome by the smell of unwashed bodies. Levi doesn't move a bit. He keeps his eyes and the crossbow on them.

"Does it ah-matter?" one asks.

"If they were cast out, then there's no one to ah-protect them. But if they're coming out, after what happened in there, then there's the lot of us competin' for the game and food. There's a lot of more of them than there is us. As long as we got the weapons then we got the upper hand. But if they keep coming we can't ah-fight them all."

"I say pick them off as they come out and that way they'll stop ah-comin'. Or if they keep on ah-comin' we can kill them all and move inside and have all their riches."

"I surely would like stayin' ah-warm this winter," one agrees.

"Then we'll ah-start with this bunch and see what happens."

I cannot believe they talk so callously about killing us. Without even knowing that we are mostly children. The same righteous anger than filled me when I struck the rover for stealing the goat comes over me again. If I held the crossbow in my hand I would willingly shoot them all. But I don't. Levi does and his head is wiser than mine. There are two of us against five of them, and they are all armed.

"We have to do something," I say in a whisper as they continue on their way. Luckily it is away from our shelter and away from the dome. I watch them go and then turn to Levi. We are so close beneath the dead tree that our noses nearly touch.

"Did you not see the guards at your camp?" Levi questions me in a voice as quiet as my own.

"Yes."

"I do not think they are so stupid as to walk in and start shooting. I believe they will take the time to look around and they will be dissuaded when they see that our people are better armed than they are."

"You sound so sure," I say.

"I hope I'm wrong," he replies. "I hope they are *so* stupid, then we can be rid of the lot of them before the night is over. Their weapons are primitive and can't compete with ours."

"You mean by killing them?" I stare into his warm brown eyes and see the untold stories hidden within. Levi might be the same age as me but he's seen things and done things that I have never imagined. He knows of what he speaks. I am not certain if that scares me, or thrills me, especially when he answers.

"I mean by surviving." He stares back at me and his eyes suddenly soften and he looks at me. At my face, at my eyes, at my lips, which suddenly feel very dry. As Levi looks at me, Pace enters my mind and I am overcome with guilt. I have been gone for hours without a word to anyone about my whereabouts. Surely he will be worried.

Levi senses the change in me because he suddenly turns away. "We should go warn my uncle," he says. "I'll come back for the deer."

I nod in agreement and we back out from beneath the tree as quietly as we can. Levi slings the crossbow and quiver over his shoulder and takes my hand. "We best hurry," he says. "They might decide to come back this way." We take off at a run with Jonah sprinting at our heels.

There is no terror as we run. No filchers or rovers nipping at our heels. No dead bodies or crimes to escape from. No bounties on our heads. I know there is a sense of urgency, but I also feel a sense of freedom. A sense of excitement. A streak of wildness and joy that makes me relish the run. There is no need for us to hold hands but we do, and our strides fall into rhythm. Levi could easily outrun me but he doesn't. For the first time in my life my lungs do not ache, instead they feel cleansed and free of the constraints of the coal and the heavy air of the dome.

There is joy to be had in such a simple pleasure. Joy in a moment that I've never felt before. Levi looks at me and grins and I cannot help myself; I laugh, which makes him laugh, and we have to stop because we are both laughing so hard.

"I don't even know why we're laughing," he says finally when he stop and can breathe again.

"I don't either," I say. "It just felt good and right."

He stares at me again with his warm brown eyes. "It does, doesn't it?"

"Wren!" I turn and see Pace running our way and I suddenly realize that Levi and I are still holding hands. I quickly release my hold and turn to Pace who grabs me into an embrace as soon as he gets close enough to touch me. "Thank God you are all right."

"Of course I am," I say. "Why wouldn't I be?" Doesn't he realize how capable Levi is? I see the concern, plainly written on his handsome face, concern that just a few moments ago I knew he would feel, yet it annoys me.

"No one knew where you were, just like last night. You can't just disappear like that. I was nearly out of my mind with worry."

"I best go tell Uncle Lyon what we saw," Levi says, and, after raising his hand in a quick good-bye, he takes off again at a run.

"What did you see?" Pace asks. "What happened?"

"We saw rovers."

"Where? How many? What happened?"

I open my mouth to speak but first I look at him. His face is tinged with red, and I realize he has been in the sun most of the day. His hair is wild and he smells of the salt and the sea. And he is wearing a gun in a belt on his hip, like Levi.

"What is that?" I ask.

"Lyon taught us how to shoot. We were down on the beach so the rovers wouldn't hear us." He puts his hand on the handle of the gun. "I was good enough that he gave me this pistol, which didn't set well with James. According to Lyon, he doesn't have the patience for it."

"I guess I was gone longer than I thought," I say. "When I left they were still asleep."

"I thought you were with Zan and the rest of the women," Pace admits. "It wasn't until we came up and they said they hadn't seen you and thought you were with us that I really got worried."

"I am so sorry," I say and I really mean it. I did not mean to worry him, nor did I mean to avoid him.

Pace puts his hands on my shoulders and kisses my forehead. "It's all right," he says. He puts a finger under my chin and tilts it up so he can kiss me. "Just let someone know next time."

I was fine until he corrected me again. I start to protest. Someone did know where I was. Levi knew. This feeling of resentment I have bothers me. There is no reason for it yet there it is. Pace does not deserve it. He is always there for me. Since the day we met he has supported me and I fell in love with him for it. Except now that support feels constraining. It's not him, it's me. I know it's me and I don't know what to do about it.

"Tell me about the rovers," he says. He takes my hand and I find myself comparing his grip with Levi's. Levi's hands are calloused and rough like mine. Pace's are smooth, but why shouldn't they be? He was a student before he joined the enforcers. His life was nothing like mine. We walk toward the airship and I tell him what we saw and heard.

"We need to make sure the children are safe," Pace says. We'll have to find a better place than what we've got now."

"Levi seems to think that when they see the guards and the weapons that they will be discouraged," I point out. "And one of the guards informed me that they are moving us closer to the airship for protection."

"Levi and the rest of them won't be here forever, Wren," Pace says. "We've got to figure out a way to survive on our own."

"I never realized that things would be so much harder once we got out," I confess.

Pace squeezes my hand. "If it was easy we wouldn't appreciate it as much," he says. "But we can make it. As long as we all work together."

· 15 ·

*W*e *need to find* their camp," Lyon said. "The smartest way to beat the enemy is by knowing the enemy."

We sit around a fire in the clearing across from the catwalk. In just a day the Hatfields have established a welcoming place away from the airship. The grass in the field I'd hid in the night before has been cut and stacked next to the new pen for the ponies and goats. They are within sight of the airship and well protected. Most of the cats have scattered, content to make it on their own, except for a few who make themselves at home on the catwalk, beneath the canopy and beyond in the darkness, where they sit, staring at us with their glowing eyes. The sky above is as clear as it was the first night, and its velvety blackness is covered once more with stars. The air has a bit more chill than the night before so the fire is most welcome.

A large tent is set up along with the awning and the table, chairs, and Pip's cage, of course. It is nice and homey, but it is only a temporary fix. We've got to find a more permanent place to live. As Pace said, the Hatfields will not be here forever.

Jane spent the day taking care of the children, bathing them, feeding them, mending their clothes and helping Sally to get them back onto a normal schedule of lessons. Only now their lessons included learning about the actual world, instead of our former closed-off one. The rest of us had lessons also, about geography and the history of the past two hundred years, which brings us all up to date. My head hurt from all the things Jane and Dr. Stewart told us about the new world. It's as if my brain can only absorb so much at a time. So much has happened in such a short time that it is hard to process it all.

Our meager supplies, scavenged from the floodwaters, have been organized so that if we need something to wear or a cup to drink from we have a place to find such. The children, along with Sally and George, are asleep in the tent and the rest of us sit around the fire, well sated after our meal of venison stew. There are guards stationed as usual. I found out during dinner that the Hatfields' airship has a crew of eight soldiers along with a pilot, a copilot, a cook, and a steward who is in charge of the mundane day-to-day things, like setting up tents and tables. They all have quarters within the actual airship, which I find amazing. Apparently Alcide does too, because he told me he'd seen the inside. I cannot help but wonder if everyone in America is as rich as the Hatfields and as generous. I certainly hope so. The world outside would be a wonderful place if it were true.

"The first thing we need to do is to set you up with weapons. We have a few extra pieces, but not enough to outfit all of you," Lyon continues.

"How about bows and arrows," Levi suggests. "There's certainly enough wood around to make some."

"Good idea," Lyon says. "You can show the boys how to make them tomorrow. We should have enough scrap iron to make arrowheads."

"Like Robin Hood?" Pace asks.

"Yes," Zan says excitedly. "You know about him?"

"I read about him," Pace says.

"Another book?" James asks.

"Another legend," Levi says from across the fire. He is sitting on the ground with Bella pressed up against him with her head in his lap. "One that is told in America too." He stretches his legs out and crosses them. "The Indian tribes hunt with bows also. They are just as deadly." I was witness to that today.

"Indians?" Alcide asks and Levi obliges him by telling him about the Sioux.

Pace sits in a chair and I sit on the ground in front of him with my legs crossed and my back against his leg. Pip sits on Pace's shoulder after showing off his tricks, and Jonah sits under the chair staring at the fire. The rest of us are scattered about. Jon sits on the ground and Beau is next to him. Jon seems sad, and I know its because he'd grown very attached to the dog in the few days they spent together. Adam sits in a chair, as do Rosalyn, Lyon, Jane, and Dr. Stewart. Zan sits on a stool next to her mother, and I can't help but notice that she and James are again stealing glances at each other when they think no one is watching. Alcide and Peter sit on the ground also. Peter is still coughing, but not as bad. I hope Jane had something in her medicine bag to help him.

"Tell us about the rest of America," I say when Levi is done talking about the Sioux. "How did the people there survive the comet?"

"Not all of them did," Lyon says. A map, similar, yet smaller than the one inside, hangs on the side of the tent, left over from our lessons today. Lyon rises from his seat and goes to it as we all watch with rapt attention. "The nation as a whole was woefully unprepared for the disaster. Everything west of the Rocky Mountains," he points to a line two thirds of the way across America, "was lost because of the massive earthquakes caused when the comet hit the earth. Everything east of the Appalachians," he points to a line less than a third of the way across the landmass, "was eventually lost to the rising waters caused by the melting of the polar ice caps. Half of the population lived in those areas, the majority of them here, in New York City." Lyon puts his finger on a dot that is now in the underwater part of the map. He continues. "The capital was moved from here," he points to another spot beneath New York City, "to here in St. Louis because of its accessibility to the Mississippi River, which leads into the Gulf of Mexico." He takes his hand and slashes it across the bottom part of America. "Once again, this part of the country was underwater, along with most of these island chains. Some survivors did make it to us by boat, but their numbers were very few. Most of those who fled to the Midwest had nothing. There was no way to sustain them because of the climate change that wreaked havoc with the seasons. Many people starved and died from the elements. Those that did survive did so by pure will power." Lyon then moves his hand to the continent below America. "This continent was devastated. Still no sign of anyone surviving. It's a shame really; the entire Amazon Basin was rumored to be quite extraordinary. The loss of it had quite a devastating effect on our atmospheric conditions."

"That makes me appreciate what our forefathers did more," Rosalyn remarks.

"They were years ahead of their time," Dr. Stewart says. "But there was no valid reason to stay inside so long. Your society would have had the advantage over any survivors around this area."

"Unfortunately we have no way of knowing what guided their decisions at the time the earth was recovering," Jane observes. "I am certain they think their reasons are very valid."

"The problem is they presume to make the decisions for everyone," Lyon points out. "No one, beyond the royal bloodline, was ever asked if they wanted to leave. They had no options beyond work for all our survival. It's just another form of slavery."

I know my father would not see it that way. For him it is all about our service for the greater good.

"I think they should give some the choice now," Rosalyn says. "Since we are out. There has to be some in there who want out also. There has to be some of our people who survived who cannot get out." I know she is talking about her husband, Colm, but she will not mention his name. She will not give voice to her fear that he is dead like so many others.

"There are," James said. "I will not believe otherwise."

"David and Lucy," I say.

"Harry," Jon says. "Jilly."

"My mother," Pace says.

"Colm and the others who were trapped on the other side of the water," Peter says.

"It's as if they are being held prisoner," Adam offers.

"My mother *is* a prisoner," Pace says.

"What can we do about it?" Zan asks. "Shouldn't we do something about it?" she asks Lyon.

"Actually we formed an idea," Levi says. "Wren, Pace, and I. We can go into the dome through the hole on top."

"What would you do once you were in there?" Lyon asks. "Is there a way down into the city?"

"There is a catwalk that stretches from end to end," Pace says. "I've been on it, I know my way around it. And Wren and I both know the streets."

"If we can make it to our friends' house," I say, "we can find out about most of the people we know. From there we can get back into the tunnels and help them find a way out."

"Why not just go back the way you came?" Lyon asks. I can tell that he's challenging us to plan things out instead of acting impetuously.

"Because of the flood in the caverns, we cannot get to our hatches that lead into the dome," I say. "But from the other side we might be able to find a way across."

"It does sound feasible," Dr. Stewart says. His eyes are bright with excitement, and I know if we decide to go through with this plan that he will want to be included. But will I? The thought of going back inside makes me feel sick to my stomach. Yet I know I will have to go because no one except Pace knows the streets as well as I do.

"That still doesn't solve the problem of the rovers," Lyon says. "We must investigate them first to see what kind of threat they hold, especially after what Levi and Wren heard today. I will take out a scouting party first thing in the morning. Dr. Stewart, if you would like to accompany us that would be fine. Meanwhile, Levi can get the lot of you set up with bows. Do any of your group know how to form metals so arrowheads can be made?"

"George does," Peter says.

"Excellent. It sounds as if we have tomorrow planned then. After we evaluate the rovers we'll talk about a venture into the dome." Lyon goes to Jane and extends his hand in a very romantic and courtly bow. "I am ready to retire my dear."

"As am I," Jane replies and takes his hand. "Good night everyone," she adds, and they leave.

"I must prepare for tomorrow's expedition," Dr. Stewart says. "If you will all give me your goggles, I would be happy to paint them for you before I retire so that your eyes will be protected from the sun." All of us that have them hand him our goggles and with a quick bow to all of us he leaves.

"I'm definitely ready for sleep," Rosalyn says and rises. "Peter, you should get some rest too. Remember what Jane said." Peters nods and yawns and follows her into the tent where George's snores are now approaching canvas-rattling proportions.

Four chairs are now empty. James and Zan quickly slide into those left behind by Lyon and Jane, which means that are now sitting next to each other. Alcide offers one to Levi, who denies it. "Give it to Wren," he says.

"I am content where I am," I say. I am. My back rests against Pace's legs, Jonah is now in my lap, and Pace occasionally drags his hand through my hair, combing out the tangles with his fingers. For the first time since our escape I feel blissful. Knowing that I did not kill the rover has taken such a weight from my shoulders, along with the fact that the Hatfields are set on helping us. A full belly and shelter from the elements go a long way in setting one's fears to rest.

Alcide slides into the chair, and Jon tosses another log on the fire from the pile the men scavenged from the forest earlier in the day. He goes back to petting Beau's large head, which rests in his lap just like Bella's does with Levi.

One of the reasons why I did not want to move to a chair is because Levi sits directly across from me and I can watch him without Pace seeing it. Perhaps I should feel guilty about being curious about Levi, but I cannot help it. He is so very different from anyone I have ever met. "Tell us more about the world," I say. "Where have you traveled to?"

"You saw the pins on the map," Levi says. "Those mark all the places we've been. China is the most exciting place."

"China?" Alcide asks, on the edge of his seat once more.

"China is across the Pacific Ocean from America." Levi points to the map. "Like us, they were able to recover quicker than most places that were closer to the comet's path. Our country signed a trade agreement with them fifty years ago, when air travel became possible."

"What about ships?" Pace asked. "Isn't that how people used to travel? Across the seas on ships?"

"They did," Levi says. "But ships are built with wood, and the forests were devastated and have only started recovering. The government has put precautions into place so that the forests can continue to recover. When airships were invented they became much more practical, although they cannot carry as much weight as a ship. Factories are at work now, designing and building ships out of metals that are powered with steam engines that can carry thousands of tons of goods."

"Amazing," Alcide says, clearly caught up in the story.

"Levi didn't mention that our grandfather is the one who invented airships," Zan says.

"He did?" Pace shifts behind me, and I sit up to allow him room to move. He puts a hand on my shoulder and eases me back into place.

"When he was just a little bit older than we are now," Levi says. "He is still at it, working on new designs that are faster and can carry more weight. Our other uncle runs the company."

"And Papa tests them out," Zan says. "Which is perfect as he loves to explore and seek out adventure."

"What about your parents?" I ask Levi. "You said they died in an airship explosion."

"One of our grandfather's prototypes that didn't work out," Levi says.

"We did not think he would ever recover from that," Zan adds. "We were just children at the time. Levi lost his older brother too."

"Lance," Levi says quietly. "He was seventeen when he died. The same age I am now." His brown eyes seem sad as he stares into the fire, and I know he is remembering his brother. "I am so lucky that Uncle Lyon and Aunt Jane took me in." He smiles at Zan, putting his grief away where we cannot see it. "Of course having a cousin as a sister is a bit of a pain at times."

Zan shoves him with her foot, and Levi pretends he is severely wounded from her blow. Bella grunts at the interruption of her rest and shifts her head from Levi's lap to the ground.

"What about China?" Adam asks.

"China is as different from us as you can get," Levi says. "Yet we each need what the other has. America has the technology and factories. China has things like silk and spices. They have so many more people too. They, like the Indians, were used to living off the land, where in America, so many were city dwellers that they had forgotten how to survive. They are so very different than us in every way. They even look different. Their skin has a different hue and their eyes are shaped differently than ours."

"I would like to go to China," Alcide says.

"Africa is the place to go," Zan said. "It is still so very primitive, as if nothing has changed in the past thousand years. And there are so many different species of wonderful animals. Lions, elephants, giraffes, antelope, cheetahs, and gorillas." She shrugs. "More than I can name. More than you can imagine. And so many treasures from the age of the pharaohs. Pyramids and the Sphinx, and other extraordinary structures that are thousands of years old and survived the comet."

We listen in wonder to their words. Pace had told me about these creatures before, but Levi and Zan have actually seen them. At least Pace has the ability to comprehend what they are talking about because he's read the books and seen the paintings in the museum and library. For the rest of us, the things they talk about are only words, and I long to have an image to place with each one.

As I listen to Zan and look at Levi I realize how sheltered we really were. Our world began and ended with the dome. The people who came before us never had the chance to experience such wondrous things, but they also were protected from the horrible elements wrought from the comet, along with not having to worry about starvation and disease. Looking back now, and knowing how hard it was for the human race to survive the disaster, I think they would say it was worth it. But now the world has so much to offer, especially for people like us who were relegated to a role no matter what they felt. People like Harry, who was expected to be a butcher, even though he cannot stand the smell of blood, and Jilly, who was told who she had to marry in order to keep the royal bloodlines from crossing too often and too close. People like me, James, Adam, and the rest of us shiners who can now be anything we want to be and go any place we want to go. It is up to us to make it happen.

Hearing about these things suddenly isn't enough. I don't want to know about them from books and pictures. I want to see them for myself. I want to fly in the airship to places like America, China, and Africa. I want to see pyramids and giraffes and elephants. I want to see the world.

Zan yawns widely. "Goodness," she says as she politely covers her mouth. "It has been a long day, and we've got a busy one tomorrow according to my father."

Pace leans forward and wraps his arms around me. Pip chirps as his perch moves beneath him. "I'm ready for some sleep," Pace whispers in my ear. "Wish we still had our cave," he adds, and I know he's talking about the privacy of it, not the location.

Levi watches us. Zan stands up and James jumps to his feet beside her.

"Good rest," he says.

"Thank you," Zan replies airily. "Good night to you too. Levi, are you coming?"

Levi still has his eyes on me as he stands up. "I am," he says. "See you all in the morning," he adds, and they leave with Bella following them.

"Good rest to you Miss Hatfield." Alcide stands and bows as Zan and Levi step onto the catwalk. Only those of us still around the fire can hear him and we know he is only doing it to aggravate James, who promptly punches him in the shoulder. "Ow!" Alcide exclaims as he rubs the spot where James punched him. "I was only pointing out that they will get a good night's sleep, while the rest of us have to listen to that all night." He jerks his thumb in the direction of the tent where George's snores have reached a louder pitch.

"I'll sleep out here," Jon says. "Beau will keep me warm."

"I've got an idea," Pace whispers to me. "Someplace soft and private. Want to see?"

"Yes," I say, wondering how soft it will be. He stands, reaches for my hand, and pulls me up. We walk by the rest without a word, stop beneath the awning where he hands me two blankets from the table and grabs Pip's cage and leads me onward to the pony pen with Jonah scampering after us. The grass that was cut from the field earlier in the day is piled next to the pen. Pace kicks it together so it will be thicker and lays the blanket down on top of it. He puts Pip in his cage and hangs it on a twig that juts out from one of the branches used to make the pen and then sinks into the blanket, taking me with him. The moon is bright overhead and the stars sparkle like candlelight in the sky. The ponies shift to our side of the pen as they recognize that I am close, and I reach out my hand to touch Ghost on the end of his nose. The goats are curled up together and Jonah gets down to the business of washing his face as we lie down.

"Much more comfortable that a stone floor," Pace says.

I settle in next to him. He puts his arm around me and I curl into his shoulder as I pull the other blanket over us. "It is," I say in agreement. It is also colder here than it was by the fire, and I press close against him for the warmth.

"I've missed you," Pace say. "I miss the time we spent together." He rubs his cheek against mine and I feel the rough stubble of hair against my skin.

"So much is happening," I begin but then I do not know what to say next.

"Just don't take off again without telling me or someone where you are going," he says again. "I don't know what I'd do if something happened to you."

"I am sorry for causing you worry." I really mean it. I remember the look on Adam's face when Peggy drowned and the sorrow he carries like a heavy weight on his shoulders. I shift a bit, trying to get comfortable. "Something is jabbing me."

"It's my pistol," Pace says. I sit up and he unbuckles the belt around his waist and lays it aside.

I look at the weapon. "Lyon must have been impressed with your ability. He said there were not enough for everyone to have one."

"I hit the target," Pace said. "But he said it was the care I took with the weapon that earned me the right to carry it. I don't think it was as much that I was cautious as it was that James is so reckless."

"Yes he is," I say, recalling that it was James's recklessness in blowing up the fans that led the bluecoats into attacking. "And James was mad after that."

"When isn't James mad?"

I laugh. "Have you noticed how Zan keeps looking at him?"

"He's looking back," Pace says.

"I noticed that too."

"Does it bother you?" he asks.

"No?" I am confused by his question. "Why would it?"

"Because you were supposed to marry him."

"No. He thought I would marry him." I point out, "There is a difference."

"Whatever the difference, I'm glad you didn't."

"Not as glad as I am," I say and we both laugh.

"Levi watches you too," Pace says.

I do not know what to say. To say I have seen him watching me, that I watch him back, that every time he looks at me I feel something dangerous and reckless inside would only hurt Pace, and the last thing I would ever want to do is hurt him.

"I don't want to lose you, Wren," he says. "I love you."

I am glad he cannot see my face. "I love you too," I say and he squeezes me tighter, kisses the top of my head, and then I hear the steady breathing that says he has fallen asleep. As for me, it is a long time coming.

· 16 ·

Why do I doubt myself so much? Since we left the dome I have second-guessed myself a hundred times. Every decision I've made I analyze over and over again in my mind, wondering if I had done anything differently, would it have saved lives. And now I doubt my feelings for Pace. Everything happened so fast, how can I be certain that what I feel . . . felt is real? How can I be certain that my feelings for him didn't come from us being thrown together and because I had no one else to turn to?

Of course my lack of sleep could have something to do with my confusion and self-doubt. My body refuses to accept its new schedule. I lie awake half the night filling my mind with recriminations and then finally fall into a restless and dream-filled sleep. If only my mind would let go of the things that swirl within it like a bird beating against a cage. When Pace wakes me at dawn I am groggy and disoriented.

"I know it's hard, but you've got to get used to being up during the daytime," Pace says as I yawn grumpily. He opens up Pip's cage.

The little bird jumps on his finger and flexes his wings. Pace lifts his finger to the sky and Pip takes off in flight and disappears into the brightening sky. The colors are still dim, as if we are inside the dome. I expect that will change when the sun finds the tops of the trees.

I fight the urge to curl up in the hay and pull the blanket over my head. To make matters worse, I smell like the ponies, or possibly the goats, neither of which is a good thing. Jonah stretches and yawns as I stumble to my feet and stagger after Pace and the suddenly pleasant prospect of breakfast. Ghost whickers at me over the pen, ever faithful. I resolve to get them out of their pen today. With all the work that is being done, surely we can find something useful for them to do.

I need a bath. It has been days since I had one. The first thing that comes to mind is the stream and the waterfall I saw yesterday when Levi and I saw the deer, but I am not really sure if I could find it again, and there is the risk of running into the rovers. I could go back down to the sea, but there is no privacy. My last resort is to go into the cave. If only I had soap and clean clothes. Perhaps I could ask Zan for some soap. I could wash my clothes and then bathe and then just wait in the cave until they were dry enough to put on. I sigh at the sight of Pace walking in front of me, handsome and cheerful and totally unaffected by the fact that he hasn't bathed in days. If anything, he looks even more attractive with the shadow of a beard on his jaw and the gun belt slung across his hips. Why is it that men seem to adapt so much more easily than women?

The area around the awning is busy with activity. Sally and Rosalyn are with the children, having the little ones wash up while the older ones sit at the table eating breakfast. I can't help but notice Freddy sitting next to Nancy a little apart from the others and wonder what Peter thinks of the budding romance going on with his little sister. It is good to see that Freddy is embracing life after losing his family.

The little boy who consoled Stella on our first day out sticks close to Rosalyn. It is our way to look after everyone. Rosalyn will never take the place of his parents, but he will be cared for. All of them will. I can only hope that they aren't left with deep scars after all the death they've seen.

James, Adam, and Alcide don't look any better than I feel as they come yawning to the awning, having just awakened themselves. We all meet at the long table covered with food and fill our plates. In the distance I hear the steady *ping-ping* of a hammer against metal and see George, Peter, and Jon gathered around a small brazier of coals. George is the one hammering. Zan and Levi drop a bundle of long, thin branches close to the brazier and come our way.

Lyon, Jane, and Dr. Stewart, along with two of Lyon's men, are busy loading supplies onto the most amazing little carts I have ever seen. They have three wheels, one in the front and two in the back. They are powered by a small steam engine, like the carts used by the vendors inside the dome, but they look to be much more maneuverable. Two people can sit astride on them, and a large basket stretches across the wide back end to carry things. There is even a leather sleeve to hold the rifles. Four carts sit on the road beside the catwalk. I can't help but wonder what else they will pull out of their airship. It seems as if its storage capacity is endless.

Dr. Stewart comes to us with a basket in hand. "Here are your goggles," he says. "You shouldn't have any trouble with the sunlight now, as long as you wear them during the middle of the day."

"Thank you," we all say. I put mine on and the world is suddenly amber. The bright colors of morning are suddenly muted and drab. I look at the others, who are all trying them out like I am. This will definitely make things easier on our eyes, but I prefer the lovely colors of the outside world.

Pace hastily consumes his breakfast and goes to Lyon, who motions at him. James snorts in disgust. I know he is resentful of the fact that Pace got a gun and he didn't. Hopefully he will excel at shooting with a bow.

I down my breakfast, sharing bites with Jonah, and then give him the plate to lick before I go to join the group with the steam cycles.

"Good morning!" Zan exclaims. Levi smiles at me and adds his own greeting to the group. Beside their golden glow I feel even more disgusting, if that is possible.

"Mr. Hatfield has invited me to go with them," Pace informs me with a big smile on his face.

"To the rovers' camp?" I ask incredulously.

"We have room for one more on the steam cycles," Lyon explains. "And it does the lot of you no good if I do everything for you. Someone needs to know where it is located, and since Pace is familiar with our weapons, I think he's the best choice."

It does make sense. I cannot help but wonder how James and the rest will react to the news. They still do not consider Pace to be one of us because he's from above. But it is not our decision, it is Lyon's to make.

"Meanwhile the rest of us have plenty to do," Levi says. "Making weapons and then learning how to use them."

I realize that it will be a long time before I can get my bath.

Lyon climbs astride a steam cycle and Pace climbs on behind him. He adjusts his goggles and grins at me, gloriously excited about his adventure. Dr. Stewart gets on behind one of Lyon's guards and another two climb on the third cycle. James, Adam, and Alcide walk up as the steam cycles start with a loud roar before they simmer to a gentle *put-put*.

"Where is he going?" James asks as they pull away.

"They are going to find the rovers' camp," I say.

James crosses his arms and looks sullenly down the road. I stand beside him and watch as they disappear into the trees, waiting to see if he has something bad to say about Pace.

"Come on," Adam says. "We have work to do."

"I promise it will be entertaining and fulfilling," Levi says. Zan rolls her eyes behind him and Alcide grins.

We go to where George, Peter, and Jon are hard at work. A pot of water sits over one fire, while another fire is open. A small table sits off to one side and is covered up with thin pieces of wood. Peter and Jon are busy with small axes, chipping away at what I realize are the antlers of the deer.

"What do we do?" Adam asks.

"While they are working on the arrowheads, we will make the bows and arrows," Levi explains. "The girls can separate the hide for us for the bowstring."

"Seriously?" Alcide asks. "The bowstring is from the deer hide?"

"Yes, but is has to be cut extremely thin," Levi says. "Fortunately Zan knows what she is doing."

"How did you learn how to do this?" Alcide asks.

"From the time I spent with the Sioux," Levi answers simply. "First we start with the bow." He picks up a long thin branch and immediately goes to work with his knife, stripping off the bark. The rest of the men do the same as Levi goes into detailed instruction.

I join Zan.

She seems so pretty and fresh in her hide pants and a white shirt with the sleeves rolled up to her elbows. Her bright hair is twisted on top of her head in a careless way that makes her even more beautiful, if that is possible. Zan picks up the deer hide and goes back to work, shaving off long strips that are not even as big as my smallest finger. I watch her for a moment until I figure it out for myself and go to work. Jonah swats at the bowstring while keeping a cautious eye on Beau and Bella who both lie off to the side beneath a tree watching everything with their kind eyes.

"Welcome to 'How to make a bow and arrow' class," Zan says with a grin. "To be followed by 'How to shoot a bow and arrow.'"

"Can we follow that up with a bath?" I ask. "I feel as if I desperately need one."

"Of course," Zan says. "Believe me, we will all need one by the time we are through."

"How exactly do you make a bow and arrow?" I ask since we are a little apart from the men and the fire, sitting on two folding stools. The sun feels warm, even though it has just cleared the trees. I am most grateful for my amber-tinted goggles because the day is already bright and the dew gone from the grass. I take off my jacket and my long-sleeved shirt, baring my arms to the sun.

"You should watch that," Zan says. "Take the sun in small doses so you don't burn up."

"Funny," I say, "that's what we were always told. That we would burn up if we came outside."

"It is remarkable how some people can twist the truth to suit them." Zan doesn't know my father yet she described him perfectly. "So here are the basics for making a bow and arrow. We cut the string for the bows," Zan explains. "Levi is soaking the wood so that it is pliable and then bends it to give it the arch. He will then tie it with the string so it will keep its shape and then you dry it over the fire. To make the arrows, first you have to make sure the wood is straight and smooth so the arrow will fly true. So you strip off the bark and any knots or splits. You make a notch on the end to slide the arrowhead into, and it is tied on with more of the bowstring. George is making the arrowheads, some from iron and other scraps of metal, while Peter and Jon are sharpening bone and antlers."

I nod, fascinated with all the knowledge Levi and Zan have at their fingertips. "Do you think we'll be able to shoot them without killing themselves?"

Zan turns her warm brown gaze upon James. "I am certain of it," she says, and a delicious grin spreads across her face as James slowly takes off his shirt. He knows that Zan is looking at him. I just shake my head at his posturing and steal a look at Levi who is doing the same. They all take their shirts off and their skin glistens in the sun with sweat.

There is something about a young man with his shirt off that is fascinating. The smooth breadth of their chests, the work of the muscles in the back, the dips and curves in the stomachs and hips. It is a strangely beautiful thing to see, especially when there are so many before me. The shiners are all sinewy muscle, lean and long, with Peter being the thinnest and James the broadest. Jon is as small as Peter due to his poor nutrition as a scarab. Levi is taller than the rest, and I realize that he and Pace are close to each other in height. I've seen Pace without his shirt on, and I know they are close to each other in build too, with broad chests that angle down to slim hips and flat stomachs that resemble washboards with their ridges and angles and strange curved muscles on their hips that dip into their pants. I cannot take my eyes off Levi, yet I feel strangely embarrassed for looking at him.

"Why did he live with the Sioux?" I ask Zan. I feel a tingle on the skin of my arms, so I pull my shirt back on but leave it unbuttoned. I hope Zan's promise of a bath comes with a loan of clothing, because the back of my shirt is quickly soaked with sweat from my work.

"His father was part Sioux. That is why his skin gets so dark when he is in the sun; he has Indian blood in him. Their skin is darker than ours, but not nearly as dark as those who live on the African continent. Of course in America we have citizens of every color. That's why it is called the melting pot. Most everyone there, except for the original indigenous Indians, came from this part of the world."

I am amazed once more at what a wondrous place America must be with all the diversity of people who are a part of it. But I really want to know more about Levi.

"Does Levi still have family with the Sioux?"

"His grandmother went back to live with them after Levi's grandfather died. Levi was only three when that happened."

"She is the woman in the photograph with him?" I ask.

"Yes," Zan says. "Levi decided to spend a year with her when he was fifteen. We were both so far ahead in our schooling that my parents thought it would be a good idea, being exposed to different cultures and all that. So while Levi was with the Sioux, I spent six months in China. The airship company has offices over there, and employees. Our cousin from my father's older brother, who runs that branch of the company, lives there, and I stayed with his family while I was there. It was quite fascinating as their culture is so very different from ours. They bind the feet of the women so that their feet are incredibly small. They can barely walk. It's a horrible tradition, quite barbaric, yet the women think of it as a badge of honor. The smaller the feet the greater their symbolic rank."

I listen to Zan but keep my eyes on the men, especially Levi and the way the muscles in his back move as he shows Alcide how to bend the bow and tie off the string. "That is appalling," I say.

"Different cultures," Zan shrugs. "We all have our horror stories," she continues with her eyes on Levi. At that moment he turns around to pick up another bow and I notice two long and jagged scars on his chest, right over his pectoral muscles.

"What happened to Levi?" I ask.

Zan looks at him and then realizes what I'm asking about. "Oh," she says. "You will have to ask him about that. It was part of a rite of passage. The Sioux culture."

"It looks like it was painful," I say.

"It was," she replies. "But now he is part of their tribe. He will always have a home with them if he chooses to go there."

"Do you think he ever would?"

Zan shrugs. "Who knows where any of us will be ten years from now? Or a year from now? Did you think, looking back at your life a year ago that you would be outside the dome?"

"I imagined it for so long that it still does not seem real," I reply.

"Tell me about your culture," Zan asks. I see that she is just as infatuated with watching the men as I am. "Do you have anything exciting and different?"

"We lived in a village underground. When we are four we go to school. We go until we are twelve and then we go to work in the mines. We die young, usually by the time we are forty."

"That is horrible." Zan hands me a length of string, and I coil it up to keep it from tangling with the rest. "You spend your entire lives underground?"

"Most of us do. Some go up to trade or meet with the dome council. Some even go up to work. We have a friend, Lucy, who did that. She's one of our friends that I'm worried about."

"It sounds dreadfully dreary," Zan says. "Did you have anything you did for fun?"

"We swam," I say. "And some of us would fly."

"Fly?"

"I guess you could say it was *our* rite of passage. A few years ago, during a tunnel exploration, a large chasm was discovered. It was bottomless, or so we thought. If you dropped a torch into it the light would just disappear from sight. On occasion a mighty wind would blow up from it. It was so strong that it would suspend you in the air."

"Like the gliders?" Zan asks.

"Exactly like the gliders," I realize. "It was the same, except they would tie ropes around their waists and someone held onto them so they wouldn't fall into the hole when the wind died."

"It sounds terribly exciting," Zan says, and I wonder if she is serious. After all, I did see her fly with the gliders the night we met. Maybe to her doing such a thing is normal. "Did you ever do it?"

"No," I admit without giving a reason for my fears. There was something about falling that scared me. It is not about the height; after all, I loved being on the rooftops. But falling into the unknown terrifies me. "But Adam and James have," I say. "Alcide, I think. I'm not sure about Peter."

"And not Pace or Jon."

"No, they are both from the dome."

"Tell me about Adam," Zan asks. "He seems so sad."

"He was newly wed when the flood happened. His wife was killed."

"Oh, I am so sorry. Did you know her? Of course you did. You had to know everyone."

"She was my best friend," I admit. "And James's sister."

Zan does not bother to hide her gaze from James. "No wonder he seems so angry."

To my mind, angry is putting it mildly. James is more like an explosive with a very short fuse, but I say nothing. Just because James and I do not get along does not mean that he will have the same result with everyone. We have very valid reasons for not liking each other.

"Alcide is funny," Zan continues. "And Pace is quite intelligent."

"His mother is a governess," I say. "He grew up taking the same lessons as the royals."

"It's more than that," Zan says. "He is observant. And he picks things up rather fast. My father said he had never seen anyone take to shooting so fast. He said he showed him one time, everything about handling a pistol, and he duplicated it properly the first time he attempted it. He called it a photographic memory, because it is just like taking a photograph with your mind. And the things he's taught Pip. That requires extraordinary patience."

"He had quite a bit of time with him when he was hiding in the tunnels," I explain. It's strange hearing someone else sing Pace's virtues. Especially when it is things I had not noticed about him myself.

"He seems confident that Pip will always return when he sets him loose," Zan observes.

"He has so far," I say as I search the skies for that tiny flash of yellow. "I hope your father and the rest don't run into any problems out there." I don't want to say outright that I'm worried about Pace, especially since I can't seem to take my eyes off Levi, yet I am. We have no idea of how many rovers are out there or how far away their camp is.

"My father will take every precaution necessary, and they are well armed," Zan assures me as Rosalyn walks up. She is wearing a woven hat with a wide brim, and she hands a similar one to me.

"Jane said to wear this to keep the sun off our faces."

I put on the hat and grin ruefully at Zan. "What is it made of?" I ask.

"Straw," Zan says. "Its starts out as something similar to grass, and when it's dried it is used for animal bedding. Or hats. Baskets too."

"It's a godsend as far as I'm concerned," Rosalyn says. "I'd like to learn how to make hats and baskets from straw. I also want to learn how to use one of those things," she says, motioning to the bows the men are now testing. "If we are at risk I want to be able to defend myself and the children."

"And you shall," Zan says with a dazzling smile. We gather up the remaining string and go to join the men.

◆

The tip of my nose burns and the muscles of my arms ache. I can tell by the way Rosalyn moves that she feel the same. Yet we share a victorious smile because we finally were able to hit the target consistently with our arrows.

"Well done!" Jane exclaims at our last volley as she walks up to where we all stand in a line. Levi has been a hard taskmaster, teaching us to shoot and then making us back up several paces in between each volley so that we are able to gain accuracy with distance.

And I was very conscious of him every time he came near to show me how to pull back the bowstring and aim the arrow. Even now I cannot take my eyes off him as he yanks the arrows free of the rotten log we'd used as our target and examines the points of them. He still has his shirt off, while the rest of the men have long ago put theirs on to protect their skin.

"I don't know about you," Zan says. "But I could do with a bath."

"It sounds like an answer to prayer," I say and hope I don't sound too anxious or the smell coming from my body is not the reason she recommended one.

Zan gives me a sly wink and calls out to the men. "If you will give me your shirts I'll have them washed while you bathe." In a much quieter voice she turns to me. "Would you like your things washed too?"

"That would be wonderful," I admit. "But I have nothing else to wear."

"Nothing to worry about," Zan says. "I have plenty. I'm sure we can find something you'd like."

Rosalyn leaves with Jane while Zan and I go to the men, who are hastily removing their shirts once more. They reek of sweat and smoke, yet they are all grinning as if they'd just fought a battle and won. I don't blame them. I feel much better about things since we are now armed with weapons we can actually use. I look down the road where I last saw Pace. I would feel much better if he were back now.

"It's nice of you to offer," Adam says to Zan as he hands her his shirt.

"It's for my own self-preservation," Zan says with a laugh. "I'm tired of smelling you."

"It's not like she's actually going to do the washing," Levi says. He bends to pick up his long forgotten shirt, and I try not to stare at the scars on his chest as he hands it to Zan. "Please?" he says with a charming smile when she hesitates.

James deliberately mops the sweat from his chest before he drops it into Zan's arms and she makes a face at him, and then turns away to roll her eyes at me. Behind her back I observe James slyly trying to smell himself.

Zan and I go to the airship with Jonah scampering along after us. We pass off the dirty clothes to the steward. "They will more than likely need a salve for their skin also," Zan tells the steward.

"I will take care of it ma'am," he says.

"Let's go to my room so you can take yours off for washing," Zan says. "You can have the first bath."

We go to Zan's room with Jonah trailing after me, curiously meowing as he looks at all the strange new things around him. Zan's room is somewhat neater now than it was the first time I came in. Several pieces of clothing are laid out on her bed and I look on them with obvious envy. I have never paid much attention to how I look or what I wear because I cannot change my looks and I only have enough clothes to cover me and keep me warm. The one dress I had, given to me by Lucy for my grandfather's funeral, was caught up in the flood. Some clothes from our village washed through to the beach, but my dress was not among them. To have so many things that you could wear something different every day is a luxury I have never imagined.

Zan goes into the water closet and turns the water on to fill the tub. I watch as she pours in something from a bottle that smells exquisitely wonderful and bubbles surge up beneath the flow of the water. "Go ahead and get in," she says. "I'll come back for your clothes." She leaves and shuts the door.

I cannot get out of my clothes quickly enough. The water is so blessedly warm. I've never felt anything like this before as I sink into the water and smell the freshly sweet fragrance that surrounds me. I can feel my muscles turning limp beneath the water. Jonah jumps onto a stool that sits by the tub and sniffs at the bubbles. I flick my finger at him and some land on top of his head. He shuts his eyes at the offense and sits there with a crown of bubbles on his head, so I laugh.

Zan knocks on the door and sticks her head in. "How is it?" she asks as she gathers my clothes up from the floor.

"Wonderful," I say.

She points out a bottle on the side of the tub. "That is for your hair," she says, and she points to a faucet that has a long flexible pipe attached to it. "Turn that on for rinsing," she explains and points to a shelf beside the tub. "Towels for drying are there."

"Thank you, Zan," I say with genuine gratitude.

"It's my pleasure," she replies with a grin. "It's nice having another girl around. I can help you fix your hair if you'd like," she adds.

"I'd like that very much."

It is hard not to feel guilty at the luxury that surrounds me. I cannot help but think how excited Peggy would be if she'd actually seen something like this. How she would squeal in delight at the clothes and the bath. How she would glow and want to look so very special for Adam. I wish she could see it. I wish there was some way she could know that we did make it out.

Thoughts of Peggy lead me around again to wondering about Lucy, David, and the others still inside. To attempt to go back inside seems to me as impossible as our escape, yet escape we did, after paying a very high cost. What if going back in costs us more?

The water is cooling, so I set about the business of washing my hair and my body, once more amazed at the ease and luxury at the fingertips of the Hatfields. Is this the way the royals live? I think not. I think they lived a better life than me, but they are still limited by the walls of the dome.

How do you measure the value of a life lived? Is it the items you surround yourself with? Is Zan a better person than Peggy because she has riches and knowledge and has explored the world? I think not. Still, I think Zan is a good person because even though she has riches, she is generous with them. She is genuinely concerned with our problems as is her family. They opened their home to us and shared food, shelter, protection, and are helping us to be able to survive when they leave. Her father has willingly put himself in danger by going out to search for the rovers' village.

Not too much danger, a little voice inside my head reminds me. Because Pace is with him.

Who determines that one person is better than another? My father thinks he can, because of his bloodline and because of his position. He makes decisions for everyone inside the dome. He decided that Alex's life was forfeit to keep the secret. He decided that Pace and mine were too. He decided that the lives of every shiner in the tunnels were forfeit, even though it meant there would be no coal to run the fans. And now he is still deciding for everyone. If everyone whom he is making decisions for had the facts, I wonder what their decisions would be.

Two hundred years ago a group of scientists, and probably the royals along with them, decided that they should be protected at all costs. I would say that the ones who were chosen, or maybe privileged, to serve at the time were grateful for their lives. But that doesn't mean that the rest of us that followed along should have to continue to pay the price for our forefathers' lives.

Everyone should be able to choose their own path. I chose mine and people died because of it. But my choice was to make things better for all of us, not just for me. Does that make me any different than the creators of the dome? Than my father? It's a question that will forever be unanswered, because no one will know for certain. They will only have their opinion of my choices, just like I have mine of the ones others made.

If the royals choose to stay inside, then fine, they are welcome to, but there are those who want to come out also. But will they be better off outside? Without the Hatfields' arrival, how would we survive? Would we have been able to? I'd like to think so. But I also like the fact that I can take a warm bath and put on clean clothes when I am done and know that there is a meal being prepared for me to eat. I cannot expect the Hatfields to support everyone that wants to come out of the dome. All I can do is learn from them and hope that the things I learn will help everyone survive.

If anyone does want to come out of the dome, they should know that it is not the paradise that any of us imagined. I suspect that some may be disappointed. But there is no turning back now. Our fate, no matter the cost, now lies outside the dome.

· 17 ·

How will you know if your father is all right?" I ask Zan.
"Haven't they been gone a very long time?" I sit on a stool in
front of a floor-length mirror while she combs out my hair as I once
more savor a piece of cinnamon toast. I am certain that if I could
choose to have only one thing to eat for the rest of my life it would
be cinnamon toast. I love the taste of it, especially when it is warm
and covered with butter. How can I have become so spoiled in such
a short amount of time, to crave something so luxurious that I will
never taste again once the Hatfields leave us?

I wipe the butter that drips down my chin and catch sight of my
reflection in the mirror. I have never seen my entire body reflected
back at me before. I have never known what other people see when
they look at me. I was always told I look like my mother, with my
dark brown hair that has a mind of its own and my brown eyes that
are not as dark as Zan's and Levi's because of the shine in my eyes.
I feel very decadent at the moment, with Zan combing out my hair
while I wear a robe of purest white that is so very soft against my

skin. Zan gave me lotion to rub into my skin that takes away the sting of the sun. She gave me a brush to clean my teeth with, along with a paste and a rinse that has my mouth tingling. I never dreamed of such luxuries, not even in my wildest imaginings of the royals' lives, and yet here I sit, wiping butter from my chin.

"I know you are worried about Pace," Zan says. "But don't. I am certain he is having the time of his life with my father. And in answer to your question, we use pigeons," Zan explains. "We have several of them. They live in cotes on the back of the cabin. My father takes one with him and sends a message back tied around their legs. They always fly back to the airship, no matter where we land. It's an instinct that they have that I can't explain."

"Amazing," I say. "So if there is a problem, he will send word."

"Exactly. And since we haven't heard anything from him, we can assume that everything is fine and progressing as he expected. The hardest part about these expeditions is keeping Dr. Stewart from going overboard on his samples. He has a tendency to wander off, following his own nose, as Mother always says."

"It all sounds so exciting," I say. To me it is the most exciting possibility I could think about. To be able to go where one wanted, when one wanted to. To have the entire world at your pleasure and whim. I never dreamed such a world existed beyond the walls of the dome.

"It is," Zan agrees. "We are very blessed."

"More so because you are generous," I say. I look at Zan's reflection in the mirror and she squeezes my shoulder as she smiles. A loud whoop from somewhere outside interrupts the moment.

"What is that?" she says, going to the window of her cabin, and then she laughs. "Oh Wren, come here and look."

I go to the window that is open to catch the breeze that flows inland from the sea. The sun sits low in the sky that is once again streaked with glorious color. Zan points down and I join her in leaning out over the sill.

"Oh my," I say as I see the boys splashing with the dogs in the water. They are all naked, and, while we are high enough above them that we cannot see anything specific, just the fact that we can see their bare bottoms shining white against the ruddy red and golden brown of their sun-kissed skin is enough to make me blush. They continue on out until they are waist deep, but we can still see the whiteness through the water.

"I never really thought about all the different shapes a man's bottom could have," Zan says. "Some are round, and some are flat. Some are wide and some are thin."

"And some are hairy," I say when George splashes out to join them.

"Some are nice and some I'd rather not see," Zan says and we dissolve into giggles, something that I had not done in years. Zan leans farther out and yells in a most unladylike voice. "I hope someone doesn't steal your pants as well!"

They look up at the two of us hanging from the window. "Enjoying the show ladies?" Levi yells back.

"Imbecile," Zan mutters. Levi grins up at me and waves while Peter, Jon, and Alcide drop beneath the water. Adam splashes water at James, who makes a show of diving beneath a gentle wave that laps into shore. "The lot of them," she says, but she smiles as she says it, and she is not in any rush to leave.

I watch also as they move into deeper water. I wish Pace was with them just so I wouldn't have to worry about him. I almost envy the men their easy play as they splash and yell and dive beneath the water. How long as it been since I have done anything so simple and fun?

As we lean out the window I catch a flash of yellow out of the

corner of my eye. It is Pip and he flies straight for the window. I
stick my arm out and he lands on it with a hop and then sticks one of
his tiny legs out as he clutches the sleeve of the robe with the other.

"He's got something on his leg," I say.

"Brilliant!" Zan exclaims. "It looks like a message, just like I was
just telling you about with the pigeons." Carefully I put my hand
around Pip and bring him inside. I carry him to Zan's bed where
we both sit down to examine his leg. "Who would have done such a
thing?" Zan asks. "Maybe it's a love note from Pace."

"I think not," I say, once more blushing. "But what else could it
be?" The note is tied with nothing more than a thread because Pip's
leg is so tiny. I do not see how anyone could write anything on a
piece of paper so small.

"It isn't paper, it's muslin," Zan says as she unties the thread and
unrolls the piece of fabric. It is only a half-inch wide and maybe
three inches long and clearly has words on it. Zan hands it to me.
"It has to be for you."

I have to squint to see the letters that are written from top to
bottom instead of left to right. I suppose it was the only way to get
the message to fit on the tiny piece of fabric. I have to read it twice
because I am so stunned by it. HELP US IF YOU CAN. And it is signed
LUCY. My heart sinks as I realize the import of the words.

"Wren?" Zan asks. "What is it?"

"It is from our friends inside." I look at Pip who has hopped over
to Zan's bedside table and pecks at the crumbs from my toast.

"You mean Pip flew inside the dome?" Zan jumps to her feet.

"He must have." I look at the tiny canary and wonder how he can
fly so high in the air when he has spent his entire life until a few days
ago beneath the ground. "It says they need help."

"Oh my," Zan says. "Is there anything else? Are they being held
prisoner somewhere? Are they hurt?"

"Help us if you can," I read the note to Zan. "And it is signed by our friend Lucy, the one I told you about that works above. Pip must have flown to the house she shares with David. He was there before with us, so he'd know it. But how? We didn't go in through the streets when we went there. We came up from the tunnels beneath."

"Would it be possible for him to fly back in the way you came out?"

"Not all the way to Lucy and David's," I say as I try to figure things out. "I do not think there is any way he would know the route. It is rather tricky and there are hatches over some of the passageways so there is no way he could get through those. Then when you get beneath David's house there was a low tunnel that they had to dig out. It was a tight squeeze and you come up through an entrance from the sewers. Pip was inside Pace's shirt the entire time." I think hard on the route and the circumstances through which we traveled. I cannot imagine Pip following that same exact route on a whim. "I do not think he went in from beneath. He must have gone in through the hole in the dome and somehow recognized the house, or maybe saw David or Lucy on the street."

"Your little bird must have the same sense of tracking that the pigeons have. Even though the airship moves from place to place they always manage to find it. Maybe tiny Pip remembers the places he's visited."

"I cannot imagine David or Lucy knowing about pigeons carrying messages," I say. "Unless perhaps Jilly is with them, as she is a royal and has the same education as Pace; it is something she could have learned."

"Or they are very desperate and this is their last hope."

Zan's words cause a chill to move down my spine. "What should I do?" I ask.

"It isn't I, Wren. It is we. What should we do? And the answer is we will show this to my father as soon as he gets home."

"I should tell the others," I say. "I need to tell Pace."

"And we will. As soon as they come up and he gets back," she assures me. "But first we need to find you something to wear."

I don't want to waste time on Zan's frivolities at the moment, but she is right, I can't just dash off down the cliff, gather the others, and then dash into the dome. Reacting, instead of taking the time to think things through and make a plan, is what caused most of the problems in the first place. If not for my decisions, and then James's rapid reactions, we might have been able to find a way out without losing so many people. I am desperate to keep the same thing from happening again. We need to plan carefully, and we need sound advice, such as the type Lyon Hatfield can give us.

Still that doesn't make the waiting any easier. My mind can only imagine the worst as I wonder about my friends. What has happened to them? What is going on inside the dome? Is someone hurt? Have they been arrested for their part in the rebellion? I imagine the worst for all of them and once more am overcome with feelings of guilt because I escaped and they did not. If only I had known beforehand they could have come down with us and then they would have been safe. But how could I predict that someone would be foolish enough to bring a flamethrower into the tunnels. That thought does not ease my mind at all. I am responsible for their lives. All of them.

"Try this," Zan says as she returns from her wardrobe with a pale yellow dress. "It should go really well with your hair and eyes."

The dress is exquisite. The fabric is beautiful, light and airy, and I realize as Zan holds it before me that it is several layers of sheer fabric sewn together. The bodice has tiny tucks running up and down it, and the neckline is low and curved with just a hint of lace around it. I have never seen anything like it. I have never seen anything that same color unless it would be the butter that melted on my toast.

"I cannot wear this Zan," I say. "It is too wonderful for me."

"Wren," Zan says in exasperation. "What makes you think you don't deserve something this lovely?"

"Because it is yours."

"And the color looks horrid on me," she says. "Really, I don't even know why I got it."

"It wouldn't be fair to the others," I continue. "Sally and Rosalyn."

"I happen to know for a fact that my mother has given them clothes. They are also working on clothing for the children from the things you brought with you. Besides, you have to wear something while your clothes are being washed unless you want to hide in my room for the rest of the day in my robe."

"But it is so very beautiful," I say in a very weak protest.

"Sorry, Wren," Zan replies. "Everything I possess is beautiful. So you can't use that as an excuse not to wear this dress. Now put it on so I can fix your hair."

It is very hard to argue with her logic and the addition of the hairbrush that she wields in her hand. Zan points to the undergarments she had placed on the bed earlier. Jonah lies on top of them, purring loudly with his eyes half closed. I push him aside and pick one up. "What is this fabric called?" I ask as I slide the smooth fabric up my legs.

"Silk," Zan replies. "It comes from worms in China if you can believe that."

"Worms? How?" I have heard of silk, but never seen it.

"They spin the threads for their cocoons," Zan explains. "It's all quite gross when you think about it. But it does make for lovely fabric."

"And you wear this every day?"

"Not every day," Zan says. "Just on special occasions. Like the first time you wear a pretty dress to dinner." Zan holds up a hand to stop my protest. "I know you are worried about your friends. But you wearing a pretty dress will not make a difference to what is happening with them at the moment. I promise my father will do everything possible to help them."

I am stuck. I feel frivolous and guilty for dressing up when so many have died and my friends are in dire need. Yet I also do not want to hurt Zan's feelings or make her angry with me. She is only trying to help, and, even though I feel more like a doll she is playing with than an actual person, I allow her to button me into the beautiful dress and fix my hair into a twist on top of my head. She does not want me to look into the mirror until she is done, so I sit on the stool with Pip on my finger and wonder what it was he saw when he was inside the dome. Pip stares back at me with his black bead of an eye and I realize how much we underestimated the canaries. We kept them and bred them through the generations to serve as an alarm for the build up of gasses in the tunnels. If a canary died then we knew not to go there. I would not have given Pip a second thought, if not for Pace needing companionship when I left him alone in the caves. I saw him only as a tool. Pace saw him for what he could be.

Is that the way my father sees us as shiners? Are we simply tools to use? I cannot help but think that is how he perceives everyone in the dome. Every person inside is a tool to be used to preserve the royal bloodline. But what happens when those tools get broken? Are they simply discarded in much the same way Pip nearly was? Is that what is happening to Lucy and the others? Are they about to be discarded? If my father has no further use for them, why doesn't he just let them go? Or would that be admitting defeat? From the few brief moments I spent with him, I readily know that admitting defeat is not something he would do.

"You can look now," Zan says.

Pip jumps onto the dressing table as I turn to look in the mirror. It takes me a moment to realize that it is actually me sitting there. Yet how could it be? I have never seen this version of me before. This version appears confident and mature, almost elegant, in a way that I've only considered the royals to be. In a strange way it is frightening to see myself this way. I've never had so much of my skin revealed, especially around my neck. The way the dress fits shows the arcs of my breasts and the valley in between. With my hair all up, except for a few pieces that dangle around my ears, I feel as if I am missing an article of clothing, and I place my hand over my breasts to cover them up.

Zan stands behind me and pulls my arm away. "Don't be shy, Wren," she says as I watch her in the mirror. "Don't you know how beautiful you are?"

"But I'm not," I say. Not beautiful like Lucy, or Zan, or Jilly. Yet I can't help but be curiously pleased with what I see and even more curious to see how Pace, *and Levi,* will react when they see me.

I shouldn't be thinking about this. I shouldn't be standing here staring at my reflection in the mirror while wearing a pretty dress. Not while my friends are hurting and need help.

"You've never had anyone tell you how pretty you are, have you?" Zan asks.

I shake my head, torn between sadness and embarrassment at her question. "All I had was my grandfather. He did the best that he could," I say.

I didn't know my mother's love, or even if she would have loved me. She might have hated me if she had lived, because I would have been a constant reminder of my father and how he turned her away.

But I'd like to think that she would have loved me. That she would have brushed my hair every night as she told me I was pretty and smart. I never had the close company of a woman, except for Peggy, who was my age. My memories of my grandmother are dim as I was barely four when she died. I mostly remember her coughing and the blood in her handkerchiefs that she tried to hide from my grandfather.

"I think he would be pleased with how you look," Zan says. I know she is being genuine, but I also know that for her fixing me up is a project, just like Levi showing the men how to make bows and arrows. Still, her generosity is genuine and I will not hurt her feelings. My grandfather might have smiled and said something, but more than likely he would have thought the yellow dress very impractical for our way of life.

"All you need now is this," Zan says and places a gold chain around my neck with a heart-shaped locket on it. "And put some of this on your lips." She hands me a tiny crock with a thick pink substance inside. "It makes them soft and shiny," she adds as she sticks her pinky in the crock and rubs some on her lips. I do as she instructs and she smiles at my reflection in the mirror. "Absolutely perfect." She pronounces me done and turns to her wardrobe. "Now it's my turn." She pulls a blue dress from her wardrobe. "Do you think James will like this color on me?"

"Zan . . ." I begin and then I do not know what else to say.

"What?" Zan practically giggles. "He is very handsome, don't you think?"

I shrug. "He is." I move from the stool to the bed. Pip pecks at a shiny piece of jewelry on the dressing table, and Jonah stretches out a paw to me as I sit beside him.

"What? Is there something wrong with him? I know Adam is sad because he lost his wife. It's strange to me to think of all of you marrying so young, but I guess it does make sense since you said you died in your forties. And Alcide is younger than me, along with Jon, but James . . ." Her chatter is rapid and nearly nonstop and I let her go on because I do not want to say anything bad about James. Just because we did not work out does not mean that things would be the same with him and Zan. Still . . .

"What?" Zan asks again.

I shrug. "I guess I think of him more like a brother," I explain. "Because he is Peggy's brother."

"The same way I think about Levi," Zan says. I can understand that. "By the way, just how serious are you and Pace? Because you know Levi really likes you."

"He does?" Heat rises up from my chest to my face and I know I am blushing. I concentrate on Jonah until I feel the heat go away. Fortunately Zan is preoccupied with her reflection in the mirror so she does not notice my reaction.

"He hasn't admitted it, but I can tell." Zan picks up the brush and works on her hair as she talks. "He's always watching you and when you're not around he's talking about you, or asking about you. Are you and Pace really serious?" Zan turns from the mirror and looks at me. "As in are you going to marry him?"

"Marry Pace?" I had not considered it. I had not considered much beyond escaping the dome. "We have not discussed it," I say. Pace and I declared our love for each other at a moment when we were certain we were going to die. But since we have been out, things have seemed different. Perhaps it is because the desperation of our situation from before we escaped is gone and we are not depending on each other as we were before. "Marriage . . ." I repeat. "I do not think I am ready for that. There is so much world out here. More than I ever imagined. I just . . ."

"Of course you're not." Zan kneels before me and grabs my

hands. "You are only sixteen years old. Why wouldn't you want to see the world? And meet other people. After all, you have your entire life in front of you." As quickly as she knelt before me, Zan is gone again, once more to her wardrobe to decide on a dress.

I have my entire life in front of me . . . It does not seem fair, especially since so many people that I know do not. And might not, if Lucy's desperate plea for help is any indication. I shake my head at my situation and myself. I am continually looking for answers, but it seems all I can find is more questions. I suddenly feel very foolish, sitting in Zan's room in her pretty dress. And there is not a thing that I know to do about it.

· 18 ·

I find myself strangely nervous as I follow Zan outside to dinner with Pip sitting on my shoulder and Jonah trailing along beside me. And, even though she won't admit it, I know Zan is nervous also. Her father has not returned and there has been no word from him at all. I saw the concern written on Jane's face also when she came into Zan's room. Even though she was very complimentary to me about my dress and hair, I could tell something was bothering her. She didn't say anything because she does not want me to worry about Pace. She might as well tell me to stop breathing. Until Pace is back I will worry about him. I know they've been gone far too long.

The long dining table sits beneath a canopy and candles gleam along its length. Lanterns are strung along the length of the canvas and cast a soft glow in the twilight air. The boys all stand around and I notice most of them pulling at their collars or grimacing in pain as they lift a glass to their mouths to drink. It's because they had too much sun today and the skin beneath their freshly washed clothes is raw. But their hair gleams in the candlelight and those that needed to shave have. I know that without the influence of the Hatfields none of this would have happened. Their arrival has helped us to keep our civility instead of falling into the most primitive ways to survive. A washed body and clean clothes will fall by the wayside when the basic needs of food and shelter are an everyday challenge.

I notice that Sally and Rosalyn, who stand with Jane, are wearing new clothes also, and George must be wearing something of Dr. Stewart's. Of all of them gathered together beneath the canopy, only Levi seems at ease in his bright white shirt and tan pants. But why shouldn't he be? He is a child of the sky and the sun.

I pause on the catwalk and take a deep breath as Zan steps off. If only Pace were here. I let Zan fix me up for him and he's not here to see it. But Levi is. Levi catches sight of me and his eyes capture me as he stares at me over Adam's shoulder.

A wide smile lights up Levi's face, and I suddenly feel shy and awkward. I don't know how to act in such a pretty dress, and I certainly don't know how to walk in the simple satin slippers that Zan gave me to wear. I'm afraid that if I step off the catwalk I'll slip in the grass and land flat on my face. I'm used to my sturdy boots and practical pants and shirts. I like hiding beneath my jacket and bandana and goggles. I feel exposed. I *am* exposed, and I fight the urge to place my hands over my breasts as Levi starts toward me.

Zan goes to her mother and Jonah trails after her, his mind set upon dinner. I see James turn and watch Zan as she walks by him without a word. Meanwhile Alcide sees me and jabs his elbow into Jon who jabs his into Peter who in turn jabs his into Adam, who punches James in the arm. James scowls as he turns and then his jaw drops when he sees them all looking at me, and I go from feeling exposed to feeling very powerful, but that turns quickly into confusion as Levi is still walking my way.

"Levi?" Jane suddenly calls out and Levi stops and turns at the sound of her voice. A large white bird lands on the railing of the airship and Levi, Zan, and Jane all dash by me in their haste to get to it. There is a small tube attached to its leg and Levi quickly takes the message from it. My heart is in my throat as I wait for Levi to finish reading.

He hands the note to Jane and comes to me. He picks up my hands and squeezes them. I can tell by the look on his face that the news is not good.

"They are under attack by the rovers. One of the guards is dead and another one wounded. They don't know how much longer they can hold out. We must go to help them."

"Of course," I say. "Pace?"

"He didn't say. Wren. We need your eyes. Are you willing to come too?"

"Yes." I am surprised that I am able to speak. "Just give me a moment to change."

"I'll find you some clothes," Zan says.

"Levi, there is only one steam cycle. Surely you don't mean to go by yourself," Jane says. "You and Wren cannot possibly hope to fight off this attack."

"Speed is of the essence," Levi says. "The rest will have to follow on foot. We will ask for volunteers. Two guards and two of our new friends. The rest should stay here and be prepared in case of an attack." By now the rest of our group has noticed the concern and come to the catwalk.

"I will inform the captain and tell the guards so they may prepare," Zan says. "Wren, give me two minutes," she says and dashes into the cabin.

"Do you think we are in danger?" Rosalyn asks.

"No. But Lyon, Dr. Stewart, and Pace are," Levi says. "We need two to go on foot and the rest to stay and defend our position."

"I'll go," Adam, James, and Alcide all say at once.

"Adam and Alcide then," Levi says. "Be ready in five minutes."
Levi turns and the look on his face is intense and frightening. Gone
is the friendly charm and in its place is a deadly warrior. And I am
about to go off with him.

In all the excitement I forgot about Pip, but worse, I forgot about
the message he carried from our friends on the inside. "Wait," I say
as Adam and Alcide turn to prepare. "I have word from the inside
and it isn't good."

"What do you mean word from inside?" James asks.

I had stuck the note inside my dress and I take it out and hand it
to Adam. He turns so the light shines over his shoulder and reads
the message out loud.

"How did you come by this?" Rosalyn asks.

"By Pip," I say and explain what happened. Their faces are in-
credulous, yet there is no denying the existence of the note or the
message.

"What should we do?" Alcide asks.

"We need to know what's going on inside," I say.

"We should go to the entrance," Jon offers. "See if we can find
something out."

"He's right," James said.

"You go," Adam says to Jon. "Take Peter. James takes care of
things here. Agreed?"

We all nod our agreement. I am surprised that James is so content to stay, and then I recall the looks he and Zan have been ex-
changing.

"Rosalyn, will you put Pip in his cage?" I ask. He's stayed on my
shoulder since I put him there, and I realize the poor canary is
exhausted from his flight into the dome.

"I will take care of him," she says and takes him into her hands.
I have taken up enough time. I dash inside to change.

◆

"How will we find them?" I ask Levi. The engine of the steam cycle is remarkably quiet as we ride deeper into the forest. The treetops close over us as if we are in a tunnel, but the darkness is not as deep and the outlines of the tree trunks are vivid to my eyes. Occasionally I see tiny glowing dots of eyes from the animals whose tranquility we have disturbed with our foreign noise.

I am dressed in Zan's clothes since mine are still damp from the laundry: a pair of hide pants that have been dyed black, a dark blue shirt, and a dark jacket of a soft and pliable fabric that clings to me like a second skin. Zan also gave me a pair of leather boots that come to my knees. They are a size too big, but the thick socks I wear help make up the difference. Levi is dressed much the same. I sit astride behind him. He gave me a new pair of goggles to wear that are not tinted so I can see things clearly. The steam cycle has a light on the front that casts a beacon onto the road. The wind comes right at our face. My hair is still pinned up, but I tie my kerchief around it to keep it from blowing in my face.

"Lyon sent his coordinates," Levi explains. "He said they were five miles due east. After that I will use the sextant to find his position."

"Sextant?"

"It's a way of finding your position using the stars. It's what sailors used when they sailed the seas."

"And the skies?"

"Yes." I feel his smile and more when he puts his hand over mine. "Don't worry, we will find him," he says and I know he is talking about Pace. "I'm sorry you're so cold."

I am cold. Colder than I've ever been in my life. But it's not the temperature of the air or the feel of the wind making me so. It is fear and apprehension that has me shivering so hard that I am afraid

I will fall off the cycle. I am glad there was no time to eat before we left. I am certain I would have emptied my stomach long ago.

We are a long way from the dome. I have seen nothing in our hasty ride that suggests there are other people out there, or that there was once a civilization, yet, from what Levi told me, this land used to be covered with farms and beneath the earth there were mines, just like the one I came from. I wonder if we would have eventually tunneled into another mine, generations from now, simply knocked down a wall and discovered another network of tunnels that eventually would lead to above.

Please God, let Pace and Lyon and Dr. Stewart be safe. I would pray for the guards too, if I knew their names. I haven't had the time or opportunity to learn them, they are just men with hair cut short who carry weapons and all dress the same. And yet one of them is dead now.

We have weapons. Levi has a pistol on each hip and two large and deadly looking knives strapped to his back. There are two rifles behind me, along with Levi's crossbow and my own primitive bow and arrows. I hope he's not counting on me to use them. I'm not sure how effective I will be in the heat of battle. Yet I have killed before and that isn't something I like to think about. Or the possibility that I might have to kill again.

The trees begin to thin out and the moon finds us once more. Levi turns off the light on the front of the cycle. The land is rolling now, like a blanket spread over a sleeper that creates dips and valleys along with rounded peaks. To my right the land gives way to the sky and I know the ocean is still there, ever present since the beginning of time.

"I see something." I point in the direction of the tower that rises up against the night sky. The remnants of some sort of structure surrounded by tumbled stone. A *castle* and I think that only because

Pace's descriptions in the stories he told me while we were hiding in the tunnels were so vivid. The trees are sparse and scattered now, and Levi stops the cycle beneath the spreading branches of one that sits alone atop a rise. He takes out the message from Lyon and hands it to me. Then he pulls a brass tube from his bag. There are several lenses attached to it, along with a brass triangle with notches and numbers.

"Read me the numbers," Levi instructs. I realize that those are the coordinates he mentioned earlier. I do and he fiddles with the sextant, first looking at the sky, and then through the tube. He moves the lenses, trying one, then the other, until he finally settles on one. "Got it," he says and puts the sextant away. I hand him the message and he sticks it back inside his jacket as he gets off the cycle. He digs in one of the bags on the side of the cycle and takes out a thin metal stake as long as his arm with a red triangle on the end. He sticks it in the ground beside the tree with the pointed end of the triangle to our left.

"How far behind us do you think the others are?" I ask.

"Thirty minutes, maybe more."

"Should we wait?"

"Do you think we should?"

"No."

"Good. Neither do I." Levi starts the cycle again and it clatters loudly for a moment, during which I feel as if every rover in the country can hear us, before it settles into its quieter rhythm and we set off, this time to the north. We ride across a field of grass, which is much bumpier than the road we just left. The cycle pitches and rocks, and I wrap my arms tighter around Levi's rock-hard body. I feel so vulnerable, riding as we are, because there is no place for us to hide and we are such an obvious target. It must be because I am so used to being closed in. I cringe until we once more reach the shelter of the trees.

"Will they be able to follow us?"

"They will see our tracks. I'll plant another marker if we have to change direction." He no more than finishes when we hear the loud report of gunfire in the distance. Levi stops the cycle and we sit and listen.

"That's an older rifle," he says. "Like the rovers carry." Suddenly we hear a barrage of shots. "That would be Lyon," Levi adds. "We should go on foot from here. You lead and let me know the instant you see anything."

Levi quickly checks his weapons. He takes the two rifles from the back of the cycle and puts one over each shoulder. He also picks up his crossbow and hands me my bow and the quiver of arrows. I feel awkward as I sling the quiver strap across my chest and put the bow on my arm. Before we go, Levi turns the cycle around so it is facing the way we came. "For a quick getaway, if we need it," he says.

Now I am terrified. We hear more shots and I jump. "That way," Levi says, pointing to the northeast. "As soon as you see something stop and tell me what it is."

I nod and set off in the direction that he indicated. Even though the goggles Levi gave me are clear, I still push them up on top of my head. I don't want anything to block my vision. I search the forest, looking left then right as I carefully place one foot in front of the other. We are not on a trail. Frothy leaves part with each footstep and twigs snap beneath my weight. We go down a slight incline and then back up again. Another shot rings out just as we reach the summit and Levi tugs on the hem of my jacket to pull me down into a crouch.

"See anything?" he asks.

My heart pounds so hard that my ears hurt. I look into the distance where I think the shot came from and I see a silhouette. It is on another small rise. Lyon, Pace, and the others must be below him.

"There." I point at a fallen tree with a man crouched on our side of it. "It looks like a man with a gun. He's aiming it."

Levi squints as if that will make him be able to see better. "We have to get closer," he says. "Find us a route that keeps us hidden."

I take off again, this time in a crouch, and Levi stays right behind me, moving with me like a shadow. I move at an angle instead of straight down so the rover won't have the high ground against us if he sees us.

"Stop," Levi whispers when we get to the bottom of the small gulley. "I can see him now." Levi eases in front of me. "Get your bow ready."

I pull my bow from my shoulder. My hands shake as I pull an arrow from the bundle wrapped in twine that I carry slung over my back.

Levi notices my shaking and puts his hand over mine as I try to notch the arrow. "Wren, I just need you to watch my back. And do what I say without question. Okay?"

I shake my head. "I don't know what *okay* means."

Levi's grin flashes in the darkness. "It's Choctaw. That's another Indian tribe. It means 'it is so.'"

I smile back at him and shake my head in agreement. "Okay."

Levi starts forward and I follow him, looking side to side to make sure there are no rovers coming up on us. He moves so silently that I take care with my steps too. Luckily there is a breeze that rustles the leaves around us and masks any sounds I make. Levi stops within ten feet of the rover who is still looking down the opposite side of the rise. He slowly takes his rifles off each shoulder and sits them against a tree. He turns to me and puts a finger to his mouth and then points to the rifles. He wants me to watch them, so I nod my agreement. Then he silently pulls one of his knives from the sheath on his back. I watch as Levi creeps up behind the rover. He grabs him from behind by placing his hand over his mouth and in one quick motion he slices his throat. I watch as blood gushes out and Levi lowers him to the ground.

It all happened so fast that I find it hard to believe it actually did happen. Yet there is the body lying on the ground and Levi waving me up to his position. I pick up his rifles and scramble up the hill. My bow slips over my shoulder and I nearly trip. I give the dead rover a wide berth before I crouch down next to Levi behind the fallen log.

"What do you see?" he asks.

I look down below. The three steam cycles form a triangle. One lies on its side. Lyon, Pace, Dr. Stewart, and one of Lyon's men are crouched behind them with their rifles pointing outward. I count five bodies lying around the cycles. One wears the uniform of Lyon's guards; the others wear the ragged clothing of the rovers. I am so relieved to see that Pace is not hurt, at least not that I can tell. I want nothing more than to run down to him and throw my arms around his neck.

"Look beyond our friends, Wren," Levi whispers. "Look in the likely hiding places for more rovers. I need to know how many there are."

I search the high ground around them. Now I know what to look for. And it scares me. I see one, then another, then another. They are well hidden, well enough that they blend into the undergrowth of the forest. If not for my ability to see in the dark I would not know they were there. But they are. I count eleven and two are fairly close, one on each side of us. The only thing that has saved our friends is their superior weaponry. The rovers' guns are not as reliable, nor do they have the range.

"There's eleven," I whisper. "I think they are waiting them out."

"Or waiting for reinforcements," Levi replies. "We've got to get them out before that happens."

"What do we do?'

"We open up an escape route. Show me where the closest ones are." I do and Levi nods when he has their position. "Ready your bow," he says. "And shoot anyone you don't recognize. This fallen log is your base. Defend it at all costs."

"Okay." My voice shakes with nerves.

Levi crouches in front of me. "You can do this, Wren." My eyes dart to the body that lies behind him and the pool of blood that stains the ground. I have killed before, but not with the casualness that Levi just showed. "You have to do this. This is the escape route. If we don't get out of there before their reinforcements arrive we will all be dead. We have to get out of here now."

His brown eyes search mine for something I am not sure I can give. But I have to, to save Pace's life, to save all our lives. "Okay," I say with a firmer voice.

"I never doubted you for a minute," Levi says with a reassuring smile. He touches his finger to his eyebrow in salute and creeps off into the brush. I watch him go. He moves silently, yet I flinch at every pop of a twig or creak of a branch that I hear around me.

I hear a whistle that reminds me of the call the men use in the tunnels. It is not the same, and I search the area around me warily for the source. Could it be Adam and Alcide? If it is I need to warm them, unfortunately I never learned how to whistle like them. I check on Levi's progress. His victim is still unaware of his approach. I take a moment to look the other way and panic fills me when I realize that I can no longer see the rover on my left. I suddenly realize that the moonlight is shining down on me and I am visible to anyone who looks my way.

Slowly and as silently as possible I stand and move into the shadows. I pull my bowstring taut and take a deep breath as I keep the arrow pointed to the ground. My heart pounds in my chest and it loudly rings in my ears. I turn my ears past it and listen to the wind caressing the leaves of the trees as it finds its way around the trunks and branches that gently sway around me. I hear a slight sound below me and I slowly turn my head in that direction. Two rovers stand behind a clump of trees. They think I cannot see them because of the darkness. I turn my head slightly behind them as if I am looking for them. They are both dressed in a combination of hides and clothes and both wear long beards and long hair. One has strange markings on his face that look as if they were done in ink. He nudges the other and they move on, coming my way. Do they know Levi is here too or do they think I am part of the group trapped below? I have a feeling I will not get a chance to ask them.

My mind tells me to run, that I cannot handle this, but Levi's urgings to defend my position at any cost ring true. This way lays escape for everyone trapped below. The two rovers are closer and I can see the intent in their eyes. They still don't know I can see them as they sneak from tree to tree. I chance a look at Levi. He is almost upon his prey, who is still unaware of his coming. Levi doesn't realize that I am in trouble as he is concentrating on moving quietly through the woods.

I take a step backward, placing a large tree between me and the rovers, who are now coming straight up the rise, not bothering to hide any longer. My arm aches from holding the bowstring taut. My heart kicks up a notch, pounding harder, and sweat dampens my brow. They keep coming, not a bit intimidated by me or my bow. I take a deep breath, count to three, and step from behind the tree. I raise my bow, take aim, and shoot.

I miss. The arrow flies wide and crashes into the brush. The two rovers take one moment to look at where the arrow landed, then as one they come at me at a full run. I fumble for the arrows slung over my shoulder. I can't move fast enough. I am unfamiliar with the weapon. They are almost upon me and I can tell by the evil leer on their faces that they have other plans for me besides death.

A vision of Jon's friend from inside being led by the rovers by a rope around her neck fills my mind, along with the face of the filcher who tried to rape me inside the dome. I will not go down without a fight. I swing the bow with all my might at the first one to reach me. I hit him in the side of his face and dance away, twisting the bow so that it comes around his neck. I yank backwards on it, making sure I keep the rover between his friend and me. I twist the bow so that it tightens around his neck and he claws at it. I keep pulling back and he stumbles as I pull, clawing and gagging while the other rover tries to get to me. The one I am choking isn't helping himself or his friend at all as he keeps flailing about. Suddenly he falls and nearly takes me with him. I have no idea if he is dead or merely unconscious. I drop the bow and stagger backwards, my eyes casting about for a weapon. I know the rover with the strange markings can shoot me, but if he kills me then I won't be of further use to him and the look on his face clearly states what he has in mind.

If only Levi had left me another weapon. I know he didn't think I would be involved in any combat. He also vastly overestimated my ability to use the bow. If I scream it will only bring more rovers down on us and destroy any element of surprise Levi has. It is up to me to somehow survive this on my own.

To my surprise the rover slowly leans his rifle against the tree, while keeping an eye on me. I watch him just as carefully as he watches me.

"What's ah-wrong with your ah-eyes?" he says.

"Not a thing," I reply. I resist the urge to ask him what's wrong with his face. I don't think it will endear me to him in any way.

"You're one of them that can ah-see in the dark. Too bad you can't ah-shoot as well as you can ah-see."

"I didn't need to shoot well to take out your friend," I say. I back away and he advances, not closing the distance between us, studying me as carefully as I study him. I can't take him on brute strength; he is twice my size, and intelligence flares in his eyes. I know without him telling me that I already took out the dumb one and it really doesn't bother him that I have.

"What are you ah-after?" he asks.

"We're not after anything," I say. "We just want to be left alone to live our lives."

"Then you shouldn't of come ah-snoopin' around." I back up against a tree and he takes advantage of the moment to close the distance between us. "You should of ah-stayed inside."

I twist around the tree and manage to extend the space between us. I move in Levi's direction in hopes that he realizes I'm in trouble. "Why do you hate us so much? Why can't you just leave us be?"

"There's not enough out ah-here for all of us," he says. "We aim to keep what's ours. Don't need none of you ah-snooping around."

"Then you shouldn't have come after our goats," I say.

"When I'm ah-done with you, a goat will be the least of your ah-troubles." He's done talking. I can see it in his eyes. The time has come for me to defend myself, and I have nothing to do it with except for my fists and my wits. I can only hope to delay the inevitable so I turn to run in the direction Levi went. I take no more than three steps when I go down. The rover tackles me and I crash to the ground. My breath leaves my body and my world goes black for a moment. When comprehension comes back to me I am on my back and the rover is sitting astride me. My jacket and shirt are open and his hands squeeze my breasts through the silk camisole I still have on. He leers at me, his eyes brilliant against the dark symbols that cover his face. I gag at the stench of him and immediately claw, strike, and swing at his head. I am no match for him. He is twice my size and the weight of him sitting on my stomach keeps me from drawing a full breath.

And then his head flies back and I see Levi behind him. He grips the rover's hair in his hand and draws his knife across his throat. Blood flies in every direction and I turn my head. Levi pulls the body off me and lowers him quietly onto the ground. His body jerks a few times, but he is silent because Levi is thorough. The cut is so deep that the rover is nearly decapitated.

Levi clamps his hand over my mouth as I try to backpedal away from the blood that covers me. I look at him in shock, and he puts the hand that holds the knife to his mouth with his finger extended over his lips to tell me to be quiet. I nod in agreement, and he takes his hand from my mouth and pulls me to my feet. I swipe at the blood on my face with my sleeve. I am trembling and Levi pulls me against his chest in a bone-crushing hug. The buttons on his jacket gouge my skin, but I don't care. I cling to him in desperation. I know the rover would have shown no mercy. Levi saved me.

"You're okay," he murmurs against my hair. *Okay.* What a simple word for the fact that my life is still mine. He lets go a bit so that I am not smashed against him, and I marvel at the fact that he can treat me with such tenderness yet kill without mercy. My heart stops pounding in my ears, and around me I hear the sounds of the forest as the creatures realize there is no longer a threat among them. I hear Levi's heart beating in unison with mine. He is a fascinating enigma and I am suddenly aware of the fact that I am nearly naked against him. The thought of his bare skin and the scars on his chest replace the horror of the previous moment.

"We still have work to do," Levi says. "I need you to be with me, Wren."

"I'm here." My voice is strong, which surprises me. Levi releases me. His warm brown eyes search my face and his pupils flare as he looks at the blood splattered on the bare skin over my breasts and upon the fine silk of Zan's camisole. With tender hands he pulls my shirt together.

"The buttons are gone," I say.

"I wish I could kill him again." Levi pulls the shirttail from my pants and knots it together. Then he pulls my jacket together. It fared better than the shirt as it has a double row of buttons on the front. Levi's hands are sure as he buttons me up. "I should have made sure you weren't splattered," he says. "I hate to admit I wasn't quite thinking right when I saw him on you."

"I'm just glad you came when you did," I say. Levi nods in affirmation, but I can tell that he's thinking that he shouldn't have brought me out here. "I knew what I was getting into," I say, answering his unspoken thoughts. "I would rather be here doing something than sitting behind and worrying."

Levi runs his hand through his hair. He picks up his knife that he dropped when he hugged me and wipes it on the pant leg of the dead rover. He sees the other rover, who must be dead, as he hasn't moved from the spot where he dropped. Still he nudges the body with his toe and then flips him over with his foot. The man's face is purple and his tongue hangs from his mouth. His eyes are wide open and stare up at the moon. "I see you put your bow to good use," he says.

"I'm thinking I should probably train with another weapon." I've killed again. Levi was right. When your life is at stake you are capable of anything. I am determined not to have any regrets. Not over this or these men.

He grins at me. "I think you are probably right." He gathers up his weapons. "Let's see about getting everyone out of here."

I leave my bow as I follow him, but I do gather up the bundle of arrows. Just because I am useless with it doesn't mean everyone else is.

· 19 ·

We station ourselves behind the fallen log once more. "We should be able to cover them from here," Levi explains. "They can make their escape on the cycles, and we'll shoot the rovers as they expose themselves."

"How will they know it's us?" I ask.

"Easy." His grin flashes and then he whistles loudly, a much different call than I've ever heard before. Apparently it's quite common for men from all walks to whistle to each other as a signal. I shake my head at the thought and watch for Lyon's reaction. He turns immediately to where we sit and puts a hand over his mouth. Instead of whistling, he emits a *caw-caw* sound. Levi answers with something else and Lyon, Pace, and Dr. Stewart put their heads together. Lyon talks to the two remaining guards.

"They'll have to leave one cycle behind," Levi says. "It will take too much time to right it."

"With only two cycles that means someone will be left behind," I realize.

"That's what they are deciding now," Levi informs me.

A chill runs down my spine that has nothing to do with the cool air making its way beneath my jacket and torn shirt. As if he can read my mind, Levi adds, "It won't be Pace. It will be one of the guards. Whichever one is fastest." He sounds so casual about it that I look at him in surprise. "They knew what they were getting into when they signed on with us," he explains. "There are no guarantees with this job. None of them has family but they do have a sense of adventure, which is required. Lyon will not risk Pace as he invited him on the expedition."

"You talk as if quite a few have died," I say.

"It happens," he shrugs. "I don't mean to sound callous, it's just the way it is. We go into dangerous places where we are not always welcome. The ones who survive retire with a lot of wealth, so they find it is worth it."

I could not imagine living the type of life Levi just explained, but this new world is full of many things that I never imagined.

"Do you think you can drive one of the cycles?" Levi asks. "Did you see how to start it?"

"I was watching," I said.

"Good. I need you to go back to the cycle and start it. Then wait for me. I will be right behind them."

"What are you going to do?"

Levi picks up one of his rifles. "I'm going to cover their escape," he says. "Go now." He smiles encouragingly. "It will all be okay."

I nod. I remember the importance of doing what he says, and I realize that time is of the essence now, but I also have the feeling that he is protecting me. Perhaps he does not think Lyon and Pace's escape will go as easily as he wants me to think.

Shots ring out as I run down the incline and back up the other side. I am familiar enough with them now to know the difference between the newer guns that the Hatfields have and the older ones that the rovers carry. I hear the sounds of the steam cycles starting and shouts ring out in the distance behind me. I am suddenly filled with a sense of urgency, and I run harder and faster until I get to the cycle. The noise behind me is loud: gunfire, the roar of the cycles, and the pops and cracks of the forest. A loud squawk sounds above me, and I instinctively duck my head as a large bird swoops a few inches over me. I run to the steam cycle and straddle it. I am suddenly nervous. What if I can't start it? I push the button on the bar, twist the handle, and kick the pedal down hard. The cycle roars to life, and it surprises me that I was able to do it so easily. I pull the lever next to the handle, but it doesn't move. Something won't let it move. Something that I don't know about. I look around, hoping the answer is obvious, but I don't see anything and I'm afraid to try the different buttons and levers I see because I am afraid I'll do more harm than good.

I hear the roar of another cycle and look behind me. One comes over the ridge, flying in the air, before it lands hard on the ground. It's Lyon with Dr. Stewart clinging to his back. Another one comes right behind it and I realize its Pace. He sees me and his eyes widen in surprise. One of Lyon's security guards rides with him, and I see a dark trail of blood on his back. Pace stops the cycle.

"GO! GO! GO!" Levi yells as he runs over the ridge. Pace isn't happy, but he does as he is told and the cycle roars away. "Move!" Levi yells at me. I slide back and he jumps on. He does something with his foot and the cycle takes off. I grab onto his waist. It's hard for me to hold on as he has his rifles, his crossbow, and the two knives on his back. I hear a noise behind me and realize the rovers are right behind us. All I can do is hold on as the cycle jumps and bucks across the terrain. I flinch, certain that a bullet will hit my back at any second, but thankfully none does. Still I don't relax until we leave the forest and come to the field we first crossed. I see the tower from the ruins against the night sky along with Adam, Alcide and two of Lyon's men standing at the marker Levi left for them.

I tap Levi's shoulder and point to the marker. He sees what I am looking at, nods, and heads the cycle that way. Lyon and Pace see his intent and head in that direction also. The cycles all pull to a stop and I slide off on trembling legs. Before I can turn around, Pace grabs me to him in a shaky embrace.

"What happened? You're covered with blood. Are you hurt?" He pulls away for a moment to search my face.

"I'm not hurt. It's not my blood."

"Then whose is it?"

"A rover's," I say. "He was on . . ." I begin to explain but before I can, Pace whirls and punches Levi in the jaw.

Levi staggers back a step. He puts his hand to his jaw, and I see the anger flare in his eyes. He is still covered with weapons, and I've seen firsthand what he is capable of. I jump in front of Pace before something else happens.

"What was that for?" Levi doesn't yell, but his voice is loud enough that I cringe.

"For bringing her out here." Pace does yell and crowds against me. I stand my ground. "For exposing Wren to danger."

"I chose to come," I say. "And it is no different than the danger you were just in." I punctuate my statement with a finger jab to his chest.

"I for one am most glad you showed up when you did," Dr. Stewart says. "Our situation was most dire."

"We lost another man," Lyon says. "We lost Stone and Bradley."

"Both good men," one of the guards says. I should learn his name. I should learn all their names since they are dying in their efforts to help us, but at the moment I am so angry with Pace. Yet I am relieved that he isn't hurt.

Meanwhile the man that rides with him is. He is trying to be strong, but he suddenly slumps over on the cycle.

"We need to get back," Lyon says as the two guards move to help him. "The going will be slow but we should all pile up on the cycles. We don't want to lose anyone else."

I am confused for a moment. Who should I ride with? Pace or Levi? Pace answers the question for me. He goes back to his cycle. The wounded man is propped up behind him and another guard sits behind him, facing backward. Lyon, Dr. Stewart, and the remaining guard do the same. Levi returns to our cycle, and I climb on behind. Adam and Alcide, who have been quietly watching everything, jump on behind, both facing backward also. The cycles move out slowly and carefully to the road that takes us back to the camp. I cannot help but wonder what additional trouble will await us when we get there.

◆

Finally the lights of the camp shine in the distance, like a beacon at the end of one of our tunnels in the mines. The trip back took three times as long as the trip out. The cycles move much more slowly because of their heavy loads, and there is no conversation. I know Adam and Alcide are desperate to know what happened. I've put that part behind me. I am more concerned about what will happen. I am worried over our friends inside. Did Jon and Peter discover anything while we were gone? I use those thoughts to distract me from my main concern over Pace and his reaction to the blood on me. A part of me is thrilled that he reacted with such passion, while another part of me feels aligned with Levi, who saved my life. Pace might argue that if I had not have gone my life would not have been in danger. I refuse to believe there is a difference between me going compared to Adam, James, or Alcide going. We are all a part of this and we must all work together, using our best assets, whether they be male or female, to survive.

A group waits to greet us in the circle of light around the Quest: Jane, Zan, James, George, Rosalyn, Sally, Freddy, and Nancy. I see no sign of Jon or Peter, which means they have not returned yet. Jane throws her arms around Lyon's neck as soon as he dismounts, while Zan waits to give her own relieved welcome. The injured guard is carried into the Quest by his friends, and Jane and Dr. Stewart follow to tend to his wound.

"Oh my goodness, are you hurt too?" Zan asks when she sees the blood on my face. Jonah runs to me with an inquisitive meow and sniffs at my boots.

"No," I reply wearily. "But I do need to wash up and change." I follow Zan to her room with Jonah trailing after me. Levi follows us to go to his room for the same purpose. I did not speak to Pace before I left. Right now I am not certain of what I should say to him. "Any news from Peter and Jon?" I ask.

"Nothing," Zan replies. "It's been a long evening for those of us left behind. But it looks as if yours has been even longer."

"Levi saved my life." I look in the mirror in the washroom. Blood splatters my face and neck. My eyes seem bigger in my face, especially with my hair pulled back. I take off the goggles, which are also blood splattered, and remove my kerchief from around my hair. I turn on the water and, with a cloth and a bit of Zan's lovely scented soap, wash my face. Jonah jumps onto the rim of the tub, then onto the sink and bats a paw at the running water.

"Levi is good at that sort of thing," Zan says matter of factly from her room. "But there are those here who might argue that if you had not have gone, then your life would not have been in danger."

"Would you have stayed behind, given a choice and under these circumstances?" I unbutton Zan's jacket and work on the knot in the shirt. Zan walks in and sees what I'm doing. A look of shock fills her face and then she shakes her head.

"No I wouldn't. Especially if someone I loved was in danger." She darts out and then back again with another shirt. "I take it your bow wasn't much use?"

"It served a purpose," I say. "Just not the one it was intended for."

"How bad was it out there?" Zan picks up a comb and goes to work on my hair, which is still miraculously pinned up. She pulls out pine needles and a small stick and flings them into a small can of trash.

"I think it was a good thing we arrived when we did. I also think Levi is very good at killing."

"He's had to be," Zan says. "I'm not saying that it's good or bad. I'm just saying that circumstances and the world being what it is, he's had to learn how."

"If we are going to survive in this world, we are going to have to learn how also."

"Oh Wren." Zan pulls me into a comforting hug. "I am sorry to say you are right."

I take comfort from her words and her companionship. I do not take comfort from knowing that in this regard, my father was right about the world outside the dome.

"Are you hungry?" Zan asks.

"Starved," I admit.

"Come on then," she says. "My father will have a tale to tell, and I don't want to miss it."

Since I am also curious about what happened before we found Lyon, Pace, and the others, I go with Zan outside to the tent where everyone is gathered and fix myself a plate. Dr. Stewart, Pace, Adam, and Alcide are just finishing up their meal. Levi joins us. He has a red mark around his eye from where Pace punched him. Adam moves off to the side to talk with James while Alcide just sits and watches everyone in turn. I am still not certain about Pace's sudden outburst of anger, so I sit down across from him and next to Alcide. Zan sits beside me on the other side. Lyon is in conference with the five remaining guards and the pilot of the Quest. The guards disperse around the camp with their weapons ready, and the pilot, Captain Manning, goes back into the ship.

Lyon goes to a small table beneath the tent that holds an assortment of glasses and bottles and pours himself a shot of amber liquid. I recognize it as the same thing my father gave me when I first met him. Whiskey.

"Will you please tell us what happened now?" Jane asks as Lyon settles himself at the head of the table. The rest of our group gathers round: George, Rosalyn, and Sally, who sends Freddy and Nancy off to bed with the rest of the children who are already asleep. I have no doubt they will listen through the tent walls to the story. I know I would, were I their age.

"We were set upon!" Dr. Stewart exclaims. "The grubbers took my samples and tossed them on the ground. An entire day's work is totally lost, along with all of my instruments."

"Excuse me, Dr. Stewart, but I am more concerned about the loss of life than the loss of your instruments," Jane exclaims.

"Oh dear, as am I," he says as he fixes himself a drink of whiskey. "It was a terribly frustrating experience."

"Do you think they will come after us here?" Zan asks

"They already know where we are," Levi says. "And if they don't by now they won't have any trouble finding us."

"Levi is right," Lyon says. Dr. Stewart places the bottle of whiskey before him, and Lyon refills his glass. "We need to establish a perimeter and make sure all of the livestock are inside it. The smaller the area in which we are contained, the easier it will be to defend it. I am afraid it's going to take all of us for this task."

"That won't be a problem for any of us," Adam says steadily. "Just tell us what to do."

"The most important thing is to make sure the Quest is protected," Lyon adds.

"We will do whatever is needed," James adds.

"First please tell us what happened," Jane implores.

"It took us a couple of hours to find the rovers' settlement," Lyon begins. "We followed the road along the coast to the ruins of a castle. It was quite extraordinary. Jethro believes its origins had to date back to the eleventh century if not before."

Dr. Stewart nods in agreement.

"Is that where you found the rovers?" Zan asks.

"No," Lyon continues. "Jethro wanted to explore the castle, and I deemed it practical. As we were in the turret I saw a stream of smoke coming up from the middle of the forest. The stream was large, so it had to come from a significant fire. I knew it had to be the rovers' camp. So we traveled a ways into the forest, parked the bikes, and continued on foot. I left Bradley with the bikes, then Jethro, Pace, Stone, Phillips, and I went to investigate."

When we stopped, Lyon said they'd lost Bradley and Stone, so Phillips had to be the name of the guard that was injured. Jane had not said how severe his injuries were. Would someone else have to die to keep us safe?

"We split up," Lyon continues. "Jethro went with Phillips and Stone and Pace with me. We went in opposite directions yet managed to come upon the rover settlement at the same time."

"Settlement?" Levi asks. "Not an encampment?"

"No, it was definitely a settlement," Dr. Stewart says. "There were permanent dwellings built in an organized manner around a central common area."

"Sounds like a settlement to me," Alcide mutters.

"Our position was not good, so we carefully backed away to find a better location for observation," Lyon continues. "I took Pace and Stone with me to a rise we saw on the eastern side of the settlement, while Jethro and Phillips went back to the bikes to send word that we'd found the settlement. I wanted reinforcements."

"For what?" Zan exclaims. "Surely you weren't planning an attack."

"No," Lyon says. "It was just the size of the settlement was so large and I wanted to keep an eye on it."

"How large is large?" James asks.

"Five hundred people or more."

"Heavens," Rosalyn says. "Will they attack us?"

"Not if we can help it," Lyon says.

"How can you stop them?" George asks.

"With our superior weaponry," Lyon explains.

"But they attacked you and killed two of your men," Rosalyn continues. "It seems like their superior numbers overwhelmed your superior weaponry."

"Rosalyn!" Sally places a calming hand on Rosalyn's arm.

"You don't know the entire story," Pace finally speaks.

James opens his mouth to retort in defense of Rosalyn but stops suddenly when Zan speaks up. "Pace is right. We don't know what happened out there. And there is much to be said for preparation. We need to know what to expect so we are ready to defend ourselves."

"We were taken by surprise," Dr. Stewart says. "We had just arrived back at the hiding place for the bikes when we were attacked by a group of ten or so. If Lyon and the others had not arrived when they did, I would be dead now."

"While we were trying to circle around to high ground we heard the shots," Lyon said. "And immediately knew Jethro was under attack. By the time we arrived, Bradley was down and one of the rovers had Jethro down with a knife at his throat. I threw myself at the man while Stone, Phillips, and Pace went after the rest. We managed to drive them back and take a defensive position so I could send out the pigeon with a message. The attackers were vicious and bloodthirsty, completely without mercy. Their brutality is comparable to the Indian wars from our colonial history, or the more current tribal wars of Africa. There is no reasoning with people like this. All they know is kill or be killed."

"Heavens, Lyon," Jane says. "Thank God you were able to send word."

"Thank Levi and Wren that they arrived when they did. If more rovers had arrived we would not have been able to hold them off. The only thing that saved us was the fact that our weapons have a greater range than theirs."

Jane puts her arms around her husband and Zan clings to his arm. "To think we nearly lost you," Jane says. "We cannot under any circumstances abandon our friends while that threat is out there."

"I have no intention of abandoning them," Lyon says. "You may all rest assured."

The thought that the Hatfields might even consider leaving nearly throws me into a panic. How will we survive if they did? We will all fall victim to the dreaded rovers without them, caught as we are between them and the dome with no shelter or basic necessities. If they had not arrived when they did we would already be gone. My father was right. The outside world is a very dangerous place and one we were ill-prepared for. I look around at our group gathered at the table and wonder how many more will die before we are safe. How many more will die because of my impulsive decision?

"What should we do?" Adam asks. "What can we do?"

"We have to prepare," Lyon says. "The presence of the children makes us vulnerable. We have to keep them out of range of the Quest. We don't want to risk a stray shot, if they do attack, igniting it. I have instructed Captain Manning to take it out to sea at the first sign of trouble. Unfortunately there are too many of you to take aboard or we could simply sail away to a safe location."

Lyon's words fill me with fear, but they also inspire me. What would it be like to simply walk on board the Quest and sail away, to a different place that had none of the difficulties of this one? A new place where I could just start over. But hadn't I thought the same about leaving the dome? Isn't that what got us all in this predicament in the first place? Was there any place in this world that was completely safe and without problems of its own? I think not. Since Adam and Eve were driven from the Garden of Eden, the world has been filled with troubled places.

Lyon continues. "The most important thing is to set up a watch tonight. This is where your extraordinary night vision will be of help. By placing a shiner with a guard, we will have the element of surprise instead of them being able to sneak up on us."

"It makes sense," Adam agreed. "We can see them long before they come into the light."

"Exactly," Lyon said. "Also tomorrow, first thing, I think the women should have weapons training also. We might as well include the oldest of the children . . ."

"Freddy and Nancy," Sally says. "Rosalyn and Wren trained today."

"Not that it did me much good," I confess. "I missed when I tried to shoot my bow."

"Practice makes perfect," Lyon says. "I assume you spent the day making weapons?" he asks Levi.

"Yes, sir," Levi replies. "A bow for everyone and enough arrows for one campaign. We also did target shooting so everyone is familiar with them."

"Excellent," Lyon says. He looks down at the plate of food Jane set before him. "Please excuse me now. I am quite hungry."

"Please eat," Jane says. Lyon takes a bite and before he is done chewing a shout rings out from one of the guards.

"It's Jon!" a voice rings out.

"And Peter."

"Where have they been?" Jane asks. "I didn't even realize they were gone."

"They went to the dome," James says. "To find word about our friends."

"Wren got a message from inside the dome," Zan explains.

"What?" Lyon asks. "How?"

I explain to Lyon about Pip carrying the message and James shows it to him. Pace looks as surprised as I felt when I first discovered it. He goes to Pip's cage where the bird is asleep with his head beneath his wing. Jon and Peter arrive at the tent out of breath from their run.

"Did you find anything?" Rosalyn asks.

Both look grim and I fear what they have to say. "We found the place where I came out," Jon says. "The door is locked from the inside."

"And?" I ask, knowing there is more.

"There were bodies," Peter said.

"Bodies?" Adam asks.

"From the fires," Peter says. "I don't know if it is from the fire that raged after the explosion or if they were executions. There were twenty-three burned carcasses. Men, women, and children."

I am suddenly sick to my stomach.

"That's not all," Jon says, and the look in his eyes scares me as much as his coming words. "They were tied to stakes." I cover my mouth with my hand as a cold fear grips me.

"Heavens!" Jane exclaims.

"Barbarians," Dr. Stewart adds.

Lyon raises a hand to silence the protests that ring around the table. Alcide looks green, and I recognize the anger on James's and Adam's faces.

"Did you recognize any of them?" Rosalyn asks in a trembling voice. Her husband Colm is inside somewhere. Alive or dead, we do not know.

Jon and Peter shake their heads. "There was no way to tell who they were," Jon says. "There wasn't enough left."

"It can't be Lucy and David," I say. "I refuse to believe that it is."

"There's not a lot we can do about it if it is," James says.

"It is obviously some sort of warning," Lyon surmises. "But for who? The rovers? Or those of you that escaped?"

"It has to be for the rovers," Levi says. "Perhaps to let them know that even though there is trouble within, that the dome is not to be trifled with."

"What makes you think that?" Zan asks.

"Wren's story of escape. As far as those in power know, everyone died in the floods. How would they know that they found their way out?"

"Whatever it is, please don't anyone panic or think the worst," Jane says. I appreciate her words, but they are not her friends inside the dome. Rosalyn leaves and Sally goes with her while the rest of us, the shiners, look at each other helplessly. I feel Pace's eyes upon me from where he stands next to Pip's cage. He is thinking about his mother. Surely my father wouldn't stoop so low. But why else would he put bodies on stakes unless they are a warning to those who made it outside?

The last he knew of me, I was on my way outside. He sent me there. It was only because his men left Jon and I alone when the explosions rocked the dome that I went back inside while Jon escaped. As far as he knows, I am outside.

Are the bodies meant for me? Am I responsible for more deaths?

"Levi, I'm beginning to think your idea of going into the dome has merit," Lyon says. "We must find out what is going on inside there. If only there was some way I could talk to the man in charge."

"Sir William Meredith," I say.

"You can't be serious," Jane says. "The man who is staking bodies up outside the door?"

Lyon smiles at her. "We've had dealings with worse my dear, and I know you recall it. Now that we have somebody that knows precisely where the door is, I don't see why we don't give it a try. If they trade with the rovers, then why wouldn't they be willing to trade with us?"

"Do you mean trade for our friends?" Pace asks. I know he's thinking more of his mother than Lucy, David, Jilly, and Harry.

"We could ask him," Lyon says. "I would love to get a feel for this man, talk to him about his motives and perhaps make him see that there is a life available to them outside the dome."

"Why would anyone want to leave the dome when they already have all the luxuries?" Alcide asks.

"They wouldn't have to leave the dome," Lyon says. "Just break the glass. They can continue to live in their homes as always. They would just no longer be trapped. They would no longer have to rely on the fans."

"They might need umbrellas," Zan said with a wry grin.

"And snow shovels," Levi added.

The answer Lyon gave was so simple that those of us from the dome sat mute with the realization of how easy it would be. Life would basically be the same for everyone; the only change would be instead of a sky of glass, there would be a beautiful sky of blue, just as Alex said. A fitting tribute to him. There would be gardens and orchards growing in the dirt and room for the cattle and pigs and chickens to roam. My mind saw a true paradise surrounding the dome, with all of us working together and jobs we chose to do because there would be room to grow and change. We would no longer need so much coal because we would no longer need the fans. We would need fuel to stay warm in the winter, but surely that could be found. We would have the entire countryside as a resource.

Even though it has been a struggle since we came out, I want it to work. The world is so beautiful. There is so much to see and explore. So much wonder to behold. Everyone should see the moon and the stars and feel the wondrous warmth of the sun upon their skin. In moderation of course. Everyone within should have the right to choose their own path.

But what if the rovers do not want to share the resources of Great Britain. What if they do fight us for them? Would we have enough manpower and weaponry to overcome them?

Lyon's remark about flying away to a safer place sounds like a dream compared to the reality of our future. Yet it wasn't that long ago that I considered this reality a dream. I also have to consider his suggestion of breaking the glass of the dome. Wouldn't doing that be the same thing as what my father did for the rest of us? Breaking the glass is the same as making the decision for everyone. If only things weren't so complicated. If only the answers were easy.

"I would not trust Sir Meredith," I offer. The thought of Lyon Hatfield boldly knocking on the door of the dome and my father's reaction to him amuses me, but I also want Lyon to know the type of man he could possibly be dealing with.

"From what you have told me of the man already, I will not," Lyon replies. "Still, there is nothing like looking your adversary in the eyes to get the true measure of his will."

"There is so much to think about," Jane adds. "Attack from rovers, pleas for help from inside the dome, and two of our own dear men dead this day. And this last bit of news is very disturbing for all of us."

"There is much to think about and plan for tomorrow," Lyon agrees. "But first we must take care of tonight. I know some of you worked the night shift. Are you able to help with guarding our little fortress tonight?"

"I am," James says.

"I will," Adam echoes along with Alcide and Peter.

"I will also," I say. "I can't seem to convince my body that the night is made for sleeping yet."

"I will stay up and help," Levi volunteers. "There is no way I can sleep after everything that has happened."

"That should do it," Lyon says. "The rest of you can take a shift first thing in the morning. Just because it will be daylight doesn't mean there will not be an attack. Those of you taking night duty, come with me. We must pair you up."

Lyon rises from the table, a signal for the rest of us that our little respite is over. We are all quiet and weighed down with the worry of today's realizations as we leave the table. George wanders off in the direction of the privy. Jon drops down by Beau's side and gives him some scraps from his plate. The rest of the group is following Lyon, as ordered, except for Pace, who simply looks at me.

"Can we talk?" he asks. Jonah jumps into my chair and with his paw scrapes a scrap from my plate. I put my plate on the chair to keep him off the table and turn to Pace.

"Yes," I agree. He takes my hand and leads me toward the ponies while I wonder what he has to say that takes precedence over the immediate danger that we face. Ghost whinnies and tosses his head at my approach, and I remember the promise I made to him this morning, to take him and the rest out for exercise. I spent the day wrapped up in my own needs and had forgotten about the needs of others. The ponies depend on me to take care of them, and I've been negligent in my duties. I lean over the pen and stroke his nose while the other ponies crowd around him. At least Rosalyn remembered them and had the children take them out. Perhaps it is a good thing for all concerned if I let the children take over their care.

"They love you," Pace says. He leans against a tree and watches me as I greet each one by name.

"They're trying to figure out who I am," I laugh. "I smell different."

"You look beautiful," Pace says quietly. "Unforgettable. I would have liked to have seen you in the dress."

The word unforgettable seems strange to me, along with his comments. He must be talking about my hair. I turn my head and look at Pace. A lamp hangs from a tree branch above him and the light surrounds his head like a halo. "Who told you about the dress?"

"Alcide."

"Of course."

"Things have been strange since we got out," he continues. "Don't you think?"

"There's a lot to get used to," I say. "So much has changed."

"Are you going to tell me what happened out there?"

"It depends," I reply. "Are you going to get angry when I tell you?"

"I got angry because you could have been hurt."

"But I wasn't."

"Because of Levi."

"Yes."

He opens his mouth and I prepare myself for his speech on why I shouldn't have been out there, but instead he says something that surprises me.

"This isn't what I expected."

"Me either," I confess. "I don't know what I expected." Jonah runs to me, sniffs at my skirt, and then ducks into the pen and trails between the pony's legs in his meandering way.

"I expected us to be together," Pace continues as he moves to stand beside me at the fence. "It feels like forever since we have been."

What can I say? There is so much going on. It does seem like forever since we have been together as we were, sharing everything and not knowing if the next moment would be our last. Fate threw us together, but since we left the dome it has been more like habit. It could be because there are so many of us now. We are distracted by those that are around us. Every day has been a struggle to stay alive. "I know," I say because I don't know where Pace is going with this conversation.

I have to admit some of the distance he feels is because of me. I haven't shared everything with him like I did before. There are things I've felt and done that I have not mentioned. It's because I did not want to change the way he sees me, but now I realize that by not being completely honest with him I've changed things in a way that I don't understand. I don't know how to fix it, and, since I cannot change the past, I keep blundering ahead and making the same mistakes.

Instead of looking at Pace, I steal a glance at the airship. James, Adam, Alcide, and Peter all have bows, and I see them flex and test them in the lamplight. Lyon's guards have been at their posts since he got back, and they stare out into the darkness with their guns cradled in their arms. Levi stands on the catwalk with Lyon, waiting on me. "They are waiting on me," I add.

"I don't want you to go." Pace puts his hand on my arm. I feel the heat of his hand on my bare skin like a burn.

Now I am really surprised. "You don't want me to go help? They need us," I explain. "They've done so much for us, how could I not do what I can to help?"

Pace shakes his head. "Of course we should help. It's just . . ." Pace runs his hand through his hair and stares off into the darkness. "It's Levi." He sighs. "I don't want you to spend the night with Levi."

"Spend the night with Levi?" I say. "You make it sound like I'm doing something wrong. We're protecting our friends. I'll be protecting you."

"I realize that," Pace says in his patient way that for some reason makes me feel as if he is patronizing me. "I know that your eyes and your ability to see in the dark will be a great help tonight. It's just that I don't like the way he looks at you. The way he watches you." Pace turns me to face him by taking my other arm and I can clearly see his concern written on his face. "The fact that he's always asking questions about you."

"He is?" As soon as the words come out of my mouth I knew they are the wrong thing to say. Unfortunately there is no taking them back, and the pain in Pace's beautiful blue eyes stabs at my heart.

His temper, along with his pain, caused by me, spouts out. "Isn't that why you put on the dress and fixed your hair tonight?" I've never seen him angry like this. Especially not at me. "So Levi would pay attention to you?"

"Pace!" I exclaim, feeling anger along with hurt myself. "What is wrong with you?"

His grip on my arms tightens, and I know when he releases me that there will be marks on my skin. "I don't want to lose you, Wren."

"What makes you think you are going to lose me?" I spout, and then I think about what he said and become angrier, if that is possible, as memories of James attacking me in the tunnel come back to haunt me. He treated me like I was his possession. He treated me badly. "What makes you think you I'm yours to lose?"

"You said you loved me," Pace explains. "We love each other."

"So love is about possession? Is that what you're telling me?"

Pace drops his hands and steps back as if I'd struck him. "No, Wren. No. That's not what I meant at all."

"Well when you figure out what you mean, you let me know," I say, powered by my anger. "I'll be keeping watch until then." I turn away.

"Wren! Wait!"

I ignore him and keep on going. Jonah runs to catch up with me but I ignore him too.

"Something wrong Wren?" Levi asks as I stomp onto the catwalk.

"I'll be back as soon as I get my jacket," I say, ignoring his question.

But yes . . . something is terribly wrong and I'm not sure if I want to fix it.

· 20 ·

I can't stop thinking about Pace and the conversation we had. Like the episode in the tunnels with James, I play it over and over again in my mind, trying to define that exact moment when things went wrong. I cannot blame Pace for being possessive or jealous. If Zan had set her eye on him, I know I would feel the same. Yet I cannot help but think he is imagining the entire thing with Levi, in spite of what Zan told me earlier today. Levi could not possibly be interested in someone like me. Could he? He knows I am with Pace. He even asked me about it the day we went hunting.

I steal a look at Levi as we make our way by the light of the moon through the woods beside the road. Lyon paired me with him because he said we proved we work well together. I could have said no, but I didn't want to draw any attention to the fact that Pace and I are fighting. I also know the real reason he paired me with Levi is because Levi is the strongest and I am the weakest.

Lyon wants us far enough out that if the rovers do come up on us, the camp will have plenty of warning. Levi and I are to set up on one side of the trail, with Alcide and one of the guards on the other. The rest of the pairs are closer in, surrounding our encampment with a direct line of sight to each other. Levi is heavily armed with his crossbow, and two pistols and a rifle. The only weapon I have is a flare gun. Lyon explained that I should point it to the sky and pull the trigger when I see something. It will serve as a signal to the others and hopefully blind the rovers. He warned both Alcide, who also has one, and me to cover our eyes when we hear it going up because the flash might temporarily blind us, which is something I never want to experience again.

I wish I knew how to use one of Levi's weapons. While Levi is well-armed, I feel as if I am more of a hindrance than a help, as our recent experience has proven. At least Alcide has a bow and his knife. I have nothing since I left my bow around the rover's neck.

"This should do it," Levi says as we stop beside a tree with a double trunk. At some point in time one of the trunks grew straight out across the ground and then up. It would take no effort at all to stand on the thick trunk and walk up its length until it stretches once more to the sky, which Jonah promptly does before settling at the height of my shoulder with a contented meow. It should be a great perch for spying down the road. "Can you see Alcide and Willis?" Levi asks.

As I peer through the darkness I hear the sounds of the night come alive around us. Levi told me the chorus was sung by tiny frogs he called peepers, along with crickets and night birds, all joining together in their evening celebration. I am used to it now and think no more of it than I did the turning of the water wheel. I search among the trees until I see Alcide some fifty feet away on the other side of the road. Alcide waves at me and I wave back. Then he grins and purses his lips into a kiss and wags a finger at me.

I make a face at him and whirl around, which nearly bumps me into Levi.

"What's wrong?" Levi asks.

"Nothing," I say, blushing furiously.

"Did you find Alcide?"

"Yes." I wave behind me. "He's over there."

Levi stares over my shoulder into the darkness. "If you say so," he says, squinting.

"Trust me, he's there."

"I do trust you, Wren." Levi leans his rifle against the tree. "How's the view of the road?"

"I can see it," I say as I look toward the east. "It's a straight run for a good while, then it curves to the north."

"Which is the direction of their settlement," Levi says.

"What if they don't come down the road?"

"They'd have no reason not to," Levi says. "Logic dictates that they wouldn't spread out until they get closer to our encampment. We're a good ways away. If there's a small party, we could even trap them between us and pick them off."

I look in the direction of our encampment. It is far enough away that I can't see it, and the lamps are nothing more than pin pricks in the distance like the stars in the sky.

I shiver. "You talk about killing so easily, Levi," I say. I keep my eyes on the road. I know why I am here. I have a job to do. Yet I can't help seeing the last seconds of the rover's life as his blood splattered all over me. "It seems to come easy for you."

"I value my life and the life of my family," he says. "Just because I talk about it doesn't mean that I think it's easy. It's never easy, Wren. You already know that."

I realize that even though I've only known him a short time, Levi knows more about me than the people whom I've known my entire life. He knows more about me than Pace. I'm not sure if it's a good thing, or bad. "Maybe it's because you talk about it like it is part of a plan."

"It's my plan to keep us alive," Levi says. "Just like today. Where would we be if we had not killed those rovers? All of us. Just like it's your plan to stay alive. Why else would we be out here?"

"I guess I didn't think about it that way," I admit. "I just thought I was helping."

"Helping protect all of us," Levi says. "Which might involve killing."

"I don't want to talk about killing," I say. "I've been lucky before, but now, if someone was to come at me, I don't know what I would do. I've proven I can't use the bow, and I'm afraid that my luck will eventually run out. I guess I could try one of the branches again." I was trying to make a joke because all of the talk of killing is making me feel morbid on top of my guilt over my fight with Pace. I failed miserably at that also I think, until Levi answers me.

"Take your pick," he says and sweeps his arm out to show the ground. "Of course a branch is only good in hand-to-hand combat. Hopefully it won't get to that." I look around the ground, debating in my mind which branch would serve me best. Levi takes his crossbow from his back. "Or I could teach you to use this. As long as we're out here we might as well do something."

"I would like to be useful," I say. "If we are attacked I'd rather be able to fight than have you worrying about having to protect both of us."

"I never doubted your self-sufficiency, Wren," Levi says. "I have no doubt that if we were attacked at this very minute you'd find a way to survive. Because that's what you are. A survivor."

His ability to see so much about me scares me. "You presume to know so much about me, Levi, yet we only met a few days ago."

"We would not have met at all if you weren't a survivor," he points out.

"That could have had more to do with luck than anything else," I say. "If I had been in the village, or on the bridge, I'd be dead right now, like most of our village."

"Then call it fate if you want," Levi says. "Whatever it was, I'm glad you survived it."

I don't know what to say to that. To say thank you would make it seem like I'd done something to deserve it. To say I'm glad too would make it seem like I wasn't sorry that other people had died. I am at a loss, so I say nothing and instead stare off into the darkness as if I see something.

"Is something there?" Levi asks as he stands beside me and tries to see if there is anything on the road.

"No," I reply. "It's just the wind." The wind has picked up, fluttering the leaves on the trees and sweeping across the grass. A few tendrils of my hair that were left down dance against my cheek. Levi slowly smiles and hooks the lock of my hair with his finger and pulls it down beside my ear where it belongs.

Maybe Pace was right. Maybe Levi is interested in me. The way he looks at me with his warm brown eyes . . .

"Your eyes are amazing," he says, and it makes me remember that Pace said the same thing to me when we first met.

"You only think that because they are different than yours," I say and turn away because looking at him is dangerous to my soul. Pace was right. I shouldn't be here with him. Levi is too tempting. Yet I cannot leave. To do so would put all of us at risk.

Why do you fight it? The little voice in my head surprised me. I don't ever recall it sounding so mischievous or being so insistent before. *You are not married to Pace,* it says. *There are no vows between you. He wants to control you like James wanted. Didn't he just prove it by the way he acted? Levi wants to kiss you.* The excuses come to me rapidly until they fill my mind and I forget why I shouldn't kiss Levi.

Not that he has tried. Or that I expect he will try. But if he does . . .

What is wrong with me? Once again I have let my mind race away to things that are impossible and improbable.

"Do you want to learn how to shoot?" Levi asks.

"Shouldn't we watch?" I ask.

"I see no reason why we can't do both at the same time." He slips the flare gun sling from my shoulder and hangs it on a tree branch where it is close at hand. "We'll just aim in that direction," he explains. "That way if someone does show up we'll be looking right at them."

"It scares me that it actually makes sense," I say and Levi grins.

"I want you to get the feel of a gun in your hands," he says. He pulls one of the pistols from the holster on his hip, turns it to the side, moves a switch with his thumb, and then extends his hand and peers down the line of his arm. "I put the safety on so there will be no accidental shooting. No need to let them know where we are if we don't have to."

"I completely agree," I say.

"Hold it like this," he says and wraps my hand around the handle. The weight of it is familiar, like holding a small pickax or hammer, yet it is more balanced in my hand than either ever felt. Levi stands behind my shoulder and lifts my arm. "You've got strong hands and arms."

"I *did* work," I say.

"Really?" I feel the flex of his grin beside my ear and his breath tickles me. "Imagine that. Now brace the butt with your other hand."

I do as he asks. "Imagine that," I echo.

"Just sight down the barrel," he says. "Put your finger against the trigger. And then you just give it a squeeze. It will jump in your hand so be prepared. Do you think you can do it?"

I imagine a rover coming at me out of the darkness, or a filcher, or one of the bluecoats who chased me through the street. "I can do it," I say. "If I have to."

"You might have to, Wren," Levi says. "You won't have time to think about it."

"I can do it."

"Good. Now let's try the rifle." He takes the pistol. "This is the safety by the way. It has to be here for the gun to work. Got it?"

"Got it."

Levi holsters his pistol and picks up the rifle. "This one is a bit different," he says. "Heavier and awkward at first."

"But it works at a longer distance."

"Yes. The pistols are more effective up close. The rifle's for farther away, when you have time to aim. You always want to aim for the biggest part of the body, so aim for the center of the chest. That way you have a better chance of hitting something."

"Makes sense," I say.

He holds up the rifle. "This is how you hold it. Brace it against your shoulder. Same rule with the safety here." I watch him carefully and do as he tells me when he places the rifle in my hands. "Pick out a target and see if you can keep it level." I look off in the distance and pick out a knot in a tree. "Do you have something?" Levi asks.

"I do."

"What is it?" I point and tell him my target, which is a bit of broken branch sticking out from a tree trunk. Levi stares off into the night. "Your eyes really are quite remarkable," he says with a grin. "I don't think it will shoot that far, Wren. You might want to try something closer. More attainable."

I nod and try again. The rifle feels awkward in my arms. I'm not so sure I could do as well with it as I could a pistol. My arms are starting to cramp from keeping them in the same position.

"You're getting a little shaky, Wren," Levi points out.

"It feels strange," I say.

"That's because you're not used to it."

"I don't think I'll ever get used to it."

"You'll be glad of this if we're attacked."

"Something to look forward to?"

"Depends on the company," Levi replies. "Let's try the crossbow. You know the basics of this and hopefully it won't ever come down to that." Levi takes the rifle from my hands.

"Hopefully," I say as I let out my breath.

"This one you can actually shoot." Levi picks up his crossbow. "Aim for that tree. The one with the branch that's hanging on the ground. Then I'll show you how to load it."

The crossbow is heavier than I expected. "You've got to balance yourself." Levi moves behind me. "Brace your body against mine," he says as he sidles up against my back. He puts his arms around me and guides both my arms up and into the proper position to hold the crossbow. I feel him pressed against me, my spine against his chest, and his legs right behind me, all hard muscle and silent strength that he wears as easily as his clothes. "Hold it just like the rifle," he instructs. "Spread your legs a bit." He pushes my left leg forward with his foot. "Now set into your stance." I settle into a more comfortable position. "That's it." Levi says quietly into my ear. "Now sight down the line of the arrow and gently squeeze the trigger. Don't hold your breath, let it out as you squeeze it."

I listen to Levi's instructions and follow them as best as I can. The arrow leaves the crossbow with a whoosh and hits the tree

with a satisfying thunk. Jonah turns his head at the strike and meows questioningly.

"I did it!" I say and turn to smile at Levi.

His face is right next to mine. "Brilliant!" he says and his eyes
dance with delight at my accomplishment. I cannot tear mine away
from his handsome face, which comes closer and closer until his
lips touch mine. I should turn away. I should stop, but I cannot. I
am captured by the feel of him, by the taste, by the fact that Levi
Addison wants to kiss me.

Pace . . . I shouldn't be doing this. Especially not after my fight
with Pace, but I can't seem to stop myself. My heart and my mind
are at war while my body enjoys the fact that Levi deepens the kiss,
moving around until he's in front of me, taking the crossbow from
my hands, dropping it to the ground and putting his hands on my
upper arms and then around my back until I'm pressed up close
against him.

I am aware of Jonah pawing at my leg and meowing. I feel the
wind pick up and twist my hair against my cheek. I hear the night
chorus around us, and it sounds as if it is getting louder, as if the
entire world has centered around this tiny dot on the map.

I shouldn't be doing this, yet I cannot find the will to stop myself. It is Levi who pulls away and stares down at me with a be-
mused expression on his face.

"So much for Pace," he says with a grin.

"Don't," I say. "That doesn't make this any easier."

"Nobody ever said love was easy."

"You don't love me, Levi," I say. "How can you? You don't know
me. You just met me."

"When did you meet Pace?" he asks.

So much has happened, I have to count the days in my head. I'm not even sure of what day it is. "Two weeks?" I guess. "What does that have to do with it?"

"It has to do with the fact that you made up your mind about him pretty quick, so why can't I do the same with you?"

"Maybe that is the problem," I say. "Maybe because everything happened so quick I can't really be sure about either one of you." I pick the crossbow up from the ground. "Show me how to load this."

"I think you deserve more than this life," Levi says as he puts the end of the crossbow on the ground, places his foot on it, and pulls up until it ratchets into place. He takes an arrow from the supply and places it in the chute, pressing it back. I watch carefully as he works so I'll know what to do. "What does Pace or anyone here have to offer you but hard work trying to survive?" Levi slings the crossbow over his back and turns to me, placing his hands on my upper arms. "Why don't you come with us when we leave and let me show you the world?" I fight the urge to shake him off. I know Levi won't hurt me, but it seems as if this is happening to me a lot. I don't want to be trapped. I've been trapped enough.

"Are you serious?" I ask. "Why? Why me?" The thought of leaving here and sailing away on the Quest is certainly a dream I've considered, but the knowledge that it is entirely possible is almost frightening. Would I have the courage to choose that future and turn my back on everything that I know? Would doing it be any different than anything else I've done so far?

Levi's eyes on me are serious, yet his face breaks into a smile. "Can't you see how special you are?"

"Why does everyone keep telling me that?" I twist away from him and turn to the tree where Jonah has once again taken up residence. I scratch his head in an absentminded way while Levi speaks.

"Because it's true."

I shake my head in denial. "I'm just a girl trying to survive. Just like everyone else."

"Oh, Wren." Levi shakes his head. "What will it take to convince you how exceptional you really are?"

"Did you ever stop to think that I don't want to be exceptional? Because being exceptional means you do things that get people killed." The sudden rush of emotion charging up from inside my body surprises me, and I have to take a moment to beat it into submission. Still I find it hard to speak. "I don't want all that responsibility. I didn't ask for it. I don't want to be responsible for anyone's life but my own."

Levi moves behind me and puts his hand on my neck where it is bare. I feel his heat against me, and I almost sigh against his touch but I can't. I am too confused, too torn, and every part of me is conflicted. "My poor Wren. You really think you are responsible for all those deaths?" he asks.

"I'm not yours, Levi," I say. "I'm not anybody's."

"I felt your kiss, Wren," Levi says. "You don't kiss somebody like that if you don't feel something for them." I cannot deny it. I turn to look at him and his hand drops away from my neck and touches my cheek. "I can see it in your eyes," he says.

"It's not that easy," I return. "I can't think clearly, especially when I feel like Pace is pulling me one way and you are pulling me another. I won't be the cause of a battle between you two. We have to work together or we'll never survive this."

Levi grins at me. "Those words are why you are special, Wren." He kisses my forehead and toys with the curl by my ear. "I won't cause trouble with Pace, I promise. But I'm not going to give up on you either. I've never felt this way about a girl before. And as you get to know me better you will find that I don't give up easily."

I nod. Even though he kissed me, I trust Levi. Just like I trusted

Pace when everything happened with us. Which makes me ask myself a very important question. How can I know what I feel for Pace or Levi is real when it seems that I am so easily torn. If my love is real, wouldn't I really know? Would I be this confused?

Just like Levi, I've never felt this way before. Or maybe I've felt this way too much. I need answers, and for the life of me I have no idea where to find them.

· 21 ·

"You *should see* the moon from the sky," Levi says. I sit on the end of the branch, in the place where it curves upward once more. Jonah is on a branch above me, and Levi leans against it beside me with the rifle in his arms. I keep my eyes on the road, watching and waiting for something that may not happen. I have to fight to keep my eyes open. Maybe my body clock has shifted, or maybe it's just the inactivity that I'm not used to. Whatever the cause, I'm glad for the distraction of Levi's statement.

The moon is now overhead and its light shines around us, casting short shadows on the ground and giving the entire area a magical glow. I look up at it, amazed that the path of my life has allowed me to see it, yet disappointed because I haven't really taken time to appreciate it. I never want to take my freedom for granted, yet I find myself just as trapped as I was before, only this time it's in the battle to stay alive.

I chose this course. I wanted the freedom to choose, so I have no regrets. I just didn't know it would be this difficult.

"What's it like?" I ask as I glance at Levi. His face is all shadow and light, yet his hair glows golden with the radiant moon.

"Some nights it's so big you think you might sail right into it," Levi says. "On nights like that, it's amazing, especially if you're over the ocean. It's as if everyone on board is holding their breath and afraid to break the spell. It's magical and thrilling." He shrugs. "Words can't really describe what it's like, it's just something you have to experience for yourself."

I peer up through the canopy of leaves. "How far away it is?"

"Thousands of miles. Ten of thousand miles. Maybe even hundreds of thousands. Technology has yet to figure out a way to measure it."

"A lot," I say, not really knowing what a mile is. I imagine the distance around the outside of the dome. Jon said it took him a day of walking and he didn't make it around. So I think about a thousand days of walking and it's unimaginable. My world has always been so small, so contained.

"It's not as big as the earth but a lot bigger than you think. Dr. Stewart says it controls the tides."

"So it's not just there to be pretty?"

"Everything in the world serves a purpose and is part of the circle of life."

I shake my head at his analogy. "Just like in the dome."

"What?"

"Everyone inside served a purpose. That purpose was to make life better for the royals."

"Everyone needs a purpose, Wren. It just shouldn't be at the expense of your own well-being."

"So what's our purpose now that we're out?"

"To learn about the world. To build a better society than the one you left behind. To live life to the fullest."

"By going with you on the Quest?"

His bright grin flashes. "You'd be amazed at the things you would learn about this world." Levi looks up at me. "You have a wonderful opportunity here, Wren. You don't have to repeat the mistakes of the past. You've got a clean slate. You can take the best the world has to offer and use it to build a new society."

"How can I do that if I'm out flying around the world with you?"

"Does that mean you're considering it?"

I can tell by the tone of his voice that he is teasing me. "It depends on how you answer the question," I reply.

"How else will you learn what works and what doesn't?" Levi says. "Experience is the best teacher of all."

I laugh as I nod in agreement. My experiences of the past few days have taught me much, the foremost being that I do not want to make the same mistakes again. "There are no guarantees that anyone will listen to what I have to say."

"What makes you think they won't?" he asks.

"Experience," I reply with a self-satisfied smile.

"Wren . . ." Levi shakes his head.

I ignore him. I don't want to have this conversation again. I look across the way at Alcide who is busy flexing his bow and aiming it at imaginary targets. The forest is quieter now, the earlier chorus having given way to the occasional hoot from a bird called an owl. I wish I had pictures to go with all the new words I've learned. I envy both Pace and Levi for all the books they've been able to read and experiences they've had. The things they've learned. While I do not have access to books, I do have access to Levi, so I ask him the question that's been burning in the back of my mind all day. "How did you get those scars on your chest?"

"You saw them?"

"I noticed them this morning. Zan wouldn't tell me when I asked her."

"Should I be flattered that you were looking?"

"It was kind of hard not to," I exclaim and Levi laughs. "Are you trying to distract me from the question?" I ask as I realize that boys are basically the same, no matter where they come from. They like it when girls pay attention to them.

"Why do you want to know?" he asks.

I study him in an attempt to decide if he's playing with me or being serious. "They look painful and tragic," I say. "I can't imagine what caused them."

Levi is quiet for a long moment and then he quietly says, "Wiwanyag Wachipi. The sun dance."

"How can a dance cause scars?"

"It's not actually a dance. It's more like a ritual."

"Zan said you lived with the Sioux Indians for a year? Your grandmother's tribe? Is that where it happened?" I try to imagine what kind of ritual would cause scars like that, and why his grandmother would permit him to be hurt.

"Yes." Levi glances up at me. "Are you sure you want to hear about this?"

"Only if you want to explain it to me."

"It's not something that we normally talk about outside the tribe."

"You don't have to tell me if you don't want to."

"No, I'll tell you, because I want you to know how diverse the world is. How many different types of people there are. People who do things that you can barely imagine. Some things are good, some are horrible. Some have a distinct purpose, and some are just because there is evil in the world."

What has he seen that is so evil? I think about the filchers, about what almost happened to me, and about Jon's friend that was traded to the rovers by my father. Surely that was evil enough. Are there worse things than the rovers out there? If there is then why would I want to go? Yet I am curious about everything, the good and the bad. I should be watching the road but I can't. I keep my eyes on Levi because I'm fascinated by what he is about to say.

"It happens during the summer solstice. That's the longest day of the year. The day that the earth is closest to the sun." I nod my head at the notion, not really sure about it, and place it in my mind to ask about at another time. "It celebrates the regeneration of life. Kind of like a rebirth. Everything is a circle and all of life is intertwined and dependent on each other. Everything on the earth is equal. The grass, the wind, a snake, a human. We all serve a purpose, down to the tiniest insect. So the sun dancer is symbolically reborn through the ritual."

"And the scars, are they part of your death?"

"Yes."

"That's the reason *why* you got them, but I still don't understand how you got them."

"The scars are part of the process of saying thank you for my life to the world. My giving of thanks requires a sacrifice. The only thing I have to give that is worthy enough and humble enough is myself. So my skin is cut in four places. Here and here." Levi draws his hands across his chest where the scars are. "A piece of bone is inserted and rawhide strips are tied to both ends of the bone. Then the strips are attached to a tree that has been spiritually prepared. And then you tear free."

My stomach flips into my chest. "You tear free? Intentionally?"

"It's not as easy as it sounds," Levi says and his voice sends a chill running down my spine. I wrap my arms around myself and realize that the entire world around us is deathly quiet, as if the trees themselves are listening. "It took four days before I was finally able to do it."

"Four days?" I stare at Levi in wonder. How did he do such a thing? "Four days tied like that? Without food? Without water? Without sleep? You were only fifteen? Why did you do it?"

"It was important to my grandmother that the tribe accept me as one of their own. And because my father and my brother did it. I wanted to prove I was worthy."

"You shouldn't have to prove anything to anyone Levi, especially yourself."

I feel the impact of his gaze. "Words to live by, Wren."

I realize what Levi has done. He's shared a deep secret with me. A very private part of his life. I feel privileged that he did so, yet more confused about how I feel about him than ever. He is much more complex than I thought. Deeper, bigger, mysterious, yet open and honest to a fault. And once more I have to ask myself, why does he want me?

A whistle rings out, and I immediately recognize it as the one the boys use in the tunnels. I look at Alcide, who points down the road, and I turn my head in that direction.

"Someone is coming," I whisper to Levi. Before I can take a breath he puts his hands on my waist and lifts me down to the ground.

"Take cover and tell me what you see," he says quietly.

I move behind a wide tree and peer around it. I see several figures darting between trees yet still coming our way. "More than twenty," I say. "I think two are women. They are all carrying weapons except for one. His hands are tied behind his back. I think he's one of your men."

"It must be Stone. He went down behind me," Levi says. He looks in the direction of Alcide and then behind us where we know James, Adam, and Peter are stationed with their partners and weapons. I can easily see his mind at work, thinking and planning. "How far out are they? Do we have time to set up a trap between us?"

"Ten, fifteen minutes," I say as I watch them approach. They are being cautious, darting from tree to tree instead of walking down the road. They move as if they have a plan. Two go forward, watch, and then motion the rest to follow until they've all caught up and then they repeat the process with the woman with Stone bringing up the rear. Alcide's call rings out again louder this time and everyone stops. "Alcide just let everyone know that someone is coming," I say as I hear three returning calls. I keep careful watch as the rovers freeze in place, trying to identify the call, which I always thought sounded like a bird until now. Will the rovers know it is not real? I hold my breath until they are on the move again.

"Can you tell him to take cover?" Levi asks. "Up a tree so we can let them go past us and then attack?"

"I'll see if he understands what you want." I wave at Alcide when he turns our way. I point up the tree, move my fingers as if they are walking and with my other hand jab my wrist. Alcide nods and immediately turns to his companion.

Levi searches the trees around us. "This one will do," he says in reference to the one I stand beside. The lowest limb is out of my reach, but I know his decision is the right one. We would be far enough up that they shouldn't notice us unless they were truly expecting us to be there. Our height would give us a great advantage and plenty of cover. "Here's a boost." He cups his hands together so that I can put my foot in it and he shoves me up to the lowest branch. I grab on and quickly pull myself up. Levi hands me the crossbow, and I sling it over my shoulder before throwing my arm over a branch and extending my other arm down to help him up. I have to hang close to upside down before Levi is able to clasp my hand and walk his way up the trunk.

"Do you have the flare gun?" he asks.

"Yes."

"When they get past us I want you to shoot it as high in the air as you can get. Find a line of sight now so you're ready. We don't want it to get hung up in the tree."

"I need to go higher I think." I glance again at the rovers. The way they dart from tree to tree makes it hard to decipher what track they will take. They could go between Alcide and us or they could go around us on one side or the other. Or they could come straight for us. It is so hard to tell.

"Go on then," Levi advises as I hand him the crossbow, which he hangs on a stout limb. "Can you still see them? How far out are they now?"

"Five minutes," I say as I climb. There is so much going on. I'm trying to watch the rovers and then I check on Alcide to see where he is and realize I can't find him at all, which is probably a good thing. If I can't see him then hopefully the rovers won't see him either. I climb up until I see an opening in the leaves that is large enough for the flare to fly through, if I shoot it correctly. I brace myself in the tree and take the flare from the sling around my shoulder. I look down through the branches and leaves at Levi, who has his eyes focused on me. He should be able to see them now.

Jonah meows. In all the excitement I'd forgotten about him and now he is standing at the base of the tree looking up and meowing again. Will he give us away? A branch snaps behind us and Levi and I both turn in the direction of the sound. Did they hear Jonah? It is hard for me to see them because I am so far up the tree. I look down at Levi, who is plastered against the tree trunk with the rifle in his hands as if he's trying to become one with the tree. His head is turned over his shoulder and I know he can see the rovers. He looks up at me and slowly squeezes his forefinger and thumb together to let me know they are very, very close.

If they heard Jonah and he decides to climb up this tree will they look this way? Levi must be thinking the same thing. I watch as he tentatively breaks off a small branch. He holds it out and drops it. It lands on Jonah's back. He leaps straight up in the air in surprise and then scampers off and jumps back onto the tree we were originally on.

"What wus that?" I hear a gruff voice say.

"More than likely ah-squirrel or ah-rabbit," another one answers.

I freeze in place and realize my hands are shaking. What if I accidentally set off the flare? The realization that someone will likely die and very soon suddenly grips me. I don't want to lose any more of my friends. What if our plan fails and the rovers get through and attack our camp? What if some of the children are hurt or even killed?

A hundred different scenarios run through my mind as the rovers walk right beneath our tree. Am I the same person that clubbed one in the head just a few nights ago? Am I the same person that choked a man to death earlier in the day? I need that brave Wren to appear, not this cowering coward that is crouched in a tree. I look down at Levi, who seems to be perfectly poised and ready to react. I cannot fail him. I cannot fail my friends.

Levi looks up at me and smiles. How can he smile at a time like this? Unless he's smiling at me for a reason, which I realize he is. Levi believes in me. He holds up a finger, signaling me to wait. I hold the flare gun in one hand and keep my eyes on him, waiting for the sign from Levi.

I count them as they go by. Twenty-six of them, all well-armed with old-looking guns and knives stuck in their belts. Some of them carry new guns, and I recognize them as the ones they must have recovered from the battle today. Two of them are women, who are also well-armed, and one is the guard named Stone, who looks as if he has suffered greatly at the hands of the rovers.

They come to a stop by the tree with the double trunk where Jonah is hiding.

Please Jonah, be still . . . "We should spread out now," one says. "I can ah-see the lights from their ah-camp." Their way of speaking is so strange. It's the same English that I speak, but the inflection is so very different, just as Levi's is different. The rovers sound more garbled while Levi's voice is more relaxed.

They are much too close to us for me to shoot off the flare. They would spot us right away and there are too many of them for us to fight. Yet if they spread out too much, there is a chance some of them could get through our trap. I keep my eyes on Levi because if I look at the rovers I might just panic. Levi keeps his finger up and his eyes on the rovers.

They disperse, six going right, which is the direction of the pony pen, six going left, which is where Alcide and his partner wait. Six go straight and six hang back with the prisoner a few very long moments before they continue on. They walk so quietly that if we had not seen them I wouldn't know they were there.

Levi must time this right. If they get too far ahead of us they will be on top of the rest of the guards along with James, Adam, and Peter. I keep my eyes on Levi until he moves his finger. It is time for me to shoot the flare gun. I extend my arm into the air, aim for the opening in the leaves, and pull the trigger.

Lyon told me to be careful about not looking at the flare, but I cannot help myself. I've never seen one before. My eyes follow the smoke trail as it moves into the sky. I hear a muffled womp noise and suddenly dancing red sparks fly out in every direction. It's a beautiful sight, except for the fact that it signals danger.

I hear shots ring out before the sparks disappear. I look down and realize that Levi is gone. I climb down the tree as quickly as I can while I hear shots and shouts ahead of me. Jonah appears by my side and follows me as I move forward, using the same technique as the rovers by dashing from tree to tree until I see someone before me.

It is one of the women. She holds an old-looking pistol to the head of Stone, who is lying face down in the forest floor with his hands still tied behind his back. The woman keeps him pressed down with her foot on his spine. She is dressed in a hodgepodge of clothes and skins, and she has a belt slung crosswise over her shoulder and waist with several small knives stuck in it. Her hair is wild and tangled and her arms bare. One has a long scar that stretches from her shoulder to her elbow.

And I have no weapon except for the empty flare gun that I still hold in my hand. But just like with the rover who stole the goat, I have the element of surprise and another hefty branch that I spy close by. Her attention is ahead of her, where the fight is crashing in the forest. I pick up the branch and on silent feet I move toward her until . . .

Crack! I stepped on another branch that cracks loud enough for her to hear. She turns and swings her arm up with the gun aimed right at my heart. All I can do is react. I fling the branch at her and it hits her arm, just as she pulls the trigger. The gun discharges with a sharp sound and something stings my upper arm. I throw myself at her, catching her across the chest and we roll on top of Stone and then over. I land on top when we finish the roll and with both hands grab the arm that still holds the smoking pistol. She tries to wrench it away and I slam her arm to the ground so hard that she drops the gun. I reach out to grab it and she claws at my face with her other hand. I manage to grab the gun long enough to fling it away when she bucks me off and kicks me hard in the chest.

I fly back, and before I can catch my breath she is on top of me with a knife in her hand. I manage to grab her wrist, and she brings her other hand down on the hilt of the knife and presses against me. She has her knee buried in my left armpit, trapping that arm so that I cannot move it.

Her face is intense, with a scar along her cheek. Her hair is wild with feathers and beads tied into the locks. She grins evilly when she realizes that I am now at her mercy, and her teeth are blackened at the roots and gums. Her stench is nearly as overpowering as her strength. I try to buck her off, but I can't. She is bigger than me, stronger, and, with the clarity of a sudden bucket of cold water, I realize that I will die soon.

I don't want to die. There is too much left unsaid, too much undone, too many people that have already died, and I have to make sure their deaths have meaning for the rest of us. The tip of her blade comes closer and closer to my face.

"I'm ah-going to cut your ah-nose off, bitch," she says and I believe her. I push upward with all my strength and the muscles in my forearm cramp with the effort. I hear Stone moving behind me. He grunts, and I realize that he is trying to stand or move or do something to help me but my time is quickly running out and he might not make it. Suddenly I hear a yowl and something strikes her face. She shrieks as Jonah claws at her and topples her over. She forgets about me and she raises the blade to stab him. My left arm is suddenly free and I grab the wrist of the hand that holds the knife. I leverage myself up and fall prone across her legs as she falls backward in an attempt to get away from Jonah, who is a writhing pile of fury. I hear his growls and his yowls and her screeching. I wrestle the knife from her hand and it flies away. I know she has more on her belt around her back. With one hand she tries to bat Jonah away and with the other she reaches beneath her.

"Stab her!" Stone yells. "Get the knife and stab her."

The knife that flew out of her hand is within my reach. I roll off her legs and grab for it just as her hand comes from beneath her body with another knife. I know without a single doubt that she will kill Jonah without flinching and I will not let that happen. I swing with all my might at her arm with the blade in my hand, and I feel it drag against her bone as I slice it open. At the same time she flings Jonah away with her other hand and shrieks in anger and pain. Her face is covered with blood. She turns to me and launches her body at me in an explosion of fury and pain. I brace the knife in my two hands and turn it outward and up. Blood from her arm spatters my face as she comes at me swinging the blade. She lands on me and the breath is knocked from my body, but I manage to keep the knife in my hands and turned. Her scream ends midbreath as she slumps on top of me.

Stone is on his feet and he kicks her off of me. I feel the knife go with her, but I manage to hold onto it, even though my hands are now covered with blood.

"Finish her," he yells. "Finish her now."

She lies on her back and gasps, over and over again. From the amount of blood, I know I hit her heart when she landed on me.

"Finish her!"

I jab the knife into the hollow of her throat and yank it out. Her face contorts and I hear her final breath rattle in her throat.

Once again I have killed someone.

· 22 ·

Cut me loose." Stone turns his back to me so I can cut his bonds. "Quickly before someone comes." I don't have time to think about what I've done. He is right, someone could come our way. I don't know how much time has passed. It could have been an instant, but it feels like an eternity. I slice through the things that bind his wrists. The knife is slick in my hands because of all the blood; still, I manage to cut them off without injuring him.

"Are you hurt?" he asks as soon as he turns around. He takes the knife from me and wipes it clean on the woman's pants. He flips her over and takes the rest of the knives from her belt.

I bend down and wipe my hands on her pants also to clean off the blood. It's hard to get them clean. I know some is on my face too. I swipe at it with the back of my hand and then try to clean them again. I don't think I'm having much luck. Jonah runs to my side and I rub his head. He saved my life. Who would have thought that a cat could save someone's life?

"Lass? Are you hurt?"

I blink. "No. Wait." I can feel the sting of scratches on my face but there is more. I look at my right arm. My jacket and beneath are torn and there is blood on the fabric.

He takes my arm and looks between the tattered and bloody edges. "You got creased with the bullet is all. It is nothing more than a scratch. You'll be fine. What's your name?"

"Wren."

"Pleased to meet you, Wren. I'm Stone. Thank you for saving my life."

"You are welcome," I say. He pulls me to my feet.

"Feel like helping the rest?" He hands me a knife while he picks up the pistol. "Damn, it's nothing but a single shot," he says. "Worthless antique." He pokes around her body and finds a small leather bag. "More ammunition," he explains as he stuffs the pistol in his belt. "Ready to go?"

I nod. Shots are still being fired ahead of us. There were twenty-five of them, now twenty-four. How many are left? How many of our people are hurt?

"Tell me if you see anything," Stone says. "I hear you can see in the dark."

"I can." I follow him onward and Jonah falls in beside us. Stone walks in a crouch, keeping his head down, and I do the same, staying behind and to his left.

"Did you shoot the flare?"

"I did." I realize he's talking to me to keep me grounded after my near-death experience. "Lyon thought they might attack and he assigned a shiner with a guard so we could see them coming."

"Who were you with?"

"Levi."

"That boy is deadly in a fight," Stone said. "He learned a lot from the year he spent with the Sioux."

"I can only imagine."

Stone holds up his hand and we both stop. Beyond us a battle is going on. Four against one, and the one is Levi, who is using his rifle like a club. They are coming at him so fast that he hasn't had time to reload. He pulls one of his pistols from his belt and shoots one who runs at him with a raised ax and quickly turns and blocks a knife strike with the barrel of his rifle while another charges at him from the back. I don't know how he manages to duck away from him but he does. There are too many of them and he will die unless he gets help.

"Stay back and stay hidden," Stone advises. "That knife you're holding won't do much against these odds." I want to say that his weapons aren't that much more than mine, but he is gone before I can open my mouth. He charges into the melee with a yell and blades in both hands. Levi must recognize his voice because he doesn't flinch or turn. He just keeps on fighting, ducking and swinging as four men advance on him at once.

I can't just stand in the shadows and watch. I move forward, looking from side to side to make sure there aren't any more rovers lurking about that may surprise us. One of the rovers turns as Stone charges in and meets him with a wicked-looking blade that is three times the size of the ones Stone holds. I hear the clash of metal as four against two do a deadly dance among the trees.

Levi manages to get off another shot with his pistol and the man staggers back, wounded but not killed. The man with the ax is not killed either and he staggers to his feet and charges at Stone.

I yell but it is too late. The ax lands in Stone's spine. His head jerks back and he falls limply to the ground as the rover jerks it free.

Now they know I am here.

"Run, Wren!" Levi yells as the man with the ax swings at him. He pulls his stomach in and barely misses being gutted as he turns and shoots his pistol again before flinging it away and grabbing for the other one.

I see his crossbow leaning against a tree on the opposite side of the raging battle. I also see the rover, who decides I am an easier target than Levi. All I can do is try to outrun him or else I will be dead too. I take off across the path of the battle to the crossbow. I feel the rover breathing down my neck. I hear Levi yelling. I hear more shots and more yells in the direction of our encampment. Something touches my back and I know the rover is trying to grab onto me. The crossbow is just ahead. I dive for it and in one motion I pick it up, roll over, and pull the trigger. I don't have time to aim, I just shoot. The arrow jabs into the rover's chin and goes straight up into his skull, pinning his mouth shut, and he falls to the ground. I point the crossbow to the ground, step on the end and slide an arrow into the chute. Levi needs my help.

Levi is fighting three now: the one with the ax and another one with long knives. He can't take a moment to shoot his pistol because all he can do is block. He's got to be tired. He keeps ducking and jumping and twisting while using his rifle to block the ax strikes. He keeps moving backward and sideways until he trips over Stone's body. As he falls I aim at the rover with the ax and pull the trigger as he raises his arm to strike at Levi. I hit him in the back and he falls forward, landing on Levi who slashes at the closest one with the knife at the exact same time the rover with the ax lands on him. There is one left and he looks between Levi and I as if he's trying to decide who is the biggest threat.

Levi shoots him with his pistol and he falls to the ground.

"Quick, Wren, reload," Levi says. I do, fumbling this time because I can't believe we are both still alive. Levi shoves the rover who fell across him away and staggers to me. He reaches me just as I slide the arrow into the slot.

"Are you hurt?" Levi shoves his pistol into his belt and pulls me to him in a bone-crushing hug. "You're covered with blood. What happened?"

I shake my head. "I'm fine. I'm fine." I hold on to him because I'm afraid I'll fall down without him. The moonlight shines down on us, highlighting the bruises and cuts on his face. He takes the crossbow from me and slings it over his arm and then pulls me close again. He puts a hand to my face and his warm brown eyes search mine as if he's not certain if I am telling the truth.

"You're covered in blood," he says.

"It's not mine."

"Wren." He gasps, and then his mouth claims mine in a kiss that is full of the heat and desperation of the battle we just fought. I feel the pull of it, down to my toes, and I give it back to him, pressing harder, and kissing deeper until Levi pushes me against a tree and picks me up by my thighs and my legs instinctively wrap around his hips. I feel his hardness pressing against my juncture and I moan.

This is passion beyond reason and my head and my heart swell with it until I cannot breathe and Levi finally pulls away with a rugged gasp for his own air.

"I'm glad to see you're not hurt, Wren."

Pace. He looks at me with such pain that I can well imagine what a knife thrust to the heart must feel like. There's a bloody cut on his head and his shirt is ripped across his chest. "Adam is hurt. He's been shot. I thought you'd want to know." He turns and walks away.

"Pace!" I cry out and start to follow, but he ignores me. I stand there torn, not knowing what to do or what to say. Should I follow? Should I stay? Should I explain what happened when I'm not even sure what it was, or should I give him time to get over his anger and hurt? Jonah looks at me and then scampers after Pace with his tail straight up in the air as if he is saying I made the wrong choice. The thing is I don't remember choosing, I just remember desperately trying to stay alive.

The air is defiantly quiet. All sounds of battle are gone. As we stand there, Levi and I, the sounds of nature come alive again. The hoot of an owl, the nervous call of a bird, the scampering of a squirrel, and farther away the heavy crashing of a stag. Levi gathers up his weapons and looks at me for a long moment when I don't know what to say or even think. I see the guilt on his face but I also see the resolve. Neither of which helps the myriad of confusion that surrounds me.

"Let's go then," he says.

I nod and follow him and we make our way silently back to the Quest.

· 23 ·

dam's been shot. Pace's words ring in my ears, but it's the memory of the look on his face that haunts me.

What have I done? I killed three people today but the hurt I gave to Pace haunts me more. And now Adam has been shot. I don't know if I can stand any more. But I have to. There is no turning back from the things I've done. Lives cannot be restored and actions cannot be undone. I might have been carried away by the moment when Levi kissed me, but I kissed him back. I can't deny it. I cannot change it. I cannot take it back.

Once more my actions have caused pain, and there isn't a single thing I can do about it. Maybe I should leave so my friends will be safe.

Yes, I am a coward. The truth is I would rather be anywhere but here so I don't have to see Adam hurt, so I don't have to see the pain in Pace's eyes. I know him well enough that he won't let anyone else see it. He will be stoic because he is proud.

And I am a coward.

Levi and I walk in silence and we walk past bodies. I know Levi has questions about how I came to be so bloody. I saved Stone, only to have him die in the next few moments. If I'd left him alone maybe he'd be alive now. Or he could have been shot by the woman I killed. From what I know of men, I know he'd rather die fighting than as a prisoner, but that doesn't help the fact that he is still dead and always will be.

I look at the bodies as we walk. They are all rovers. None of my friends is among them, nor does it look like Lyon lost any more men, although they could have collected them already.

We're on the road now and still we walk in silence. I can see the lights from our encampment and the shadows of people moving around. I am terrified to go there, terrified of what will be waiting for me, afraid that everyone's eyes will be on me and they will know how I hurt Pace, even though I know his pride will not let him say anything.

I dwell on that and let it consume me because I am so afraid for Adam. If he dies . . .

"I'm sorry, Wren," Levi says without looking at me. "It's all my fault."

"No," I reply. "We're equally to blame."

Levi nods and says, "Thank you for saving my life."

I don't know what to say so I say nothing as we come to our encampment. It bustles with purpose. Guards are stationed close in and lamps light the entire area. Rosalyn, Jane, James, and George, along with Dr. Stewart, are gathered around Adam, who lies prone on the table.

"Wren! Levi!" Zan exclaims from the catwalk and runs to us. I see Sally and some of the children behind her in the door of the Quest cabin. They must have brought the children inside at the first sign of attack. Lyon is also on the catwalk, talking to the airship pilot. Zan hugs me and then hugs Levi. "You're not hurt?"

"Just a few scratches. If not for Wren I'd be dead."

"What happened?" Zan asks.

"Later," Levi says. "How is Adam?"

"Shot in the shoulder at close range, but he should recover," Zan explains.

"Thank heavens you're not hurt." Jane looks up from Adam as we come closer.

"We were just sending out a search party," Lyon says.

"Wren!" Alcide joins us from the side and gives me a quick hug. "You survived!"

"So did you. Adam?"

"The bullet is still in him," he says. "If not for Pace he'd be dead right now."

Of course he wouldn't mention that. "Where is Pace?"

"Out looking for you," Alcide says. "Do you know you're covered with blood?"

"It's hard to miss." Alcide gives me a half smile and I go with him to Adam while Levi goes to his uncle Lyon.

"You survived," Adam says. "And thanks to Pace so will I."

"That's what I heard," I say with a smile. "I want to hear all about it when you're feeling better." Adam's shirt is off and Rosalyn washes the blood from his shoulder with a cloth. A hole is there, right next to his collarbone, and blood continually seeps from it.

I look at Jane and she smiles and nods in agreement. "First we have to get this bullet out, which might be a bit tedious."

Dr. Stewart feels the wound area when Rosalyn moves the cloth away. Adam grunts in pain. "I'm afraid the bullet may have broken this bone. You will likely be out of commission for a while. I'll just fetch my bag and we'll fix you up, good as new."

"Don't you worry." Jane soothes Adam's forehead as Dr. Stewart leaves. "He is a qualified physician, along with being a brilliant scientist."

"What happened?" I ask James.

"We saw the flare and started shooting. They were mostly in front of Adam's position, so it took a while for us to come in on one side and Peter and his partner on the other."

"There were so many of them, they over ran us," Adam continues. He grimaces in pain as he shifts his position on the table. "I got shot and it knocked me flat. Then another came at me with a sword. I'd lost my weapon and had nothing to defend myself with. Pace came out of nowhere and took him out."

"I almost hate to admit this, Wren," James adds. "But your guy gave it his all. If not for him things could have gone horribly wrong. I guess it was all that bluecoat training he had."

James's praise shames me. While I was kissing Levi, Pace was risking his life for my friends. The fact that James says anything speaks for how impressed he is by Pace.

"He didn't even pause when it was over," Alcide says. "He was so worried about you."

If only he had paused, then maybe he wouldn't have seen me with Levi. But him not seeing does not change the fact that it happened. I look around, hoping beyond hope that Pace will show up, but there is no one about, except the guards, Pip in his cage hanging in its usual spot, and . . . then I realize who is missing. "Is Peter hurt?" I ask. "Jon?"

"They are both fine," Alcide says. "They're taking care of the animals. The ponies panicked when all the shooting started and scattered."

"I should help."

"They didn't go far," Alcide assures me. "Freddy and Nancy are helping them. We all know how much you love them. We got them back and they're fixing the pen."

Of all the things that have happened to me, this is the thing that makes me tear up. I'm ashamed for anyone to see me crying, especially now after everything that has happened. Adam is the one who notices since I have my head down.

"We're going to be fine, Wren," he says. "All of us." I smile and nod because it is quite a bit easier than explaining why I don't think things will ever be fine again. I've made a mess of things with Pace.

"Why don't you come wash up?" Zan slides her arm around my waist. "You look a wreck."

"I feel a wreck," I say. I turn and look once more into the darkness that surrounds us. "I should go find Pace."

"You shouldn't go out there by yourself Wren," Alcide says. "More rovers could be about."

"Pace is out there and he doesn't have the benefit of our eyes," I say. Alcide puts a hand on my arm as if to stop me. "I'll be fine too," I assure him.

"Let her go," Levi says from behind me. "Take this." He hands me his crossbow that is fully locked and loaded while his eyes search my face. "I know you know how to use it," he says as if we're the only two there. I see the apology in his eyes, along with a longing that is very familiar to me. Mine is for answers that I still don't have the questions for.

"At least wash your face first," Zan says. She strokes my hair. "You've come undone," she adds with a grin. If only she knew how undone I really am on the inside.

"There's water over there." Rosalyn points to another table that has two basins of water and a stack of cloths. I go to wash my face and Levi follows me. A small mirror hangs on one of the supports for the awning, and I catch his reflection in it as I wipe the blood from my face.

"I need to do this alone," I say.

"I know, Wren. Pace is hurting and you're hurting too." Levi looks at his hands. They are battered and bruised, and he washes them in the other bowl. My face is scratched from my fight with the woman, and I hold the cloth against it to soothe the wounds. "Jane has some balm for that," Levi adds.

"Later," I say.

"You've been through a shock," Levi continues. "What you did was remarkable. Right now you might wish otherwise, but what you did saved my life. We talked about killing. I just want you to remember that tonight was either kill or be killed."

"I've killed too many people now to worry about it anymore," I say.

"Wren, it's only bad when you stop worrying about it. The rovers wouldn't think twice about it. Believe me, they came to kill us, and if they couldn't they would have used Stone in the worst way to get what they wanted from us and then killed him just for the fun of it. I don't know what drives them, but I do know they are ruthless and none of us had a choice tonight."

"Do you think there will be more attacks?"

"Lyon thinks that they will wait awhile, until they figure out what happened. I tend to trust him on such things. He's usually right."

I look at my reflection in the mirror. The blood is gone, but I have three scratches down my left cheek from my fight with the woman. My arm burns from where the bullet creased me but I ignore it. I've got to find Pace. He's what's important now.

"There's more," Levi says. I don't think my mind can handle

anything else at the moment, but I wait for him to tell me. "We're going into the dome tomorrow."

◆

I have no idea what to say to Pace when I do find him. If I find him. There is a lot of area out there that we've yet to explore. We've been concentrating on staying alive so much that we haven't had a chance to pay attention to the world around us. We've only been to a few places, and the only one that I can think of that Pace could get to without anyone noticing him is the place we spent the first night above.

I release Pip from his cage, confident that he will lead the way to Pace. I no longer worry about the little yellow canary returning to us. He's proven over and over again that he will come back. He takes off in the direction that I thought he would go and I follow, stopping by the pony pen to thank everyone for caring for the ponies.

"Glad you survived it," Peter says. "If not for Pace . . ."

"Adam told me."

"Did any of the rovers get away?" Jon asks.

"Not that I know of."

"We're to go out and gather the bodies when we're done here," Peter says. "Lyon wants to dispose of the bodies and leave the rest of them guessing as to what happened to them." Peter speaks so matter of factly about all of it. He's been in the middle of all the fighting since everything began and he's not but fifteen years old, a year younger than me. I study his face. He looks better now, healthier, robust with color in his cheeks and no more cough. Leaving the mines probably saved his life. Now if he can just stay alive and not get himself killed fighting in battle after battle. Will the fighting ever end?

"Do you think they'll attack again tonight?" Jon asks.

"Lyon doesn't think so," I say. "He seems to have a plan and so far he's been right, so I see no need not to trust him now."

"I agree," Peter says. "And I'm so grateful that they showed up to help us. Without them I don't think we would have survived this long." The past week has matured him in a way that I never would have considered. It's made all of us grow up in much a different way than the mines did.

"It would have been impossible without them." Ghost butts his head against me. I know he feels neglected, especially with all the troubling things that have happened lately. "I promise I will take care of you," I whisper in his ear. When that will happen I have no idea. Levi's words haunt me. We are going into the dome. I know Lyon has a plan, and I will do my part, but going back in terrifies me more than the battle we just fought and for the life of me I don't know why.

"Has Pace been this way?" I ask.

"I haven't seen him since he took off looking for you," Peter says. "I'm guessing he didn't find you."

"I hope he didn't run into some rovers we didn't know about," Jon says.

"I'm sure he's fine," I say, not having considered that possibility. "I think we just missed each other on the trail. I'm going to circle around and see if I can find him."

"Be careful," Peter says, "although I can see that you're well-armed if you should run into someone."

"I will." I leave, going in the direction of the ruins. I haven't gone far before I smell the comforting scent of a fire as I make my way through the tumbled stone foundations. Several cats come out and silently observe my passing. It is nice to see that they've adjusted so easily to life outside the mines. They are used to hunting as they survived on rats and mice down below. This new world must seem like a paradise to them.

I see the fire flickering then disappearing in the same way it did the first night we sought shelter. I take the crossbow from my back and hold it before me, just in case, as I go down the stairs. Jonah greets me on the steps.

"Traitor," I say quietly, although I'm thinking more of myself than Jonah. Pace looks up from where he sits cross-legged beside the fire with Pip on his finger. The pain in his eyes has not diminished since I last saw him.

"Adam?" he asks.

"He'll be fine," I say. "They still have to get the bullet out and his collarbone may be broken, but they expect him to recover."

"Good."

I take the crossbow from my shoulder and sit down opposite Pace by the fire. I really don't know what to say because I'm still not certain of how it happened or why. It isn't something that I intended to happen. It just did. It's the first time since I met him that silence stretches between us. Jonah, oblivious to our problems, sits down between us and starts his bathing ritual.

"I heard that you saved his life," I say, and I smile ruefully. "James was even singing your praises."

"I must have walked on water without realizing it," Pace says and we both laugh nervously.

"Thank you," I say.

"I'm certain Adam would have done the same." Pace shrugs. "James not so much, but Alcide and Peter for certain."

"They would. We all would. Even James, although he'd never admit it."

"I never doubted you, Wren." Pace leaves the "until now" unspoken. "I always knew you had my back."

"Without you it didn't matter," I confess. Not because of what he knew about Alex's escape from the dome, but because of what he meant . . . he means to me.

"I felt the same." He moves Pip to his shoulder and the tiny bird picks at a thread on Pace's jacket.

Felt . . . which means that he feels differently now? Or is he just saying it because he's hurt. Because I hurt him, something I never thought I'd do. My days have been filled with things I never thought I'd do. Cause a rebellion. Be responsible for death and destruction. Kill people.

I didn't plan on any of this, and I certainly didn't ask for it. But maybe I did. Maybe I tempted the fates when I went to the rooftops every morning to watch the light come to the dome. Just like I didn't plan on Levi, still I tempted him and myself. I have to make Pace see that it wasn't intentional. None of it.

"I didn't mean for that to happen," I finally say, after the interminable silence covers me with an oppressive blanket of guilt.

Pace gives me a fleeting smile and shakes his head. "I'm sure you didn't plan on kissing Levi, but I know he was thinking a lot about kissing you. Why shouldn't he think about it? I know it's all I think about." He pokes at the fire and then looks at me. "I asked you not to go, Wren."

"I went because they needed my help."

"I needed your help too. I needed you to help me figure out what's going on with us."

"How can I help you figure it out when I don't know myself?" I say. "So much has happened I haven't had time to think. I don't know what's going on around us, and I don't know how we're going to survive, and I'm not certain that us coming out was the right decision anymore."

"You don't have to figure these things out on your own," Pace says. "We can figure them out together. Except you don't talk to me anymore. You don't confide in me. I feel like a door has closed between us. I don't like feeling that way. I don't know how to fix it."

His words ring true in my head. Ever since we got out I've shut him out. No. Ever since I woke up alone in the cave when I was blinded I've shut him out. Looking back now I can see that it was juvenile of me, especially with everything else that was going on. Feeble excuses on my part won't make it go away, but that doesn't stop me from trying. "I'm sorry Pace. I don't know how to explain it. It just happened."

"Here's how. You got caught up in the heat of the moment." Pace stares as me, pinning my guilt to my body as if it were a tangible thing. "Which makes me think the same thing might have happened with us."

He gives voice to the same thing that I've been thinking. Did we declare our love for each other only because we were certain we were going to die? Did we fall together because we had no one else we could go to or depend on? Were we together because of circumstances or because of genuine feelings of the heart? How am I supposed to know for certain if my feelings are real?

Once again I envy the certainty of love that was so obvious between Adam and Peggy. Yet their love was never challenged, never tested; it was all so very easy for them. I guess it was more perfect than I thought. Adam will always have that memory of it, and nothing else can ever live up to that perfection he shared with Peggy. But will that memory be enough to keep him company for the rest of his life? I think not.

Pace is waiting for me to deny it. He's waiting for me to say something that will take us back to the place we were before we left the dome. Unfortunately I don't know what it is because I am so twisted up inside that I cannot think straight.

"You can't deny it, Wren," Pace says finally.

"I'm not agreeing with it either," I reply. "We've known each other for how long, two weeks?" So much has happened that I can't even count the days. "I'd like to think that if we'd met under normal circumstances that there would still be something between us. But I really thought we were going to die and I know you did too. Being with you make it seem more worthwhile."

"Just like tonight with Levi?"

I shake my head. "It's not the same with Levi. It might seem like it but," I take a moment to try to think, "it's not the same."

"But you do feel something for him."

I hate saying the words, but I will not lie to him just to make him happy. I respect Pace. "I do. I just need time to think things through. I need time to know what it is I feel for both of you."

Pace's beautiful blue eyes, once so full of affection, are veiled and shadowed, as if he's closed his heart to me as he looks at me from across the fire. "What you're saying is you need time to decide between me and Levi."

"No," I protest, but I quickly realize that he's right. But the way he said it makes it sound so horrible. It is horrible of me to say it, much less think it. How did I get myself into this terrible predicament? I didn't ask Levi to be attracted to me any more than I wanted James to be. But I have to admit to myself that I was flattered by it and maybe, just maybe, I encouraged it. "I never wanted to hurt you, Pace. I would rather die than hurt you."

Pace rises from his place by the fire and his anger, always buried deep, flares forth. Pip senses it and takes flight, landing on the ledge beside the staircase. "I appreciate the sentiment, Wren. I really do. But wouldn't that make things too easy? If you die then you don't have to make a choice. You could just go on to your reward leaving both me and Levi behind with a broken heart. A tragic end to a tragic young life. You can have all the glory and none of the responsibility that the rest of us have to deal with of building a world out here. A world that I thought we were going to share."

Pace's words are bitter and they slash through my skin like a hundred blades before they stab painfully at my heart. It is no more than I deserve. I hurt him deeply and it is natural that he wants to hurt me back. There is nothing I can say to take his pain away any more than there is anything I can do to resolve the situation.

Because I still don't know what to do.

Pace turns and goes to the staircase. He's leaving me because he's too angry to be around me. "Lyon is sending us into the dome tomorrow," I say.

Pace stops in place and he shifts his shoulders as if a great weight is on them. "What are we supposed to accomplish by going into the dome?"

His question surprises me. I thought he would be happy about it, so he could hopefully find out about his mother. "I don't know beyond helping our friends find a way out. And possibly helping your mother."

He turns to look at me again, and I see the heavy sorrow in his beautiful blue eyes. "I just thought of a way to solve your problem, Wren. And mine."

His words frighten me. I don't know what he is thinking and I am too terrified to ask.

"Get some rest. You look done in. I'll see you in the morning." Pace leaves and Pip flits after him, a dash of bright yellow against the darkness of the night. Jonah stares after them and then looks at me with a questioning meow. I put my head on my knees and stare into the fire. How am I supposed to rest without Pace by my side?

· 24 ·

I dream about the dome, sometime after dawn, because I can feel the light of it against my eyes as I stare up at the cracked glass and yearn for the small patch of blue sky I see above it. Beyond that my dream is fuzzy, as if I wore blinders. The details of it are there, but they lie just out of the reach of my memory. I wake with an ominous foreboding weighing upon me, something more than the anguish of Pace's disillusionment with me and the heavy regret of my many sins.

Someone found me in the night because when I woke up there was a blanket over me. I have no way of knowing who it was, but for some reason I think it was Pace. I can only wonder where he spent the night without me, and if any one of our friends noticed. I am stiff and sore from the unforgiving stone floor and damp, cold air, and I slowly crawl to my feet and then stretch my cramped muscles. Jonah joins me, making me envious of his ability to make it all look so easy and painless. I pick up the crossbow and blanket.

When I climb the stairs from the shelter I am greeted by clouds, which is the perfect foil for my dreary mood.

When I come to the pony pen I find Sally and George there with the children and Rosalyn busy milking a goat. Stella runs to me and throws her arms around my thighs.

"What's that for?" I ask as I kneel and return her hug.

"For saving us," she says.

"She overheard us talking about your exploits at breakfast," Rosalyn explains.

I feel my blush heat my cheeks. I'm fairly certain my exploits of the night before are not something Stella, or any of the other children, should know about.

"I like living outside," Stella says. "And Mommy says we're going to build a house like we had in the cavern."

Rosalyn shrugs.

"When you go back inside can you find my daddy and bring him outside?" Stella asks. "I miss him."

"I'll do my best," I say.

"Come on little one." George lifts her up and puts her on Ghost's back. "Time to exercise the ponies."

I pet Ghost's nose. The littlest ones are on the ponies' backs and the older ones lead them by the halter. Stella wraps her hands in Ghost's mane. "We take them out to graze a bit," George explains.

"Thank you for caring for them," I say. I drop a kiss between Ghost's milky eyes. "Take care of her," I whisper in his ear.

"They were still at the table when we left," Rosalyn says. "Can you carry this for me?" She hands me a bucket of milk.

"I will." I take the bucket.

"Wren," Rosalyn says, "thank you for everything you've done."

"I'm not sure I've done anything right," I say.

"You've given us hope," Rosalyn says. "And that's more than we've had for a long time." She hugs me and I return her embrace awkwardly since I am laden down with a crossbow, a blanket, and a bucket of milk, which Jonah swats at in hopes of getting some. "Bless you," Rosalyn says as I leave.

"Wren!" Zan exclaims as I arrive at the encampment. "I was so worried about you."

"I'm sorry," I say as I lay the crossbow and blanket on another table. "I fell asleep in the ruins we stayed in the first night."

"I told you she was fine," Alcide says, and I look at him curiously. Was he the one who gave me the blanket?

The only empty chair is between Pace and Jane, with Levi across from it. I nervously slide into it and keep my eyes on my plate. Pip pecks at some crumbs above my plate that Jane feeds him.

"How is Adam?" I ask as Pace quietly passes me a dish.

"Doing exceptionally well," Jane says. "We have him set up in the parlor and he's been asleep ever since. The surgery was quite painful, but he came through it like a champ. We expect he'll make a full recovery, given enough time and rest."

"That is good to hear," I say. "What about the rovers? Any sign of them?"

"Nothing," Lyon says. "We have guards posted on the road and the bodies have been disposed of. We recovered quite a few weapons from them that have been distributed among your group, with the proper instruction provided for each. I really don't expect we'll hear anything out of them for a few days. At best I think they might send an envoy of some kind to investigate our threat potential, under the guise of negotiation of course."

As Lyon talks I realize once again how grateful I am for his presence. If the Hatfields had not arrived when they did, God only knows what would have happened to us. We would either have been killed by the rovers or captured. I can't decide which one would be worse.

Pace and I would still be together . . . Even though he sits next to me, I can feel his distance and the wall he's placed between us.

Without a true leader we are scattered and ineffective. I had no idea what we were getting into when I started this journey, and I see now the mistakes that were made by all of us. We could have worked together better; I should have told my grandfather everything and sought his counsel. I thought I had the answers, but it turned out I didn't and because of that we all could have died. But that doesn't mean I think my father's way was right. There has to be some middle ground somewhere, a place that will help us all survive and build a better world for everyone, not just the royals and not just the shiners, everyone, including the people in between. I believe Lyon, with his experience, can help us find that way, if everyone is willing to listen.

"We need to take advantage of the lull to investigate the dome," Lyon continues. "Before I speak with Sir Meredith I want to have a concept of what things are really like inside there now, since the disasters you have mentioned. It would help your position immensely if we can catch him off guard, and the best way to do that is to let him know that we know how dire his situation actually is."

"What if the situation inside isn't as dire as we believe?" James asks.

"Smoke is still pouring out and there are bodies staked outside. I would say the situation is extremely dire," Lyon says. "We will go at dusk, which will give you all time to prepare," Lyon continues. "For now you can practice by going off the cliff. When it's time to go into the dome, we will take the Quest up and we can launch from there. We have four gliders. Zan and Levi will each pilot one with Wren riding tandem with Levi and Pace with Zan to balance out the weight. I will take the third one and James will be our fourth pilot. From what I've seen of James this morning, I am certain he will have no problem piloting on his own."

"It's just like flying over the pit," James says.

"With the same chance of dying a tragic death," Alcide adds.

"It's perfectly safe," Zan says. "And loads of fun."

"I'm just wondering how you convinced the first guy to try it," Alcide says. "Did someone say put these on and go jump off a cliff?" Everyone laughs at Alcide's comment.

"We were showing James how they worked this morning," Levi explains. It's the first time he's spoken since I arrived. "So we've pretty much spent the morning jumping off the cliff."

"He caught on to it a lot quicker than I did," Pace adds, and I realize that the two of them had spent the morning together while I slept. I cannot help but wonder if they talked about me.

"You flew the gliders?" I ask Pace.

"I tried to fly one on my own," Pace confesses. "It didn't go well. Thank goodness for Zan. We were strapped into that thing together."

I steal a look at Zan, who grins widely. Is Pace trying to make me jealous? And him wanting me to be jealous means he still wants to be with me, doesn't it? Or is my ego merely getting out of control like everything else in my life?

"Wren, we need to get you used to it so there are no surprises later on," Lyon said. "You're not afraid of heights are you?"

"No sir," I say. "I'm used to being up high." There is no need to tell him that I'm terrified of falling. I've gone too far to stop now. "I spent a lot of time on the rooftops."

"Which is why we've chosen you and Pace to go in. You know

the streets best, and combined with your and James's knowledge of the earth beneath, you should be able to find a route out for any of those inside who want to escape."

"Shouldn't we tell them what's out here first?" I say. "Shouldn't we give them a choice?"

"They are your friends, Wren. What do you think?" Lyon asks.

"I think they should have a choice."

Lyon smiles at me, and for some reason I think he's proud of the conclusion I've come to. "Exactly. And that is why we're going into the dome."

◆

Standing on the edge of the cliff is much different than standing on the edge of the chasm beneath the dome. The chasm is deep and dark, bottomless. It is full of blackness and the unknown. The cliff only shows the light and the never-ending horizon. The cliff doesn't scare me like the chasm does. Or maybe it's just that I know Levi will keep me from falling.

The wings that we wear now have a bar attached to them. The first time I saw Levi and Zan fly it seemed as if the wings were directly on their backs. Now I see that it is more complex than that. There is a set of harnesses and a bar for turning.

"We have to run as one," Levi instructs. He stands behind me with his arms on either side of the bar. "You just have to hold on. You won't fall because of the harness. Let me control it and make sure you do what I say."

I nod, too excited and scared to speak. Zan gave me leathers to wear, explaining that they make the body more streamlined and keep you warm against the colder air we will find higher up. My hair is stuffed inside a leather cap and I wear my goggles. James and Pace are similarly dressed.

"Watch what James does," Levi says. "It's like he was born to fly."

James stands to the left side of us. Zan is doing a final check of his harness. Pace is beyond, watching all of us. There is no need for him to train anymore. Since he's not flying on his own he learned all he needed to know this morning. I feel the wind blowing in from the ocean and wonder if it is enough to keep us aloft.

James grins at me and takes off at a run, jumping off the cliff just as he did when he flew over the chasm. He falls and then is carried upward by the wind. He lets out a whoop and sails out over the ocean, turning back and forth in lazy circles until he gently coasts down to the beach below. When he lands he looks up at us and waves before taking off his harness and folding the wings into an easy size to carry back up the cliff.

"See how easy it is?" Levi asks. "Are you ready?" Once more I nod. "On my count take off running, starting with your right foot. Don't stop when we get to the cliff. I know you'll want to, but don't. You're going to have to fight the urge."

"I will."

"You can do it, Wren," Pace says encouragingly. I look at him and see nothing but concern on his face.

"One. Two. Three." Levi completes his countdown and I take off. I feel his body in step with mine. "Don't stop!" The edge of the cliff is right before us and I hold my breath as I step into space. "Stretch out your body like you're reaching forward."

It's all about trust. That's all I can do as I feel my body falling to the ground. "I got you," Levi says. I reach out and imagine myself flying and suddenly I am. I feel the jerk as the wind catches the wings and suddenly we are soaring out over the waves. I look at the surface of the water below me and catch the reflection of Levi and I gliding above. A flash of yellow catches my eye and I see Pip, rushing to join us. He flies in front of us as Levi begins the turns, back and forth, back and forth until I see the ground slowly approaching. Pip leaves us, soaring upward on the wind to return to Pace.

"Try to bend your knees when we land," Levi says.

The ground moves up as we float down, and, without me knowing it, my legs drift down until I am hanging below the wings. Then we touch the ground with the wings sheltering us from those above. I hear a whoop from Zan and Pace and another one from James, who is still climbing back up the cliff.

"What do you think?" Levi's words rumble against my ear and I turn to look at him with excitement until I realize that we are in the exact same position that we were last night. I will not kiss him. Not with Pace watching.

"I think it was the most amazing thing I've ever done," I say and quickly turn away. My hands shake as I unbuckle the harness and step away from beneath the wings.

"It could always be like this, Wren," Levi says. "If you want it to be." He steps out of his harness and folds the wings. I look up the cliff face and watch Pip disappear over its edge, back to the safety of Pace.

"That's what I am trying to decide, Levi," I say. "What it is exactly that I want."

"There's an entire world out there waiting on you," he says. "I'd love to show it to you."

"I know," I say, "but first there are some things I must do."

"I realize that," he replies. "And I will help you until you've seen it through."

"That might take a long time," I say.

"I got nowhere else to be at the moment." He extends his hand in the direction of the trail and I begin the long trek back up. I realize as we climb that, like everything else in this new world, the moments of excitement are few and the work is long. We only have time for the one flight. There is much to be done before we can go back into the dome.

♦

The clouds grow heavier and the wind sharper as the day progresses, with the same heavy threat from the night we climbed the cliff face. A storm is brewing off the coast. I stand on the balcony of the Quest with Pace and James, waiting for the lines to be dropped. Lyon's plan is for the Quest to drop us above the dome and then we will coast down with the gliders. On the horizon the sun sinks from beneath the clouds and into the water in a dim replica of the sunset we saw on our first night out of the dome.

It gifts me with a sense of foreboding that is as heavy as the clouds.

Lyon has done everything possible to insure the safety of those left on the ground. All the guards are to remain on the ground and Alcide, Peter, Jon, and George are now armed as well with the weapons taken from the rovers, whose bodies I learned had been weighted and dumped far out to sea. Stone was also put into the sea, but with a proper ceremony to note his passing. It was the same way things were done in the before time, Zan explained as we dressed in leathers. Except now the sailors sailed the skies instead of the oceans.

I can't help but remember what Pace said about the bodies buried in the dirt. Is it any worse than being at the bottom of the ocean? I would rather be burned so that my remains travel on the winds.

But only after I am dead. The memories of Alex's death still haunt me. Dying by fire has to be the worst possible way to die. There could be something worse. One thing I know for certain is men can be creative when they need to, and desperation will drive you to do things you never thought possible under normal circumstances.

The children, along with Rosalyn and Sally, are in the tunnel Jon found his first night. It was the safest and most secure place for them. The ponies and goats are still in their pen. There is no place to hide them. If the rovers do attack while we're gone, they will be sacrificed. I can't help but worry about Ghost, and I bid him a long good-bye before I leave. I can only pray that he will still be there when I return.

Jonah is in the cabin, along with Jane, who is caring for Adam and Dr. Stewart, who wants to be part of the boarding party, as he calls it. Lyon answers him with a simple "Next time." I have no idea where Pip is. I haven't seen him since he flew with me.

Zan joins us on the balcony, and Lyon and Levi release the cables that keep us attached to the catwalk and hastily jump onto the ship, pulling the staircase up behind them and bolting it into place. The engines engage, and I am amazed at their silence. It is more of a feeling than a noise, a slight vibration. I look up at the pilot's cabin, which is beneath the nose of the ship, nothing more than a large room that fades into the body of the dirigible with windows all around it. The entire thing is a total wonder to me. How does it all work?

There is so much about this world that I don't know. So many things to learn, yet I feel as if I am going backward instead of forward. I have not voiced my fears about returning to the dome to anyone. Just like Pace said, I've kept everything inside since we came out. Perhaps I shouldn't, but with this venture it is too late to turn back.

We float higher and higher into the air. How something this heavy can stay afloat is another wonder. We wave as our friends at the encampment get smaller and smaller and the dome grows larger before us.

We sail upward and onward until the only thing in our field of vision is the dome. We are so close that I can see the cracks on the surface and the rusty flakes that cover the mighty girders. We stand on the balcony, all of us, at the front of the airship and look at the dome. My hands rest on the railing and Pace places his on top of my mine and squeezes them gently. His parting words from the night before come back to me. I look up into his beautiful blue eyes and he smiles at me.

It feels as if he's trying to tell me good-bye.

"We need to make sure we stick together once we get inside," I say. "We can't risk getting separated."

"I agree," Pace says.

"Zan is to stay with the gliders," Lyon says. "We cannot risk losing them."

"While the rest of you have all the fun," Zan pouts playfully.

"The only fun part is getting there," James says. He adjusts the pack on his back that holds the clothes we're to put on once we land so we will blend with the people inside. The tight fit and high quality of the leathers we wear now would quickly identify us as people who do not belong to the dome. James, Pace, Levi, and Lyon all wear pistols also, along with each having a brace of knives. I have a knife also, tucked into my boot. I have no qualms about using it. Not now. Not after everything that I've done.

The air is cooler the higher we go and the wind stronger, tossing us about. Dusk quickly becomes darkness as the sun sinks below the horizon and the clouds take possession of the night. The dome is nothing more than a soft glow as we rise above it.

It is time to go. We put on our harnesses, and the gliders are unfolded and locked into position. Jane and Dr. Stewart both come out to assist us in preparing for the jump. We are all quiet as we prepare our minds and bodies for what is to come.

Jane kisses Lyon for luck and hugs Zan and Levi both before buckling Pace and I in with them. Zan stands before Pace in the same manner I stand before Levi. The only difference is she will be the one steering the glider. Jane grasps James's hand, then Pace's, and then mine.

"Godspeed," she says.

"Thank you for everything," I reply, and I slide my goggles into place. The amber coating Dr. Stewart gave them turns the world as dark as the tunnels below, and it takes a moment for my eyes to adjust. Even with my ability to see in the dark, I cannot see through things. I concentrate on the soft glow of the dome. That is the only thing I need to see clearly.

I shiver uncontrollably as Levi and I wait our turn. "Cold?" His breath is warm against my ear.

"Yes." I keep my eyes on Lyon as he climbs to the railing and dives off. James follows him.

"You're about to get colder," Levi says as we climb into place. "There's no running this time. Just jump out. Ready?"

I look out into the darkness and I realize it is just like standing over the pit. There is nothing before me, just a yawning emptiness that never ends. This is what I've always feared, falling into the unknown, and here I am, ready to take that first step. I have no choice. I have to do it. There is no turning back now. "Yes."

"Jump."

I close my eyes, because really there is not much difference, and I step out into the darkness. We fall, and it is all I can do not to scream, and then suddenly we are soaring.

"Are you with me, Wren?" Levi shouts above the wind.

I open my eyes. My hands are clenched so tightly on the bar that my arms cramp in pain. I see the dome below us, and the shadows of Lyon and James flying to it. I hear a *whoop* and look toward the sound to find Zan and Pace sailing beside us. I am so cold that I cannot stop shaking, and all I can do is hold on and trust in Levi to get us down safely.

Lyon and James land and the dome rises quickly beneath my feet. I see the massive hole torn in the glass by the explosion and the deep cracks that travel outward from it. "Get ready," Levi says. I bend my knees and get ready to land. The dome is much slicker than the sand and not forgiving, and we slide and stumble as the high wind beats us forward. And then we suddenly stop and I pitch forward onto my hands and knees with Levi sprawled on top of me. Lyon and James come to our rescue and I see that Levi closed the wings, which kept the wind from blowing us off the dome.

Zan and Pace come in right on top of us, and we all duck our heads since they are traveling fast. I watch as Pace puts his hands around Zan's waist and sits down, while Lyon and James grab onto the wings and fold them shut.

I roll over on my back, push my goggles up, and look up at the sky. My heart is racing in my chest and I find it hard to believe that I survived it. We all survived it. Levi reaches for my hand and pulls me to my feet.

"We made it," he said. "I didn't want to tell you up there but I was a bit worried with this wind."

"Thanks for sparing me," I say. "I'm fairly certain I was scared enough without that bit of information."

Levi laughs as we form a group on top of the dome. The sides stretch out in every direction without end. They just fade into the night. The wind howls unceasingly around us with a deep sound of pipes as it flows over the hole. The smoke is gone.

Lyon takes his pack from his back and pulls out a long stake that resembles a claw. "This is something we use for mountain climbing," he shouts. "We'll attach it to one of the girders and lower ourselves down." We follow Lyon to the hole. I feel the glass creaking beneath my feet. It was weakened by the explosion, but it is so dense that we walk on, unafraid. The hole is right by a girder and Lyon, Levi, and Pace go to work on attaching the stake while I peer down into the hole.

The inside air is smoky and thick, like the clouds that hover above us. I barely see the catwalk and the tops of some buildings. Everything else is lost in the smoke. It takes me a moment to orient myself. We are over the government section, on the royal side. If I can see rooftops it means the cave-in must have happened someplace else. For some reason I thought the cave-in would be under the hole, that one caused the other. The bad news is we will be coming down into one of the most secure parts of the dome. The good news is, we are not that far from David and Lucy's.

"You should go ahead and change," Zan says. She holds James's pack. I quickly dress into my shiner clothes, pulling my pants on over the leathers and trading the leather shirt that I wore over my sleeveless top for my usual shirt and jacket. I comb my fingers through my hair after taking off the cap and tie it back with my bandana and hang my goggles around my neck. I notice James has done the same with his and, except for the fact that he is clean, he looks just as he did when he came out of the mines after his shift.

Pace changes into his old clothes, and Levi and Lyon put on some things they borrowed from the rest of our group. They busy themselves with concealing the weapons they carry beneath their jackets, but none of the four will pass a close inspection, especially Lyon and Levi. They are dressed appropriately, but I know they will stand out. They are both too bold and bright to go unnoticed.

"Will you be all right up here on your own?" Lyon asks Zan. "If something should happen and we can't get back, someone has to inform your mother. And she will be much more generous with you than me."

"As long as I don't freeze to death," she replies. She empties the pack of the remaining items that include a fur-lined coat, gloves, and a hat.

"If you see a flare, take the gliders and leave," Lyon instructs. "Here is hoping we will be back soon to all fly back together."

Zan nods as she gathers everything together into a neat pile. "Good luck!" she says to all of us.

"James goes first," Lyon says. He looks down into the dome and spots the catwalk. "We'll lower him down and then swing him to the catwalk. He can tie the rope off and the rest of us can slide down with hooks."

It all sounds terribly difficult and frightening, but once again there is no going back. Our friends' lives depend upon us. James puts back on his safety harness from the glider and Lyon ties the rope to it. Even though the rope is anchored, Pace and Levi wrap it around their arms to swing James, who has his feet braced against the hole and is leaning back into his harness. He looks at me and grins before Lyon signals to lower him into the dome.

The grin was genuine and contained none of James's false charm or the manipulation that he is so good at. As I watch Lyon instruct Pace and Levi, and James casually swings to and fro below us, I realize that James relishes this. He was meant for more than digging coal beneath the earth. He felt the restrictions of his life and he acted the way he did because he was frustrated. Now he is able to live to his potential. My anger at the things he's done to me in the past fades because I understand him now. I forgive him.

"You're almost there, James!" I say. He floats beneath the glass, swinging back and forth while Levi's and Pace's arms strain with his weight. He reaches his arm out, hoping to catch the catwalk. He misses and Lyon encourages Levi and Pace to swing harder.

"He's got it," I say as James grabs onto the restraining bar on the catwalk. He flops over the rail and quickly unties the rope and then ties it to the bar, pulling up all the slack.

Lyon attaches a handle to the rope with a much thinner rope attached to the handle. "Levi first," he says. "You two watch what he does so you can follow."

"All you got to do is hang on," Levi says. He grabs onto the handle and walks off the dome into the opening. The handle slides down the rope and Levi is at the catwalk and climbing over the side before I take my next breath. Lyon pulls the handle back up with the smaller rope and Pace goes next, jumping off with a grin.

"Boys," Zan says with a shake of her head. "It's all an adventure where they are concerned."

"Ready, Wren?"

I look down at the catwalk where I see Pace, Levi, and James all looking up at me, all ready to catch me on my descent. I take a deep breath and take the handle firmly into my hands and squeeze it tight. "I am ready." I step off the glass and glide downward. Pace catches me on one side and Levi on the other and gently they lift me over the rail of the catwalk.

I am in the last place I ever wanted to be. I am back in the dome.

· 25 ·

Pace knows the way off the catwalk, so we follow him in single file as we traverse the dome. I look up at the thick glass. From here would the inhabitants have been able to tell if the flames still burned? Maybe during the daytime they would have seen the bright glare of the sun and thought yes, but at night?

How submissive a people had we become that our forefathers trusted without doubt what they were told? Or maybe it was the sight of so many others like Alex, burned alive, that kept them at bay. Was someone in each generation sacrificed by leaders like my father as an example? Were those that came before us compliant because of fear, or did they just not care? As long as their bellies were full and they had a dry place to sleep they kept quiet because doing otherwise was too much effort?

I should not condemn those who lived before because I do not know their reasons, any more than those who come after should condemn or condone me. I can only assume that everyone in their time did what they considered best for themselves and the ones that they loved.

All I know for certain is that I wanted better. Whether I have that now still remains to be seen. Things are not what I expected, and the things that are to come are still a mystery to me. My immediate need is all I can concentrate on right now. I desperately need to know that Lucy, David, and our other friends have survived.

"Amazing," Levi says. "It looks as if they simply built the dome around an existing city."

"Dr. Stewart would be beside himself," Lyon agrees. "Here's hoping we can get him inside."

"How about if we hope we can get back out first?" James says.

We have come to where the dome curves and a series of ladders lead down into the smoke. "Where does this come out?" I ask Pace.

"The industrial side, below the coal lift. There's an access on the royal side also. I thought this one would be less conspicuous."

It also led us a far piece away from David and Lucy's, but I know he was correct in using this one. We would be spotted as outsiders immediately in the royal section.

"Zan is going to have a long, cold wait," Levi says as we begin the long, downward climb.

"I told her to leave at dawn if we weren't back," Lyon says. "She'll probably sleep most of the time anyway."

"Poor Zan," James says. "She's missing out on all the fun."

The smoke surrounds us and we are suddenly quiet. I cannot see Pace beneath me or Levi above me. All I can do is concentrate on the rungs of the ladder. They are rusty and they shake with our weight. I have no idea how high we are, but I can feel the ominous presence of structures around me and I imagine windows with people watching us, even though we surely cannot be seen.

After climbing down for what seems like an eternity I step onto a rooftop. A stench rises around us, part of the smoke. I take my kerchief from my hair and wrap it around the lower part of my face. "What is it?"

"The slaughterhouse," Pace explains. "Without the fans, there's no place for the smell to go."

"Or the smoke," James says. "Good. I'm glad they're suffering."

"Some of them are our friends," I say. "And a lot haven't done anything to deserve this."

"We also lost a lot of friends in this," James returns. "And you're worried about people you don't know being inconvenienced? Maybe if they suffer enough they'll rise up, just like we did."

I know James is expecting an argument out of me, but I see the wisdom of his words in the same way I now look at him in a new light. "You're right," I say. "Maybe this is what everyone inside needs."

"We should just give them all sledgehammers," Levi observes. "And tell them to break the glass."

"It's so easy when you say it like that," Pace says. "But you've yet to meet Wren's father."

I cringe at his words. Because I had not been confiding in Pace, he did not know that I omitted telling Lyon who my father was.

"What does Wren's father have to do with this?" Lyon asks.

"I thought you were an orphan," Levi echoes.

I see the apology in Pace's eyes, but once again, there is no turning back. "Wren's father is Sir William Meredith. The man in charge."

◆

I have never seen the streets so deserted, not even at this time of day. I have a sinking feeling in my gut that has nothing to do with Lyon's obvious disappointment that I was not totally honest with him. Everything around us is eerily quiet and the heavy smoke that lingers at street level gives the area a mystical dreamlike quality that does nothing to help our mood.

"I got a weird feeling about this," Pace says as we come to a corner. We have stuck close to the side of the dome, coming up the street that is parallel to the coal lift and I can see it to the right as we stop. We are close to Scarabtown but we've seen no sign of anyone on the street.

"So do I," James agrees. "Aren't there usually people around here? Scarabs?"

"They pick up the coal that falls off the carts," I say. "Look at the street. There's nothing there." The streets are picked clean. It looks as if they've even been swept for coal dust. The lift hangs at an awkward angle, damaged, no doubt, by the explosion.

"We should check the body lift," I say. "Peter thinks some shiners could have gotten out this way."

We turn that way. We startle a cat and it runs for the coal lift with its ears flattened, as if we are its mortal enemy. I am hesitant to cross the street to the lift. My skin prickles as if a thousand eyes are focused on me, yet there is no one about, and it impossible to see any distance in the cloud of smoke.

We check the lift. The chute is empty, and even with my and James's exceptional night vision we see no sign of the car as we peer down into the depths of the mine. James flips the lever and nothing happens. But why should it? There are no engines running because there is no coal to power them. The eerie quiet is because the fans aren't running, but there is more.

"I haven't heard a dog bark, or a voice," I say. "I don't even remember hearing the sheep or cows when we walked by the stockyards. I haven't even heard a bird."

"Is it because the fans are down that is seems so quiet?" Pace asks. "Maybe we haven't heard any birds because they've all flown out of the hole in the dome."

"I think there's more to it," I say. "Maybe we can find something out from the scarabs."

We move onward, cautiously, peering around corners before we take to the next street as we work our way to the part of town where Lucy and David live. We will have to pass through the center of the dome and cross the promenade and I want to do it on this end of the dome before we get into the central business district.

I stop. Pace does too and James slowly turns in a circle. We are in an alley. An alley that used to be crowded with people.

"What's wrong?" Levi asks.

"Everyone is gone," I say. "The people who lived in this alley. They are gone. Even their homes."

"Homes?" Lyon asks.

"Scraps of wood and canvas mostly. Some nothing more than fabric walls. Everything is gone. They were the street people. We call them scarabs because they had to scavenge for everything. They were descendants of the ones who snuck into the dome before it was closed. There was no allowance made for them, so they lived on the edge of our society. Generations of them with nothing ever gained," I explain. "Jon is one of them."

"Good Lord," Lyon exclaims. "What could they have possibly done with them?"

"I'm afraid I know," I confess. "I think some of them are the bodies that are staked outside."

We move onward, even more cautiously than before. We are silent, each of us lost in our own thoughts of where the scarabs have gone. I'm afraid mine are the most dire because I know what my father did to Alex. Surely he wouldn't do that to an entire group of people. But where does someone like my father draw the line?

A noise startles us. It is hard to identify. It could be the slamming of a door or a crate falling over. We stop and turn, trying to discern the direction through the heavy cloud that surrounds us. Lyon and Levi both pull their pistols from their jackets. Pace shakes his head. "A shot will bring everyone down on us," he whispers.

"Maybe not," James says. "Remember, the bluecoats have guns too. Maybe they'll think it's another one keeping the law."

"Keep walking," Lyon says. "The sooner we're at your friends', the sooner we can relax and know what's going on in here." We cross a street and I lead everyone into an alley that opens into the promenade, which we have to cross at some point.

We hear another noise behind us and together we pick up the pace, walking quickly. The end of the alley is nothing more than haze. A sound erupts above us. Pigeons frightened of something. They arise as one from a ledge and fly into the smoke before us.

"Stupid birds," James says. "Freedom right above them and they're still hanging around inside."

"Kind of reminds me of us," Pace says in his dry way, and I grin at him.

The end of the alley is in sight, and then suddenly our way is blocked by a bevy of bodies. The smoke clears a bit and I see the leather masks.

"Filchers," I gasp.

"Behind us too," Lyon says.

"Run for it," James yells. "Right through them."

"Don't be afraid to shoot," Lyon adds. James and Levi take off with their pistols in their hands. Lyon pushes me forward and Pace grabs my hand. I latch onto it, wrapping my fingers around his, just as we did when we were being chased before.

We run. Lyon turns and shoots at a filcher coming up behind us and he drops like a stone. The rest of us barrel into the promenade, crashing through the filchers who grab for us. James and Levi shoot and knock arms away while Pace and I dart through, dodging and dancing away. A hand catches in my hair and my head is yanked back. Pace pulls out his pistol and shoots the filcher who holds me and he drops too.

"Go! Go! Go!" Lyon yells and we careen onward with filchers right on our tail. There are so many of them, at least a dozen, and another group joins the chase. I try to think where we should go. I don't want to lead them to David and Lucy's, and we are on the opposite side of the dome from our secret hatches that might even be gone now. We cross the promenade and dash into another alley. This one has crates against the wall, and we shove them as we go by to slow down our pursuers.

I have to do something.

"I'm out of ammo," James says.

"Me too," Levi announces as we run. "No time to reload."

"There's too many of them," Pace says. "We've got to do something."

And just like before, I know what to do. I might not know my father well, but I know him well enough. And I know Pace too. I know what he was thinking when he said good-bye to me the night before. His sacrifice will accomplish nothing. But mine can accomplish a lot because I am, after all, Sir William Meredith's daughter, whether he likes it or not.

"James," I say as we run. "You've got to get Lyon out of here. He's the only one who can get us out. Levi too."

James looks at me and nods. It's just like before, when I told him to save Pace at any cost, even if it meant someone else got caught. He knows what I'm thinking and he knows what to do.

"Wren?" Pace says.

"Maybe we'll find your mother this time," I say.

"What are you thinking?" Levi asks.

"We're trapped and we've got to get you out." We dash around a corner and stop. Levi quickly reloads his gun and Lyon sends some shots down the alleyway. I know we only have a few moments. "James will get you to safety."

"And what are you going to do?" Lyon asks.

"I'm going to have a talk with my father."

Lyon shakes his head.

"It's the only way and you know it," I say.

"She's right, Uncle," Levi says.

"Go," Pace says. "I have to stay. I have to find my mother."

"I will negotiate for your release," Lyon promises. James grabs his arm and they fade into the smoke.

"Levi?" Lyon calls out.

Levi finishes reloading.

"Go," I say.

"No," he replies. "I'm going to see this through, with the both of you. Perhaps your father will see my value as a hostage."

The filchers are closing in. We can see them behind us, and I hear them coming around from the other side. I can only pray that James and Lyon are gone and will find their way back to the outside.

"Let's make them work for it," Levi says.

"I'm right by your side." Pace has his pistol in his hand.

"If we're going to do this, let's make it count," I say and take off running again. Only this time I have a certain destination in mind. I head back to the promenade, darting down the next alley. The filchers are on our heels once more and Levi and Pace keep shooting at them, hitting some, and hopefully killing some. I know the shots will draw attention. I just hope I can keep the bluecoats from killing us with their weapons when they find us.

I turn onto the promenade and run with all my might for my

father's building. It is much easier to run now, even with the smoke, because my lungs are clean. They have been breathing free air for days. They know what it feels like and they never want to lose it.

Sometimes the path to freedom is not a direct one. Sometimes it is blocked and you have to work your way around it. Freedom is not appreciated unless it is earned. Everyone needs to know that they have a choice, and it doesn't have to be the one my father has made for them.

We run past the fountain where Alex died. Lamps are lit on the corners now and around the fountain, casting a warm glow against the grayness of the air.

"Get them!" a filcher yells. "Don't let the bluecoats have them. We won't get the reward."

I grin as I run up the steps of my father's building with Levi and Pace by my side. A squadron of bluecoats spins and aims their weapons at us. We've surprised them.

"My name is Wren MacAvoy, and I'm Sir Meredith's daughter!" I yell. "And I surrender in the name of my father." I drop to my knees and put my hands behind my head.

"My name is Pace Bratton, and I surrender to Sir Meredith!" Pace yells, drops his gun, and does the same.

"My name is Levi Addison, and I surrender to Sir Meredith!" Levi echoes.

My heart is racing and I pant, trying to catch my breath. I see Pace kneeling on one side of me and Levi on the other; several bluecoats surround us with their own guns pointed at our heads.

"Well, well," a deep voice says, and I recognize it as belonging to my father. I look up and the bluecoats part as he walks to me. "Stand her up," he instructs, and I am hauled to my feet by two of his men. "What have you been up to, daughter?"

I am pleased that he's called me daughter. It means he's

acknowledged me in front of his men, and, I notice, in front of some royals because I recognize the cut of the cloth of the two men and a woman who stand in the doorway of the building with looks of horror on their faces.

I smile. "I've been outside, Father. And you were right. It is a frightening place. But it is also very beautiful and new and we can have a life out there. All of us if we work together." A dash of color catches my eye. Something bright yellow against the drab gray stone of the building. Pip warbles a song and then he takes off in flight for the top of the dome.

"You should see it, Father. The sky is so very blue."